A past that will not die, whether that of an individual bound to a time or place, one held by the memories of others, by a need to avenge a wrong, or to pay for some action taken. These are just a few of the scenarios in which the haunts, specters, and spirits who roam these pages are to be found. So venture if you dare into such unforgettable adventures as:

"Jennie in the Field"—Her sister's death had haunted her since childhood, but now memories of Jennie seemed to be leading her on a very special quest. . . .

"In the Chief's Name"—They were rebels with a cause, out to overthrow the technological present and big corporations, and return civilization to a simpler time. And now they were calling upon the spirit of an Indian chief to help them in their war. . . .

"Warrior in the Mist"—She was a dedicated reenactor, a Norman through and through. But this year's climactic battle against King Harold would truly bring history alive. . . .

HISTORICAL HAUNTINGS

More Imagination-Expanding Anthologies Brought to You by DAW:

CIVIL WAR FANTASTIC *Edited by Martin H. Greenberg.* In *Civil War Fantastic* some of science fiction's finest take us back to this turbulent time with their own special visions of what might have been. So don your uniform, load your cap and ball rifles, raise the colors, and prepare to charge into *Civil War Fantastic* with such top authors as Nancy Springer, Robert Sheckley, Mike Resnick, Brendan DuBois, Josepha Sherman, Willliam H. Keith, Jr., Gary A. Braunbeck, David Bischoff, Kristine Kathryn Rusch, and many more.

SPELL FANTASTIC *Edited by Martin H. Greenberg and Larry Segriff.* Fantasy is fueled by spells, from those cast by simple love potions to the great workings of magic which can alter the very nature of reality, destroy seemingly all-powerful foes, offer power or punishment, immortality or death. In *Spell Fantastic* thirteen of today's finest word wizards—including Kristine Kathryn Rusch, Nina Kiriki Hoffman, Robin Wayne Bailey, Jane Lindskold, Dennis McKiernan, and Charles de Lint—have crafted unforgettable tales with which to enchant your imagination.

WARRIOR FANTASTIC *edited by Martin H. Greenberg and John Helfers.* Alan Dean Foster, Jean Rabe, Diana L. Paxson, Fiona Patton, Tim Waggoner, David Bischoff, Janet Pack, Pauline E. Dungate, Nina Kiriki Hoffman, Kristine Schwengel, Jody Lynn Nye, Bradley H. Sinor, Bill Fawcett, Gary A. Braunbeck, and Charles de Lint let you share in the challenges and victories of those who fight to hold back the darkness. Fron an old arms master hired by the Sheriff of Nottingham to teach him how to best Robin Hood . . . to a betrayal of hospitality that would see blood flowing more freely than wine . . . to a band of warriors who attacked on four legs rather than two . . . here are stories of both legendary warriors and of mighty heroes drawn entirely from the imagination. All of them are memorable adventures that will have you cheering for these magnificent champions as they rescue the downtrodden and mete out justice.

HISTORICAL HAUNTINGS

Edited by
Jean Rabe and
Martin H. Greenberg

DAW BOOKS, INC.
DONALD A. WOLLHEIM, FOUNDER
375 Hudson Street, New York, NY 10014

ELIZABETH R. WOLLHEIM
SHEILA E. GILBERT
PUBLISHERS
www.dawbooks.com

ACKNOWLEDGMENTS

Introduction © 2001 by Jean Rabe.
Fighting Spirits © 2001 by Roland J. Green.
Jennie in the Field © 2001 by Stephen W. Gabriel.
Ravenmere © 2001 by Andre Norton.
In the Charnel House © 2001 by Brian M. Thomsen.
When You're Dead . . . © 2001 by Michael A. Stackpole.
Spirit of Honor © 2001 by John Helfers.
Danny's Desire © 2001 by Janet Pack.
The Mummies of the Motorway © 2001 by Elizabeth Ann
  Scarborough.
In the Chief's Name © 2001 by Bruce Holland Rogers.
Hatshepsut's Revenge © 2001 by Peter Schweighofer.
Those Taunted Lips © 2001 by Leslie What.
Warrior in the Mist © 2001 by Lisanne Norman.
Where the Bodies Are Buried © 2001 by Pierce Askegren.
An Answered Prayer © 2001 by Gene DeWeese.
Stars, Won't You Hide Me? © 2001 by Tom Dupree.
Pretender of the Faith © 2001 by James Lowder.
Knowing She Would © 2001 by Donald J. Bingle.
Diving the Coolidge © 2001 by Brian A. Hopkins.

CONTENTS

INTRODUCTION
by Jean Rabe

A curtain flutters, yet the shutters are drawn tight.

The floor in the hallway creaks, but no one is stepping there. The candle flames dance eerily, though the air is still. In the darkness, you sense that you are not alone.

Is it your imagination?

Or are there ghosts about?

The notion of ghosts has intrigued writers for centuries—from Greek playwrights to Shakespeare to Charles Dickens and his *Christmas Carol* to modern day screenwriters whose ghosts are given vivid and gory life by elaborate eye-popping special effects.

In this volume, our writers and their ghosts will intrigue you.

Eighteen of the best voices in fantasy and science fiction were asked to pen tales of haunts drawn from history—shadows of the past, as it were. There are spirits whose presence is barely noticeable, a suggestion playing in the back of your mind. There are malevolent spirits as well, tormented souls bent on disturbing the living. And there are capricious spirits, too—as ghosts are as diverse as the writers who try to capture them in stories.

Andre Norton drew upon her love of a particular fantastical era to find her ghosts, while Janet Pack drew upon her own family history—a distant and wronged relative from the Revolutionary War.

Roland Green found his specter linked to World War II, while John Helfers discovered his in the ancient Orient.

9

Lisanne Norman called upon her own experiences reenacting famous battles of long-dead armies to find her ghosts. And Brian Hopkins took to the open water to seek his "Davy Jones."

Mike Stackpole unearthed one in a ruined building. Pierce Askegren found one at a construction site. And Donald Bingle discovered one in . . . well, that would be telling, wouldn't it?

Apparition, shade, specter, spirit, haunt, revenant, phantom, spook, wraith, phantasm, visitant, bogy, shadow, shade—call them what you will, use whatever name makes you feel most comfortable. They are all here—in this collection meant to give you a shiver or two.

And when you're reading this book . . .

And the curtains happen to move

or the hallway creaks.

or the lamp by your chair flickers . . .

Maybe it's not your imagination. And maybe you aren't alone.

FIGHTING SPIRITS
by Roland J. Green

Haiku by Frieda A. Murray

Roland J. Green writes science fiction, fantasy, men's action fiction, nonfiction, and book reviews. He is also a voracious reader of military and naval history, and is married to Frieda Murray, a voracious reader of folklore. This explains, but does not excuse, the subject of "Fighting Spirits" in this anthology. Roland and Frieda live in Chicago with their teenage daughter, Violette, and a large black cat named Thursday. Roland's latest book is *Voyage to Eneh,* seafaring science fiction, and the first in the Seas of Kilmoyn trilogy.

Officially, this never happened.

I'm real. So is Dr. Okubo. So is Iwo Jima. I'm not going to bet either way about anything else being "real" as the normal world understands it.

In my business, betting is a bad idea. It attracts the attention of what I'll call by their Greek name, the "luck gods." People like Okubo. And I want their attention about as much as we want the attention of the *National Inquirer.*

Unofficially, who am I? A Marine (there's no such thing as an ex-Marine) who carried a BAR on Iwo Jima in 1945, a retired pharmacist, owner of an organic-food store outside Sacramento, occasionally doing some work with—call them "paranormal phenomena."

Don't call me a "ghostbuster." Please. There are ghosts and there are ghosts. Also, don't ask who I work for. It's classified "If I told you, then I'd have to kill you," in both the United States and Japan.

As to why Iwo Jima, I can save you the trouble of looking it up in a history book. In 1945, about a hundred thousand Americans and Japanese piled onto seven and a half square miles of volcanic rock and sand in the northwest Pacific. About thirty thousand of them did not leave the island alive, or in many cases at all.

That's a pretty dense population of ghosts, if you look at it from the point of view of my current profession.

*   *   *

I wasn't there, obviously. But afterward I studied the records of the three men whose deaths brought me back to the island, and I know where and how they died. So Okubo and I reconstructed the—the deaths something like this . . .

Gunny Wade was the farthest down the tunnel, because he was the shortest. (Some Marine Gunnies look more like welterweight wrestlers than Conan the Barbarian.)

Sergeant Haab held the light up, so that Gunny Wade could see and still have both hands free. Behind Haab was Lance Corporal Shimizu. Hawaiian Japanese, he was the team's linguist. Right now, he was ready to let his M-16 do the talking, if there was anybody to talk to.

Gunny Wade was the senior Marine NCO on a joint Japanese-American remains retrieval team. (Remember all the dead who never left the island.) This far down in the caves and tunnels that honeycombed the island, any remains would most likely be Japanese. Remnants of General Kuribayashi's tough troopers, who'd fled down into the darkness and died of wounds, thirst, or starvation if they didn't commit *seppuku*.

So Wade's job was to mark any remains for the Japanese retrieval people. He was also to learn what had happened to two Japanese and one Marine who had gone into the tunnels for body retrievals two days ago and hadn't come out.

Cave-ins, falls, getting lost? Maybe, but Wade suspected something else—illegal souvenir hunters. The Japanese Self Defense Force garrison was hardly big enough to fill the hangar for roll call, let alone patrol an island where even above ground you sometimes couldn't see fifty feet ahead of you. (Nature made Iwo Jima rugged. The battle made it worse. Then the engineers tried to smooth it out. Typhoons and seismic activity have been trying to roughen it up again ever since 1945. You can walk from one end of the island to the other in a short day—if you have good boots and sprain-proof ankles.)

Some World War II souvenir collectors had no morals and lots of cash. Enough to make it pay to take a Zodiac from a fishing boat over the horizon, across the beach in the middle of the night, search half a mile of the underground by daylight, then retrace steps.

It would be easier, for people armed and ready to kill anybody who stumbled on them while you were looting the dead. Most of the time, an M-16 can prevent that.

So Wade knelt and studied what he saw on the floor in front of him.

"This one's American. Not from the battle either. Too new."

"Have we—is it Linuzek?" That was the missing Marine.

"Too old. He's wearing Vietnam jungle boots, and—Jesus!"

"What?"

"Something just ripped him open right down the rib cage, then scattered the bones."

The darkness must have felt even darker for a moment. It would probably have been Haab (the solid type you want on your flank when it hits the fan) who said, as he drew his .45: "We'd better check the records of our garrison here before the Japs came back in '68. Could be they lost one, could be sightseeing around here goes back a ways."

"Dumb," Shimizu might have said.

"Dumb people go back a long way, too," Haab could have replied.

I don't know if they said anything else, before they heard something that made them all shut up. The next noise would be three clicks as they snapped off safeties on two M-16s and the .45, and the one after that a crash as the ceiling cracked open.

I don't know if Gunny Wade yelled when the chunk of stone crushed his leg and pinned him to the floor. He must

have said something when—whatever it was—lunged down
from the hole and scooped out his guts, then slammed into
his jaw so hard it broke his neck, snapping his head
backward.

By then, Shimizu must have been shooting, because he
had a target. But seconds later another rock smashed the
light, so maybe Haab didn't fire because he was afraid of
hitting Wade in the dark. Of course, he couldn't have hurt
Gunny by then, or the enemy at all.

Haab got his knife out before it killed him, maybe to try
fending off the enemy while Shimizu pulled Wade's body
out from under the rubble. Marines don't leave their dead
behind if there's any chance of getting them out.

When another chunk of ceiling came down, Shimizu was
right under it. He couldn't have known what hit him.

*   *   *

Whether or not everything happened just this way, three
missing Americans made waves the size of small *tsunamis*.
Eventually the waves broke on an office in a seventeenth-
century building outside Kyoto. (It's in a lot of guidebooks,
listed as "Private Property," without anybody knowing what
goes on inside. Most of our other offices also hide in plain
sight.)

The people at the office consulted a certain Yasatuke
Okubo, a retired doctor now a priest at a nearby Shinto
shrine. He sent a coded message, which my office relayed
to me. A week after Gunny Wade and his team died, I
landed on Iwo Jima.

My cover was EOD (Explosive Ordnance Disposal, or
cleaning up dud shells and bombs, for you civilians), so I rode
in an SDF transport along with six Self-Defense Force people
and bits and pieces of high-priority cargo. (At least, I assume
a bonsai tree for somebody's office was high priority.)

I was the only American on the flight, so Japanese politeness eventually gave way to human curiosity. Fortunately, nobody asked me a question I couldn't answer convincingly.

So we came into Iwo just after dawn, about the same

time we hit the beaches in 1945. The place didn't look much prettier than it did when I was evacuated on March 27. There wasn't any fighting going on, the vegetation had come back, and the late spring weather was better than the late winter weather we'd had so long ago.

I stayed seated until the ground crew pushed the boarding stairs up against the door. Then I took my cane in one hand and my suitcase in the other and walked down the stairs to set foot on the soil of Iwo Jima for the first time in much more than half a lifetime.

*   *   *

I didn't recognize Okubo at first. He not only wasn't wearing his yellow priest's robes, he wasn't wearing his glasses. I saw several men about the right size and shape in a variety of uniforms, plus a couple of civilians, but none of them looked quite right, and addressing the wrong man would attract notice. It wasn't until one of the civilians came up to me and bowed as to an equal, that I caught on.

"Okubo-san. It is an honor to see you again," I said, in Japanese. There are enough Japanese speakers where I live so that I have plenty of practice between assignments. The prewar Japanese mostly didn't come back after they got out of the relocation camps, but Japanese businessmen have taken their place and become some of my steadiest customers.

I returned the bow, as Okubo replied, "Schumaker-san, the pleasure and honor are equal for both of us, I believe. Would you care to rest before we speak?"

I had spent seventeen of the last twenty-four hours in airplane seats, even if I had flown first class from San Francisco to Tokyo. Also, the SDF transport was an ancient C-46 Commando, uncomfortable even for passengers a lot younger than I am.

I also knew the answer that Okubo expected, which wasn't the one my aging frame wanted me to give.

I looked over a straggling hedge, across a dusty lawn, to a line of concrete-slab workshops, then let my eyes rest on the ashy landscape beyond. Here and there chunks of concrete dotted the ash, some of them old enough to be veterans, and you could still see dips in the ground that had once been shell or bomb craters.

"Would it have been possible to declare this island neutral territory during the war, and then give it to the loser?" I asked, so that nobody but Okubo could hear me.

"Perhaps. But now the dead have consecrated it, as your President Lincoln said. All we can do is meet—*undeath,* as best we can."

*   *   *

It took us a rugged five minutes to reach Okubo's quarters, in the back seat of a Toyota four-wheeler. I was getting old enough to prefer a cushioned ride.

Hell, I was that old when Okubo and I visited Bali in— a year quite a while back, before Japanese and Americans could admit to cooperating. The Jeep we used then practically bounced my kidneys up into my throat.

I held my cane and my tongue. It would have been a twenty-minute walk, but Okubo could have started my briefing. As it was, he tried to make polite conversation after he had run out of politeness, which is a very face-losing thing for even a fairly Westernized Japanese. Fortunately the Toyota's muffler was faulty. I couldn't hear half of what Okubo said, and the driver hadn't a chance of getting suspicious over any pauses.

I also got a dusty throat, but Okubo had a quick remedy for that when we got to his quarters. It's known as Kirin Beer. While I cut the dust, he pulled out three incense burners and mixed the incense in each one with a pinch of herbs. The herbs came from pouches stowed in that ivory-inlaid chest he has carried everywhere I've seen him, and which will remain a mystery until long after I'm dead. It's certainly an antique—early Tokugawa work, at the latest— and as usual, some of the herbs smelled as if they'd been around as long as the chest.

But the herbs turned the incense burners into jammers,

effective against both electronic eavesdropping by humans and other kinds of eavesdropping by other orders of beings. I appreciated the caution, didn't like what it said about our mission, but suspected I already knew the worst.

I was wrong.

"Two more men have vanished since you agreed to come," Okubo said. He reached under the low table and pulled out a map of Iwo Jima, disguised to look like a Meiji-era scroll. The handles at either end were weighted to keep the paper lying flat.

He gave me a tour of the island as the map showed it. Take my word for it—you cold walk the length of the island, from Suribachi to Kitano Point, *underground*. Kuribayashi and his engineers figured that you always dug five different ways of getting somewhere, then added a sixth just to be safe. Which is why the Marines had to saturate the island with steel, explosives, and flesh before they took it.

"The last two were installing lights in a cave that is being opened to tourists," Okubo said. "They stayed behind to finish the last connection. When the people above tested it, one man thought he heard a scream. They went down again, with guns, but found nothing and no one."

"No blood or remains?"

"Not this time. The next time—"

"There'd damned well better not be a next time," I said, with more bravado than I felt—a hell of a lot more. "Otherwise we'll have the whole island on alert, and 'tourists' from everybody's intelligence agencies crawling all over it and us. We want to fight the Second Battle of Iwo Jima without kibitzers."

"What makes you think this will be only the second?"

Nobody could have heard Okubo's words, but anyone who saw his eyes wouldn't have needed to. They said enough—enough to make me reach for another Kirin.

"I think I shall prepare dinner," Okubo said. "We have red beans and rice, cabbage, and some not despicable beef. If I remember correctly, you have little taste for sushi."

I sipped the Kirin, although I wanted to chug it. "If God

had meant us to eat raw fish, He would never have let us discover fire."

*   *   *

It wasn't a silent night. Planes and helicopters took off or landed several times, and the air conditioner was almost as noisy as the planes. Also, Okubo snored, and I was sleeping in a Japanese bedroll on the floor.

I still slept like a brick.

Over a breakfast of rice balls, scrambled eggs, and tea, Okubo outlined the plan.

"We will seek our point of contact with the demon-world here," tapping the mark for where the last two men disappeared. "We can reach it directly, without traveling above ground long enough to risk being seen and stopped. Also, it is the most recent site. That has been known to help, with prey such as ours."

I agreed, from both reading and experience. But another look at the map made me wonder who was going to be prey and who the predator. We would have more than a mile of underground hiking (or crawling, or scrambling) to the site from the nearest entrance to the underground. Plenty of time for an enemy with only normal senses to hear us coming and lie in wait.

"I have the ingredients for the—the medicine—you took in Bali. It helped against the heat, as I remember. It should help your knee."

The stuff tasted awful, and my heart wasn't in the same shape it had been, back before Maeve died. But I didn't want to crap out and either abort the mission or force Okubo to execute it alone.

"As long as it's not mixed up in Suntory." A small amount of ethanol seems to be necessary for the medicine's effectiveness.

"We have more Kirin."

"Good enough."

*   *   *

The entrance to the underground was only about five hundred yards off the end of the airfield, just outside the security perimeter. We had to carry our gear in backpacks because a couple of obvious cavers wandering across the base would make people turn and look where they were going. Then the big sign over the entrance—WARNING: POISON GAS CONTAMINATION—might not be an adequate cover story.

We reached the entrance, climbed down the thirty-foot shaft (an old well) without any problem, then pulled on our gear. No warm clothing, since Iwo Jima has plenty of geothermal heat, but plenty of water and a few quick-energy-type rations. Also a belt for each of us, on which we slung our weapons and pouches of herbs from the ivory chest.

Those weapons were another reason for keeping out of sight. I was carrying a Ka-Bar knife that the son of a friend of mine had used in Vietnam to tighten a tourniquet around the stump of a Marine's leg. Okubo was carrying a Swiss army knife that he had used to save a fellow passenger on the Tokyo subway with an emergency tracheotomy.

That was a rule hammered out over generations, maybe centuries, of our business. The weapon could be cold iron or bamboo, but it had to be something capable of killing that had also been used to save life.

Don't ask me why. That's a secret so closely guarded that even *I* don't know the details.

It was all low tunnels, built for World War II Japanese prepared to rough it, except for one large cave. That one had clearly been entered from the surface and cleaned out of remains and souvenirs years ago. Then why did I feel more like bait there than anywhere else?

"What we seek has been here," Okubo said. "I hope this does not mean that it searches for a way to the surface."

The next length of tunnel led out of the far side of the cave, about sixty feet away. Our lamps could just light up the entrance—enough to show a figure standing there.

I put my hand on the hilt of the Ka-Bar, then noticed that Okubo had not drawn his knife. He had reached behind his back and put his hand on one of the herb pouches, though. I'm not in his class as an herb-lorist, but I recognized a mixture that you can throw in front of you, to halt an evil spirit in its tracks or get the attention of all the other kinds long enough to talk to them. If they want to talk.

This one apparently didn't. It—*he*—took another step forward. Then Okubo bowed so deeply that he nearly overbalanced and fell on his nose.

"Greetings, Kuribayashi-*san*," he said.

I didn't need the greetings to recognize our visitor. He was a middle-aged man, above average height for a Japanese, heavily built and with the beginnings of a paunch. A pencil mustache didn't soften his broad face. He wore a khaki shirt, brown riding breeches, and polished boots. No insignia, but his whole bearing said "military."

It also told the truth. This was General Tadimichi Kuribayashi, the Japanese commander of Iwo Jima. I didn't doubt his presence—at least in spirit—or what I ought to do first.

A Marine salutes superior officers. I saluted General Kuribayashi. That made him notice me for the first time. I hoped he didn't notice the faint chorus of wailing spirits I thought I heard from a long way off—Marines who couldn't stand seeing an American salute Kuribayashi. Considering how much American blood Kuribayashi had shed, I was not surprised.

Kuribayashi was not a stoical sort. I'd read his letters to his family. I imagine he was surprised. But discipline held him, too. He returned the salute.

"It is an honor to meet a Marine," Kuribayashi said. He had a distinct accent, which suggested that he was one of those high-ranking spirits who is allowed to retain characteristics of the living person, to provide peace of mind while they do important work. From the way Okubo had greeted him, I suspected that the important work had involved my friend before. I now understood that look when I said "the Second Battle of Iwo Jima."

I did not want to be the first Marine casualty of the Third (or Nth). I also didn't want to even *think* less than courageously, in the presence of any aspect of a Japanese soldier of Kuribayashi's day.

"I thank you for recognizing me as a Marine," I said, in Japanese. This got a bow in return, the one to somebody only *slightly* inferior—say, a field grade officer.

"I have recognized the wisdom of Dr. Okubo since he was a much younger man laboring to return our wounded to the battle or to give them an honorable death," Kuribayashi said. "For such a matter as we must consider now, only a Marine and a veteran of Iwo Jima would have the necessary power."

"Will even the three of us be enough?" Okubo said.

"That depends on both our fighting spirit and our weapons," Kuribayashi said. "I am familiar with Dr. Okubo's skill. And I would never question the fighting spirit of a United States Marine."

It occurred to me that the Marines finally had their tribute from Kuribayashi, just as they had given him theirs in 1945, a backhanded "I hope the Japs don't have any more like him."

But Okubo and Kuribayashi were talking now, in Japanese and so quickly that I had to listen carefully to keep from missing something important.

*   *   *

Kuribayashi had a real head for details—but nobody who'd spent a week fighting their way through his defense system could have doubted that. Obviously, he'd carried it over from Iwo Jima into the spirit world—another mark of high rank there.

But he'd need more than details and rank for dealing with our enemy. Our mystery killer was a naval lieutenant named Hattori, who had died in Captain Inouye's *banzai* charge. He'd fallen even before blooding his sword, and left the world broadcasting fury and frustration so loudly that an *oni* heard him.

Onis are a form of Japanese demon—big, ugly, fierce, always horny, but usually not very bright. This one realized that he could have a human serving him for centuries, if he promised Hattori a chance to kill more Americans or traitorous Japanese.

"He promised Hattori that he himself might become an *oni* in time," Kuribayashi concluded. "As I lacked power in either the human or the spirit realms, and the war was still going on, I did nothing to restrain Hattori's spirit. After the Emperor commanded that the war cease, I sought him, but he and his master appeared to have left the island.

"Now, I fear that the *oni* has promised Hattori his final transformation, if he will return to Iwo Jima. I do not doubt that Hattori has forgotten all honor, and believes that Americans and Japanese alike desecrate the graves of his comrades.

"With your help, Sergeant Schumaker, Medical Corporal Okubo, this old general will try to return one of his men to the paths of honor."

That's a mission statement you wouldn't find in any business-school text, but it was the right stuff for us.

*   *   *

I won't go into details about how we got from where we were to where we fought. A lot of it's either technical, secret, or both. Also, there's a certain amount of memory loss involved. Your memories of what happened before and after the passage are intact—or they're supposed to be; I suspect that some of our people who didn't come back weren't lucky that way. Your memories of the passage itself are blurred.

So all I can say is that a crack opened in the nearest wall of the cave. It grew wide enough to show us a flight of rough stone steps dimly lit from above by what seemed to be sunlight. Odd bits of iron stuck out of the floor, ceiling, and walls here and there, and we had to maneuver around them as we climbed. I noticed that my knee wasn't hurting *at all*, and that Okubo was practically scampering up the stairs.

Neither of us, however, wanted to push ahead of General

Kuribayashi, who climbed at a steady pace, as dignified as an Emperor and as unstoppable as a tank.

Suddenly we were in sunlight, within sight of Iwo Jima. Or a place intended to look like Iwo Jima, just after the fighting stopped. We could see Mount Suribachi looming to the south, and ridges and ravines gouged by shells and bombs all around us. Great lumps of concrete showed where explosions had blown whole pillboxes out of the ground. Burned-out Shermans showed where Japanese anti-tank gunners had got lucky. A huge hole at our feet looked like the crater from a battleship's gun or a spigot mortar.

The sky overhead was a uniform, unnatural gray, which I was afraid to look at too long. And the *smell*—it took me back all those years. Natural sulfur, explosives, burned flesh, and the peculiar mix of excrement and decaying bodies that nobody who was on that island can ever forget.

I saw that Kuribayashi now had a lieutenant general's insignia on his shirt, a sword at his belt, and another sword wrapped in silk slung across his back. His boots were dusty.

I looked at Okubo, who now wore threadbare Japanese Army fatigues, bloodstained canvas shoes, and a first-aid bag. So I wasn't surprised to feel the familiar weight of a BAR under my arm and a bandolier of magazines for it slung across my chest—a chest now covered with an olive-drab shirt, with a crumpled pack of Lucky Strikes in the breast pocket. And the rest of what I wore now was what I'd worn then, down to the gouge a grenade fragment left across the top of my left boondocker.

Kuribayashi started to lead us around the shell crater, then Okubo held up a hand.

"Wait. I think he—*they*—will come to us." He reached into his first-aid bag, pulled out two pouches of herbs, and slit one of them open with the Swiss Army knife. Then he began sprinkling its contents around the rim of the crater. I only hoped he had enough. Meanwhile, I unslung the BAR and checked the bolt, trigger, and magazine. I didn't bother with the sites. This would be a close-range fight, where a Thompson or even a .45 would be accurate enough.

Okubo hadn't quite finished circling the crater when I felt the ground shake, as if a large shell had burst close by. Kuribayashi drew the sword at his belt and motioned me to step back. I was torn between being a sergeant ordered by a general and being a Marine who wouldn't stand behind anybody.

Before Kuribayashi could notice my hesitation and read me the riot act, the ashes and debris at the bottom of the crater heaved up into a kind of dirty bubble. Then the bubble burst, showering us with ashes, bits of rock, and other kinds of debris. Lieutenant Hattori soared out of the crater as if he'd been fired from the spigot mortar, and landed halfway up the slope.

Or rather, what had *been* Lieutenant Hattori. I thought for a moment that the *oni* had come to do its own dirty work. Hattori's arms dangled below his knees, his legs in their ragged trousers were bowed, and each hand had four claws in place of fingernails and a longer claw with a serrated inner edge in place of the thumbnail.

I wondered how far his transformation into an *oni* had gone. Too far for him to understand us?

Hattori landed on all fours, but sprang up with the agility of a gymnast and swarmed up the slope toward us. Okubo just had time to throw the second pouch into the last gap on the rim, raising a cloud of herbal dust mixed with ashes. Hattori ran straight into it, stopped, wiped his eyes (human-looking, even if his face had turned green) with the back of one hand, and sneezed.

That sneeze was oddly reassuring. All his humanity hadn't gone. How to reach what was left?

Then Kuribayashi strode forward, his face twisted as if he were about to chew out a drunken private. He walked straight through the fading cloud of herbal dust as if it wasn't there, another proof of his powers in the spirit world. ("His round belly is packed full of fighting spirit," the Japanese wrote about him at the time. Death, defeat, and time didn't seem to have changed that.)

"Lieutenant Hattori!" Kuribayashi barked.

"Hai!" Hattori replied, bracing to attention and saluting

as best he could with those grotesquely altered demon-arms. I thought he was going to poke out an eye.

"You disobey your Emperor, you dishonor what little uniform you have left, and you shame your ancestors and comrades who obeyed the command to surrender."

"You surrendered Iwo—"

"Silence!"

Lieutenants do not interrupt generals. This applies on all planes of existence.

Kuribayashi continued. "The war is over. The Americans had fighting spirit equal to ours, and they had superior weapons. Shall I show you how the war came to an end?"

I did not see what Kuribayashi put into Hattori's mind, but Okubo winced and clapped his hands over his eyes, as if to protect them from a blinding flash. Hiroshima or Nagasaki?

"After these, and after Okinawa, the Emperor knew that we must end the war or it would end the Yamato race, in both body and spirit. So Japan surrendered, and received more honor than we would have dared expect."

This time I had glimpses of what Kuribayashi was showing the recalcitrant lieutenant. The surrender on the *Missouri*. Marine occupation forces going ashore at Yokusaka. MacArthur installed as a quasi-Emperor at the *Dai-Ichi* palace. Then a fast forward through the long, painful, but ultimately triumphant recovery, as rubble vanished from the streets, rags vanished from people's backs, buildings rose again, factories hummed—

"Ahhhhhh." It was an entirely human wail of despair, from a man too filled with shame to find words. "Unless you are lying . . . ?"

Kuribayashi stepped forward. I thought he was going to slap Hattori into the middle of next week, in the old Japanese Army style. Instead he stepped within reach of those ghastly claws, and put both hands on Hattori's head. I hoped that I could miss Kuribayashi if I had to use the BAR on the lieutenant.

Instead, Hattori fell facedown in the ashes and muttered

several particularly choice Japanese obscenities. Then he
sat up and went into lotus position, his eyes on the ground

"The *oni* lied."

"They often do," Okubo said gently. "But they offer
such temptation, that a desperate man—or spirit—can find
it easy to believe them."

Kuribayashi was not going to let Hattori off that easily
"You not only believed the *oni*, Lieutenant Hattori. You
obeyed the commands to perform dishonorable acts. So you
threw away your chances of learning that he had lied."

"Then there is nothing left for me." Hattori looked
around, to see if any of us was carrying the ceremonial
short blade used for *seppuku*. His eyes fell on my Ka-Bar

"That is honorable steel, made for honorable warriors
with fighting spirit and carried by them in many battles
Would it offend the spirits of dead Marines if I used it as
I must?"

I was just about to hand over the knife when something
surged out of the ground no more than fifty yards away. It
came up on all fours, and for a moment I thought it was a
rock thrown up by a hot spring or volcanic activity. Then
it stood up, and I saw that it had a head rising at least nine
feet above the ground, a tail, and four arms ending in claws
like Hattori's.

It howled its rage, and lumbered toward us.

"My master comes," Hattori said, quite unnecessarily. "If
I can distract it long enough—"

"With Hachiman's favor, you can do more," Kuribayashi
said. He unslung the sword across his back and tossed it to
Hattori. In midair the wrappings peeled off, and a dazzling
katana made three complete circles before Hattori snatched
it—with hands that were suddenly tanned, callused, dirty,
normal human hands.

Meanwhile the advancing *oni* halted. He must have
sensed that powerful enemies were ready to help his rebellious servant, because he began changing his shape. Gray
flesh flowed, limbs shortened and spread out, the head flattened and the snout extended—and before us stood a tank.
It looked like a sketch of a tank done by a third-rate *manga*

artist after the fourth drink, but it had everything a tank needs—including a turret that was rapidly swinging to bring its gun to bear on us.

The first shot missed. Shapechanging can throw off anybody's aim. I knew that the *oni* would improve its aim before we acquired an antitank weapon. At least I had good company to die in—which is not something I would have called three Japanese in 1945.

Hattori raised the sword. I hoped he wasn't going to do anything suicidally stupid. Instead he shouted, "Hachiman, in the sword of a samurai rests his soul. Now I offer my soul again, that I may find honor."

He ran toward the tank, zigzagging to be a more difficult target. He made good time over the ashes, particularly since he was no longer holding a sword. Hachiman—or somebody—changed it into one of the Japanese antitank pole charges, a hefty shaped charge on a bamboo pole or length of pipe. I'd talked to Marines who were inside Shermans when one of those blew, and knew that we finally had a tank killer.

The *oni* now had more targets than its feeble wits could track. So Hattori got in too close for it to depress the tank gun. It started to turn, but on the ashy soil the tracks couldn't dig in fast enough. Hattori rammed the charge into the left track, and when the cloud of smoke and ashes had cleared away, Hattori lay still and bloody, while the left track had spilled off the bogies onto the ground.

Another soul-torturing howl, and the *oni* changed back to its original form. But now one leg was an oozing, smoking, reeking stump, and its belly gaped open, like a very sloppy job of *seppuku.*

Okubo threw another pouch, and it flew like a major-league pitcher's fastball straight to the *oni*'s face. The pouch burst in a purple cloud. The *oni* shrieked and tried to protect eyes now oozing a stream of yellow slime. But only three of its four arms were usable now.

Kuribayashi ran forward, drawing his sword as he moved. He was not built for track and field events, but he covered ground pretty fast. He didn't try to jump, either, or to do anything fancy with the sword. (Maybe it was a cheap wartime model; the books said he'd left his own ancestral blade at home when he went to the island.)

With Kuribayashi's muscles behind it, the sword was good enough. One cut, and the *oni*'s head flopped to one side. A second cut, and only the spine held it on. The last cut severed the spine—and Kuribayashi flew backward, to land almost at our feet.

I was relieved to see that he'd been slapped rather than clawed. Then the relief vanished, as I saw the *oni* groping blindly about, all three working arms feeling their way across the ashy sand, toward the severed head.

I could do something about that. I crippled the most outstretched arm with one magazine from the BAR, then sent the head rolling out of reach of the others with a second burst.

Okubo grabbed my arm. "Only fire can destroy the head for eternity."

At that moment I would have given *my* soul for a white phosphorous grenade, but I was luckier than that. Suddenly my knees sagged, as I felt seventy pounds of weight on my back, and my hands were grasping a flamethrower projector.

The BAR had fallen muzzle-down. Kuribayashi flashed me a thin smile. "I did not think Marines were allowed to be so careless with their weapons."

I thought of flipping him the bird. Instead I advanced, at what might be charitably called a fast lumber. Fortunately it was only a few steps before I was in range, but even then I was up to my ankles in the sand.

The flamethrower did the rest. I burned the head until it was a charred, shrunken, smoking *thing* the size of a football. I was searing the neck stump when the tanks ran dry—and the weight of the whole deadly equipment lifted off my back and legs as it vanished.

I picked up the BAR and felt in my pockets for a cleaning kit. Kuribayashi and Okubo stared at me. Both had to be handling ugly memories—Kuribayashi of the number of his men who had died from flamethrowers, Okubo of the number of men he'd seen dying the ghastly death of large-area burns.

I had just decided that the BAR was going to have to stay dirty (and believe me, that really gripes a Marine!) when the landscape swirled around me, as if part of it was turning to mist and the mist was blotting out the rest. I went to my knees, then flat on my face, and I don't think I had any form of consciousness for a while.

When I came to, Okubo had just finished sprinkling another pouch of herbs over me. I would have said I felt like hell, except that I'd just been there and hadn't felt nearly this sore. All my work in a younger body was coming back to make my aged muscles scream.

I sat up, emptied a canteen (most of it into me, and the rest over my face), and looked at Okubo. "This wasn't the first time you—worked—with General Kuribayashi, was it?"

"No. Nor will it be the last. Both of us have much fighting, before we are allowed to rest as purified spirits."

At the moment I would rather rest as a purified body. The last time I'd needed a bath this badly was the last time I was on this island. Then I saw Okubo staring at something lying on the floor of the cave. It looked like a package wrapped in silk.

The wrapping was silk. On the silk someone had brushed a *haiku;*

> My own land, Nippon
> Honor have I kept with you
> And my Emperor.

—then wrapped it around two fresh peaches.

"He did say his spirit would continue to defend Japan," Okubo said. "But this is the first time he has left anything behind. Did you make the difference, Marine?"

Probably I did. Before I had to go into the nursing home, I went back to Iwo Jima three more times on legitimate remains-retrieval assignments, as well as to keep an eye on the spirits.

And each time, I had a fresh peach to eat on the plane home.

JENNIE IN THE FIELD
by Stephen W. Gabriel

Stephen W. Gabriel holds a Bachelor's Degree in Architecture from the University of Wisconsin–Milwaukee and served in the United States Air Force during the Gulf War. Currently, he works in information systems management and design engineering, while writing fiction, playing games and attending game tournaments, and pursuing other various creative outlets in his spare time.

Maggie stared out the window of the bus as the rain hammered down, graying out the details, making the world appear like an impressionist painting. Not the weather she had hoped for.

It was spring break and she was on her way home from college. All her friends had gone someplace warm—someplace with sand and sun, loud music, and cheap wine and revelry. For some reason, Maggie had felt compelled not to join them, and to instead come home for the week-long break. It might have been the thought of parading around in a bikini in front of strangers that drove her to the Greyhound station, she told herself. But she knew that wasn't it. She had packed a single suitcase, put on one of her old sweaters, and paid the man at the counter fifty dollars for the round-trip ticket.

She switched on the overhead light and turned back to her book, her eyes falling on the beautiful paintings. It was art history, one of her more tedious but enjoyable courses. Maggie had been interested in art ever since she was a child. It probably had a lot to do with her father's love of paintings—he had scores of them hung around the old

Victorian house, and many more stored away or in various galleries she used to visit with him. She continued to read about the Renaissance masters as the miles and the rain passed, and finally the bus stopped. She closed her book almost reverently, packed it in her bag, and trudged out with the rest of the passengers.

Her mother spotted her and waved.

"Hey, Mom, wonderful weather for this time of year!"

"Oh, yes," her mother replied, glancing up at the overcast sky. "But be happy it isn't snowing. It was snowing this time last year." They hugged each other briefly, then headed for the car. Maggie threw her bag into the back seat and slid into the front next to her mother.

She shook her head as the car pulled out of the parking lot, a few sprinkles hitting the window. "So, where's Dad? I thought he would be here, too."

"He's at a new exhibit in New York. But he should be home tomorrow. He's looking forward to seeing you."

Maggie nodded.

"So . . . how are classes?"

She let out a sigh, the air fairly whistling between her teeth. "Classes are fine, Mom. Professor Mulligan is a little dry, otherwise everything's going well. I set my schedule for next fall with Daniels—she's the head of graduate studies."

Her mother took her eyes off the road, a look of joy spreading across her face as she locked eyes with her daughter. "You've been accepted? That's wonderful, dear!"

Maggie pointed, and her mother returned her attention to driving, swerved back into the right-hand lane.

With a guilty shrug, Maggie replied, "Yeah, I've been accepted. Sorry, I thought I'd told you. I found out early last week."

Her mother laughed. "You're about as absentminded as your father."

*   *   *

Maggie smiled as she carried her bag up to her old bedroom, its walls decorated with her own early artwork, dating all the way back to kindergarten. The old drawings brought back fond memories of pleasant days spent coloring and playing in the sun. One crayon drawing in particular caught her attention—a man sitting in a muddy field under a brilliant blue sky in which hung a bright summer sun.

Maggie recalled when she drew it—*copied it*—sort of, she corrected herself. She was about eight, and she had been mesmerized by a painting that had hung variously in the living room over the mantel and in her father's office between the high-reaching bookshelves. It was over the mantel now.

She remembered that painting well because of its somber nature and its overbearing sense of despair. The child she had been had captured the essence of the man's form from that painting, but she had replaced the leaden sky with the bright sun and sky of her youthful imagination.

She began to unpack, unconsciously putting clothes back into drawers that had been unused for nearly four years. She rarely came here for a visit. Maggie put her case of oils on the floor near her old easel and stool. Her father had converted the attic into bedrooms when she was young and gave her the north room when she showed signs of becoming an artist. He had told her that the best light to paint under came out of the northern sky.

It felt good to be home again. The place was familiar and comfortable. The stresses and worries of her final semester slipped far into the back of her mind.

Maggie finished unpacking and then stepped out, passing her sister's room. She peered in for a moment. It was as though time had stopped just beyond the doorframe, as the room lay in perfect order, the toys arranged precisely on the shelf and the pretty lace comforter tucked neatly on the bed. The sun had broken through the clouds briefly, sending shafts of light across the hardwood floor, filling the room with a warm glow.

Maggie remembered the day that her mother came to get her at school, her eyes full of tears. She was twelve and had just started her first year at the middle school. Her sister, Jennie, had been eight and was still in the elementary school. Her mother didn't speak at first, she simply hugged Maggie tight, and Maggie had found herself crying without knowing why. Maggie collapsed in shock when her mother told her of the death of her sister, struck by a car on the way home from school during lunch.

The girls had been close, despite the age difference, playing together often. It was years before Maggie was able to look at a picture of Jennie or talk about her without breaking down in tears.

Maggie choked down a sob and headed down the stairs, thinking how odd it was that something so long ago could still hurt so much. She could still hear Jennie's laughter ringing through her thoughts.

* * *

They ate dinner in the kitchen, cleaned up, and then talked until nearly midnight. Her mother felt it was her duty to catch Maggie up on all of the happenings in town and with the family. Maggie just nodded and smiled, adding an appropriate comment here and there, laughing when required or when a bit of gossip truly amused her. Then her mother headed up to bed, while Maggie browsed over the evening's newspaper for a little while.

The clock struck one as Maggie turned out the kitchen light, negotiating the short hall to the front stairs by memory in the darkness. A sudden chill overcame her when she reached the base of the stairs, like a cold wind blowing through an open window. Maggie froze, straining to see anything.

"Who's there?"

Someone was. She could sense it.

"Who?"

She felt something brush by her legs and heard the pounding of paws going up the stairs. She let out a heavy breath, her body relaxing. It was Claude, her father's pet tabby, coming back from his late-night romp.

She climbed the stairs, changed into her flannel nightshirt

and shooed Claude off her bed before curling up beneath the covers. Maggie dreamed that her sister was walking through a field.

*   *   *

She slept in the next morning and came down to find the house empty, save for the cat. A note explained that her mother had gone to pick up her father at the airport and would be home around lunchtime. She grabbed an apple, then padded toward the den.

"Oh." She stopped in the hall, spotting a picture in an ornate and heavy silver frame. It showed two young girls, both with long blonde hair and wearing pink lacy dresses, glints of mischief in their eyes. Jennie looked the same as Maggie remembered.

Car doors slammed, and she scurried to the kitchen.

Her mother came in first, saying, "Good morning, dear. Did you sleep well?"

Maggie nodded, waiting for her father.

He followed shortly, dropped his luggage, and reached out to hug her. "Hello, Mags! How's my little precious doing?"

"I'm fine, Dad. And you can stop calling me that. I haven't been little for quite a few years."

He laughed deeply and released her. "Still my girl. Full of spunk. Your mother told me the good news. We're both very proud of you. A full graduate fellowship, that's wonderful. Will you spend much time teaching?"

Maggie shook her head. "No, Professor Daniels said I can only teach up to six hours a week. Basically, two studio sessions. It's not much, but it will pick up in the second year." She grinned impishly at him. "How was the exhibit?"

Her father peeled off his coat and his eyebrows rose. "They had two newly rediscovered paintings, both were Renoirs and were lost during World War II. We're really seeing more and more of these as people start going through old possessions and the governments start raiding their own vaults. These two are especially fine. They won't need much restoration work. So, how was your first night home?" He led her to the table.

"It was good. Nice and relaxing, except for when Claude decided to spook me in the hall last night."

Maggie's mom dropped a can she'd tugged from the cupboard, and quickly recovered it. Maggie didn't see her lean against the counter for support.

"About what time was that?" her father asked.

Maggie shrugged. "I don't know, around one or so. Why?"

"Claude's been getting rather active that time at night."

* * *

They spent the rest of the weekend catching up on each other's lives and watching the rain come down in an unending drizzle.

True to form, Claude tore through the house at one again, ending up on Maggie's bed and waking her. She sat in the dark for a while, stroking his head and the back of his neck while he purred softly. He had interrupted the dream of her sister in the field.

* * *

On Monday, Maggie's parents returned to work. After breakfast, she stretched a new canvas and broke out her oils. Maggie always painted whatever came to mind, and today the dreary weather outside helped to provide the subject. It was nearly noon before she stepped back and looked at the rough painting. It was unmistakably a copy of the picture over the mantel—the man in the field, done more as she remembered it—an exhausted and disillusioned man sitting in a muddy field, surrounded by craters half-filled with water under lead-gray skies. She could see the sun striving to break through the barrier, but failing, and noticed that maybe she'd put a little too much blue in the gray for the clouds.

The metallic clink of the mail slot told her the postman had arrived, and she decided to use it as a distraction. The mail contained the usual stuff, plenty of advertisements, some magazines and catalogs, an electric bill. Maggie quickly sifted through it, sorting out the art supply catalogs and dumping the remainder onto the table by the stairs. She grabbed the catalogs and headed into the living room. No sooner had she sat down than Claude was in her lap, circling until he was in the perfect position and then plopping down. The cat purred contentedly as she absently stroked the top of his head while browsing through the pages.

Maggie was halfway into the second catalog when she heard an odd sound, like the one a metal coin makes when it is dropped on the floor and spirals around on its edges until it comes to a rest. Claude stiffened and Maggie looked up in time to see the candlestick holder on the coffee table in front of her wobbling. Claude leaped from Maggie's lap as the candlestick holder came to a stop.

The air turned chill and Maggie gasped, her breath escaping in a white cloud. She shook, more from fright than the unnatural cold. Then she sat still for a few minutes, slowly looking around the room, her breath still steaming away from her.

"Who's there?"

She sensed someone. Just as she had a few nights ago.

"Who?"

Then the sensation passed, as the cold passed. Claude returned to her lap.

*   *   *

Maggie made meatloaf for dinner and had it ready and on the table when her parents came home. They discussed the day's happenings, the latest news, and how work had gone. Then Maggie prompted, "Have either of you noticed a cold draft in the living room?"

It was as though somebody had pressed a pause button. Her parents sat stock still, their mouths hanging open. They looked at one another, and her father finally answered, "We've noticed it gets a little chilly in there from time to time."

Maggie nodded, "Yeah, cold enough that I could see my breath today. And how about the candlestick holder? Have you seen it dance without anyone touching it?"

Maggie's mother started picking up the plates. "She always loved to play with those, you know."

That night when Claude climbed into bed with Maggie, he didn't interrupt her dreams.

*   *   *

At breakfast the next morning the mood was somber, and few words were said before her parents left for work.

Maggie threw on an old oversized T-shirt and sweatpants and returned to her easel.

"How . . ."

Yesterday she had painted a somber gray sky full of heavy clouds with only a little light from the sun penetrating at one point. She remembered thinking that she had used too much blue in the mixture, but it wasn't nearly what she saw now. The sun was a dim orb visible through the clouds, and the sky was a dull blue-gray with all the detail of the clouds faded out.

She shook her head. "The light from the window is different this morning," she told herself. "Brighter and yellower than yesterday. Makes the painting look different."

Maggie picked up her brush and began to paint, stopping when she again heard the clinking of the mail slot.

She considered letting the mail lie there, but then stretched her arms and back, tight from hours of painting and walked downstairs. Claude was sleeping on his back in the middle of the stairs and she reached down and scratched his belly as she stepped over him. He flicked his head up and glared at her for waking him.

Maggie picked up the mail and flipped through it, then set it on the table beneath the silver-framed picture of her and Jennie.

"Jennie." She picked up the picture and carried it into the living room and sat down, placing it on the coffee table in front of her, memories of happy times with her sister flooding her mind. Jennie had always been a happy girl. Maggie remembered the way her sister used to draw, how she held a crayon, the way she bit her tongue with the tip sticking out the right side of her mouth. Jennie had been like a little image of Maggie, as though Maggie were looking at herself only four years younger. She missed her sister terribly, imagining what it would be like to have Jennie still alive and here today.

With a deep breath Maggie stood up, her stomach telling her it was time for lunch. She passed by the painting over the mantel, its dull gray imagery dampening her mood. Her father had gotten the painting while he was in Europe after the war. His unit had landed at Normandy two days before he turned eighteen. They fought their way in toward Paris, where her father spent the rest of the war after being injured. He bought the painting from a woman in a private gallery. It had captured his attention, the drabness of the muddy grays and browns, and the dejected look of the soldier reminding him of the feeling of the battlefield after the combatants had left it.

Maggie stepped closer. The lone man sitting in the midst of the war-torn field under heavy gray clouds emoting hopelessness and despair at the same time bothered and captivated her. She was nagged by a thought that it wasn't right, that the field and the sky and the clouds and the man weren't *right*. That there was something wrong with the painting.

It was painted by a man named Giroud, and according to art historians it depicted his interpretation of a battlefield during World War I. Giroud was an unknown artist, and for all she knew this might be his only piece. From close up, Maggie could see that the painting was not handling the passage of time very well. Cracks crept across its face, and it was beginning to blister near the center. She realized that the painting was also quite dirty, a film covered the paint, making the strokes and colors indistinct.

Cleaning the painting would be routine, but the other restorations would take time.

"But now it's time for lunch," she announced, patting her grumbling stomach. She fixed a sandwich while Claude made love to her legs, rubbing and stroking his head and body along them, hoping for a scrap of the roast beef from her sandwich. A crash from the living room caught the attention of both Maggie and the cat.

Maggie rushed into the room, Claude following cautiously. The picture of her and Jennie lay on the coffee table, tipped over on its face. She reached for the picture and quickly pulled her hand back. So cold! She could see frost forming on the metal, even though the room was quite warm. Nervously glancing around, her breath coming in short uneven gasps, she reached down again and this time picked up the picture, the frame still cold to the touch, returning it to its normal spot in the hallway.

"Jennie?" If it was Jennie, why would she knock over the picture? If it wasn't Jennie, then what was it? And what did "it" want? Maggie was normally skeptical of ghost stories, but something seemed to be going on here. Something that defied explanation. Her parents had obviously noticed the occurrences, and the cat had as well. Still, she had no answers, only a growing number of questions.

Her mother had told her last night that she believed it to be the ghost of Jennie. Her father wouldn't say one way or another. However, they made it clear that they didn't want to discuss the matter. But Maggie was determined to get some answers.

She returned to her lunch, and Claude resumed his begging.

"You win. I'm not hungry anymore." Maggie set her plate on the floor, and the surprised cat dug in with little hesitation, a contented purr coming from his throat.

*   *   *

The dinner dishes were washed, and the three of them were in the living room, her father flipping through the *TV Guide* to see if there was something worth watching.

"How long have these things been happening?" Maggie broke the silence.

Her mother pretended to be interested in Claude.

"Mags," her father finally said, "I'm not sure. The first incident I remember was about a year after Jennie died. But, I didn't notice anything else for another couple of years. It was with the candlestick. Sometimes a knick-knack."

"Have these . . . incidents . . . been getting more frequent?"

He smiled. "Yes. Mostly when you stop by for a visit. This is the first time you've noticed them, though. We didn't say anything because, well, we didn't want to upset you or make you think that perhaps we were losing it."

"Do you think it's Jennie?" she pressed.

Her mother looked up, but said nothing.

"Your mother does," he said. "But I'm not so sure. I would have thought it would feel more familiar. If it was Jennie. It seems, I don't know, *different,* like whatever is doing this doesn't belong here." He contemplated the table for a few minutes, nervously chewing his lip before asking, "Do you think it's Jennie?"

Maggie shook her head, "I don't know, Dad. I just don't know."

*　　*　　*

Maggie spent the rest of the evening working on the painting in her room, recalling the details of the original that hung downstairs and laying them down as accurately as she could. It helped occupy her mind. She crawled into bed around eleven and was soon fast asleep. Immediately she began to dream of her sister, running around the backyard in the dress she had worn in the picture. Jennie was daring Maggie to catch her, hiding behind trees and bushes. Maggie chased her and chased her, laughing along with Jennie, careful to always let Jennie stay just out of reach.

Jennie broke through a line of bushes, and Maggie heard a muffled scream followed by a splash. Maggie froze for an instant, her breath catching in her throat as her heart began to race and a feeling of dread came over her. She slowly approached the bushes, hearing Jennie's cries of fear and frustration coming from the other side.

Maggie looked through the bushes at a gloomy vignette. The ground was covered in gray mud for as far as she could see, broken apart by thousands of craters partially filled with water. The bushes and grass and flowers had simply vanished. The sky had become heavy with clouds, their sullen weight bearing down, blotting out any vestige of sunlight. Jennie was trying to climb out of a crater, all the color drained from her, her dress and hair covered in the oppressive gray mud.

Jennie was crying, pleading, "Help me, Maggie. Get this off me!"

* * *

The echoes of a crash jostled Maggie awake. She glanced at the clock's luminous dial. It was one, and the room was cold. Maggie looked around for Claude, but he was nowhere in sight. Then she thought about the painting.

Maggie turned on the light near her bed and got up.

The painting had been knocked from the easel and was lying facedown.

"Claude," she softly cursed, believing the cat responsible.

She pulled the painting up from the floor with a sickeningly wet peeling sound, and Maggie let out an exasperated sigh. Half of the paint had adhered to the floor, the other half to the canvas.

She pulled out a spatula and began scraping the paint off the floor, putting it into a can. Then she wiped up the floor with a dry cloth and then with linseed oil to remove the last stains of the oils.

Maggie sat back, looking at the remains of the painting that sat once again on the easel. In desperation, she turned the spatula on the painting, intending to peel off the layers of oils right down to the canvas.

When she started to take the second pass, her eyes grew

wide. She quickly scraped another pass of paint off, clearing another stripe on the canvas and another. Then she stared, thunderstruck.

Under the layers of gray and gray-blue of the sky, the canvas was stained in a staggered pattern of intense blue, a yellow coronated ball denoting the sun.

Maggie didn't remember running down the stairs. The next thing she knew she was pulling the painting off the wall above the mantel. She looked around, and seeing no suitable lights, took the painting into the kitchen and placed it on the table. Her mind was racing.

Was the ghost or whatever it was trying to tell her something about this painting? Was it changing what she did each time to her own painting, trying to show her what should be there?

Maggie held one of the linseed oil soaked rags in her hand and began dabbing at the corner of the painting, watching as the layers of soot and dirt came loose.

The top layer of paint came away as well, revealing an intense blue sky painted in a staggered pattern of shades of blue. She let out a deep breath, unaware that she had been holding it.

It all made sense, it had happened so many times. An unknown artist had painted over someone else's work in order to hide it.

Maggie ran upstairs and grabbed her art box, returning quickly to the kitchen where she continued cleaning the painting.

*   *   *

Her mother and father came down for breakfast the next morning into a kitchen littered with paint-soaked rags. Maggie sat on a chair near the table, looking at the painting standing propped up on the counter.

The painting depicted an intense blue sky with a golden sun, a green field spread beneath it rendered in the same blotchy and nervous style as the sky, a little girl with long blonde hair walking along a trail through the field.

Maggie looked up.

"It wasn't Jennie, Mom. And it's not a Giroud," she said, indicating the painting. She pointed at the trail near the edge of the canvas where the name Vincent was clearly written.

"It's van Gogh. There's a title written on the edge in French. It means 'Jennifer in the Field.' "

A chill puff of air teased Maggie's face briefly—it was a sigh of relief and thanks, she knew. Then the air in the house warmed.

RAVENMERE
by Andre Norton

Andre Norton has been writing for more than sixty-five years. The author of more than one hundred novels, she has produced tales in numerous popular genres. However, her best-known work has been done in fantasy and science fiction, in which fields she has won many honors, including the Nebula Grand Masters Award. She presently resides in Murfreesboro, Tennessee, where she oversees a writers' library and makes time to read and recommend historical mysteries. Miss Norton's dual fascination with the legends of King Arthur and unique forms of art—particularly those practiced by women—finds expression in her story "Ravenmere"; there, the bead-weaving created by the heroine suggests the "magic web" wrought by Tennyson's Lady of Shalott.

"Heard as how they has sold Ravenmere—to foreigners. Have to be such."

I had nearly reached that portion of the general shop sacred to Her Majesty's mail before the two women at the other end of the crowded room noticed me. For my part, I paid no visible heed to the silence that ensued as they did; in the small towns of my American homeland, strangers were equally suspect.

Mrs. Jones propelled her considerable bulk around the end of the counter. "You was a-wanting your package, Miss? Jimmy the Post brought it in last night." She produced a box from a pile of parcels and slid it toward me.

"Mighty lot of stamps on that," the proprietress observed. Though her delivery duty was concluded, she did not turn away but stood watching. The little eyes in her broad face flitted from me to the box and back again.

I decided that, the sooner I gave my new neighbors something real to discuss, the quicker I would be accepted as relatively harmless.

"Yes, there are," I agreed; then I took my first step toward acquaintance. "Some children collect stamps. Do you know any youngster who would like these, Mrs. Jones?"

The shopkeeper nodded. "If you'd be so kind, our Jamie does that, miss—Miss Tremayne."

Out of nowhere a pair of scissors appeared, and I carefully cut out the much-bestamped corner of the parcel's wrapping. Enid had certainly made sure of a safe delivery of my order, I thought as I passed the scrap to Mrs. Jones.

Encouraged by this minor ice-breaking, I voiced my real concern. "Could you direct me," I asked, "to someone who could help in the house?"

Silence again, except for a kind of hiss from the other customer, who was now looking at me intently. The shop's owner retreated a step or so, and her mouth pursed as though locking itself on any answer.

"I can post a notice if you want," was the curt reply. The woman nodded toward the door, where a small board hung to which a few tags of paper had been pinned.

"That would be most kind," I answered. "I would like help every day but Sunday—just general cleaning."

Mrs. Jones nodded once more, then abruptly turned back to her other patron. "More o' them cream biscuits for you today, Missus Calder?"

I had been dismissed but accepted the fact without irritation. I was far from certain I would be here very long; however, though I am not a gregarious person, there are shades of loneliness that even I did not wish to darken my days.

As though bodying forth my thought, the overgrown trees and shrubs on the path leading back to my lodging cast their own darkness over me. It was most apparent that this was not a well-traveled way, yet its budding promised an early spring that I longed to see.

A few minutes of travel brought me into an uneven clearing that contained my temporary home: a cottage larger than those in the village. When Ravenmere was in its glory, this place must have housed the bailiff. But what, I had wondered from my first sight of it, had it been in the very beginning?

Two slabs of rock resembling menhirs flanked either side of the door, and stones even larger and apparently more ancient formed the base of the walls. The structure had been created by additions—quite a number of them. Each succeeding century had left its own mark here.

The great house of the estate was now merely a tumble of stone half-hidden by vegetation long out of control. I had no desire to explore that area; none of the locals had warned of snakes, but such a miniature jungle seemed a place where snakes might well set up hole-keeping. What the present owners intended to do with the long-deserted estate they had not yet decided, but meanwhile I had settled here at their invitation for an indefinite stay.

On so promising a day, my chosen workplace was not inside. I set the box I had just acquired into the top of my handy wheeled tote, then pushed past bushes that clutched at my jeans, heading for the discovery I'd made on my second day of residence.

They were called "follies" two centuries ago, such fantastic small buildings placed in formal gardens. Some, of which I had seen pictures, were modeled after classical temples or hermits' caves, and a few were large enough to be used for sheltering picnic meals or staging amateur theatricals. This one, set to front a weed-choked lake, must have indeed been a folly where money was concerned. Its shape was that of a square tower, as though to suggest it had once been part of a now-vanished fortress. Fortunately for my needs, real windows, not arrow-slits for the convenience of castle defenders, had been built into the four sides of the structure. All gave good light, but that was best at the side where I chose to set up my worktable in the single room: facing the water.

The lake was framed by coarse reeds that formed an oddly-precise ring about its murky liquid. One could easily imagine strange life going about its own affairs beneath the surface; yet, while I had been drawn several times to study it, I had never thought of menace.

I unloaded my tote with the ease of long practice, setting out assembly trays, then glass bottles of beads, boxes of threads, and a container of tools—needles and the like. Next I took out my pattern sheet, which I had fastened to stiff backing. At last I was free to deal with the contents of the parcel.

I lifted away the packing material, and what lay within came to life with color. For a moment I simply feasted upon those many hues. Enid had been more than generous. Glowing ember of garnet, molten lava of ruby, noon sun of gold—bands of fire appeared to pulse across the beads dyed with the warm tones of the spectrum. Farther along, the colors cooled to water-tints of green and blue, then chilled to silver, gray, and black. Every nuance was present, from the lightest to the darkest.

Yesterday I had set up the embroidery frame. Now I rose and pulled it from the wall, untied the protecting cover, and drew it into the strongest light; the casters on its legs would make it easy to move as the sun shifted. Finally I arranged the pattern, creasing it so it might be readily consulted. When I had subsided again into my chair, I let myself relax and become absorbed in studying the lines marked on the long banner of gray silk tight-stretched before me.

This was an old art. Exquisite examples had been brought into being in the far past but were now only to be marveled at in museums; however, such "painting" had recently been reborn to enchant beadworker and beholder alike. Considering the challenge of the craft, I flexed my fingers nervously, so much in doubt of my own skill that I almost shrank from threading the first needle.

I continued to gaze at the waiting fabric, picking out the lines I had set there as guides no more than an afternoon ago. But—quickly I pulled my chair closer, reaching at the same time for the large magnifying glass I kept always at hand— *No!*

I snatched up the paper pattern with its intricate markings. Leaf and branch were gone! A drawing remained there, right enough, but it no longer showed the picture I had so carefully designed in days of planning. The glass tilted in my shaking hand.

There was no possible way this could have happened. The new lines had obviously been set down by someone experienced in such work; however, I could not believe that what I had created with such labor had simply vanished—or rather been exchanged for this alien motif which bore no resemblance to it.

Shaking with anger fast growing into such a rage as I had never known, I lifted one hand to rip the cloth from the frame. All my limited time—wasted! And by whom? In this small village, which person could have the expertise to do such a thing—and why?

With this thought, my hand fell again to the table, and I cowered in my seat. The unnatural—impossible—nature of the act had smothered my fury with a fear as icy cold as the anger had been hot. Such a thing could *not* happen!

Every movement was an effort; still I forced my head around and twisted my body so I could view the room without trying to get to feet I did not believe would support me at present. I listened, too, though I could hardly demand an explanation from emptiness.

Then an answer came. Like a hand gripping me by the nape of my neck, some compulsion forced me to bend forward, examine again those marks I had never made. As I did, I began to understand the meaning of this and that traced line. They formed a picture, yes, but one very unlike what I held in mind. The more I studied the artistry of that unknown hand, the greater grew my fear. The only word I could put to the feeling of what I detected in the new pattern was—*Power.* My fear became awe, then envy. This was masterwork, as far above my own labors as they would be beyond the stumbling stitches of a clumsy child.

I laid down the magnifying glass, pushed out of my chair, and stepped through the door, leaving all behind me unprotected. A wind, not yet more than a breeze, had arisen.

Careful to keep away from the edge of the reed-bed, I stood for a long moment facing the lake.

The rising air was light, but it drew ripples across the surface. As I watched, though without truly concentrating on what I observed, I saw colors moving wave-wise in my mind: green of standing water, blue of sun-touched shallows, gray of shadow-play.

Thus—and thus—and thus—

I swung around and ran back to the workroom. Throwing myself into the seat, I faced the smooth stretch of waiting background. *Yes!* There could be no mistake: the design had been altered to represent the pond. But by whom had it been drawn, and for what purpose?

Curiously, those questions no longer troubled my mind. It seemed enough that the scene without had been brought within. I might be caught up in a mystery, but fear had departed.

Touching the fabric, I gasped. My probing finger had been stung with a sharp burst of force like that of an electric shock. I felt filled with energy, consumed by the need to bring to life the image I could now see on that expanse of cloth.

* * *

When I looked up from my labor, the light had moved; the hard jewel-glitter of the beads had softened to a stained-glass glow. For the first time, I was aware of the ache in my hands, my shoulders, and I felt dizzy as I straightened up. My mouth was dry, too. I had never worked thus before, so utterly absorbed in what I was doing.

I glanced away from the small section on which I had been concentrating, then back again—a device I used to sharpen sight dulled by fixed gazing and to catch any error.

I saw the green of velvety sod, the blue of liquid unclouded by murk and laced with a silver glint that expertly created the illusion of breeze-wakened ripples. And at the nearer edge of that body of water was the outline of a pacing bird.

Close-mown grass, not the rank growth I knew to exist outside my window; water of such freshness that it might be rising from a clear spring; a bird in stately pose. The deft shading and setting of the beads made it alive—all of it. I drew a breath of wonder. I had prided myself on my work, but *this*—this was perfection such as I had aspired toward but never before attained.

Thus began my bondage, for imprisonment—and forced labor—it came to be. Luckily, the cottage had been stocked with provisions when I moved in, as I begrudged any time away from my task, even the brief length needed to prepare a simple meal. I sustained myself by oatmeal made in quantities and swallowed speedily when I came out of bed; then by soup and crackers, or a mess of canned vegetables, heated up at dusk when the light had faded too far for me to put in even one more bead. I did not break my absorption for any midday meal.

During the hours when I was not occupied with needles, beads, and tiny stitches, muscles I never knew I owned protested their hours of being pulled as taut as the threads they had sent into the silk. However, while I labored, I felt nothing but excitement, a relentless drive to accomplish as much as I could. That in itself was new, for it was clear that I was now somehow able to complete far more work at each sitting than I had ever done before.

On the third day I was interrupted. Without warning a shadow fell across the backing of the bead-picture, and I glanced up, startled, to see someone standing at the window that faced the lake. At the same instant, the passionate desire to continue my crafting vanished.

The woman was tall, and her body was concealed in a dark garment so that only her face was visible. That was an ivory mask in which the eyes alone showed life; but once I had raised my own to look into them, I could not turn away. Out of that muffling cloak emerged a pale, long-fingered hand, and she beckoned.

Nor could I delay my answer to that gesture. I rose and

went to the door and, as I opened it, found myself facing my visitor through the window in another wall. Again her gaze held me mute and waiting. She herself was in no hurry to speak; instead, she shrugged almost lazily, and her covering slipped from her. That garment never reached the floor—suddenly, it simply *was not*.

The dress she wore beneath fitted far more snugly and was of a now-familiar green-blue shade touched here and there among its folds with a flick of silver. Her hair had been divided into a pair of heavy braids, one of which fell across her left breast while the other disappeared behind her right shoulder.

By now I was shivering—this *lady* (she surely owned no lesser title) could not be anyone from the village come in answer to my note posted in the store. Not by the greatest stretch of imagination could I envision her wielding broom or duster, or bustling about a kitchen with cooking pots!

She ceased to hold me with her measuring stare but rather advanced boldly so that I was forced to move aside as she strode past me. When I turned, she was standing before the frame and tracing with her first finger a pattern in the air, at a few inches' distance from the patch of completed work. Now and then she nodded, as though with approval. I was still trying to summon the courage for a question when she spoke.

"Nimuë ever chooses well. You are truly of her service, Maid of the Needle—"

Nimuë . . . that name . . . Deep within me, a memory struggled to awaken.

At last I succeeded in speaking. "Lady—who are you?"

My visitor smiled enigmatically. "Who am I? Well, I have borne many names in my time: Traitor, Challenger, Destroyer, Dealer-in-Death. How like you such titles?" Now she laughed, on a mocking note. "You will find them told in chronicles long kept, but said to spring only from bards' fancies and to have no force of true life in them."

I backed away, believing by now that the woman was not only attempting to frighten me but also that she was working herself up to an act of violence. Clearly she was insane.

"No," she replied as though she had read my thoughts. "I am not twisted of mind—I am, in truth, more sane than this world with all its strains and stresses. But this work," she indicated the bead-picture, "will alter that. For you there will be payment, when the labor is complete. And that must be soon."

I began to shake my head. The gesture of negation grew ever faster, until I could hardly see and only the supporting wall behind me kept me on my feet. Still I could not voice the denial that seemed dammed behind frozen lips.

Now my legs, too, obeyed orders that were not my own, carrying me to my seat and planting me firmly in it. I twisted my hands together, resisting the pressure that came next to pick up a needle, choose another bead.

The woman had likewise moved, and I could still see her. That she was enjoying the sight of my resistance—and relishing my grinding-down into subordination—was very plain.

"What name do you bear in this age, Maid of the Needle?"

That query swung a lash of force against which I could not stand.

"Gwen—Gwen Tremayne."

Once more the water-gowned one laughed, and her gaze swept over me slowly from head to feet, as though she were appraising me in some way.

"This time is not so fortunate for you, is it—my Queen?" she drawled, her tone close to insolence.

What she said had no meaning as far as I was concerned—or so I thought.

"So you are yet lost; still, you can make yourself useful." My captor held out both hands brought together to form a cup, and into that improvised vessel liquid began to splash, though from where I could not tell.

This meeting had passed so far beyond the bounds of reality that I closed my eyes. Had I labored with such intensity during the past few days that I was hallucinating?

"Nine we were . . ." intoned a voice, one so distant that

I heard it only as a whisper. *"Nine we divided the Great Wheel . . ."*

And then I saw—though with some sense of the mind or memory, for my physical eyes were still shut—that there was, indeed, a Wheel. Lines of silver crossed, overscoring one another to form a disk, and adorning it were nine glimmering stars of argent light.

"Turn with time!" the voice ordered crisply.

One of the stars moved forward, expanded, and eclipsed the Wheel. It formed a frame that enclosed the head of a woman. Her piled gray hair supported a crown, or what seemed the ghost of such a diadem: a tarnished circlet pocked with empty settings for now-lost gems. Her face was near as hueless as her hair.

"Greetings to thee, Dindrane, Queen of the Wasteland," chanted the speaker.

"Greetings to thee in turn, Mistress of the Wheel," the gray woman answered, "but I am not for your summoning again. What we wrought, we wrought, and that is long past."

With that speech, she vanished. The silver-traced disk became visible again, though briefly, for another star flung out of it to front me. Once more a woman appeared; however, this lady had free-flowing black hair beneath a crown of clouded silver, and she wore a countenance as deeply tinted as her predecessor's had been wan.

"Hail," the voice greeted her, "Dark Woman of All Knowledge."

The answer of this high one, too, came swiftly. "The Storm Winds blow no longer; I am not for your calling."

So they came and went. Some were young, others in the fullness of life. Each was crowned, and every one was saluted by the speaker as a woman of Power. However, when the seventh star swung outward and grew, the frame it formed was empty, save for the likeness of an apple behind which hung an argent branch.

"Aye, you still linger." The voice rendered no formal greeting but a curt phrase chill with anger. "Yet your power is long since wasted, Flower Queen, and the Wheel has thrown you off—though not so far that I cannot bring you to my service. For I am Morgan, and the Wheel answers to me in this world, which I once lost, as well as in Avalon!"

The frame vanished, and the nine-sectioned disk once more appeared—but one of its blazing stars was gone.

"Look—with the eyes of the body!" The speaker sharpened those words into a compelling order.

I opened my eyes. No Wheel any longer hung before them, but the dim light of the setting sun made of the window another sort of frame for the woman who had intruded. Now she took several long steps that brought her to me, holding out her still-cupped hands. That chalice of flesh she presented to me with a command I dared not disobey:

"Drink!"

Lowering my head, I sipped. The liquid was cool, and from it rose the scent of ripened fruit which, as I mouthed it, I knew for the juice of new-pressed apples.

I drank—and I understood—but part of me still refused to believe.

"I am *not*—" I began to protest.

"Remember—do not deny memory!" Morgan gave her third order.

A tapestry of doings and dealings that were certainly not mine in this life unrolled in my mind. So fast it happened, and so galling were many of the recollections, that I covered my face with my hands and felt them wet with tears.

Fingernails dug painfully into my shoulder as the witch-woman brought me back to the present. "May Queen you no longer are," she declaimed, "yet you remain the key that will open the door. I have not lost my power but have gained more while I slumbered. Mistress of the Wheel and of Time is Morgan, daughter of a king, wife of a king, sister and first love of a king!"

"And," I answered bitterly, "one who brought about the destruction of a world that might have been." For the past was now mine, though I wanted none of it.

Yet somber legends of an age agone seemed no more unreal than the waking nightmare of my present imprisoning. Dusk had now sealed the window behind me; however, light still lay all about within the room—it might have been flowing from the walls. As I fronted the frame with its stretched silk, I found I could see as well for my work as though the sun were standing at full noon.

And labor I did, without hesitation and untiringly—needle and bead, green of this shade, blue of that hue. The picture before me grew magically, but in the border only—the very center of the scene being created remained blank.

Time no longer had any meaning. All that mattered was the place I was bringing into existence; yet with the only part of my mind that remained my own, I did not forget the one whose predatory-bird gaze watched my efforts and whose power kept me at them.

Those of the Wheel—those women I knew, as well. Queens they had been, and priestesses also; and in a time so distant from this that no mind could rank up the years between, they had held the rule of this land which had, in turn, mothered that of my birth.

Dindrane . . . Kundry, the Old One of Death and Knowledge (the lore of both being intertwined). Enid, Lady of Joy . . . Ygraine, the Hallows Queen, bearer of Him Who Was, Is, and Will Be. Nimuë, holder of the strength of Merlin . . . Dame Ragnell . . . Argante, who dwelt beneath a lake and gave the world's most famous Sword to the greatest of champions . . . Guinevere—

Like a finger that touches flame, my whole being drew back from the last of those. With fierce concentration, I centered my mind wholly upon my task. I wanted to deny that I had ever answered to the name of that Queen who had compassed the destruction of another Wheel, the Round Table; but the same mystical sense that forced me to own that truth revealed what I now did—though in spite of myself—as another act of betrayal.

Completed, the work I labored upon would, I knew, be seized by Morgan, and for a second time an act of mine would change the world. It was a world already deep-stained with blood and heart-gnawed by evil, true; yet the release of Morgan's full power would transform it from a

place merely shadowed to one utterly enshrouded by the
Cloak of the Dark.

That must never come to pass—not, at least, through
my hand, my needle, my beads. Still I sewed and could
not stop.

*   *   *

Save for the empty space at its center, the picture was
finished as the dawn's rays touched the window, warring
with the witch-light about me.

"Done—well done!" The praise was not meant for me;
it was my captor's pleasure in her own accomplishment that
she was voicing.

Morgan had stood by my side as I labored through the
night. Now she stepped in front of me, gripped the beading-
frame, and swung it to face herself. A large needle gleamed
suddenly in her hold, and she leaned forward until the point
of that implement touched the fabric. There was a flash of
pallid fire, then another, a third . . .

When the sorceress stepped back, her contribution to the
design was revealed: the Wheel, web of a spider freed once
more to spin her nets of shadow. Yet the labor was still
not complete, for she issued an order to me, her gaze still
fixed on her work:

"Crystals—"

Again her power held me, moving my hand against my
will. Crystals . . . yes, a small tube held such clear mineral
spheres, part of the treasure Enid had sent. I laid them out
in a line, eight in number—but a ninth I grasped tight in
my hand and did not add to that gleaming row.

This time I did not need to thread the needle I had set
upon the edge of the sorting tray. Once the crystals had
been released from their vial, they arose of their own accord and, flying toward that nine-pointed web, fitted themselves one by one to each star on the Wheel. Hidden in
my palm, the remaining bead, icy cold, was stealing all sensation from my flesh. Still I clutched it close.

Morgan gave a near-purr, a sound like a cat well satisfied;

she seemed to have forgotten me. In that moment I took
my chance. Clenching my left hand to match my right, I
raised both fists and brought them down onto the worktable with all the force I could summon. Under that assault,
a rich shower of color geysered up as beads by the hundreds, the thousands, filled the air like a shattered rainbow.

I heard words screamed out like a curse but paid no
heed—I was intent on something else. The ninth crystal I
held must be meant to center Morgan's own star—the top-
most on the tapestry—and I saw nothing but that. Groping
without looking, I closed my free hand about chill metal: a
pair of keen-honed scissors.

The fist crimped round my own bead had numbed to the
point of uselessness, yet my left hand still obeyed me. Leap-
ing to my feet, I slashed down at the unfinished picture
with the open blades. But I had leaned forward to aim that
blow, and now I overbalanced and—*dropped.*

Water closed about me—water, such as had ever been
the medium of Power for the Sisters of Avalon, the Women
of the Wheel.

I fought as slime-laced liquid surged up to draw me
down, hearing as I did so the thwarted sorceress screaming
as a raven might screech above a battlefield. My right hand
a weight dragging me to the depths, I flailed with my left,
kicking my feet to keep my head above the surface. Knowing that I must open the clenched fist or be pulled to my
death, I forced its fingers apart with a desperate order from
my mind. The crystal, loosed, tumbled away. But now my
other hand was a dead weight!

Morgan was coming, striding across the surface of the
water. Her features were twisted into such a malevolent
mask that she seemed a very demon.

Somehow I was able to raise the lifeless thing my left
hand had become. As it moved up through the water, I
could see a gleam of metal; but when it lifted into the air,
that glimmer became a light. Yet I did not hold my work-
shears, as I believed; instead, I clutched a clump of reeds,
each darkening fast, and growing heavy—oh, so heavy.

The witch-woman was almost on me, no longer voicing

a battle-bird cry but rather keening sounds in no language
I knew.

I made my last and greatest effort, swinging my leader
arm up to meet the blow she aimed my way. I was not
even certain I had touched her, but she flinched away and
bent over, nursing one of her own arms against her body.
Then her mouth opened to show pointed teeth, and she
howled, maddened and dangerous as a wounded beast.

I was sinking, the noisome waters rising past my shoulders to neck, then chin. My resistance grew feebler as the
last of my strength ebbed. Yet still Morgan made no move
to slay me—instead, she retreated a little, mouthing words.

"Sisters." I could understand her now. *"To me!"*

Did seven shadowy faces show for a moment behind her?
And from whence came the cry that I myself choked out
fighting to keep my lips above the liquid?

"Iron, cold iron!"

I lost myself in darkness.

*   *   *

Pain found me all too quickly and brought me out of
that friendly nothingness; every bone in my body ached.
But I was content to lie as I was for a space, eyes closed,
for nothing threatened now—of that I was sure.

Slowly, as one might assemble scattered pieces of a puzzle, I strove to understand. I opened my eyes. Above me
rose the cobweb-curtained ceiling of the folly. By the light
it was near to noon. My back protested, but I managed to
lever myself up in spite of even greater discomfort in my
palms—strange sharp stabs. My throat was painfully dry
and my head swam.

Swam—

In a rush, memory returned.

Morgan! I scrambled up, catching hold of the edge of the
table, and somehow got into my chair. For some moments I
sat brushing beads from my clothing and dusting them from
my hands, where many had left small bleeding pocks. At
last I looked toward the tapestry.

The picture showed a great rent scoring its center, and caught in the frame hung a streamer of green that, even as I watched, crumbled into gray ash.

The wreckage in this room might be thought proof of my victory. I must accept it as that—accept it, yes, but never let it be known. Though how I had done it I might never understand, I had won my way from the Wheel—

Wheel! On the floor near my feet lay an object bright enough to attract my attention even now. A crystal star, its symmetry marred by two broken points. Steadying myself in the seat, I stamped it ruthlessly into dust.

Had my actions destroyed those others—the Ladies of the Lake? I do not know, but I remain free, and of this I am sure: the triumph I gained was not a passing thing, but for all time, and perhaps, also, not for me alone, but for all the world.

IN THE CHARNEL HOUSE
by Brian M. Thomsen

Brian M. Thomsen has been nominated for a Hugo, ha
served as a World Fantasy Award judge, and is the author o
two novels, *Once Around the Realms* and *The Mage in th
Iron Mask,* as well as more than thirty short stories. His mos
recent publications as an editor include several anthologies i
collaboration with Martin Greenberg for DAW Books, includin
The Reel Stuff, Mob Magic, Oceans of Space, and *Oceans o
Magic,* and as a coauthor with Julius Schwartz on his memoir
entitled *Man of Two Worlds—My Life in Science Fiction an
Comics.* He lives in Brooklyn with his lovely wife Donna an
two talented cats by the name of Sparky and Minx.

Smoke.
Cold.
Darkness.
*The smell of the detritus of society . . . too man
bodies . . . crammed into too little space.*

The club was really hopping tonight.

It was "Jackboots Night," and most everyone was decke
out in full storm-trooper regalia to strut and gyrate to th
latest noise that was passing for music. Despite the healt
codes, people were smoking, and occupancy limits were ex
ceeded by at least twenty-five percent.

Dov didn't care. He didn't dance, and he wasn't int
dress up and drag. And as long as he had a seat at the bar
a pack of smokes, and—as he was frequently known t
say—"a bottle in front of me or a frontal lobotomy, which
ever comes first or lasts longer"—all was right with th
world. At least for the time being.

Dov had been a successful lawyer until he was disbarred. Of course, the Park Avenue law firm he once was a part of had been generous with his severance package. The firm had even represented him gratis on a subsequent lawsuit for a back injury that netted him a nice disability settlement with a none-too-likable landlord for whom he had been doing some work when the building around him sort of fell apart.

Dov wouldn't have to work for a while, and if his wife ever got around to divorcing him, his share of her Madison Avenue salary might see him through for who knew how long.

If it wasn't for the boredom, being unemployed might even be a pretty good life.

Sure, he still went out on the occasional interview, pretending to press old contacts for paralegal work.

Nobody really held the disbarment against him. Well, not much at least.

The sweet-sour stench of not enough soap and too much sweat intruded.

They must be getting ready to close the doors to keep any more folks from joining the party—if they haven't closed them already. Even Chelsea clubs have to draw the line somewhere, which is not to say if some celeb or powerful muckymuck or friend of a friend was really persuasive they wouldn't be able to jump the queue.

Dov tapped his glass, and the attentive bartender gave him a refill. He always made sure to tip the bartenders with a flourish so that he would be remembered and be able to reap the benefits on his next visit—even if it was for just that little extra bit of attention on a crowded night like this one.

The bartender tarried a moment, so Dov sipped and nodded his approval. Then the bartender tapped the bar and left the cash in place, as if saying that this one was on the house. Then he blew Dov a silent kiss as he went back to serving the masses.

Dov just smiled back. An automatic smile.

"He a friend of yours?" a foreign voice inquired.

Dov turned toward the inquisitor, finding himself face-to-face with a long-haired bearded fellow in an ankle-length dark coat. He looked like a refugee from some Yiddish production of *Fiddler on the Roof*.

"The guy with the pink triangle?" the inquisitor in Orthodox drag pressed.

"The bartender?"

"Is he a friend of yours?"

Dov was still early enough in his alcoholic glow to be mellow. "You mustn't have gotten the invitation to the club right," Dov said by way of an answer. He gestured toward the dance floor. "Wednesday is 'Jackboots Night.' Don't you think you're a bit out of place?"

"Who is to question why God's chosen are where they are?" the inquisitor replied.

"Whatever." Dov turned his back on the man.

The stench of bodies in this place was even stronger. Something must be wrong with the air-conditioning, Dov thought. "Really stinks," he whispered.

Dov stole a look back to where the inquisitor had been, but he was gone. A scan of the crowd didn't turn him up either.

Maybe a street person who had managed to slip in, Dov concluded, and who was ushered out just as quickly.

*   *   *

With an hour to go before closing, Dov settled for a little alleyway action with an NYU Goth gal who was grateful for a few drinks and a cab ride to her dorm. She apologized that she couldn't invite him upstairs—something about an uptight roommate or a curfew or something. But that was all right. Dov really had to be getting on home. He was married, after all.

With a peck on the cheek, she said good night and pressed a piece of paper with her phone number into his hand. Then she skipped inside. The paper was a napkin

from the club, with Charnel House emblazoned across it
on the diagonal. He used it to wipe his cheek to remove
any telltale signs of her black lipstick, then he threw it out
the cab's window as it turned left and headed back
uptown.

No one was left on the streets except for the few late
night-early morning walking dead who were shuffling home
or elsewhere.

Gray faces without hope.
Piles of rags.
Mounds of flesh.
Fighting the scavengers for anything worth saving.
An emaciated figure, face pressed against the cab's win-
dow was trying to get in.
The figure began to scream . . . fingers clawing out to
Dov . . . the window clouding with his breath as the lost
soul strained against the glass . . . the glass seeming to
buckle . . . to give way. . . .

Dov sprang back and looked out the cab's window. The
figure had vanished.

"Sorry about that, Mac," the Asian cabby apologized.
"The bums aren't normally that brazen when they're looking for a handout. But it's getting cold, and the mayor is
making things really tough on them."

"Things are tough all over," Dov mumbled.

"You can say that again," the cabby agreed. "First the
mayor came down on us, then on the street vendors, now
on these unfortunates. Who knows who's next?"

"The Jews, probably," Dov answered absently.

"You really think so?" Then the cabby quickly pulled
over to the curb. "That'll be seven even."

Dov handed him a ten and didn't wait for the change.
He just shambled out into the cold and then into the building. He didn't remember how he got upstairs.

*   *   *

He was chilled to the bone, and his lungs felt heavy with congestion. His back ached from too much lifting and bending. Still, it was better than the alternative.

He had a pallet to sleep on and an extra shirt, and a threadbare blanket to wrap around himself.

The soup had been good tonight. And the storm outside would probably slow down the next day's shipment. That meant there would probably be no digging tomorrow, just sorting.

A well-earned break in the routine that would allow him time to regain his strength.

He would regain his strength. And he would survive.

It was good having a job.

It kept him going.

He would survive.

A jab with the butt of a rifle to the ribs disturbed his momentary respite.

He had been distracted. Maybe fatally so.

Once again he joined his coworkers for inspection, using every ounce of concentration to stifle a cough that was working its way up from the ever-congested bottom of his lungs.

A cough could mean a sentence of death—sooner rather than later.

One of the newer arrivals to the processing team began to weaken and stumble. Things had been awfully busy since he had arrived, and he hadn't had time to recover from his journey.

The guard noticed—they always did—and motioned for the newcomer to take a step forward.

The unlucky soul's knees buckled.

A replacement would be picked tomorrow. There were always replacements willing to do anything to survive.

The newcomer never stood again, a bullet to the back of his head ended his misery. His body would join others in the ovens.

Inspection was over, and he returned to his pallet, grateful for the few hours he would be able to sleep.

Dov's head was heavy from the night before. His mouth was dry, and his throat felt coated by a combination of crust and fire. It felt as if he hadn't slept at all.

He turned his head slightly and looked at the side of the bed normally occupied by Susan. But she was long gone. A glance at the clock revealed that it was well past noon.

Of course she isn't here, Dov told himself. Some people have jobs. Commitments.

"I used to have a job." He looked at the night stand as he got his bearings. Next to the clock was a note.

> Dov,
> See you at Malka's at one.
> Try to be on time.
> > Susan
>
> P.S. Remember to pick up your tux
> from the cleaner's for the benefit tonight.

"Shit," he muttered.

Even if he skipped showering, a prospect neither he nor anyone downwind of him would relish, he'd miss at least half of their assigned fifty-minute session of counseling. No loss. Malka and Susan could rag on him without him being there. After all, wasn't that what counseling was about anyway?

Men bad.

Women good.

All parties agreed, and anyone with a penis was exempted from having an opinion.

Not that it really mattered. It was over between him and Susan. They were just going through the motions until it became official. Any day now he expected to find a note saying that she had found a new place or a new lover or something.

The condo was in his name, and money from the severance agreement had paid things up for at least another six months (that had been at her insistence).

No regrets. Sure, they had been together for more than ten years . . . but no one thought it would last forever. She the Scandinavian ice princess, perfectly proportioned,

blonde and petite. He the swarthy Bohemian. She, Miss
Smith College. He, CUNY all the way.

Who'd a thunk it?

She had been there for his overnight success, and for his
equally overnight decline. And when he hit what she
thought was the very rock bottom (he knew otherwise), she
said all of the appropriate things. "This is just a temporary
setback." "You'll show them." "Things will fall into place in
no time." "Just take your time and get your head together."

Shit.

What he really needed was a drink. Just two fingers, an
aspirin, and a shower.

A crowded room with naked and smelly people.
Everyone feared the showers.
Sometimes you never came back from your appointment
with hygiene.
The door would be closed, and the crowd would wait for
the showerheads to rain down the ice cold water or. . . .

Instinctively, Dov rushed through his shower. He was
trying to overcome his unease and enjoy the hot water
cleaning and renewing his flesh. He was valiantly trying to
wash away the sins he couldn't really recall committing the
night before.

A towel wrapped around his waist, he contemplated another hit of the hair of the dog, and instead decided on a
cup of coffee. It was never good to tie one on this early—
it only led to distractions. And he was going to need every
bit of focus to make it through Susan's ire at his missing
their "session," and to stay awake through tonight's benefit.

What was the benefit for again?

Another publishing thing? Or was it some sort of guilt
thing about the sad state of the environment that was supposed to make him happy for wasting a few hours of his
busy schedule? When he was employed, such things passed
as opportunities for business—with drinks for free.

Now they were just a bother.

Dov looked at the elegantly engraved invitation that was

attached to Susan's note. A matte finish Star of David took up most of the square card. It was cloth-quality paper emblazoned across the center with the words: THE RINGEL-BLUM FUND . . . lest we forget! The date, time and location were in the lower right-hand corner.

What was the Ringelblum Fund?

* * *

The balding middle-aged executive was still droning on. "If not for the efforts of such men as Emmanuel Ringelblum, not an extraordinary man at all—just a university-trained historian who happened to have been born Jewish in the shadow of the Reich—we would not have these documents of life in the Warsaw ghetto. He and others compiled a complete archive of everyday life during the captivity. He was shot with others during the revolt of 1944. But the product of his work lives on today to give witness to the atrocities that we can never forget. It is proof against those who wish to claim it never happened."

The crowd clapped politely.

Dov picked through the assembly and finally caught sight of the scowling Susan—who had also obviously just caught sight of him.

"Where were you?" she hissed.

Dov held up his hand, as if waving to someone he'd just recognized. The gesture held Susan at arm's length.

"I overslept. And this is not the time or the place," he said, cutting her off with one of his favorite expressions, then adding, "and why are we here?"

She shrugged. "Don't ask me. You're the one who never missed a single UJA shindig. We're probably on one of their eternal lists. They still think you're Mr. Six Figure Contribution."

"What's this one for?"

Susan smiled politely. "Some fund named after a dead historian." Then she added, remembering that she was still pissed off at him, "not that I would know, being a dumb shiksa and all."

* * *

Lest we forget. . . .

Dov felt a cold breeze slice through the overly-crowded hall, sending a chill down his spine.

"What's the matter?" Susan asked, probably fearing that a DT bout was setting in.

"Nothing. I just felt a chill."

Susan looked concerned. "It's roasting in here," she countered. "Listen, maybe you're coming down with something. Let me hit the ladies' room, and then we can head home."

He nodded. "As good a plan as any."

Dov accompanied her to the back of the hall, to a table where they had picked up their name tags. He decided to amuse himself as he waited by looking at a rusty milk can that was mounted on a platform by the entrance. As he stepped closer, he couldn't help but smell an odor of decay and rot coming from it. And he wondered what that thing was doing on display.

"Memories of the past," a heavily European-accented voice offered from behind.

"Come again," Dov said. He turned to face the speaker, a somber, dark Semitic-featured academic type who seemed to be in need of a good meal and a vacation.

"You were wondering what such an ugly thing as this could be used for," the man explained, pointing at the milk can. "It held the memories of the past, or, more accurately, the actual archives of a small group of historians who put together a record of day-to-day life in the Warsaw ghetto."

"Really?"

"We knew it would be necessary. That is why we sealed the records in it and buried it beneath the street before the uprising. We knew that even after we had long gone, the records would exist."

Dov could tell the stench was growing stronger, the rot mixing with stale sweat. Maybe Susan was right. Maybe it was too hot in here.

"It is not just the artifacts of the past that leave a stench."

"Whew," Dov said. "How can you stand the smell?"

"I've been around worse," the stranger replied. "As have we all." Then the gaunt man extended his hand to shake Dov's.

Dov noticed a strange tattoo on the man's forearm. Numbers.

"So I guess you were a concentration camp survivor?" Dov ventured.

"Not really."

"Dov?" This came from Susan.

He turned to see her coming their way, jacket draped over her arm.

"Well, gotta go," Dov said, turning back to face the fellow. But there was no one there.

As they grabbed a taxi back downtown, Dov still smelled a trace of the stench that came from that milk can.

He decided that playing ill was probably the best way of avoiding a heated tongue-lashing from Susan. So he decided to go straight to bed.

Wake up!
The new arrivals are here!
Get up or you will join them.
And you know what that means!

The next morning Dov roused himself just as he heard Susan closing the door. She was off to work. She had held him close most of the night, as if trying to will his body well with her own warmth, her smell mixing with his and almost being enough to block out the traces of the milk can stench from the night before. They had not made love, but they had shared each other's presence. And strangely enough, Dov could not recall any dreams that disturbed his sleep.

"Good," he said aloud, as he sat up and reached for his robe. A faint stain on his arm caught his eye.

"What the . . . !"

There was a numerical tattoo, not unlike the one the fellow had last night.

Some sort of a joke, he thought. Has to be. But it wasn't funny!

Dov darted to the bathroom, where he scrubbed his arm red, his skin raw and bleeding. Still, the number would not come off. It had indelibly taken to the skin, feathered at the edges as if it had been there for some time.

Shaking his head, Dov glanced up from the sink. The face that looked back at him in the bathroom mirror was as haggard as a skid row junkie. The fringe of his closely-cropped hair seemed to be going gray—as if he was prematurely aging.

Even during his workaholic early years he had never looked so worn. He had to be sick, even though he didn't really feel sick. Just tired.

An amusing thought crossed his mind. Tired. I've been out of work for six months—and now I'm tired.

It was as if being without a job was more draining than being on the job—the distraction of work providing a salve on the brusque grit of everyday living.

Arbeit macht frei.

That was a funny thing to cross his mind. Must be leftover from last night's festivities. All of the morbid Holocaust stuff. What was done was done. Why dwell on it? His reason for attending those kinds of things never had anything to do with his own Jewish heritage. They were just savvy business connections, places to move and shake with the movers and shakers. When he was working, he had spontaneous sincerity down to a science.

Just ask Susan.

But that was when he had a job, something to keep him busy and something to feed his habits. Now he was just another member of the walking dead of the charnel house called New York City. A place where the unemployed partied till they dropped—or at least partied until their money ran out.

A chill passed through him again, a sensation that

gripped him as harshly as if a winter wind had cut a path through his bathroom.

Dov started coughing.

That doesn't sound good, he thought to himself.

Stop that!
Not now! a voice hoarsely whispered.
The guards will hear you.
You don't want to be put on report for inspection, do you?
You know what will happen then.

Dov couldn't stop coughing. He spewed a gob of black gunk into the sink. Definitely time to see a doctor.

Dov was going to shower before visiting the walk-in clinic downtown, but decided against it. The ringing in his ears—probably just another symptom from some bug they were testing in the subways—wouldn't stop. And it seemed to get louder as he approached the shower.

Fear of showers? Fear of water? Wait, hydrophobia! That's another name for rabies! And rabies was worse than any of the traditional STDs he had suspected he might have picked up along the way.

Jeans on, topped by his heavy fisherman's sweater, he dashed downstairs, then downtown to the clinic that was three doors down from the Charnel House club he'd recently been frequenting.

The clinic had taken care of that mild case of clap he'd caught a few months back. He had even dated one of the attendants there (and Susan never found out).

The clinic would help him.

He just wished he looked better going there. His clothes were so loose today. Had he lost a lot of weight in only a couple of days?

A taxi was unloading, and he grabbed it, barking the clinic address to the driver, then rubbed at his cough-ravaged throat.

It was as if the taxi was filled with smoke. He couldn't catch his breath. And his cough wouldn't stop.

He looked out the window.

*   *   *

Trains kept passing by, arms outstretched from slits in the cattle cars.

The trains were endless, all traveling in one direction.

Last stop coming up!

Dov must have dozed off again.

Enough with the freaking nightmares! That was definitely his last UJA function. Small loss for them—he hadn't donated a single red cent in the past three years.

The taxi pulled up to the hydrant in front of the clinic. Dov paid the fare and exited, his whole being filled with vertigo. He paused a moment to regain his balance, and caught sight of the waves of homeless who were milling around the street, all of their worldly belongings stacked in front of them. People upon people.

Dov shuffled to the clinic's entrance, only to find a handwritten sign. BE RIGHT BACK. With a sigh of resignation, he took a few steps back to the curb, lit up a cigarette—which he knew wouldn't do his cough any good thank-you-very-much—and waited.

"Bum a smoke?" The voice came from behind him.

Dov was about to answer with an offhanded obscenity as he turned to face the bummer. But instead he offered his pack to a neatly dressed fellow with a Roman collar.

"Thanks," the man replied. "Who says New Yorkers aren't generous?"

"Aren't you going to give me a blessing or something?" Dov's manner bordered on being snide.

"If that's what you want."

"What I want is a cure for what ails me."

"Sorry. Can't help you there." He held out his hand. "Name's Martin."

"Father Martin." Dov shook it.

"No. Reverend Martin, of the Protestant sort. Reverend Martin Nieomoeller. But you can call me Martin."

"Dov."

"Glad to make your acquaintance, Dov. And thanks for indulging my bad habit. The cigarette, I mean."

"Don't mention it," Dov replied, feeling vaguely reassured by the presence of someone who didn't seem to be either a plague victim or a homeless wretch. "Come here often?"

"No, not really," Martin said in a measured tone. "Just came to lend a hand."

Dov inhaled and nodded knowingly. "Urban mission, homeless stuff."

Martin shook his head. "Nothing that simple. You might say everyone is the flock for whom I am the pastor."

"Plenty of lost souls around here."

"Indeed."

"There but for the grace of God go I, and all of that," Dov said casually. He was losing interest in trading platitudes with the do-gooder in the funny collar.

"One has more to do than just be thankful for one's own safety and comfort."

Dov stamped out the butt and looked to see if there was any activity at the clinic's door. There wasn't. He started to leave, when Martin took his arm and stared into his eyes, and in a hushed tone stated: "First they came for the socialists, and I didn't speak out—because I was not a socialist. Then they came for the trade unionists, and I did not speak out—because I was not a trade unionist. Then they came for the Jews, and I did not speak out—because I was not a Jew. And then they came for me . . . and there was no one left to speak out for me! And some, like you, even aid and abet the monsters."

Dov jerked back and broke Martin's grip.

"You're crazy!"

Martin shook his head and continued, "You said you have no choice. You abdicate your free will and you do their dirty work. And for what? Survival? For a few more wretched hours or days?"

Dov tried to dart away but was blocked by the crowd of homeless who had gathered.

Throng upon throng of naked bodies.
Young and old alike.

*First, they had to be shaved and sheared, men and women,
and then everyone into the showers with a promise of soap
and hot water.*

It was all very necessary to assure proper hygiene.

*Then the door was closed, and the task at hand turned to
sorting of the rags, a tedious but welcome respite from the
next task in the unending assembly line of death.*

Dov was racked by another coughing fit, bending him in
half by the force. When he finally stopped long enough to
catch his breath, he noticed the street was now oddly
empty. The door to the clinic was open.

Then the door was open, and the really odious task began.

*It was easier to think of the bodies as cords of wood or
piles of refuse.*

*A rag was fashioned around his mouth and nose, but he
familiar smell of death still pervaded—along with human
feces and piss and sweat that never seemed to leave the facil-
ity no matter how hard he and the other crew members tried
to remove it with disinfectant and scrubbing.*

*Soon, but usually not fast enough for the guards' satisfac-
tion, the bodies were removed and passed onto the ovens,
where others would do their part in the extermination cycle.*

The clinic waiting room was filled with all manner of
hopeless people. Dov was about to leave and go somewhere
else, but the receptionist motioned him forward.

"The doctor will see you now," she said.

Dov hadn't seen her here before.

"But what about . . ." Dov motioned to the others in
the waiting room.

"They can wait," she replied. "It's your turn. Room B.
The doctor will be right in."

*   *   *

Room B was a typical examining room, a mixture of
white and chrome, with the sterile smell of germ-free anti-

septic. The doctor came in, a small man, balding and bespectacled.

"I . . ." Dov began to explain his symptoms. But the doctor held up his hand as if to say "silence," and began to poke and prod and examine, while taking notes on a pad.

"Much of a lice problem?" he asked.

"No," Dov answered, shocked at the question.

"How long have you been coughing up blood?"

"I d–d–don't think I . . ." Dov stuttered, moving toward the door. "I'd better be going. There are others in the waiting room who are worse. I mean . . ."

The doctor put his hands on his hips, and with a sardonic grin, said, "You know what will happen to you if you can't work, don't you?"

"I haven't worked in months," Dov cut back, trying to find the doorknob while not taking his eyes off the doctor.

"I doubt that," the doctor said.

Hand on the knob, finally, Dov pulled the door open and headed toward the rear exit at the far end of the hall.

"You're all crazy," he muttered fearfully. "Or maybe I am."

The doctor leaned out the doorway as Dov escaped, and said something in German.

Arbeit macht frei, is what Dov thought he heard.

* * *

The rear door opened on a back alley that Dov recognized as passing behind the Charnel House club. He remembered that he had scored some blow here not too long ago. The alley was deserted, and the sky, partially visible directly overhead and framed by wires and tenement overhangs, seemed to be getting dark.

He felt exhausted, cold and weak and getting worse by the minute. It was as if the trip downtown and the stopover at the clinic had drained most of the life from him. He longed for the usual morning curse of a hangover. At least that was of his own making.

I'd better get some help, he thought.

Hastening along the alleyway, he tried the back door of the Charnel House. Open. He stepped inside.

"A little early, aren't you?" This from the leather-clad bouncer.

"I just want to use the phone," Dov said.

"Make me no never mind. You know where it is."

Dov put a quarter in the slot and dialed Susan's office number.

One ring.

Two.

"Pick up," he whispered. And then the dead line.

"Shit!" Dov reached into his pocket for another quarter, but came up empty. "Double shit! Now what is my calling card number?" He strained to remember. Then he once again noticed that tattoo on his arm, and a peculiar gray complexion that had taken over his skin.

Dov panicked for a moment and glanced around the Charnel House. A breath of relief. Everyone had the same gray cast. It must be the club's lighting.

Maybe the bartender will give me some change.

Dov took a seat at the bar and was greeted by the bartender—who turned out to be the Hasidic inquisitor from Jackboots Night.

"Shalom," the bartender greeted. "Are you here to give me a haircut again?"

Dov coughed, feeling the blood-laced sputum rise again.

"Guess not," the bartender said. "Too bad. If you can't work, you know what happens."

"What happens?" Dov was afraid that he was losing his mind. His body was itching and aching now, and his frame seemed barely able to support his slight weight.

"What happens to everyone who comes here."

"Tell me, Rabbi," Dov begged.

"Death." The rabbi paused. "True, some postpone their fates, doing the devil's work in the changing and sorting areas or in the showers or in the ovens. But eventually it all comes to an end. If you ask me, I don't know how you have managed to do it. Oh, I suppose some manage to just apply themselves to the hellish work at hand as if they were soulless golems. Others might imagine themselves to be far away, in a better place. But eventually reality intrudes."

Dov looked in the mirror that hung over the bar, his jeans and sweater were gone. In their place he wore the striped uniform of the condemned capo, the Star of David neatly in place, his head scabbed and shaved.

"What can I do?" Dov implored.

"Don't ask me," the rabbi said with a chuckle. "I'm already dead. Don't you remember?"

The Hasidic rabbi continued to pray as Dov sheared and shaved his head, careful to catch each of his long locks for the piles of hair that would fill the officers' pillows and mattresses. Dov also remembered the rabbi being kicked by one of the jackbooted guards as he entered the shower room where the gas awaited.

The rabbi's skin had already begun to welt and bruise before Dov closed the chamber door.

"You were safe enough while you could work," the rabbi explained. "*Arbeit macht frei!* The work will set you free! It wasn't a total lie. You were free from the fate that you abetted for others. But now you can't work." The rabbi shook his head and turned his back on Dov.

Dov started to remember his life in Berlin before he had been rounded up with the others and placed in the ghetto in Poland as he awaited further transportation.

What about Susan?

His career?

New York City?

What about the sins, the decadence, the fun? What about his life?

Dov felt a kick to the side, a rib snap, the bone piercing the skin. He fell to the floor of just another of Auschwitz's cold waiting rooms outside the showers.

It had all been so real!

"You there!" the guard ordered. "Join the others inside. Schnell!"

Another kick, and Dov struggled forward, inching toward the room that he knew held his death.

It had all been just a dream, he realized in pain. The others in his life were ghosts, specters of those who had died before him and who haunted him until it was his time.

He looked at the bleak surroundings, knowing that no one would help him. Slowly, but with determination to avoid further humiliation, Dov removed his paper-thin cloth uniform and joined the rest in the shower room, waiting for the deadly gas that would soon take his life.

During his last few seconds he tried to recall the New York he had "lived" in, a New York that was out of his reach.

All that was left was the crowded room of the naked damned, lost souls all. All that was left was the promise of death, a promise that was fulfilled with the coming of the Zyklon B.

WHEN YOU'RE DEAD . . .

by Michael A. Stackpole

Michael A. Stackpole is a writer and game designer best known for his *New York Times* bestseller *Star Wars* novels. His most recent novel is *The Dark Glory War,* the first of a four-book epic fantasy series.

I felt dead, and it was all Lancaster Dean's fault.

Pain pulsed through my head. I was pretty sure my skull was cracked, but at least it wasn't crushed like the hard-hat that had protected it for a short while anyway. I saw the remains of it flattened beneath a broken concrete beam, with a twisted piece of rebar stabbed straight down through it. Something about that prompted me to smile, and then I felt the blood coating the right side of my face crack.

Despite having my brains feel like someone had used an in-the-egg-scrambler on them, the cracking of the blood registered and sent a jolt through me. I'd been out long enough for the blood to clot and dry. That wasn't good, because I didn't hear any sounds of digging. *And if they aren't digging . . .*

I did a quick inventory of body parts and found all of them still attached—many things bruised, but nothing busted. I snorted once, blowing out a bubble of bloody mucus that I cleared away with a hand, then, for lack of anything better, I wiped it on a pants leg. If I was going to get out of here, neatness points wouldn't count for much. Then I laughed, knowing my mom would be happy to know I had clean underwear on for when they took me to the hospital later.

*   *   *

One solid knock on your head, and your thinking takes on a distinctly nonlinear nature.

I forced myself to think past the fog of pain, and began a search for my cell phone. The only light I had came from a few of those battery powered emergency lights, and the other ones that Lancaster Dean—"the Elusive Dean of Magic"—had placed around for his TV special. As near as I could tell, that was the *only* favor he'd done me. And it wasn't close to enough as far as I was concerned.

For a half second I considered that it might not all be his fault. The Scottsdale Galleria was this pink monstrosity of a building that had been erected in downtown Scottsdale as an upscale mall. It had failed miserably in that job, being more of a ghost town than a commercial center. It went bust, then got used as a set in a couple of movies. *Tank Girl* was the most notable of these, giving you an idea of how bad things were. Then it housed a traveling Smithsonian display for a bit, but only after it failed to become a sports bar complex and, after that, failed to become a corporate center.

The building was so snakebit, I don't think they could have made it work as a homeless shelter.

Some genius at City Hall decided it had to go, and what better way to attract attention to Scottsdale than to have the building blown up on a magician's made-for-TV special? Lance Burton and David Copperfield passed on the project—they were just too classy. I guess it's good Sigfried and Roy also passed, or I'd have been trapped with big cats who were pissed off. I'm sure other modern Houdinis turned the city down, and then they got to Lancaster Dean.

I don't know magicians from a hole in the ground—just those I see billed on signs in Vegas—but folks made a big deal about getting Dean. The usual press kiss up went on, so all the local news outlets told of his background. You know local TV—all press releases, all the time.

*   *   *

According to the legend, he died when he was eight—a Cub Scout pal of his still swears he had no pulse after a fall—and he said he escaped from death and came back. Having accomplished that greatest escape, he launched a career as an escape artist. None of the newsies described his career as "modest," but they used all the words they use when they wished they *could* say modest.

All I know is that for me, he was a pain in the ass. I'd gone into the Galleria to make the final check on the explosives, just to make sure things were wired up perfectly, that the right pillars would be blown so the building would come down folding in on itself, and not take out the other buildings nearby. Controlled implosion it's called, and we'd set up to do it right. Dean made the inspection a pain by having his set dressing scattered around and insisting he'd do a final inspection after mine, "just to make sure things were all set."

If everything that clown knew about explosives was C-4, it wouldn't have been enough to blow his toupee an inch off his scalp.

And certainly all the C-4 we had in the Galleria couldn't have cracked his ego.

I only found pieces of the cell phone. My Walkman survived fine, stayed clipped to my belt and everything. I'd not been listening to it while making my inspection. I'd just taken to wearing it when having to deal with Dean, putting it on and cranking up tunes when I couldn't stand listening to him tell me how to do my job.

I tuned it into the local talk station and got confirmation of what I already knew. "Welcome back to 620 Talk Radio. We have with us Lancaster Dean. Mr. Dean, just to recap . . ."

I could see Dean preening as he spoke—not caring that it was radio—and it set my teeth on edge. "We have one man down in there. A very brave man, very brave. He was doing an inspection of the explosives and . . . I should have been in there with him, but he's a trained professional."

* * *

"Now, pending notification of next of kin, they've not released his name, but we know he's thirty-five, a demolitions engineer . . ."

"Right and, well, Tom, if by some miracle you can hear my voice, you have to know we're coming for you. I swear to you, Pat, and all your listeners, that I'm not going to let Tom die down in there. I've been talking with the rescue team and when we go in . . ."

"Did you say 'we'?"

"He's in there because of me. How could I not . . . ?" Dean's voice broke, then returned thick with emotion and subdued. "The team is working on some initial problems, but I'm in constant consultation with them, and I'm sure we'll be moving fast."

I turned the Walkman off and hugged my knees to my chest. The reason there was no digging, and no rescue team coming in yet was the same reason I'd survived. Something had set off *some* of the charges, not all of them. Static electricity could have, but that was unlikely. Thunderstorms blow up quickly in the desert, but it wasn't the season and I'd have been called if that looked possible. Could have been some idiot ran a truck into a power pole or substation and caused a huge arc; but whatever it was, it blew some of the charges, leaving an unstable building sown with explosives for the rescue crew to try to figure out.

This building was a danger for them, and that meant it was a tomb for me.

"There you are. C'mon, let's go. You don't have much time."

*   *   *

I whipped my head around, which was *not* the thing to do with a concussion, which I'm sure I had. The world kind of sizzled, as if a sparkler had been pressed up close to each eyeball, then things came back into focus. I saw this little guy, little ball of muscles, wearing a white shirt and tuxedo pants standing there. His sleeves were rolled up to the elbow and his dark eyes half-glowed. Grim determination settled over his face, and he impatiently waved me onward.

I got up to follow, with about a billion questions lining up in my brain, but the world began to defocus again, scattering everything. I reached up and touched a low ceiling, steadying myself. "How did you . . . ?"

He glanced back at me from within a narrow crack in a wall. "We've got to get out of here. It's not going to be easy, but given what it took to get this far, the rest will not be impossible."

I shook my head, which is also not recommended with a concussion. "Can't get out." I tapped the earphones. "Radio says the building is unstable."

"Radio? Where?"

I shifted to show him the unit on my hip. "It made it through better than I did. We're stuck."

"So that's it, you're just going to give up?"

"Don't have a choice, do I?" I slowly lowered myself to my knees. "They'll think of a way to get us out."

"The only person getting you out is you." He came back into the small chamber where I knelt and towered over me. "Let me tell you something, son. Life is a grand adventure, and you don't live it by waiting. If you do nothing, then you'll stay here and faint from thirst and die. If you try working your way out, you might still die—but they'll see that you didn't lie down and die. You kept fighting to the end. It might be that you're going to be remembered as the guy who died here, but better to be remembered as the guy who died trying to get out."

Then he winked at me. "And, if I'm right, this will be the greatest escape this town has ever seen."

*   *   *

It wasn't like he hypnotized me or anything, but something in his words just thundered through me. I struggled to my feet, and he made no attempt to help me. He let me do it on my own, reinforcing what he'd said. I smiled—

cracking blood be damned—and followed him as he melted through the hole in the wall.

Being a bit bigger than he was, I got a little scraped up going through. I had to shift my butt around and tore a pocket on my jeans. I reached out with my right hand, hoping he'd take it, but found a good piece of rebar and pulled myself along. I slipped free and leaned against a half-collapsed slab to catch my breath.

My partner stood there, arms crossed over his chest. "That's the first step, let's go."

"Give me a second here, will you?"

"You have the remainder of your life to rest."

"Which is likely to be fifteen minutes if you don't let me catch my breath."

"Less. You don't have fifteen minutes." He frowned at me. "Are you really that out of shape?"

I straightened and grabbed a double-handful of beer belly. "Everyone gets a little thick around the middle as they get older."

The man slapped his own flat stomach. "Only if they don't have discipline." He flopped down on his back and tapped a dark triangular hole in the wall. "In through here."

"You're crazy."

"It will work. Drops to the left halfway through, then up for a while. Don't go left, go up." He wriggled his way into it and was gone.

*   *   *

I walked over to the hole, but couldn't even hear him scrabbling along. I debated for a second not following and didn't like the silence. I pulled the headphones on and heard just enough of Dean's voice to decide the silence was better. I did a quick check for size, realized the Walkman would hang me up, so I left it behind. That didn't get rid of Dean, though, because in my mind I could hear him some time in the future talking about how they found my

Walkman and how he hoped his words of encouragement had given me solace in my final moments.

I wanted to puke, and I was pretty sure it wasn't because of my concussion.

The little tunnel *was* a tight squeeze. I pulled myself along, reaching up with my hands, pushing off as I was able with my feet. Things raked my flanks, tugged at my belt, and clawed at my gut. In the pitch-black it was easy to imagine them to be the talons of strange creatures, which made me wonder about rats that might be lurking, or snakes or scorpions or black widows. I decided even the tiniest of God's creatures had sense enough to be leaving the vicinity, but that didn't stop me from shivering whenever something brushed my face.

Halfway through, my left leg did dangle into space, but things were so cramped I couldn't look down. I kept on moving, even though without left leg purchase it was harder. My fingers started tingling and hurting from pulling myself along. The fact that I felt air flowing up past me helped me to keep going; aided and abetted by determination that I'd *not* be found wedged in some cement tube like a hot dog in a fat man's throat.

Finally I wiggled my way free, swaying to this side and that like one of those time-lapse photography images of a seedling stalk emerging from the earth. I plopped onto my back and lay there for a moment, sweat stinging my eyes. I was breathing hard and had started wheezing a bit. I figured that was from the dust.

My partner stood over me, looking down disgustedly, his fists planted on his hips. He had that commanding presence, sort of like Rudolf Valentino. Very dramatic, very forceful, and clearly not pleased with my performance so far.

I shrugged. "Sorry."

"Sorry for whom? Your wife? Your kids?"

*   *   *

"No kids. I want them—but, my wife, she has her career. She's a lawyer. She's probably soon to be my ex-wife." I slowly rolled onto my belly, then worked myself up onto my knees. "You got kids?"

He shook his head. "Bess and I . . . it's one of my regrets."

I gave him a gentle nod, then sighed. "Sorry I'm not making this getting-out-thing easy."

He cracked a smile. "You couldn't make it easy. Easier, perhaps, but not easy. If it were easy, it wouldn't be worth doing because anyone could do it."

"Yeah, but if Dean were trapped in here . . ."

The man waved that idea away dismissively. "Better a thousand of you than one of him. C'mon, let's go. One more ordeal and you're out of here."

I stumbled to my feet and shambled after him. We picked our way along a corridor that had survived the collapse pretty well, which suggested to me that some undetonated explosive lurked nearby. My best guess is that I'd awakened on the second subground parking level and was moving up through the first. Then we rounded a corner and I stopped dead in my tracks.

A chunk of the mall courtyard had collapsed and dropped down, forming an archipelago of tiled islands linked by twisted threads of rebar. They floated above a black chasm in which dimly burned a couple of emergency lights. The darkness made it hard to judge how far down they were, but they illuminated jagged hunks of broken concrete. No matter how shallow the drop, the landing would be painful.

My companion walked to the edge of the chasm and squatted down. He pointed off toward a triangular island. "That one is the key. Once you get there, it's a simple walk out."

* * *

I closed my eyes for a second, then opened them again, but the islands had not shifted. "Um, getting to that one will be the tough thing. There are those three there, which get smaller and smaller, and a good eight feet up and over to our goal."

"Easily done. Watch." He backed up past me, got a six foot running start, then leaped to the first little island. He landed square in the heart of that oval, skipped high in the air and landed on the next one, six feet along. Another step and his powerful legs launched to the smallest island. He landed in a crouch, then shot up and off again, flipping through the air like a gymnast, sticking the landing on the higher island.

He held his hands up as if waiting for applause, but only the reboant click-clacking of debris falling into the blackened pit echoed through the ruins. He turned slowly, his face lit by a glorious smile, his eyes shining, then he nodded to me.

"You can do this, Tom. Come on, you can do it."

I shook my head slowly. The throbbing pain built until I was pretty sure the top of my skull was going to explode clean off. "I can't do that."

"You can." His voice hardened. "You *must!*"

"I *must?* Who the hell do you think you are?" With my head pounding, I straightened up to my full height. "It might be that they find me here, or they find me down there, but they find me where I decide I'm going to be. There is no *must* about this."

"But there is, Tom, there is." He crouched and pointed out toward where I felt certain the rescuers would be waiting. "If you don't do this, Lancaster Dean wins."

"He wins?"

*   *   *

"Yes, he wins." The man shook his head. "I've seen his kind hundreds of times, thousands. They have no real talent, save for marketing themselves. Now I know something about that, I really do, but when you market something, you have to have something there, something real. He's done nothing but use the ideas of others forever. If you don't do this, you know what will happen. He'll dedicate a performance to you, maybe a tour. You'll become a friend he lost, a momentary pause in his show when he can't go on. Your death will be what humbles a great man before his audience, and that will make him greater in their eyes.

"Do you want to do that? Do you want to make the man who placed you here into a hero for shedding a crocodile tear in your memory?"

I growled. "Yeah, so I try and fail, and then folks know how horribly I died. I know this media crap, I see it all the time, right? I'm not stupid. How I die will be forgotten fast enough, and he'll still win. He's Lancaster Dean. He's a star. He's the man who escaped death!"

"HA!" The man shot to his feet and gave me a glare that drove me back a step. "Don't tell me you believe that nonsense. He never died. It was a trick."

"How do you know that? Were you there?"

"No, but I *know*." His voice grew a bit softer. "When you die, it puts things in perspective. Winning the applause of millions doesn't matter. You learn what's important in life. He's clearly not learned that lesson."

I nodded slowly. "Maybe you don't have to die to get an angle on those things." Not being a very deep guy, and having been whacked on the head, what was important to me in that moment was some sunshine, a smile from my wife, a cold beer, a barbecued burger, and, maybe, just maybe, a chance to poke Lancaster Dean in the nose.

I backed up to where he'd started his run, then took off. I made the leap to the first island easily, perhaps too easily. I didn't get as much of a push off as I wanted, but still made the second island. I got a spare step there, then launched myself at the third. It hung there like a tiny speck of land in a black ocean, but I was on target. All I had to do was crouch there, then spring up again just as he'd done. . . .

*   *   *

Yeah, then flip through the air like some little girl gymnast. . . .

That thought, and the impossibility of my duplicating his action, isn't exactly what doomed me. My friend, being smaller and lighter than me, hadn't impacted the islands the same way I had. He was a little velociraptor, where as I was a *Jurassic Park* tyrannosaurus rex, setting everything to shaking and quivering as I bounced along.

My target shook on my landing, listing hard to the left. A tile crumbled beneath my foot and I went down. I landed on my right hip and started to slide. I could feel my feet flailing in the air, my rump sliding off the edge. I grabbed at the island, tearing the nails off my right hand as I clawed for any hold at all. I still was slipping then, and all of a sudden I jerked to a halt.

My legs dangled and pain shot up from my left hip. I felt around and found a hooked piece of rebar had caught my belt back by my right cheek. I started to tip forward, but my right foot hit a long piece of rebar below, steadying me. Shivering, I clung to my little piece of rock.

"You're okay. You're okay." I heard his voice from the triangle, which hung above me. "Are you okay?"

"Oh, hell ya, for someone caught on a rock in the middle of the goddamned air. Sure, I'm just ducky." I growled again, then looked up. "Don't even think of coming down here. Even if you could free me, there's not enough room and you couldn't get back up. Go on without me."

"I'm not leaving you here." His voice took on the edge again. "You *will* get free, you *must*."

"No shit, Sherlock, I'm the one dangling here."

"You can do it, Tom."

"Will you shut up? I need to think here for a moment."

"Yes, of course."

*   *   *

His voice softened, and I knew he wasn't going to stop talking. I almost told him to shut up again, but since I couldn't see him, hearing his voice meant I wasn't alone. Where I was at the time, not being alone took on a lot of importance in my life—which, all things considered, was looking pretty close to being over at that point.

"Want to know how he did it, Tom?"

"Did what?"

"Faked his death?"

"Um, sure." I reached down and began to unlace my left work boot. I hooked my little finger through the laces so it couldn't fall off as I loosened it. Very carefully, I worked it off and brought it up to my island as my companion explained Dean's trick.

"It's a pretty common thing, Tom. Fakirs in India used to do it. You get a hard little ball of rubber and place it up near your armpit. As you squeeze your arm down against your chest, you shut off the flow of blood to the artery there in your wrist. Dean's friend checked his wrist, found no pulse, and ran off for help."

"You don't say! Why that son of a bitch, been lying all this time." I smiled and shifted around enough to grab an unseen piece of rebar with my toes and then bring my right foot up to where I could unlace that boot. "I guess that's why you said he had no real talent."

"Part of it, yes. And, Tom, I trust you will keep that secret to yourself."

"Dean's secret?"

"The secret of the ball. It's frowned upon to reveal such things."

"Your secret is safe with me." I brought the right boot up to land on the tile by its mate and unlaced both of them, down to the last three eyes on each boot. This gave me a good four feet of doubled-lace between them. Using my teeth and left hand I knotted them together good and tight, giving me two boots linked by over a yard of laces.

*   *   *

I glanced up at the triangle island and could make out a rebar fringe. "Okay, look, get back from the edge. Hang on to something up there. I have only one choice here and I don't want it killing both of us."

"Don't give it a second thought, son. Just do what you have to do."

"Okay, here goes nothing." With the boots dangling from my left hand, strung together the way sneaker pairs are when hung from high power lines, I started my small island bouncing. I know that sounds insane, but I really had no other choice. My weight had lowered my island to the point where I couldn't reach the triangle. Only by using the springiness of the rebar could I get up high enough.

The rocking motion did nothing good for my head, other than to sync the throbbing with my movement. As I rose, I made the first cast with the boots, but they missed. I rocked more and harder, but bounced the boots off the rebar. I could hear chunks of rock pitching down below, clattering around, and knew the whole network might give way.

I gave it one last solid heave, and timed it beautifully. The right boot arced over a metal stake and wrapped around twice. With my right hand I jerked my belt buckle back, loosening my belt and letting the rebar that had held me up slip free. The little island did batter my right leg as it descended, then just quivered below, with the shaking rebar webwork angrily chattering at me.

I stripped my belt off as I hung there, doubled it and hooked it over another piece of rebar. I held on tight, and started to pull myself up. I let go of the laces and grabbed more metal, then shortened my grip on the belt. My left foot found another long strand of rebar, and I latched on with my toes.

"Now just hook your chin on the top here. Handhold to the right." He stayed on the high side of the triangle, nodding and pointing.

*   *   *

It was that nod, that acknowledgment that I was on the right track, showing his confidence, that got me up on the triangle. Being able to chin myself like that and haul myself up, I'm sure adrenaline gave me some help there, but his nod told me I'd make it. Not disappointing him seemed somehow as important to me as getting out alive.

I crawled up onto the triangle, then reached back down for my boots.

"Leave them, we've not much time."

"No. They saved my life." I smiled over my shoulder at him. "Besides, you know how long it takes to break in a good pair of boots?"

He laughed and nimbly moved to a long strip of tile. Looping my boots around my neck by the laces, I followed carefully and we quickly reached a solid portion of the flooring. I turned to look back and saw the islands bobbing, bits and pieces of them beginning to crumble. From higher up pieces of debris fell cometlike, trailing dust. One large chunk pulverized the island where I'd hung.

I shivered. "Another minute."

"Another minute you don't have, Tom." He pointed to a tunnel that sloped up and, at the top, I could see the artificial glare of klieg lights. "Get going."

I started to scramble up and got past a tough point. I turned back to give him a hand, but he hadn't moved. He just stood there at the opening. "C'mon, we're safe, we made it."

"You're safe, Tom. You've made it." He gave me a salute and a smile. "I have to go back for my mother."

At the time those words made no sense to me, mainly because of the thunderous crack of concrete breaking and riding over them. Major chunks of what had remained standing chose that moment to collapse. Situated where I was in the tunnel, well, I was pretty much a BB in the barrel of an air rifle. A heavy gust of dust and air slammed into me, hurling me up and out of the ruins. I arced through the artificially lit night, an ill omen for Lancaster Dean, but feeling very lucky indeed.

*   *   *

Because of all the media coverage and cameras, I've been able to watch my flight many times, from many different angles. The landing is always the best part because there he was, Lancaster Dean, sitting at a makeshift desk, being interviewed, when I came down. He and the anchor had turned toward the building with the crack. The newsie fell one way, Dean another, and his toupee yet a third, with me smashing Dean through the table.

The doctors told me that I was pretty much out of it because of a concussion and loss of blood. They even had a shrink come in and explain to me that my traveling companion, about whom I kept asking, never existed. "It's normal, in a time of stress, for some people to imagine another person being there, so they won't be alone. Don't worry about it."

Sure, don't worry about it, but take these pills until you stop talking nonsense. I stopped talking nonsense pretty quickly, especially after someone leaked my story to a tabloid and I found myself in print saying an angel had helped me escape. But even though I stopped talking, I knew I wasn't wrong. I had proof.

And that little red ball of proof was great for draining the blood from the face of first-year medical students taking a pulse—and not finding one.

Kim, my wife, brought me the ball. My almost being dead helped her reorient what she thought was important in life, too, which meant our paths merged again. She was the one who discovered that the power unit that had shorted, triggering the explosives, when Lancaster Dean plugged a nose-hair trimmer into an overloaded socket in his trailer.

And it looked like the settlement would more than cover the cost of the new house we were going to need, being as how the kids would want their own rooms as they grew up. The settlement with the tabloids for misquoting me was what would get them through college.

*   *   *

About the time my bruises had healed up enough for me to be photogenic, Lancaster Dean arranged to meet me at the Doubletree Resort for dinner. It was a photo op, pure and simple. We were being billed as the two men who

had cheated death, and the photographers loved it when
suggested they get a shot of Dean taking my pulse.

The expression on his face when he doesn't find any i
priceless. Pity those shots never get into his publicity
packet.

But it wasn't until three weeks later, when I was watching
one of those tabloid TV shows while working out at the
gym, that the last little bit of things put themselves togethe
for me. It was right after the segment where Dean an
nounced he was retiring from performing. They did a little
piece on me and my escape, comparing it with the bes
escapes of famous magicians. And that was when I saw my
companion again.

The only footage of him they had was black and white
but the smile and the eyes, the eyes especially came
through in the stills. In reviewing his career, to tie thing
all together, they said my escape was better than any escape
he'd ever performed.

Of course, they were wrong. Harry Houdini's greates
escape was passing over that gulf that separates life from
death. He plucked a reluctant volunteer from the audience
brought him along and got him out. And, true to himself
only Harry would believe he could make the trip twice, the
next time to bring back his mother.

And, you know, I don't doubt he's done it.

SPIRIT OF HONOR
by John Helfers

John Helfers is a writer and editor currently living in Green Bay, Wisconsin. A graduate of the University of Wisconsin–Green Bay, his fiction appears in more than twenty anthologies, including *Future Net, Once Upon a Crime, First to Fight,* and *The UFO Files,* among others. His first anthology project, *Black Cats and Broken Mirrors,* was published by DAW Books in 1998. Future projects include more anthologies as well as a novel in progress.

Kyoto Island, Japan, May 18th, 1645

Kitsune's teeth chattered as the freezing rain plastered his worn kimono to his body, making him shudder uncontrollably. He raised his head to feel the drizzle patter on his fevered skin, then dragged his hand across his face, wiping the clinging raindrops from his eyelashes. A series of deep coughs racked his young body, doubling him over as he fought for air.

He clung to his mule, his upper body draped over the animal's relatively warm neck. The muddy trail in front of him lurched and spun, the water and his weakened condition making the narrow path blur and double. All this, and the mule wasn't even moving.

Two figures approached him out of the darkness, a smaller man having a spirited, if one-sided, conversation with the larger man next to him. Kitsune straightened up, trying to look as alert as possible under the conditions.

"Good night for traveling, eh, Kitsune?" the smaller man said as he drew near. He looked strangely ageless, his face lined yet strong, like oft-read parchment. With bushy tufts of white hair peeking out from under his hat and eyes that sparkled with intelligence, he could have been anywhere from thirty to sixty summers old. Dressed in a simple red woolen robe that hung to his knees, he looked comfortable and dry underneath the huge straw hat that protected him from the rain. All of the rain, even the drops that blew in underneath the hat, was stopped as if they'd hit an invisible barrier.

He carried a staff that was as tall as he was, topped by a carved wooden ring through which two brass circlets had been placed to chime pleasantly as he walked. All in all, he looked like he was strolling in a flower garden on a warm spring day instead of here. Kitsune didn't bother to look at the man's feet, but he would have bet the next warm bed they came to that even his wooden sandals were perfectly clean, free of the mud and filth of the road.

"Maseda-san spotted a light farther down the trail. It appears that we are coming to a small village. Do you think you can make it?" the small man asked.

"No . . . choice . . . Asano," Kitsune gasped before a fresh coughing spell seized him. "No place to rest . . . here." The boy frowned as he looked at the diminutive man. *If he's such a powerful wizard, why can't he cast a spell that would keep us all warm and dry?* he thought.

"Don't worry, a little rain never hurt anyone," the man said as if he had just plucked the thought from his student's mind. Ignoring Kitsune's shocked expression, Asano looked at the other man. "Let's keep moving, Maseda-san." With that, he walked on down the trail.

The tall man, dressed in a brown traveling kimono with his hair pulled back in the traditional topknot, watched Asano, his face impassive. Although soaking wet, he seemed oblivious to the weather and their situation. Taking the mule's rope bridle in one hand, he kept his other hand around a sash slung over his chest, with the handle of a katana jutting up behind his shoulder, and started walking.

If Asano inspired respect and awe, then Maseda was the most fearsome person Kitsune had ever known. Asano claimed that he was a *ronin,* or masterless samurai who had been hired by the court to protect the wizard, but sometimes Kitsune suspected the emotionless warrior was a demon that Asano had spellbound into human form. He had no proof, but little things he had witnessed made him wonder. Like the fact that he had never seen Maseda sleep in all the months they had traveled together. Ever. Or that the samurai was the fastest human being Kitsune had ever seen. Regardless of the man's origins, Kitsune knew he could place his life in Maseda's hands, because he had before, and no harm had come to him or Asano. For a samurai was nothing if not loyal, and Maseda's loyalty to Asano and Kitsune was absolute.

The trail wound down the mountain slope into a small valley. As they traveled, Kitsune saw a flickering light below. At that same moment, a jagged bolt of lightning split the heavens, casting an unearthly silver glow on the valley and surrounding peaks. In the flash, Kitsune saw a cluster of small huts surrounding the light. He began to say a prayer of gratitude to the gods for leading them here, but stopped in mid-sentence as his gaze traveled elsewhere.

On the other side of the valley stood a tall castle, its structures rising from the thickly forested mountainside like a sleeping dragon. In the flash of another lightning bolt. Kitsune spotted the main building, its several stories of arched pagoda tile roofs and white stone walls standing out in sharp relief against the night sky. A tall wall delineated the perimeter of the castle grounds, with the roofs of a few small buildings barely visible from Kitsune's vantage point. Although the castle looked to be in good repair, no lights could be seen, not a single torch. Then the lightning vanished as quickly as it had appeared, plunging the valley into darkness again.

Kitsune rested his head against the mule's neck and pondered what he had seen. *I don't remember Asano saying anything about a* daimyo *ruling this area,* he thought. *Unfortunately, we're too far from the castle to get there tonight. Too bad, it would be wonderful to sleep in a real bed instead of on a straw mat.*

He felt Maseda pull on the mule's bridle as they continued descending the trail. Although the going got progres-
sively more treacherous, Asano skipped down the trail
without a care. Maseda plodded steadily onward, leaving
Kitsune to fight to remain seated on the mule, a battle he
was constantly in danger of losing.

By the time the three reached the floor of the valley, the
rain had lessened, falling almost gently instead of being
whipped by the wind. As they approached the village,
Asano trotted ahead, bowing in greeting to the heads that
popped out of a hut door. A quiet conversation followed,
and Asano motioned for Maseda and Kitsune to come
forward.

As he tried to slide off the mule, Kitsune felt the last of
his strength slipping away. Asano and the villagers blurred
in front of him. He felt the dizzying sensation of falling,
then the cool wetness of mud on his skin, then blackness.

*   *   *

Kitsune awoke to warmth and quiet. As his eyes fluttered
open, he saw the roof of a hut over his head. A woven mat
hung in the doorway, keeping out the rain he heard pat-
tering on the roof. A single burning taper illuminated the
simple room, which was bare except for the straw mat he
was lying on. Hearing the sound of someone breathing next
to him, Kitsune turned to look.

"Awake at last. To see you lying there, one would have
thought that you would have slept until the Yama kings
themselves rose from the nine hells to sweep across our
land," Asano said, holding out a small wooden bowl.
"Here, drink."

Kitsune took the proffered bowl, his stomach rumbling
as he smelled the delicious *miso* broth. He rose to a sitting
position and bowed before drinking. When he had finished,
he bowed again. "Thank you."

"Do not thank me, but rather thank my new friend Hiroko here, who has prepared the fine soup you thoughtlessly
slurped down," Asano said, shifting slightly to reveal a

young girl, about Kitsune's age, kneeling on the floor. When she saw Kitsune, she bowed her head to the ground, remaining there for long seconds before straightening. Kitsune responded by giving the deepest bow he could under the circumstances.

"Please forgive the poor fare we have offered," Hiroko said, bowing again.

"It was a delicious meal such as I have not enjoyed in many days," Kitsune said, partly because his complimentary response was expected in answer to her apology, and partly because it *was* the best meal he'd had in days, delicious, hot, and filling.

"Ah, I take you everywhere with me in this magnificent country, show you sights such as you have not seen in all your inexperienced years, and you have the temerity to complain about the food the gods have seen fit to grace our humble mouths with. Sometimes I wonder if you will ever truly follow in my footsteps, Kitsune." Asano's voice was stern, but his face impassive.

Kitsune glanced past him for a second to see Hiroko hiding a smile behind her hand. Catching her gaze, he smiled in return, then looked back at Asano. "Perhaps I would be more fit to take up the mantle of your station if we did not clamber up and down mountainsides in the pouring rain, leaving me to catch my near death of fever."

Asano sniffed. "And yet here you are, braying like a mule, when it is obvious that you are not the least bit hampered by illness."

Kitsune's smile faded as he realized that Asano was right. His cough and fever were gone, in fact there was no pain throughout his entire body. He felt like he had just slept for two days, and could get up and travel from the northern mountains to the southern islands without stopping, if need be.

Asano continued, "Indeed, I might suspect that you feigned the entire thing just so we would stop in this village, no doubt entranced by the rustic charms of this peasant girl whom you probably glimpsed on our way in, and whom

even now you are trading witless smiles with for your
own amusement."

Hearing this exchange, Hiroko bowed again, this time to
Asano. "You are far too kind, my lord."

Asano rocked to his feet. "Please, please, dear girl, I am
certainly no one's lord, well, except for this vagabond lying
before us. Rise, my child." The girl did so, and Asano examined her with a critical eye. "Yes, not unpleasing at all.
Rest, Kitsune, and I will speak with you later." He turned
and strode out of the hut without a backward glance, leaving Kitsune and Hiroko alone.

When he was gone, Hiroko knelt again, this time averting
her eyes, and held out another wooden bowl. "He said you
would be hungry."

Kitsune, who had been watching Asano leave, looked
back at her with another smile as he accepted the bowl,
filled with hot rice. "He's right, as always. Thank you for
your generous hospitality."

"He seemed like a kind old man at first, but now I think
he's terribly stern," the young girl said, still not meeting
Kitsune's gaze.

Between mouthfuls, Kitsune nodded. "That *was* him
being kind. It is just his way. Believe me, he's satisfied that
I'm all right, although he probably had everything to do
with that."

"Then it's true, what the elders are saying," Hiroko said,
now looking directly at Kitsune, her eyes filled with wonder. "He is a sorcerer."

Kitsune chewed a bite of rice while he considered his
answer. Yes, it was true that Asano had a reputation as a
sorcerer of high renown, especially at the Emperor's court,
but traveling incognito as they were, he often just passed
himself off as the Emperor's physician. Of course, why the
Emperor's physician would be out here in the middle of
nowhere, instead of at the Emperor's side, was never asked.
In fact, the last time Kitsune had asked Asano when they
were going to court, which he had never seen, Asano had
replied, "I will know when my *daimyo* needs me." They

had been traveling ever since, up and down the kingdom, going wherever Asano's whim directed that particular day.

"Obviously rumors of my master's skill have preceded his arrival in your village," Kitsune said, trying to adopt a suitably humble tone. "It is true, my master does have some degree of skill with medicine, and it is that skill which has caused mention of his name to spread beyond an ordinary physician's reputation. Rest assured, there will be no spirits haunting your dreams tonight."

"Oh, that is very . . . good," Hiroko said, casting her gaze down to the hut floor again as the smile faded from her face.

Surprised by her reaction, Kitsune stared. "You do not seem pleased."

"No, it is a great honor for our humble village to provide shelter for our most revered Emperor's physician," Hiroko said, then closed her mouth as if biting off her next sentence.

Putting a lesson he had learned from Asano to good use, Kitsune did not reply, but instead scooped up another bite of rice while he waited for the girl to continue.

"It's just that what we really need is a sorcerer, not a physician," Hiroko said at last, her shoulders slumping as she realized what she had just said. "Please forgive me, I meant no offense."

"No offense was taken," Kitsune replied. "But, please, stay a while and tell me about what is bothering your village. Surely it cannot be as bad as you say, for a problem needing a sorcerer would be difficult indeed."

"I will tell you, but it will make no difference," Hiroko said. "Only a sorcerer can drive away the evil that plagues the castle on the mountain."

"Ah, so that is why the castle looked unoccupied when we approached," Kitsune said. When she nodded, he continued. "Please, tell me whatever you know. My master has a fondness for stories of the unusual. If your tale interests him, he may consent to look into the matter."

The girl looked up. "But what can a physician do against something that has killed more than a dozen samurai?"

Kitsune hid his smile behind his bowl of rice, not wanting to offend the girl. "Every problem has a solution. It would appear that samurai are not the key to this one. Please, tell me more."

"I don't know very much, and the elders have forbidden anyone to speak of it. But I do know that two winters ago the fever swept through Sudoken castle, leaving not one member of the Yoshioka family or their guards alive. Not wanting the word to get out that our province was undefended, we immediately sent word to our revered Emperor telling him of this unfortunate occurrence. When spring arrived, the Emperor's retainer came with it, and announced that the Shingeda family would be living in the castle, having been given the fief as a reward for the lord's courageous behavior on the battlefield.

"Some weeks later the Shingeda clan arrived and took up residence in the castle. That same evening, several of the palace guards reported seeing the figure of an unfamiliar man walking around the courtyard, as if he was looking for something. The next night, two of the guards who had been patrolling the courtyard were found dead, but untouched, as if their hearts had simply ceased beating. The next night, the clan head—Shingeda Satomi himself—along with six of his personal guard, waited in the courtyard to face whatever it was that had killed his guards. No one heard a sound from the courtyard during the entire evening. In the morning, they found Shingeda and the guards dead, all without a mark on them. Satomi's katana had not even been drawn from its scabbard. The house guards swore no one had got past them. Upon discovery of the body, the captain of the house guard killed himself over the disgrace of what had happened to his master. That afternoon the rest of the family, after ceremonially burying the body, fled this place."

She shook her head sadly and met Kitsune's gaze. "Since then, the castle has gained a reputation for being haunted, although no one has ever seen any indication of it and lived. A few weeks afterward, apparently over an ill-advised wager, one of the local boys, Tokugawa Fujikage, took his father's old *no-dachi* and went to the castle to spend the night. He was found dead the next morning, his sword also never drawn.

"Since then, we have sent messages to the Imperial Court, but have heard no reply. Over the past few months, several samurai, *ronin* by the looks of them, have come into town, usually lured here by hearing about Sudoken castle and hoping to make a name for themselves by vanquishing whatever it is that resides there. They made a name for themselves all right, all becoming victims of the ghost as well. It's obvious that word of the curse has spread, for there have been fewer and fewer travelers lately. In fact, you're the first we've seen this month."

"Well, if people are leaving you alone, then what's the trouble? As long as you pay your taxes, no one will bother you unless a war breaks out nearby," Kitsune said.

"It's not that simple. First, no travelers means no merchants, so we have to journey over the mountains to get supplies. Second, since word of the abandoned castle got out, we've been plagued by bandits. They grow stronger and stronger, and soon they're just going to walk in here and take everything. Then what will we do?" Hiroko demanded.

"Hmm, you're right. This problem is more difficult than I thought," Kitsune said. "I think I can persuade my master to investigate this matter. At the very least he could make a report to the Emperor regarding the weakened status of this province." He let out a deep breath and set down the now-empty bowl. "I need to rest now. Please, let whomever else is tending to me know that I will be sleeping for the next few hours. Take that message to Asano as well, if you please."

"As you wish," Hiroko gathered up the bowls and began to leave the hut. At the doorway, she stopped and looked back at Kitsune. "Do you really think he will be able to do something"

"If the gods favor it, yes," Kitsune replied with the utmost sincerity. *And if I can talk him into it, which shouldn't be hard.*

After Hiroko had left, Kitsune lay back on the mat and closed his eyes. He did not fall asleep, however, but cleared his mind of all thought and waited. It could have been seconds or hours, but a while later he felt a tiny breeze waft across his face, as if the air had been disturbed by someone entering the hut.

"It is good you have come back, Asano," Kitsune said without opening his eyes.

The diminutive sorcerer grunted. "Well, at least you remember some of those lessons I've tried to teach you. The girl claimed you were sleeping." Asano's voice sounded like it was right next to him.

"I told her to say that. It was the surest way to get you here," Kitsune said with a smile as he sat up and opened his eyes, then gaped in shock.

Kneeling next to him was Maseda, who stared impassively down at him. With a start, Kitsune sensed a presence behind him. He tried to roll out of the way, but was too late. A sound like thunder exploded in Kitsune's head, and the next thing he knew, he was sprawled out on the mat, his ears ringing from the blow Asano had given him.

"Ordinarily I would not have been so harsh on someone so recently ill, but your clumsiness at sensing who was coming into the room was intolerable. To think that I could be mistaken for that man-mountain. Disgraceful," sighed Asano as he walked to the other side of the mat and knelt down.

Kitsune rolled to his knees and bowed, his forehead touching the floor. "I apologize for my arrogance, Asano."

"Your apologies would be meaningless if I were a *shinobi* and had split your skull open with that blow. Always use every sense that is available to you, Kitsune. Never put your trust in just one or two, for any of your senses can be deceived."

Kitsune bowed again. "Thank you, Asano. I will remember."

"The headache you will have tonight will be reminder enough." With a wave, Asano dismissed the looming samurai, who took up his customary station outside the hut. "I trust you paid more attention when you spoke with the girl."

"Yes, and she had a most intriguing tale," Kitsune said.

"So, just what is it that has taken over the castle and driven the owners out?" Asano asked, forestalling Kitsune, who had been just about to launch into the story.

"Um . . . they don't know. Before the Shingeda family left, there were reports of an apparition walking around the courtyard. Apparently it is this ghost that killed the guards, Shingeda himself, and a local boy."

"You seem very confident that it is this spirit doing all the killing. Who has seen this ghost of Sudoken castle?"

"Well, no one—who lived to tell about it. What else could it be, Asano? Hiroko described the guards being killed without a mark left on them, as well as the master of the castle, who was dead before he could even draw his sword. Who else but a ghost could do that?"

"Perhaps. Regardless, it seems there is quite a mystery here. I think we will be paying this 'ghost' a visit tonight. That is, if you feel up to it."

"I am ready," Kitsune said, fighting back a grimace as pain lanced through his head.

Asano looked at Kitsune in bemusement. "Perhaps you should truly rest now. I will return at dusk, and we will make our preparations."

Kitsune began to nod, then stopped when he realized what the movement would do to his aching skull. "I will be ready when you arrive."

"Excellent." Asano rose and headed toward the exit.

"A question, Asano."

Asano paused.

"How did you know about the castle?"

"It was simple," Asano replied. "The castle showed no signs of occupation when we arrived, and the villagers did not send a messenger there bearing the news of our presence. Since no castle is ever unoccupied for any reason, especially during these times, it was easy to surmise that something was keeping people out. Rest now."

The moment Asano left, Kitsune gradually lowered his

head to the wooden pillow on the mat, stopping every time
the pounding in his head grew too much to bear. He
stopped often. Finally, he was able to lie down and, before
he had time to think about his mistake or what they were
going to do that evening, immediately fell asleep.

* * *

Kitsune awoke just as the sun was beginning to sink
below the western horizon. He sat up gingerly, still feeling
the effects of that afternoon's lesson. Rubbing his head, he
left the sleeping mat and walked to the center of the hut
floor, where he assumed the lotus position and closed his
eyes, attempting to clear his mind again. It was harder to
concentrate this time, mostly due to the dull, throbbing
ache behind his temples. He had almost succeeded in relaxing when he again felt the presence of someone entering
the hut. Kitsune remained motionless, sensing the person
moving closer to him. The figure stopped in front of him.
Kitsune sensed a tenseness in whoever was standing before
him, and he readied himself. The air around him shifted,
splitting apart as if the person was swinging a fist. Kitsune's
hand shot up—and grabbed the other person's hand just
before it would have struck his forehead.

Kitsune opened his eyes to see Asano standing before
him. "And so you have learned today. You saw me as
clearly as if you had been watching me from the moment
I entered the hut. With no assumptions to blind you this
time, you were ready for anything, and blocked the possible
attack. Excellent."

Kitsune released Asano's hand and bowed.

Asano smiled. "The only thing is," he paused, then his
hand blurred toward Kitsune's forehead, tapping it lightly
with his index finger. "I was only going to rid you of your
headache, since I will need all of your faculties intact
tonight."

Kitsune experimentally looked up, then down, then
moved his head in a circle. The pain was gone, vanished as
if it had never existed. "Thank you, Asano."

"I'm sure you will repay me by keeping those wits about you tonight," Asano said. "Come."

Outside, the storm had dissipated, and only a few clouds scattered across the sky marked its passing. The ground was muddy and treacherous, with many standing puddles that Kitsune noticed only after stepping in one, so intently was he looking up at the castle. Asano, with his usual deftness, casually stepped on the tiny patches of dry land to higher ground.

Maseda was waiting for them, carrying several sacks and earthen jars tied to a long pole, much like the yoke of an ox. Kitsune expected to find the villagers there to see them off. Instead, the public square was deserted, every hut quiet and dark. As he scanned the small village, however, Kitsune felt the distinct sensation of being watched.

"Asano—" he began.

"I know. They fear the spirit may come down and seek revenge if it sees them with us."

Led by Maseda, the three walked through the village and started up the path toward the castle. As they left the last cluster of huts and passed out of sight of the village, a hiss from a nearby bush caught Kitsune's attention. Stepping closer, he asked, "Who's there?"

With a rustle of leaves, Hiroko stepped out of the foliage, bearing a small bouquet of lotus blossoms. Extending them to Kitsune, she bowed and said, "For luck."

Kitsune bowed deeply and accepted the offering. "Thank you. Now I know the gods will favor us this day."

Hiroko smiled shyly, then turned and vanished into the woods. Kitsune saw Asano watching him, a mysterious smile on the older man's face. Still holding the bundle, Kitsune fought to control the blush rising on his cheeks. Asano did not say a word, but simply turned back to the path. With one last look at where Hiroko had disappeared, Kitsune scrambled after him.

The path was wide and smooth, and showed little sign of abandonment. Maseda set a brisk pace, and soon they found themselves standing before the main gate of the castle, a massive construction of thick wooden beams upon which two huge iron-bound doors were set, flanked on either side by tall guard towers, now empty and lifeless. One of the doors was closed, the other open, revealing a flagstone pathway that led inside the castle walls. The rays of the setting sun cast a crimson hue on the white stone walls and red-tiled roof of the buildings, making the castle appear painted in blood. Kitsune shivered at the thought, then tried to distract himself by watching Asano.

At Asano's signal, Maseda, his hand on the hilt of his katana, cautiously approached the entrance. Reaching the door, he looked inside, alert to the slightest disturbance. After a moment, he stepped through, then motioned for Asano and Kitsune to join him.

The stone path continued to the main building, with another trail branching off to what looked like the courtyard. The main path appeared to have been swept clean that morning, as did the courtyard, with low rounded bushes arranged around a large circular slab of stone set into the floor of crushed gravel. In one corner of the yard Kitsune saw a small *koi* pond, empty save for a little rainwater that had collected in the bottom. In the corner directly opposite it, the remains of a small flower garden, arranged in an octagon, lay crushed and lifeless. Except for the pond and dead garden, the rest of the grounds looked immaculate. Everything was so clean that Kitsune half expected someone to walk out of the castle at any moment and inquire what they were doing here.

"Do you feel it?" Asano asked Kitsune, his inscrutable black eyes pinning his student. Kitsune again studied the courtyard and castle. He saw nothing except the buildings, guard towers, and wall, and yet something was tickling the back of his mind.

"There is a sense of . . . something unfinished here," he said.

"Yes, I sense it as well. We do not have much time. Already Amaterasu sinks ever lower. Maseda, Kitsune, follow me," Asano said as he strode toward the courtyard.

Once there, he positioned himself in the center of the stone slab. "Kitsune, bring me the sash and the jar of salt.

Also, the red clay jar, the third bundle of herbs from the left, and the mortar and pestle."

Kitsune trotted over to Maseda, who had set down his load and stepped away, his hand still on his sword. Sorting through various bags, jars, and other containers, Kitsune found what he needed and brought it to Asano, who took one end of the sash and gave Kitsune the other.

"Walk out five paces, and pour the circle," Asano instructed.

Kitsune did so, and by holding onto the sash, laid out a perfect circle of salt on the stone, stepping inside just before he closed it.

"A circle within a circle. This ward will be powerful, which I think we will need this evening," Asano mused.

"Shouldn't Maseda be in here, too? After all, if the spirit has killed all samurai who have encountered it—" Kitsune said, glancing at the impassive *ronin* standing a few paces away.

"Just as Maseda-san has never tried to tell me how to work my magic, so have I never told him how to hold his sword. It is an arrangement that has worked admirably for many months, and I see no reason to change it now. Maseda-san knows what he is doing," Asano said as he crumbled the herbs into the pestle and ground them to powder. Uncorking the jar, he sniffed cautiously at the contents, then poured a dash of the liquid inside into the mortar. With a snap of his fingers, a single spark appeared out of midair and floated down into the bowl. There was a loud pop and a puff of green smoke as a thin wisp of vapor began streaming out. As the smoke thickened, it flowed to the ground and began to spread across the stone floor, wreathing the courtyard in a layer of unearthly vapor.

By now the sun was below the horizon, and the last rays of light were fading, returning the castle walls to their pristine white color. The emerald smoke was giving off a dim glow of its own, growing more intense as the sunlight grew weaker, and illuminating the courtyard with its flickering green light. A breeze sprang up from the east, swaying the barren tree branches, but failing to disturb the vapor.

Kitsune tried to watch every direction at once. Beside him, he saw Asano sit cross-legged on the ground, the smoke-producing mortar still held in his hands. Maseda had adopted the same position, and might as well have been carved from stone. Gulping, Kitsune slowly lowered himself to the ground, his legs disappearing in the green smoke that now covered the entire grounds.

The last crimson sunbeam disappeared behind the high palace wall, and night crept in. Except for the green vapor, the garden was dark, with no moon or stars to light the stone paths. During all of this, Kitsune, Asano, and Maseda silently watched and waited.

The moment the darkness fell completely, the figure of a man appeared on the path leading up to the garden. The green mist parted where he walked, only to close up again behind him. He was dressed in the simple robes of a priest, his arms folded near his chest in a position of rest. Kitsune's eyes widened as he realized that, as the man drew closer, he could see right through him to the wall of the castle itself. The man was insubstantial, a pale wraith gliding among the remains of the once-proud fortress. Kitsune noticed that his head was shaved bare, lacking the traditional topknot of a nobleman.

Kitsune tore his gaze away from the spirit to glance at Asano. The old man's face was still as he watched the ghost come nearer. Kitsune wanted to say something, but the words stuck in his throat, unwilling to break the silence that permeated the garden.

Strangely, it was Maseda who rose to his feet and walked toward the man. He had stuck his hands inside his kimono, making it appear that he had no arms, just empty sleeves. He walked boldly, making no pretense of stealth. When he reached a point about five paces in front of the circle, Maseda stopped and waited for the ghostly man to approach.

The ghost drew ever nearer, until it seemed that, with one more step, he would pass right through Maseda's body. Maseda bowed deeply and held the position for several seconds, then straightened. At the movement, the spirit halted, standing silently in front of the *ronin*, then bowed slightly, acknowledging the samurai's show of respect. Maseda said a few words, none of which were understandable to Kitsune. The ghost nodded his head once, then again. Maseda nodded, then bowed deeply again.

This time the ghost bowed more deeply than before, turned on his heel, and slowly drifted out of the garden. As he walked, the green smoke dissipated around him, leaving the garden shrouded in darkness.

Maseda watched him leave, along with Asano and Kitsune, neither of whom had moved during the entire one-sided conversation. When he was gone, Maseda turned and walked toward Asano and Kitsune, stopping just outside the salt circle.

"Yoshioka Genzaemon would rest with honor," Maseda said. It was the longest sentence Kitsune had ever heard the samurai say.

There was the sound of a spark being struck, and Asano's face was suddenly lit by the dimly burning remains in the mortar. His expression was calm, as if he had expected everything that had happened during the evening.

"Whom does he need to see?" Asano asked.

"Miyamoto-san," Maseda replied.

"I think we can provide some assistance," Asano murmured.

*   *   *

The next morning, Asano was maddeningly obtuse about the whole encounter, cautioning Kitsune to keep silent about what had transpired. He met with the village elders and told them that, if all went well that evening, the curse of Sudoken castle would be lifted. The villagers had greeted this news with cautious optimism, but upon seeing the look on Asano's face, had refrained from pressing him further.

Kitsune had gone back to the hut where he had recovered, only to find Hiroko eagerly waiting for him. "Did you see it?" she had asked.

"Yes," Kitsune said.

"And? What did it look like? Did it try to kill you? Did you defeat it?"

"I'm sorry, Hiroko, but Asano told me not to speak about what is happening up there, for fear that the spirit might hear its name and come down to the village to investigate," Kitsune said, wincing inwardly at the white lie.

"So you can't tell me anything " Hiroko pouted.

"Only that if all goes well, the castle will be free of its curse tonight," Kitsune said. He didn't dare say anything else, for he knew that if he mentioned anything about the spirit in the castle, Asano would somehow know. And Asano's punishment for willful disobedience was strict indeed.

That evening, Kitsune, Asano, and Maseda again began the long walk up the mountain to the castle gate. Asano was unusually quiet, seemingly lost in thought. Kitsune divided his attention between the path and his mentor. Maseda, bent under an even more heavily-laden yoke than the one he carried the previous evening, only had eyes for the path ahead.

The three reached the open castle gate when the sun was just beginning to slip below the horizon. Now the crimson-tinged walls did not bother Kitsune so much. Again they headed for the barren garden, where Asano set up his equipment, this time on a smaller stone slab next to the large circle he had been in last night. When Maseda set down the yoke, Asano surprised Kitsune by stepping over to the bundle himself and rooting through the contents. As he did so, he began speaking.

"You are familiar with the name Miyamoto Musashi, are you not?"

Kitsune nodded, although in confusion rather than understanding. Of course he knew who Miyamoto-san was. Everyone knew the name of the greatest swordsman of Japan, the man who had developed his own unique style of fighting with two swords, and who had dueled with and defeated more than sixty opponents.

Asano continued. "This happened when Musashi was very young, and had just set out on his *Musha-Shugyo,* a warrior's pilgrimage to seek out opponents to test his ability. Musashi arrived on Kyoto Island with the intention of challenging the samurai here to a contest of *Taryu-Jiai,* a competition between students of two fighting schools to determine which is superior.

"He issued a challenge to Yoshioka Genzaemon, the head of the Yoshioka clan. The Yoshioka family had served the Ashikaga Shogunate as martial arts instructors, so their skill was not inconsiderable. Genzaemon could have refused the duel with no loss of honor to himself, as he was a high-ranking samurai, and Musashi was, at this time, still unknown. Nevertheless, Genzaemon accepted the challenge, and the duel was scheduled for the next day.

"The morning of the duel dawned, and Genzaemon arrived at the appointed site and waited for Musashi. And waited. And waited. Two hours later, a messenger sent to locate Musashi found him at his inn—still asleep. Musashi told the messenger to apologize to Genzaemon and assure him that he would arrive soon. He rose, took the time for a leisurely breakfast, then set off to the duel site, arriving two hours later.

"As you can probably guess, Genzaemon was furious at having been kept waiting four hours by a lowly samurai of no name. Therefore, when the duel began, he was impatient and careless, whereas Musashi was calm and deliberate.

"The duel ended with Genzaemon stretched out upon the ground, unconscious. When Genzaemon recovered, his shame was so great that he shaved off his topknot, set down his sword and turned to the priesthood, never to fight again.

"I can only assume that, for whatever reason, even the contemplation and meditation required of the Buddhist priests has not cleansed his soul or the stain upon his family honor, therefore he wishes to face Musashi one last time. Shingeda-san, his guards, and the *ronin* just got in the way and suffered the fate of those who accost spirits.

"Since Miyamoto-san died a few days ago, his soul should be almost ready for reincarnation on the great wheel. With a little persuasion, it should be a simple matter to entice him to make one small stop before he ascends."

As he was relating the story, Asano had been working, selecting various ingredients and grinding them into the mortar. When he finished, there was an inky black liquid at the bottom of the bowl. Asano selected a writing brush and walked to the middle of the stone circle. Bending, he dipped the brush into the ink, paused for a moment, then fluidly drew an ideogram on the rock.

"This castle has been built, unintentionally no doubt, at a crossing point between dimensions, and as such contains a portal to the spirit world. With this ritual, we will open a door into that other world and call forth Miyamoto-san's spirit. While I am preparing for the rest of the ritual, pour the circle around that stone, leaving a break for me to step through." Asano then lit a stick of pungent incense, waving it over the ideogram he had just created and chanting in a low voice.

As he chanted, the thin smoke from the incense hung in the air, beginning to form the shape of a doorway. Asano kept chanting and waving, and the portal solidified into a round opening ringed in rich jade green, sealed with mystic energy. A white light emanated from the portal, and every so often Kitsune could see a blur of movement behind the glow, as if something had passed between the doorway and the light shining through it.

Asano stepped through the break into the circle, then snatched up the salt jar and poured it out, sealing the gap. Now all three were inside the unbroken circle of salt.

"Kitsune, wash the mortar and prepare the components for the binding spell," Asano commanded.

"What are you going to do?" Kitsune asked.

"I am going to open the doorway. Unfortunately, often there are portal guardians on the other side who demand appeasement before letting anyone pass. With good *joss*, I will be able to use the guardian to summon Miyamoto-san. Go now!"

Kitsune grabbed the mortar and carefully washed all traces of the ink mixture out of it. He took a different stick of incense and crumbled it into the bowl, then added a pinch of herbs from a brown leather bag, mixing the ingredients. He was about to snap his fingers for a spark—Asano had taught him that much—when he stopped and looked up, aware that Asano had not told him to light the mortar's contents.

Asano had assumed the lotus position on the ground in the center of the salt circle. There was a small gong in front of him, and he held a small mallet in his hand. When he judged the moment to be right, he beat the gong five times, waiting for the previous sound to die away before hitting the gong again.

At the fifth beat, the doorway shimmered as the light faded, revealing a hole of utter blackness that flickered with occasional shapeless pale white wisps. Kitsune was about to ask if this was supposed to happen when a form appeared.

The thing, for there was no better way to describe it, hunched down to see into the garden. It was as tall as the main level of the castle, and grossly obese. Its naked, gray-scaled body was covered with dozens of small orifices from which snakes and spiders emerged, crawled, or slithered around on its folds of flesh, then disappeared into other holes. It had two arms, and underneath those were two writhing, slime-covered tentacles. Its hands were massive, easily the length of its spindly forearms, and tipped with what looked like stingers which dripped with a foul yellow liquid. It squatted on four armored legs that resembled the limbs of an insect. Its face, what there was of it, consisted of a ring of bright blue eyes encircling its pointed head, a lipless slit of a mouth containing far too many rows of jagged teeth, a vestigial nose, little more than two slits in its broad face, and long green antennae which quivered as they attuned themselves to the doorway and the garden that lay beyond it.

Kitsune simply stood there, holding the mortar in his hands, and stared at the monstrosity. He looked at Asano, who was bowing to the creature.

"Nani ga hoshi dess ka?" the thing hissed in a corrupted form of the Court language. "What do you want?"

"O sagashte i-mass Miyamoto-san. Kare wa muko ni i-

mass ka?" Asano replied. "I'm looking for Miyamoto-san. Is he over there?"

"Ga ari-mass ka sonaemono?" the demon hissed. "Do you have offerings?"

In response to this, Maseda stepped forward and unsheathed his tanto. Drawing the blade across his forearm, he let the blood trickle from the cut into a small wooden bowl Asano held up.

The demon leaned out of the doorway, his antennae wriggling as he inhaled the smell through the flaring slits in his face. The tentacles shot forward, reaching greedily for the bowl of blood, only to stop as they encountered the invisible spirit barrier Asano had erected. The creature hissed in frustration, then settled back onto its haunches.

"O kure-masen ka ketsu-eki?" the demon asked. "You give me blood?"

Asano nodded. *"Mitskeru Miyamoto-san. Mot-te kuru koko. Sorekara ketsu-eki age-mass,"* the old man said. "Find Miyamoto-san. Bring here. Then I'll give you blood."

The demon nodded once, turned, and lumbered off into the darkness.

"Now we wait," Asano said.

Kitsune glanced up at Maseda, who was about to wrap the cut on his arm with a clean cloth. Asano shook his head and traced the cut on Maseda's arm. As his finger passed over the wound, it closed up, leaving only a thin white line.

"Asano, aren't you worried that something else might come through the gate?" Kitsune asked.

"Guardians like that one hold complete power over their gate," Asano replied. "Nothing can come through without permission from it, and they never let anything through without payment, which spirits almost never have."

"If that thing controls the gate, why doesn't he come through into our world?" Kitsune asked.

"Most demons are not comfortable in our material world. When they take an interest in mortal affairs, they use humans to do whatever dirty work they have in mind, usually by possessing them or hypnotizing them in some fashion.

A demon bound into a weapon or object is the most dangerous kind of all, instantly able to take over whomever touches its prison. I've faced something like that only once, and its power almost defied understanding . . . ah, I believe he's coming back already. I just hope Miyamoto-san hasn't traded his earthly form for something more . . . exotic."

"That makes two of us," Kitsune said. "I don't think I could take anything much more exotic than that."

The demon returned with a human figure behind him. Asano looked at the man closely, then nodded. The demon, however, shook what amounted to its head.

"Mot-to ketsu-eki."

Asano sighed. "He wants more. Very well." He rolled up the sleeve of his kimono and slit his own arm with a long fingernail, letting several drops of his own blood mingle with Maseda's. The demon sniffed even harder when Asano's blood hit the air.

"Mot-to, mot-to!"

"Mo kek-ko dess!" Asano snapped. "No more!" He waved his hand at the bowl, and it began to tip to one side, threatening to spill its contents.

"Ie!" the demon screamed, shoving the human through the gate. "No!"

Asano concentrated on the bowl for a moment, then gently blew on it, sending it floating through the air toward the demon, who reached for it with his tentacles, eyeing it possessively all the while.

"Honto ni arigato gozai-mass," Asano said to the demon, who was licking greedily at the bowl, consumed by his own hunger. "Thank you very much." The demon ignored him. Asano rang the gong five more times, and with each sound, the gate grew more and more insubstantial. When the fifth ring faded away, so did the doorway.

Which left them all looking at Miyamoto-san.

Miyamoto Musashi certainly did not look like a man who had fought more than sixty opponents and never lost. He was clad in a torn and stained kimono that looked as if it had been left outside all winter, then picked up and put on without even shaking it out. His topknot was a matted, bedraggled mess, with the rest of his hair, untrimmed and unwashed, streaming from his head like strands of black wire. Even though Kitsune knew he was a ghost, he thought he could almost smell the odor of the swordsman's unwashed body. The ghost did not carry the traditional set of metal katana and wakizashi of the samurai, but instead had a wooden sword stuck through his obi, which was carelessly knotted around his waist.

Musashi's face was unremarkable save for his eyes, which flickered past Kitsune, paused for a moment on Maseda, paused longer on Asano, and finally turned toward Genzaemon, who had appeared by now. For the second the spirit's eyes had rested on Kitsune, he felt like the ghost had evaluated him, found him to be inconsequential, and had therefore moved on. *His gaze is like Maseda's,* Kitsune thought, *it is the look of one who knows he has already won the battle before it has begun. If anyone could get past the spirit barrier, I think he could.*

Genzaemon had knelt before Musashi and bowed low, his forehead touching the ground. Musashi, in an unusual show of respect, bowed deeply to the older man. As he came out of the bow, Genzaemon revealed a tanto, or dagger, held in his right hand. Musashi drew his sword instantly and took a step away and to the rear of Genzaemon, his weapon held in the down ready position.

Genzaemon faced Asano, Kitsune, and Maseda, and bowed to them as well. Kitsune bowed deeply, following the other men's example. Kitsune raised his head just in time to see Genzaemon put the dagger to his left side and, without hesitation, plunge the blade into his own abdomen. Genzaemon stiffened, then drew the tanto across his midsection in a long horizontal slash. The spirit sat for a moment, then slowly bowed his head.

The instant his neck was exposed, Musashi's arm blurred into motion, the wooden sword arcing downward, slicing off Genzaemon's head.

Before Genzaemon's head could hit the ground, both it and his body vanished. Musashi nodded once, then stuck his sword through his obi and waited.

"Kitsune, hand me the mortar," Asano said, never taking his eyes off the swordsman.

Kitsune looked down to see the bowl still clenched in his hands. With an effort, he handed it over to the older man, who turned the bowl over, letting the mixture spill out. As it did, he blew on the drifting powder, sending it wafting toward Musashi.

The powder swirled around the ghostly swordsman, enveloping him in a twinkling brown cloud. It moved faster and faster around him, spinning like a stationary dust devil. Then, all of the dust scattered to the four winds in a soundless explosion, and when it had cleared, Musashi had disappeared.

"Even though he had lived the last decades of his life as a priest, for his soul to find rest, Genzaemon needed to die as a warrior," Asano explained. "We will go down to the village and let them know that the spirit has been dispelled, but you will not tell anyone what has transpired here tonight. I'm sure you will come up with a suitably heroic tale for yourself to impress the young woman, eh? We will stay with them for a few days, at least until word can be sent back to court, and a new *daimyo* appointed for this province. Would that suit you, pupil?" Asano's eyes twinkled, much like the brown powder had.

Kitsune nodded, still staring at the space where the two spirits had been. He looked up at the castle, which no longer seemed so forbidding or ominous as when he had first seen it. *The spirit has been laid to rest with honor, and now it is time for life to return here,* he thought.

"Well, then, what are you waiting for? Surely you have not forgotten your duties so soon? You have to pack all of this up before we can go. Move!" Asano snapped, shaking his head.

Kitsune started, then jumped to his task, turning away from Asano to hide the smile on his face.

DANNY'S DESIRE
by Janet Pack

Janet Pack lives in a slightly haunted farmhouse in Williams Bay, Wisconsin, with cats Tabirika Onyx, Syrannis Moonstone, and Baron Figaro di Shannivere. She writes science fiction, fantasy, and mysteries in the dim morning hours, then works as the manager's assistant at Shadowlawn Stoneware Pottery in Delavan, Wisconsin. In rare free moments, Janet composes music (some of which has been printed by TSR/WotC and in *The Death Gate Cycle*), reads, plays with her cats, watches good movies, collects rocks, cooks, designs costumes and jewelry, and avoids housework.

The mob dragged the man toward the old oak, shouting maledictions against him and the British.

"Please," the captive managed in a tenor voice which sound thick and peculiar to his own ears. "Please, I am not what you think." He struggled futilely against the rope binding his wrists, feeling the warmth of blood for his efforts. His coat felt strange on his shoulders, so stiff and heavy; even his words felt odd in his mouth, a slightly different patois than he normally spoke.

"Traitor!" snarled a burly man dressed in a tricorn hat and ragged vest that halted just above his knees. "You're nothin' but a traitor!" He shook a flintlock rifle in morning air perfumed by woodsmoke. A Minuteman. The description leaped easily into the prisoner's brain as the man continued his cursing. "Stinkin' English pig!"

"I beg you, wait for the courier," the hostage panted, pulling against the bruising grips of two strangers walking on either side of him. But they and the rest of the folks who made up the mob weren't listening. They just shoved him inexorably toward the tree and its stout limb hanging almost parallel to the ground. "All will become clear when General Washington . . ."

"You sully our leader's great name!" A fist slammed into his mouth, rocking his head backward. The captive spat blood and a broken tooth. Crimson blood from a split lip dribbled down his clean-shaven chin and dripped onto his once-white cravat. "You have no right to speak of our General Washington, dirty lying loyalist!"

Now beneath the tree's reach, the prisoner straightened, trying to accept the fate he could no longer deny, praying that somehow the courier might arrive in time. But there was no sign of such a man riding into the howling throng.

"So be it," he stated in a voice full of doom, catching the fevered eyes of the instigators. "But I will haunt each and every one here who is responsible for my death."

"Loyalist!"

"King-lover!"

"Tory!"

"Hang 'im!"

They heaved him onto a restive horse and cinched the rope around his neck. The crowd couldn't see the phenomenal strength of the man through their hatred. He was steel inside, willing to die for a cause he'd upheld for years behind the mask of a mild-faced English merchant. He'd been a prime agent of freedom for this new country, a proponent of Benjamin Franklin and Thomas Jefferson—but only in his thoughts. He had no regrets, except for the ignoble manner and suddenness of his death at the hands of his own countrymen. They had no inkling of the path to freedom he'd made more accessible for them. Despite his threat, he felt sad for their incensed misunderstanding.

He heard the slap, felt the horse jolt from beneath him. The noose's knot slammed against his ear, but unfortunately not hard enough to break his neck. He choked, fought the bite of the hemp, and struggled for long minutes against the pain. Finally succumbing to its shrinking clutch, the man sucked in a last burning breath as darkness surged over his final whispered thought:

"I will be remembered!"

* * *

Dr. Edward Kharman bolted upright in bed, gasping, tangled in sweaty sheets. He'd never had dreams so vivid or so violent until he'd bought this old Virginia house. Disoriented and trembling, more fatigued than he'd been last night when he went to bed, he fumbled for his glasses and settled them against his nose before swinging his long legs over the edge of the mattress and pulling on a pair of jeans.

Barefooted, he padded into the kitchen and made coffee. The rich smell of Jamaica Blue Mountain soothed his twitching nerves a little, but he required sunlight to dispel the clinging flannel shreds of the dream.

He wrapped a hand around his favorite mug and slipped through the back door and onto the small porch. Leaning one shoulder against a wood-stained support warming in the sun anchored him to the real world again.

"Mornin', Perfessor!"

Hot coffee sloshed onto Ed's hand as he jerked in reaction to the sharp soprano. Grinning at his nerves, he nodded to the person in the next yard.

"Good morning, Mrs. Sheridan. You're up early."

"Always. And call me Nettie. Everyone does." The feisty octogenarian studied him with vulturelike intensity. Edward was suddenly uncomfortably aware of his unshirted chest, bare feet, and worn jeans smeared with paint. He was grateful his short dark beard disguised much of his blush.

"How's she comin' inside?"

"Fine, thanks." A yawn escaped him. "Excuse me," he offered, yawning again. "I'm a bit tired this morning. Finished painting the parlor last night, so I was up late. That Federal blue you suggested for the upper walls looks great with the oak chair rail and the wallpaper."

"Thought so." Her scrutiny didn't abate as she stabbed

her spade into the garden plot. "Those nightmares started, too, didn't they?"

His cup sloshed again as the memory of his dream eclipsed the sunlight. Kharman shivered, and for the briefest of moments he felt the burn of a thick rope around his neck. "How do you know?"

"Somethin' about the look of you. Seen it in previous owners of the place. None of 'em lasted long." She cocked her head, crowlike. Sunlight gold warred with the bright silver of her cropped hair. "Mebbe you won't either."

"Why . . . why would anyone who owned this house get nightmares?" Ed wondered, not meaning to say the words aloud as he stared into his coffee.

"Somethin' about stones from the first foundation still existin' in those walls. Tale deals with a British sympathizer in the Revolutionary War. Heard he met a violent end. Owners of that place say they had peculiar feelin's sometimes, and nightmares." She shrugged an end to her interest in the subject, aiming her attention at the new shoots by her feet.

"Hanged," Kharman muttered. "He was hanged."

Honed by a boyhood fascination for personal stories associated with Old World civilizations, Edward's curiosity was piqued. "What kind of peculiar feelings?" he asked her, remembering an unusual sense of nervousness as if an invisible Sword of Damocles hung over his head since he moved in.

"Dunno," the old lady returned. "Didn't pry."

"I don't know much about that period. I teach Western European history. Where'd you hear about it?"

"Just picked it up somewhere."

"Do you remember anything else about the story?"

"Young man," Nettie snapped, straightening, "I don't clutter my mind with such trivia. If you're that interested, go to the Recorder of Deeds and the Surveyor's Office. Also the library. Check with my granddaughter Cassie at the latter—she's a research librarian there. Cassie Bloodworth. Very pretty. You'd like her." The old woman re-

turned to her work with energy, obviously terminatin
their conversation.

Ed considered his options. Since it was Sunday, neithe
the Recorder of Deeds nor the Surveyor's Office wer
open. But the local library certainly was. Feeling a bit les
spooked, he returned to the kitchen, fortified himself wit
another half mug of coffee, replaced his jeans with presse
slacks topped by a sports shirt, slipped his feet into loafer
and headed for his worn Honda parked in the driveway
Wallpapering the study could wait. It was a fine day to d
some research.

* * *

"Cassie Bloodworth?" Ed stopped at the research desk
The attractive copper-and-honey-haired young woman pag
ing through an oversized antique book looked up.

"I'm Cassandra Bloodworth." Her wide brown eyes wer
as sharp as her grandmother's, owning a glint of smok
quartz in their depths. Her voice claimed soprano registe
but possessed an intriguing huskiness, making it easy on hi
ears. "May I help you?"

"Yes, please." His baritone clouded, and he cleared th
tightness nervously. "I'm Dr. Edward Kharman, a professo
at the university. I live next door to Nettie Sheridan."

"Nettie told me she had a new neighbor." Her smile wa
slight, but she held out her hand. Ed shook it, marvelin
at the cool delicate fingers. "What may I do for you?"

"Well, uh . . . I'm looking for information on a . . ." H
couldn't force the word "haunting" past his teeth. It jus
didn't sound right in full daylight. ". . . a subject beyon
my expertise. I teach Western European history, and wha
I need to know concerns the American Revolutionary War
I've got a minimum of facts and a great deal of curiosity.

"This library has an excellent collection of books an
quite a good database on that time period," Cassandra said
rising. "Let me get you started. I've got a bit more informa
tion to look up for another patron, then I'll be able to help
with your search." She led him past rows of dry-smellin

tomes on wooden shelves to a large alcove marked "American History."

"There's the computer." She pointed, the wisp of an impish smile playing across her expressive mouth as she turned to leave. "I'll be back shortly."

Ed settled down and sat flummoxed by the menu until he found "Legends—Hauntings." Unfortunately, the few references he came across dealt with soldiers killed during various battles now tied to the field or grove where they fell, or sweethearts and wives of soldiers who died of disease or in childbirth, their last words cries for their loved ones. There were very few structures on record listed as haunted, and none by a British sympathizer. He had just called up the list of known loyalists in the colonies and printed it out when the research librarian returned.

"Any luck?" She stopped behind his shoulder.

"Not much. I should have inquired at the real estate records office before coming here. I just don't know enough about my subject to look this up.'

"Here, let me try."

Kharman gratefully relinquished his chair. He sucked in a deep breath and commanded his courage not to desert him. "I'm looking for the history of the spirit who's haunting my house."

"Oh."

"Yeah," Ed replied, letting his frustration and fatigue show. "I don't even know his name. I shouldn't have bothered you with this."

Dark brown eyes shiny as polished bayonets met his reflected in the screen. "When I was younger and that house was empty, a couple of friends and I sneaked in and tried to talk to that ghost. It wouldn't deign to communicate through an Ouija board."

"It gets to me through dreams." Edward shuddered, the memory of his nightmare chilling sunlit reality. "He was hanged."

"How do you know?"

The professor sighed. "At the risk of you thinking me completely crazy, I was forced to experience his death last night, from his point of view. It happened the night before, too. The scenes get worse each time, more graphic. And the nightmares have been increasing in scope since I moved in. They started as just garbled vignettes. Now I get a full march to the hanging tree, and more." He smiled wanly, unable to keep his fingers from searching his neck for the tingling rope burn. "If this keeps up, soon I won't be getting any sleep at all."

Ed felt as though he'd passed some sort of rigorous emotional test when Cassandra finally nodded acceptance after several moments of silence. "He may be able to communicate with you more easily because you're male. Or perhaps you have something else in common. Let's see. Nettie always called that place the Winthorp House. Don't let her fool you, she knows a lot more than she admits. We'll start there." Her nimble fingers tapped code words in fast sequence as the professor drew up a chair and watched. Information flashed on-screen.

"The original house on that site believed built by the owner in the late 1760s," Edward read the lines on the monitor aloud in a low voice. "Partially torn down in the mid-1770s. Rebuilt on the same foundation, incorporating the two incomplete ground floor walls left standing. Owned by Paul Winthorp, merchant and farmer, during the 1800s. House burned in late 1800s, again leaving two walls and the foundation. Stood abandoned for nearly twenty years, then was rebuilt. Finding the remnants in surprisingly good condition, the current owner ordered them worked into the construction. The original limestone foundation was expanded and a small wing added including a second guest room above the new kitchen."

"Here's a suggestion," murmured the librarian.

"What's that?"

"I'll bet if you sleep in that room above the kitchen, your nightmares won't be as bad. It's not part of the original house." She twisted to face him. "What's odd about this description is that both times the place was torn down or burned, parts of two walls and the foundation were left. They're probably the same ones each time. You've still got stones and who knows what else left in your house from the first residence. Your nightmares might be associated with those. They sometimes form a spiritual anchor for the tortured spirit. That's purely conjecture, you understand."

"I'll try sleeping in the guest bedroom," Ed said, studying the information. "There's no owner's name linked with the first house."

"That's another odd thing," Cassandra replied, turning back to the computer. "It's as though someone has intentionally erased the record of the first owner. Reminds me of the female Pharaoh Hatshepsut: her son tried to obscure her claim to the afterlife by obliterating all the cartouches inscribed with her name from stelae and her tomb in Egypt.

"Most of the old houses in this area are very well documented—we get information all the time from people doing research on their families or on old homesteads. Considering the exhaustive details we have on other old places, this file should have several pages in it, not just one."

She hit "Print," and they waited in companionable silence until the machines communicated and the single sheet spat out. He reached for the paper as she leaned from her chair and grasped the edge. Their fingers collided.

"Sorry," Edward said awkwardly, his hand retreating as she rose and offered him his house's sparse history. "Thank you very much, Ms. Bloodworth. You found much more information than I expected."

Her half-smile returned. "I can't resist mysteries. That's why I'm good at this job." She cocked her head as a soft female voice with a Southern accent called her name over the library's paging system. "Someone else needs my help."

"Would you . . . uh, would you like to see what I'm doing to the place? I'm refurbishing the interior myself. Since you've been in it, I thought you might be interested. . . ." His voice floundered to a halt. The professor, normally a reticent person with new acquaintances, couldn't believe the words that had just marched from his mouth. He held his breath as Cassandra studied him with a bird-bright expression twin to her grandmother's.

"I'd love to." It was her turn to be shy. "I've got next Sunday off."

"Sunday afternoon, then, around three. I'll ask Nettie to come, too. We'll have tea. Bring your . . . your partner if you wish."

Cassandra laughed, a frothy rich sound, as she disappeared beyond a bookshelf on her way back toward the main part of the library. "I don't think so. My cat doesn't travel well."

Kharman whooshed out a breath. He'd gained less information than he'd hoped about his house, but more than he'd expected about the lovely research librarian. Clutching the printout in one hand, the professor strode out of the library into a day brimming with spring optimism.

*   *   *

He spent the rest of the week drowning in grading research papers from his students. Cassandra had been correct—his visions of the hanging were less horrific in the kitchen and the guest room above it, but still they persisted. Night by night, Ed achieved less sleep. Night by night, the urgency and reality of the dream grew no matter where he closed his eyes. He began mainlining coffee from soup mugs to stay awake, and dreaded the increasingly late hour of his bedtime. His head felt consistently muzzy, and his burning eyes saw the world through the thin gauze of fatigue.

He read at the paper-stacked kitchen table rather than in his wing chair in the parlor or at his desk in the study just because the strange feelings of panic that occasionally overwhelmed him from nowhere and the peculiar whisperings he couldn't quite hear seemed farther away. Over a particularly boring composition, however, tiredness betrayed him and he nodded off. Kharman jerked awake sweating and gagging as soon as his body—the loyalist's body, he corrected himself—dropped to the end of the rope.

Details. Details might help Cassandra locate the British sympathizer. Beginning his own research, he started lists of the things he saw in the dream: clothing, weapons, buckled shoes, men's hair pulled back in short ponytails, trousers ending in cuffs just below the knee, long hose, even the words he'd heard and how they were spoken. Edward realized he'd become the cultural anthropologist of his own nightmare.

He was very glad when Saturday afforded him the opportunity to sleep late after staying up until 3 AM wallpapering the study. The physical labor had been a welcome respite from grading papers. A strange noise forced him out of the dream during the loyalist's threat to haunt the mob hanging him. Ed lay in the guest room bed trying to place the irregular thudding, then rolled over and looked at the digital clock.

"Seven!" he groaned, groping for his jeans and a shirt. "Who's knocking on the back door at seven?" Stumbling down the wooden stairs he slipped, pitching headfirst toward the braided throw rug at the bottom of the flight.

A gust of wind with the pressure of two strong hands slammed against his chest, pushing him back with enough force that he somehow managed to stop his headlong flight and get his feet beneath him. Ed stood shaking on the treads, trying to make something from the nothingness his eyes beheld. He blinked furiously into ether wobbling like the heat shimmer that resides on warm highways. Trembling, he reached out and passed a hand through the area. His skin prickled with sudden cold.

"Show yourself!" Kharman panted. "Please! I must know your name! Why are you doing this? Why are you here?" The pressure against his pectoral muscles dissipated. He felt air stir around his ears, but whatever the phantom tried to say seemed pushed away or garbled before it translated into sounds he could understand.

Knocking came again, more urgent. Ed stepped carefully down the rest of the stairs, snapped on the light in the kitchen, and threw open the wooden portal, ready to whip the intruder with stinging words. They died on his tongue.

"Nettie!"

"Looks like you just been through somethin' awful.

You're white as a bleached sheet." She thrust out a china plate. "Anyway, figgered you could use some good food with all those night owl hours you're keepin.' Muffins for breakfast." She peered at him with all-too-knowing eyes, lowering the fragrant bread and hefting another heaping plate covered with a paper doily. "And you probably don't have time to bake in that fancy computerized oven of yours, so I'm providing cake for tomorrow's soiree. Heaven forbid my Cassie havin' to eat those wretched store-bought things."

"Thank you. Will you come in?" Edward suddenly realized how much his hands were shaking, also how overwhelmed with research papers his kitchen table was. "I'm making coffee . . ." He relieved her of the plates and stood back for the spry old lady to pass.

She sniffed in disgust. "Never touch the disgustin' stuff. Just burned beans. I suppose I'll have to bring some decent tea tomorrow, too."

"No, ma'am," he announced, smiling at her acerbic retorts. "I have tea, Darjeeling to be exact, and I know how to prepare it in the finest British tradition."

"Welllll," she replied, lifting one eyebrow in surprise. "Perhaps he'll do after all." She whirled, raising one hand in farewell, and strode across his yard to the gate in the wooden fence separating their properties, let herself through, and returned to her garden.

Kharman shut the door with a toe. He crowned the pile of graded papers with the muffins, then wrapped the cake with foil and slipped it into the refrigerator. The warm, homey smells of bread and cake made his empty stomach complain loudly. He brewed coffee, fetched butter and a clean plate, and sat down to breakfast while he considered his options.

The Recorder of Deeds and the Surveyor's Office might be open Saturday mornings. It would be good to meet Cassandra and her grandmother tomorrow with information instead of offering them only hospitality. He'd also ask their opinions about the list of details he'd built regarding his nightmare, as well as his near-tragic tumble down the stairs.

But first he'd have another muffin and more coffee. His hands quit quaking as the dark liquid and fresh bread comforted him. Licking the last crumb from his fingers like a schoolboy, Ed washed his dirty dishes in the sink, set them in the wooden drainer, and went to his bedroom to change clothes.

*   *   *

The knock on the front door shouldn't have startled him, but it did. He'd been dozing at his desk. Edward stole a moment to take off his glasses and swipe a hand across his aching eyes before repositioning the silver frames on his nose and answering the summons. His guests stood on the doorstep, both dressed in spring-weight skirts and pretty frilled blouses.

"Thank you for coming, Nettie. Ms. Bloodworth."

"Cassandra, please."

The old woman assessed his condition in one glance. "You look terrible, Perfessor."

"And you both are Spring personified," he replied gallantly as they stepped past him. "The parlor's on your left."

The librarian glanced around. "You've done a lovely job with the hallway. I really like the flagstone floor."

"I appreciate that," Edward returned. "It took a lot of work." He led them on a tour of his house, then settled the ladies in the parlor like roses amid the grouped candles with tea, coffee, and thin slices of Nettie's rich cake. Detailed descriptions of what Kharman planned for the rest of the house and backyard dominated the conversation for half an hour.

"So what happened yesterday?" the elder woman finally asked, appreciatively sipping the amber liquid from her china cup. "See the ghost?"

Ed sighed, reluctant to approach the chilling memory in such a warm, friendly atmosphere. "Almost," he answered slowly. He related the tale of nearly falling down the stairs and the invisible hands that had likely kept him from breaking his neck. He finished and waited for their reaction. Surprisingly, Nettie was silent, studying him shrewdly.

"I think it's trying to tell you something," stated Cassandra suddenly, setting down her cup. "Maybe when you know its name, it can communicate with you more easily." She looked at the ceiling, the walls. "I wonder which ones were left after the demolishing and the fire. I also hope the ghost is listening."

Nettie tapped her wrinkled fingers on the armchair. "Cassie told me about your visit to the library. Mebbe it's not the spirit of the person who died who's been feedin' you those nightmares, Perfessor. Mebbe there was so much hate he had to live with for so long that it's in the walls. Perhaps your ghost is battlin' against it, just as he tried to do 'fore he was hung. Somethin' definitely on your side saved you yesterday. But the hate blocks him whenever he tries to communicate directly."

Ed returned her stare. Nettie definitely knew more than she let on. "My nightmares aren't direct communication?" he asked, his mind trying to encompass the bizarre details.

"I think what Nettie's trying to say is perhaps the only way the ghost can talk to you right now is by messages mixed with plenty of hate," said Cassandra. "Those get through, others don't. I'd say since the spirit helped you on the stairs, that's a strong indication it means you no harm."

Edward nodded. "I've been writing down observations I make during the nightmares." He passed half the list to each woman to peruse. "The strange panic attacks that start for no reason and whisperings I can't quite make out words to are less in the kitchen, so I've been doing most of my grading in there. And I did have some luck yesterday at the Recorder of Deeds Office."

"Don't leave us sitting here in suspense, young man!" Nettie snapped.

The professor smiled and poured her more tea. "Paul, one of my students, works there, so he was willing to donate more time than usual looking things up for me. He's also been doing some research on his own because he's fascinated by the spies General Washington employed before and during the Revolutionary War. Intends to do his Master's thesis on the subject. He went way back in the files, put two and two together, compared his facts with my story, and came up with a possible name for my ghost."

"Who?" his guests chorused.

"He thinks it's likely a man named William Daniel Deaver, who was often called Danny."

"Different from the Danny Deever in Rudyard Kipling's poem," mused Cassandra.

"Definitely. That was more than a hundred years later. William Daniel Deaver lived somewhere in this immediate area, but there's no existing record of precisely where. Like you suggested last week, Cassandra, any papers relating to him were probably burned or otherwise destroyed. The nightmare leads me to believe he was a merchant or businessman, and was apparently a staunch loyalist. At least on the surface. Paul found some interesting passages in Washington's papers regarding an unnamed man the general referred to as 'my most daring spy.' "

"Go on," Nettie urged when Kharman paused for breath and a sip of coffee.

"The references are necessarily vague, but Paul is pretty well convinced it was Deaver." Ed looked at them both. "He was a double agent, a very good one."

"Hanged by his own side," Nettie stated, shaking her head. Her short silver hair appeared burnished in the candlelight. "Poor man."

"How horrible," murmured Cassandra. "That would certainly account for all the hate left, and possibly for the first destruction of the house. The mob may have pulled most of it down after his hanging. Time and motivation both fit."

"Paul said Washington was worried about his agent during the time when feelings against the British flared most hotly among the colonials. Many loyalists abandoned their houses and businesses, fleeing to Canada. The general may even have tried to save Deaver's life with a letter sent by courier, but the message never got here. In my dream, the victim urges his captors to wait for the courier, but they're so driven to rid their land of loyalists they won't listen. That's why Danny was hanged. The loss was unnecessary. Washington did what he could, but it wasn't enough. The general mourned the loss of his best source of information about the British for the rest of the war, and for the rest of his life."

"No wonder Danny became a ghost." Nettie punctuated her statement by setting the china cup in her saucer with a musical *chink*. "Now what?"

"I think," Cassandra said slowly, "that this ghost wants something." She looked at Edward. "When you figure that out and do what it requires, the nightmares will probably stop."

"I look forward to that. I'm about at the end of what I can take and still remain functional. But how do I learn what this spirit wants?"

"What does anyone want, young man?" Nettie's voice was soft and atypical. She stared at the hardwood floor. "To be remembered, of course. Our own tiny gleam of immortality. This man's was taken away, and his spirit wants it back. Mebbe that will give his ghost the power to fight the hatred still flowing around here and hold it at bay. Recognition may make him stronger."

Cassandra patted her grandmother's wrinkled hand. "Nettie, you're brilliant."

"I know," the old lady returned in her normal brittle tone. "I just can't understand why no one but you knows that."

"Any suggestions on how to remember him?" asked Ed. "Hold a posthumous wake? Put up a monument or a brass plaque?"

The librarian smiled. "Publish his story. You've had research papers printed. Get this student of yours to do one on Deaver. Better yet, work on it together. That way he can take advantage of your name and get a print credit that will look great on his scholastic record. And you can pick his brain for knowledge of the time period and more details about Danny."

"Deaver's story would make a great book," the professor

admitted. "I hope Paul's got that in his plans." He sat in silence watching Cassandra, openly admiring the graceful movements of her hands and her delicate face. He finally remembered his manners. "Well, we've found out quite a bit, but I don't intend to let this rest. There has to be more. I'll keep poking around until I can say most of the puzzle pieces are fitting together. We'll probably never know all the details."

Cassie stood, smiling. "Thanks for the coffee and the tour. I hope you'll let me know how things here are coming, especially what happens with your nightmares."

The invitation stood open. "You'll be the second person to know," Edward promised, with a smile for the librarian alone. He escorted his guests to the door. "May I see you home, Nettie?"

"I'm very capable of seeing myself home, young man!"

"Then allow me the pleasure of escorting you to the gate in return for those excellent muffins. It's the least I can do for such kindness."

The old woman considered briefly. "In that case, of course."

Kharman held out his arm. Nettie took it. As they moved into the yard, he traded amused, understanding looks with Cassandra above her grandmother's head.

*   *   *

Ed felt unusually restless that evening. The feeling grew worse as the night added hours. He finally went into his study and flipped the "On" switch of the laptop computer sitting on his desk. Making himself comfortable in front of the blank screen after the word processing program booted up, he understood what he needed to do to appease the ghost.

"Remembering Danny," he typed as the title, then paused to order his thoughts. The house seemed to sigh and settle a bit more firmly around him, as if finally accepting him as a partner.

As if the ghost was finally achieving rest.

Edward typed on, setting down the bones of his experience. He'd add the details later. He felt good, his mood becoming so buoyant that he determined to conquer his nerves and ask Cassandra out to dinner. Nettie, too, if the crafty old bird acquiesced. It was the least he could do for their help and moral support. And he'd catch his student Paul after class tomorrow and suggest writing the paper together. He'd also call his friend Nathan who directed the university's press and propose the idea of publishing the story to him over lunch.

A wholesome tiredness swept over Ed as he saved the file and shut the lid of the laptop. Turning out the lights in his study, he ascended the stairs to the master bedroom, shucked off his clothes, and dropped into bed. Despite his fatigue, ideas kept buzzing around in his mind and whispering flitted past his ears. Or was there something else going on, like a war between Danny Deaver's spirit and the hate of the colonists. Had the hate grown so great it had become an entity in itself?

He didn't know, and didn't have time to find out before the first restful sleep he'd had since moving into his house claimed him.

                    *   *   *

Ed slowly stretched, the cool cotton of the pillowcase feeling good beneath his bare shoulders, as one of the first crisp breezes of fall fluttered the lace curtains at the window. It had been quite an experience—this six months since his moving into the Virginia house and the episodes of nightmare which followed.

His occasional visits with the pretty librarian had bloomed into nightly phone conversations, highlighted by occasional dinners, a picnic, and a movie or two. Things were going well—at a comfortable pace, allowing a deep and appreciative regard to grow in his soul as the woman's delightful personality and talents unfolded their petals. Edward fervently hoped she felt the same way toward him. He couldn't be absolutely certain, but he suspected she did.

Even her crusty grandmother seemed pleased by the relationship, a minor miracle.

Today he'd invited Cassie and Nettie to Colonial Williamsburg. The trio wandered among the displays in the old wooden buildings and listened intently to the costumed docents explaining and demonstrating how things were done three hundred years ago. He wondered if General Washington's daring double agent had ever traveled to Williamsburg to do business.

Since the "Danny incident," a term Nettie had coined for the unrestful period when they were trying to discover his ghost's name, the professor found his attention captivated by the era and had made it a hobby. It was amazing how his nightmare had begun a sequence of events which brought him into contact with first Nettie, then Cassie. It also started his intense research for the paper he'd published with Paul a few months later in a historical magazine, followed by their book proposal to the University Press.

Kharman's appreciation for the hardy, determined colonists of the mid-1700s burgeoned during that time. His interest in Danny Deaver turned into admiration as he and his student sleuthed facts and traced the agent's undercover movements.

After treating the ladies to a lingering dinner at an excellent restaurant on the way home, he'd dropped Cassie off at her apartment. Her thanks and good-bye had felt extraordinarily tender. Perhaps the time was finally right to suggest their engagement, or barring that, at least openly declare their steady dating. Kharman endured Nettie's pointed regard and did his best to turn her intuitive questions away from the subject of her granddaughter as he drove to the house he now called "Danny's Rest." After seeing the old lady securely behind her locked door, he entered his own place, scooped up the mail scattered on the flagstones beneath the brass flap, and headed upstairs to his bedroom.

"Hi, Danny," Ed addressed the air in a quiet salutation that had become habit. Since that night when he began writing Deaver's history, the house seemed to embrace him with an atmosphere Kharman could only categorize as friendship. There had been no discomforting intrusions into his dreams, no peculiar itchy whisperings, no panic that he couldn't tie to a solid reason. He intended to do what he could to keep it that way as long as he owned the place.

Switching on the table lamp next to his bed, Edward hung up his shirt and slipped off his shoes. He tossed back the star pattern handmade quilt, then fluffed a pillow against the iron and wooden headboard. Settling down, he thumbed through his mail, feeling pleasantly tired and extremely contented.

An envelope of thick linen-weave paper bearing the University Press return address caught on his fingers. Dropping the rest of the pile on the sheet beside him, he thumbed open the seal.

It was from his publisher friend Nathan Allyn. "Dear Dr. Kharman," he read the formal phrase half-aloud. "Thank you for sending me the proposal for the book *The Lost History of Danny Deaver* by yourself and Paul Harrington. I'm pleased to inform you that the editors of the University Press and I are accepting it for publication on next year's list. A contract will follow soon under separate cover.

"We agree with you and your coauthor that this story needs to see the light of day. It's intriguing, unusual, well-researched, and well-written, which is the type of work we look for. Thank you for your submission. Congratulations. I'll be in contact by phone in the next few days." The letter was signed, "Best, Nathan Allyn, Director of Publishing."

Edward couldn't help laughing with delight, holding the paper out as if inviting the ghost to read the wonderful news. "Did you hear that, Danny? Paul and I are going to write your story, and this time it's going to be a book. No one will ever forget you again!"

He scooped the unread mail onto the table beside the lamp, got ready for bed, and slipped between the sheets. With the light out he listened to the breeze, grateful that its susurrations held no disturbing near-words. Despite his excitement, sleep sent him sliding down its dark corridor almost immediately. His last thought was the hope that Danny's spirit had heard the good news.

A man dressed in mid-1700s attire with a rope burn partially hidden by his white lace-edged cravat waited at the edge of the professor's dream. His wrists were scarred but unbound. A soul-deep smile lighted his features, replacing the pain that had become all too familiar during Edward's nightmares. William Daniel Deaver held arms forward as if he wished to embrace a brother or cherished friend.

"Thank you," Danny intoned with feeling. "Thank you so very much."

THE MUMMIES OF THE MOTORWAY

Elizabeth Ann Scarborough

Elizabeth Ann Scarborough is the author of twenty-three science fiction and fantasy novels, including the 1989 Nebula Award-winning *Healer's War* and the *Powers* and *Acoma* series cowritten with Anne McCaffrey, as well as the popular Godmother series and the Gothic fantasy mystery, *The Lady in the Loch.* She's a prolific short story writer as well, and has edited collections of short fiction, among them *Warrior Princesses* and *Past Lives Present Tense.* She lives in a Victorian seaport town in western Washington with a lot of cats, beads, and computer stuff.

Scarborough, UK
March 25th
Dear Mom and Bro,

Just wanted to let you know that no matter what the kids write to you, I really have done my best to show them a good time over here. Please don't blame me if they tell you that next time I offer to treat my only niece and nephew to a trip to England, you should say they have come down with bubonic plague.

We had a great time in London, where there were more indoor activities and it didn't matter so much that it's been raining since we first arrived in England. The kids loved everything, Madame Toussad's, the museums, and especially the plays. Rain in England is part of the atmosphere, really. Just like it is in Seattle. Maybe we should have paid more attention to the news before we left London, but the B&Bs I could afford for us did not have TVs. We got on the last train coming or going before the mudslides washed out sections of both the roads and the tracks. With the roads washed out, and the postal service on strike again, I may have to send this via carrier pigeon relay, but there's not a lot else to do under the present circumstances, so I am writing to you.

Needless to say, Monte, your offspring are bored. Jason was monosyllabic all the way up to Scarborough and Cindy could only talk about how much she missed her cats, which is of course making me really miss *my* cats. I can't blame them. There isn't much for an eighteen-year-old boy or a fifteen-year-old girl to do here, really. Or a fifty-three-year-old aunt who's already been here, for that matter, and we did most of it today.

We seem to be the *only* nonresident guests in this whole heap of a hotel. The resident guests are more like patients—as in nursing home patients. Scarborough doesn't get enough visitors in the off-season to keep the hotels open. So apparently the large ones like this one, which *was* suspiciously cheap, take in people who spent happy holidays in their youth here back in the days when people still came for the mineral baths and played at the seashore.

It looks like here's just one couple that runs the whole pile, the snooty woman at the desk who took one look at us robust and sturdily built Scarboroughs and insisted we had to use the stairs, even though she stuck us up on the fifth floor. The lifts, as they call elevators here, are for the disabled only.

The kids took it pretty well, Jason got all macho and took the stairs four at a time. Cindy pretended to prop me up and reminded me that I had told her this was a spa. "And see, Aunt Annie, they give you the exercise class free with your room. Anyplace else we'd have to pay for a Stairmaster!"

We made it upstairs, lightened our knapsacks, strapped on our bum bags and flipped our ponchos dry, then hurried back down for lunch. One look at what they were serving, again in deference to the residents, and we decided to risk being washed out to sea by walking down to the tacky little tourist traps on the beach and seeing if we could find a fish and chips joint.

I tried to call a cab but because of the weather, even with so few visitors in town, none were available. So we slipped on our ponchos, opened one of the big front doors and took one step out before the wind, which had whipped itself into a gale, tried to pick us up and carry us in the opposite direction from town. It didn't just whistle. It shrieked and howled and the ocean that had been so placid on my previous visit crashed and roared as if auditioning for a surfer movie.

I put my head down and splashed forward. The kids trailed behind at first, but once they could see the strand, as they call the beach around here, Jason plunged forward as the leader of the expedition. Of course, when he got to the place where the sidewalk ended at the cliff, he had to stop. Turning a streaming face to me, he shrugged and asked, "Where to now?"

"Aha!" I gurgled through the rain. "This is the first of the many wonders of your ancestral town, nephew." I led them past a couple of bushes to the little cage at the top of the cliff. "Behold, the funicular!"

Cindy rolled her eyes and Jason gave another shrug questioning my sanity and whether or not their aging aunt had begun speaking in tongues. But they were as glad to get in out of the wind and rain as I.

"A *what?*" he demanded.

"This little tram," I said. "It's called a funicular. They've had them since the days when people came for the baths, back before the wars."

"How does it work?" Cindy asked.

"You put a coin in here," I told her. Which I did. It had been fifty pence when I was there five years ago. Now it was a pound.

"Big whoop," Jason said at the bottom.

I peered through the rain at the straggle of fairy lights bouncing above the beach, and the neon lights and cardboard signs proclaiming the wonders of each and every gift shack that was open. There weren't very many of the neon signs lit.

"Hold that thought," I told him. "That may have been your big thrill for the day."

We asked at the first souvenir shop if there was likely to be a chip stand open, and the fellow jerked his thumb and said it was two doors down. Cindy bought some candybars and pop and stuck them in the empty knapsack she had had the foresight to bring along. I found the notebook and authentic Scarborough, England, pen with which I am writing to you now.

The man was a little cheerier when he saw we were after something besides free directions, and he chatted a bit with Cindy, who I suspect kept him talking to hear his Yorkshire accent. "He sounds like those guys in *The Full Monty*, Aunt Annie," she giggled behind her hand as we left.

The chippy, as they fondly call fish and chip shops hereabouts, was almost cheerful. Just about every person still working on the strand came and went from it or stood around talking. There was no place to sit except outside in the rain, so we stood around, too, and ate our greasy fish and French fries out of newsprint cones and drank our Cokes and lemonades, which is like 7-Up.

"So, you're here on holidays, are you?" the lady at the chip stand asked. I felt like saying no, we were all very frail and puny, obviously, with the three of us all looking as hefty as is the Scarborough clan legacy from Dad.

"Yes."

"Pity about the weather. It's generally much finer in summer."

"Yes, but the airfares are higher," I said. "And the kids had their Easter break, so I thought I'd bring them over."

"We don't get a lot of American youngsters here this time of year," a bearded man remarked, also in a Yorkshire accent.

"We have a special reason," Cindy said. "See, our last name is Scarborough. Our Grandpa Scarborough died last year and Aunt Annie thought we ought to come over and see where all our English relatives came from."

"Your grandpa was from here, was he?"

Cindy shook her head. "Oh, no. Kansas City."

"My history teacher, Mrs. Martinez, says people usually only got named for a place after they left it," Jason volunteered.

"Did she now?" The man asked gravely. "Well, then, you'll be needing to see my place. I have a museum and historical exhibit of the history of this town from the time it were a Viking village. You can see the castle from my place as well."

"We don't have any kings in our family, do we, Aunt Annie?" Jason asked suspiciously.

"No, honey. They just named the castle after the place. A king or two stayed there once in a while when they were passing through."

"Oh."

"But *my* history professor told me that a king once killed his son the prince's homosexual lover by throwing him out the window at Scarborough Castle."

"Cool! A murder!" Jason said with typical teenaged bloodthirstiness.

We toured the exhibit, asked questions, bought booklets and souvenirs, and looked out the window at what we could see of the castle's ruins through the gusts and sheets of rain. The kids were really disappointed when the man said we couldn't visit the ruins. Since we had probably paid his expenses for opening that day, though, he asked, "Where are you staying?"

I told him and he said, "I'll give you a lift in the tour bus then, half price! I'm needing petrol anyway. Name's Bert Hoskins."

Once aboard the bus, Bert turned on the radio instead of giving us the tour, and that's when we heard that the railroad bridge had washed away.

"Wow! We just went over that one."

"Do you think they'll get it fixed before we're supposed to leave tomorrow, Aunt Annie?" Cindy asked.

"I wouldn't count on that," Bert said. "Probably won't

be fixed for weeks. I'm afraid you'll have to take the bus back."

Just about then we crested the hill in time to see one of the hotels that teetered on the edge of the cliff like a mud-slide mansion in California do exactly what those houses did during heavy downpours—it listed toward the sea for a few moments while our driver, his brakes on, waited for it as if it were a dog crossing the road.

The kids thought this was pretty neat, especially when the five-story brick building began its slide, picking up speed as it toppled, eventually dragging a portion of road with it, shaking the bit we were sitting on so that the kids and I glanced nervously at each other. It was a huge crash, and Cindy covered her ears, even as we all craned our necks. However, we couldn't see much for the dust and smoke and little spurts of flame from the severed electric and gas lines. Apparently the staff had enough warning of their domain's imminent demise to disconnect the necessary and evacuate before the disaster. The staff, the old and disabled residents, and probably a good portion of the town watched from the swampy overgrown green quadrangle, formerly a garden, around which the hotels primly perched.

"The bus doesn't need to run on *that* road, does it?" Jason asked Bert. Jason had that skittish horse look in his eyes that he gets when his voice is perfectly calm but he is very worried about something.

Bert laughed. "This is a good one for these parts. We don't see much of our tax money for new roads up here. Save all that for the cities, they do. During the war when asphalt was not to be had for civilians, me old dad told me they ground up all them mummies the museums had dug up in Egypt and brought over here."

"Ugh!" Cindy said. *"Why?"*

"Well, the way Dad told me, the bandages the bodies was wrapped in were coated with something like pitch, and it worked almost as good as the genuine article. So, they recycled them, you might say. Used 'em as fertilizer, too, and to fuel the fires in the trains."

Jason glowered. "That's horrible."

"Practical, more like," Bert said, and then added, slyly, "But they do say when you have these wet spells, washouts and the like, it's them mummies tryin' to bust their way loose from the roads so's they can drag their bandagedy arses back to t' Nile." Jason rolled his eyes and made a spiral motion with his finger by his ear. "I'll be turning at t' square."

I thanked him and told him we'd get off. We spent the rest of the afternoon helping the hotel staff and a few other able-bodied people taking the now homeless old folks into the various hotels that had agreed to shelter them.

We finished up a few hours later, and the kids were both tired. They slept through dinner, and we had to make do with the candy and crisps (Brit for potato chips) we bought on the strand. Sorry, Mom. Since little British towns like this one roll up the sidewalks at five, the kids decided to go to bed early. I plan to get us on the first bus out if at all possible, so I'll go downstairs and call the bus station recording pretty soon to see when we have to get up. Our plane for home leaves day after tomorrow.

* * *

Later.

When I woke up to go to the bathroom at about midnight, Cindy was gone. I had been having restless dreams of my cats crying for me to come home and seemed to still be hearing them as I woke up. Vaguely, I remembered hearing Cindy arising and the toilet flushing, but now the bathroom was dark and her bed still empty.

I pulled on my own black leather jacket and a pair of sandals and padded down the hall to the communal bathroom. Maybe she'd decided to take a shower or something, I was thinking. But there was no light down the hall and the doors to the loo and the shower room both were dark and empty. My heart stopped. I knew you were going to shoot me, brother, if I lost your little girl. She is so sensible and calm most of the time I forget she's just a kid, and though we are all of us a bit large for anyone other than

Hercules to drag off into the bushes, still there are a lot of creeps who prey on young girls, and Cindy is so friendly . . . I reminded myself of your family's karate lessons all the way back to our rooms, where I woke up Jason and told him to get dressed, then shucked out of my jacket, pulled on my own socks and shoes, sweater over my nightshirt, and shrugged back into the jacket.

Jason, still wearing his sweat-pajamas, padded sleepily to his window, frowning as he gazed out.

"What are you *doing*?" I'm afraid I came very close to snarling at him as he returned to my room, still wearing the sweats he had worn to bed.

He gestured with elbows bent at the waist, hands extended, bouncing up and down, telling me to cool it. "I was just *checking* to see if I could see her out the windows," he said. "But you can't see anything out there. It's really foggy. Besides, she's probably not out there. She probably found someone to talk to." That was not unlikely, Cindy being your daughter, you most sociable of brothers, and her garrulous grandpa's granddaughter. In which case, since except for the distinctly unfriendly staff here, there was no one much under the age of eighty, I hardly saw how she could be in any danger. But her coat was missing and on closer inspection, I saw that her running shoes were gone as well.

Jason had on his jacket and his own unfastened shoes and handed me a flashlight. "Where'd this come from?" I asked him.

"I brought one for each of us," he said in that very matter-of-fact way he has, then added, "I decided we might need them more than I'd need my tuxedo. Cindy had one, too. I was looking to see if she was using it a minute ago." Sometimes that boy actually seems to have a sense of humor. Not to mention that he seems to have learned what a tuxedo *is* since he turned down the girl who asked him to the prom because he thought she had to be joking.

We heard the wind howling and moaning around the corner of the hotel as we trudged down the stairs. That seemed funny to me because usually when the wind is high, the fog gets blown away.

Instead it was as if kidnappers had pulled a gray woolly sack over the entire area. The only distinctions from the pervading dark fuzziness were the occasional wisps or blobs of white floating through it.

I unlocked the hotel's outer door (they always give you a key for after hours) and we had only taken a few steps out toward the road when I glanced back. The hotel's looming bulk had been swallowed by the fog.

"Cindy?" I called, trying to keep my voice pitched so that if she were near, she could find her way back to us but I wouldn't be waking the old-age pensioners. I couldn't help feeling that if I had screamed my lungs out, the fog would muffle my racket as it muffled everything else.

Jason strode past me, cupping his hands to his mouth and bellowing, "Yo, Cynthia Dawn!"

Something scrabbled off to the right and I said, "Cindy!" sharply.

There was an answering "Rrrow?"

Though that is not, of course, Cindy's normal voice you will understand, brother, why, I, cat-mother of Treat and Kittibits, instantly felt relieved. I understood Cindy's motivation for being out here. Obviously she had heard the cat crying and came out to investigate. I'd have done the same thing if I'd been aware of it. She was very possibly trying to find her way to the hotel kitchen to get it some fish or milk or something. I handed Jason the key to the outer door of the hotel and told him to go check out the kitchen and see if his sister was there. I would stay and try to entice the cat to stick around until the kids got back either with or without a tidbit.

"Here, kitty," I said, kneeling and rubbing my fingers together. "Kitty, kitty? Mrrow?"

Now, yes, Mother, I know that not even my animal-loving niece and nephew and I can't save every stray cat in England, but what you don't seem to understand is how awfully lonesome I get for my kitties when I'm away from them for any length of time. I was not cajoling the cats for their benefit so much as for my own and I can safely say that Cindy's motives were similar.

Jason had already turned away, and I heard the key turn in the lock of the door. I didn't even look back, however, knowing that with the fog so thick it wouldn't do me any good.

"Kitty?" I asked again, since I hadn't heard it since that first time. "Cynthia? Are you out here, too?"

"Yow," said another, higher pitched feline voice from the other direction.

I took a step into the fog toward it.

It's a good thing I was looking for a cat because I was looking down, hoping to see those coin-bright eyes reflecting the beam of my flashlight. Where the road should have been, blackness gaped. I shone my light directly into it. Water and rock, broken asphalt and jagged edges of earth and cement rimmed a hole so deep the beam couldn't penetrate the bottom.

The sameness of the fog and the depth of the abyss—I'm not exaggerating. It really was an abyss, not just a hole. I have never seen sinkholes in permafrost that deep—plus being jerked out of a sound sleep combined to give me a sense of vertigo. "Omigod!" I know I said aloud, and yelled, "Cindy, are you down there? Are you okay? Say something, honey? Make a noise!"

The pavement crumbled from under one foot and I stumbled backward. As I did, my heel encountered something soft and yielding. An angry hissing and the scream of a cat pierced my ears. I almost jumped back into the hole again but instead tripped over my own feet and fell on my butt, which did not endear me to the invisible feline at my feet. Trust a cat not to come when it's wanted but to be right underfoot when it's sure to trip you up.

"Sorry, kitty," I said, falling on my rear. I tried to stand, but found my ankles wouldn't separate enough for me to rise. As I reached toward my feet, my hand encountered a strip of fabric, something that felt like rough cotton, snaking up my legs toward my knees. Now instead of the angry teakettle noise, a loud purring twined around my legs as the cotton strips did the same. "That's enough of that, cat!" I said sternly. "Naughty kitty!"

I swear I could hear it laugh, and maybe it was just the stars in my head from my fall, but looking around me, I seemed to see teams of golden eyes surrounding me in the fog, an occasional "mrrup" of encouragement punctuating the thrum of purrs.

And then, suddenly, something infinitely larger loomed out of the darkness throwing its huge shadow across the frail beam of my flashlight.

"Nope, Aunt Annie, she's not in there either," Jason said.

"Shine your light on my feet so I can get untangled here, will you?" I asked. He did. There was nothing around my ankles but little wraiths of the white fog, that trailed away as I got to my feet. "These cats seem to be practical jokers."

Jason started off.

"Watch out!" I cried, and he stopped. "There's a big hole there. I thought maybe your sister had fallen in. . . ."

He shone his beam, considerably stronger than mine, into the hole. "Nope," he said and started off again.

"Where are you going?"

"To look for my sister," he said.

"Well, yeah, but watch the ground. I bet that's not the only new hole in the road."

"I *know* that, Aunt Annie," he said disdainfully, as if I were treating him like a baby.

We walked and walked, with only our flashlight beams to guide us. At first the walking was flat, then it went uphill and down, and though we walked slowly, my feet were getting tired. Despite my coat and the exercise, I began to shiver. I heard Jason sneeze and thought something was blooming which was no doubt bothering his allergies. That's about the time I realized my hair was blowing into my face and plastering it over my eyes, and wind was cutting through my leggings. Then a big fat raindrop—the gulls weren't up yet, so I hoped it was a raindrop—plopped on my nose, followed by a lot more of them.

The wind tore ragged chunks from the fog, revealing that the white blobs were not simply different colored foggy bits, but raggedy, lumbering forms that looked as if they were the heavily bandaged victims of terrible accidents. As the rain moaned, it seemed that these bandaged forms did, too, their gauzes bannering like dirty, tattered ribbons away from what was no doubt their corrupted bodies underneath. Although, hadn't Bert said they were ground up?

"Aunt Annie?" Jason asked.

"Huh?"

"How come the mummies of people and cats we saw in the museum had their legs tied together, but these guys are walking and the cats are even waving their tails?"

"I don't know," I said. "Don't ask me. I'm no special effects expert."

Most of them *did* look fairly indistinct, and then the fog before us also got blown away and we saw a larger mummy, taller than me, and under its bandages the pale triangles of orange reflector cloth winked back at us from its jogging shoes.

"*Cindy!*" I yelled. Jason yelled, "*Cynthia,*" at the same time.

This is the point at which many of my students would write, "and then Cindy turned around and we saw that the bandages were just wisps of fog wrapped around her, as were all the other things we thought were mummies. She lowered her hands, blinked her eyes, and said, 'I must have been sleepwalking!' and I hugged her and said 'Yes, it was all a dream.'"

But at any rate, that is not what happened, though she did seem to be sleepwalking. However, contrary to what they say in the movies, waking a sleepwalker is not dangerous to his or her health and it certainly doesn't kill anyone.

Cindy simply blinked at us through very sloppily applied bandages, which she brushed from her face like cobwebs when she stretched and yawned. "Aunt Annie, Jason. Hi, what are you guys doing here?"

"You go first," Jason said. My sentiments exactly.

Cindy said, "I heard a little cat cry and I came out to

find out where it was and if it was hungry. Then a bunch of bandaged kitties came out of the fog to play and wrapped me all up. Then they wanted me to go someplace with them."

"Where?" I asked.

As if in answer, the wind roared itself into a gale and blew away the last of the fog. We were standing on a lonely stretch of road beyond the strand, beyond the main part of the city. The road gaped with holes and in one of these was lodged the front wheel of the bus that had driven us back up the hill that afternoon.

"That's Bert's bus!" Jason said.

It was indeed and Bert himself, albeit Bert looking like a refugee from a casualty ward, swathed in bandages as seemed to be the style, tottered forward with his hands outstretched. "I am the ka of the Pharaoh Hamen-Ra. Woe to those who disturb my rest."

"*Us* disturb *your* rest?" Jason complained. "We haven't slept all night because of all you Band-Aid guys and cats."

"Izzat so?" demanded Bert/Hamen-Ra. "Well, maybe you'd like to have what was s'posed to be your immortal body ground up and put on the road for lorries and tour buses to lumber over, eh? See how well you'd sleep then, my lad! Not to mention the sacred moggies ground up for somebody's rose garden. We've had a rum deal since we was taken from our tombs and brung over here! We demands to be took back to t'Nile right away."

"Bert, this is all very funny," I told him. "Cut it out. The Nile is definitely not on our itinerary. And listen, if you're going to play at channeling ancient entities, you're not doing it right. You're not supposed to use your own accent. I live in Port Chetzemoka, where there are lots of channelers and past life relivers and all that stuff, and I can tell you for sure you have to use the ancient spooky voice the whole time you're channeling or the effect is just ruined."

"Silence, mortal woman!" Hamen-Ra said, continuing in the same mixture of stage-mummy and Yorkshirese. "If you'd been lying in the road, listening to kids squabbling in back seats, old folk nattering about the plumbing, and complaining the food gives them gas, or talking about what was on telly last evening, you'd not have a posh accent to channel with either. You're just lucky I've deigned to learn your bloody tongue so's I can make meself understood through Bert here."

"He's not kidding, Aunt Annie," Cindy said urgently. Maybe it was the rain dripping down my face, or maybe it was the rain dripping down her face or the fading beam of the flashlight, the batteries of which had put up a valient but now losing battle, but Cindy's eyes still looked a bit strange to me.

"Oh, yeah?" I argued. "Surely you've had enough theater to recognize the amount of ham in Hamen-Ra."

Then *she* started speaking in a deep spooky voice, claiming to be a priestess of Bast's shrine at Memphis, reciting her lineage, Hamen-Ra's lineage, and the lineage of the dynasties and so forth leading up to her time of life. That was when I knew we had a real supernatural manifestation on our hands for sure. Cindy and Jason are, as you've often told me, Mom, both great students, but Cindy is not really crazy about history and the movies don't go in for that sort of boring "begat" detail.

I inquired again if the kas of the pharaohs, cats, and courtiers wouldn't like to come home with me to Port Chetzemoka in America, where we had a nice seaport and lots and lots of nutcases who would be thrilled to channel their immortal essences, but they stubbornly declined in favor of the Nile.

Well, I was sympathetic of course, and certainly didn't want to bring Cindy home with an ancient cat priestess cohabiting her body, so there seemed to be only one thing to do. The family build came in handy for us Scarboroughs then, because between Jason, Cindy and her priestess, and Bert/Hamen-Ra and me, we managed to get the truck's tire out of the hole, and turned around. Hamen-Ra wisely let the inner Bert take over the driving, since he knew the back roads out of Scarborough heading south.

Which is why my writing is a little wobbly as I sit here between the sleeping kids, bumping along in Bert's tour bus with piles of bandages and scraps of bone and pitch swept into lots of paper marketing bags taken from Bert's newsagent friend. We should be making our delivery in London and then hopefully the priestess of Bast will vacate Cindy at that time. If not, I hope the Church Camp she is going to attend when she comes home is multi-denominational.

*   *   *

March 26th, Evening

Dear Mom and Bro,

You'll be pleased to know we are sitting at Heathrow waiting to board our red-eye special, having made it to the British Museum by noon today. Other than Bert having a hell of a time finding a parking place outside the museum, we had no real trouble, much to my surprise.

I was very much afraid the museum people would think I was a nutcase, even with exhibits A and B, Bert and Cindy and their respective guest entities, but when I told the security guard that I had somehow inadvertently become the head of a Motorway Mummy Liberation Front and we wished very much to speak to the acquisitions direction for the Egyptian exhibits at the museum, he simply grumbled, "Oh, yeah, we get a lot of that sort of thing with this wet weather," and led us to the rather tacky steam-heated office of the director.

I had been hoping for an Indiana Jones type perhaps, or at least a Sean Connery type, someone with distinguished strips of gray at the temples and maybe a slight foreign accent. Instead, the director was a very earnest and nerdy young man with rabbity teeth and scant hair pulled into a ponytail. All of that was forgiven because his manner was most sympathetic and his eyes understanding and full of apology as Hamen-Ra and Cindy's priestess poured out their stories, with a few interjections and explanations from me. Jason just looked disgusted but helped the security people and the grad students interning at the museum haul the bags of mummy material into the museum.

"It was very good of you and the children to come forward, Mrs. Scarborough," he said to me. "Most conscientious, especially since you are not, ahem, British. We are, in the interest of international harmony, religious tolerance, and respect for the customs of others sadly ignored in former times, attempting to repatriate many of the mummies and have them returned to their tombs. I don't suppose your niece or Mr. Hoskins would care to come with us to interpret for us the original location of the remains you've brought?"

I said absolutely not, and if that priestess didn't get herself out of Cindy this instant, the deal was off. At that point, Cindy had a little coughing fit, and one of the female grad students, a girl who looked Indo-Asian, stood a bit straighter and got a weird look in her eye.

Cindy glanced at me a little regretfully and shrugged.

"We at the British Museum certainly appreciate your efforts on behalf of the offended parties and to show our gratitude, would like to offer you a gift certificate for the postcard of your choice at our gift shop," the director said.

I chose this one of the mummy I'm enclosing with this letter.

Should be home well—today, by your time, about five in the evening. See you then!

*   *   *

Port Chetzemoka, WA
Dear Mom, Bro, Cindy, and Jason,
It's very nice to be home again after the trip to England. The cats are glad to see me. I'm sorry, Brother, that every cat within five miles has flocked to your house to see Cindy, but I don't know what I can be expected to do about it. As far as I know that priestess is back home again in good old Memphis, maybe enjoying a new incarnation as kitty litter for the descendants of her former goddesses.

I am very happy to hear, however, that Wizards of the Coast is considering adding Jason's new deck, The Eyes of Hamen-Ra, to their pantheon of Magic Cards.

Egyptian-ness seems to be quite the thing these days.

Several of our local channelers have added—uh—new stations, with Egyptian entities as their guides or whatever the heck they call them. Makes me wonder what I brought back in my coat pockets and on the soles of my shoes when I came home.

But on a more practical note, Mom, you'll be glad to hear I've become more active in city government. I am our neighborhood's liaison with the public works department for having potholes on our street filled. Can't stand the damned things. Guess this wraps it up.

Love, Annie

IN THE CHIEF'S NAME
by Bruce Holland Rogers

Bruce Holland Rogers lives in Eugene, Oregon, home to a famous community of anarchists. His short stories have received a variety of honors, including a Pushcart Prize, the Bram Stoker Award, and two Nebula Awards. He writes a column for *Speculations* magazine on meeting the psychological and spiritual challenges of full-time fiction writing, and his instructional audiotape, *Writing in Spite of Everything,* was recently published by Panisphere Books and Audio. His personal Web site is at: http://www.sff.net/people/bruce.

Rain pattered on the metal roof of the van. Wolf sat on the carpet scraps in back with his eyes closed, listening, waiting for Peach and Raven to finish setting up the antenna. He opened his eyes when the van's rear door opened with a groan.

As Peach and Raven piled in, Wolf could see the lighted second-story windows of the houses on either side of the alley. Inside the van, he could see the jumble of radio gear and tools on the floor, the tangle of wires. The door shut. It was darker than ever.

"All set," Raven said. He dropped something. It sounded like the vise grips. "You ready?"

Wolf clicked on a dim red bulb overhead. He checked his meters and put on his headphones. "Here we go."

Peach donned her own headphones and leaned close to Wolf. She smelled of wet hair and patchouli oil. "Gonna play the loop?"

"Of course, baby."

The loop had been her idea. She'd heard something like

it while listening to shortwave radio. It was supposed to help listeners find the station they were searching for, although in this case, it was just window dressing. The broadcast signal from the van wouldn't even carry across Lake Washington to Bellevue most nights, and the broadcast schedule was necessarily irregular.

Wolf started the loop. Over his headphones he heard the hoot of an owl, then a howling wolf, and finally his own recorded voice: "This is Radio Free Seattle, FM." After a beat, it repeated. He could also hear the signal of the commercial radio station whose signal they were treading on just enough to pull listeners away from it.

Raven's hands were cupped over his own earphones. "Sounds good, man. This was a good idea, Peach."

Wolf gave Raven a glance that he meant as a warning, but the red light was dim enough that expressions were hard to read. Raven didn't seem to get the message.

"I mean it," Raven said. He put his hand on Peach's shoulder. "It sounds totally professional."

Wolf snorted. "Oh, great. We sound totally professional. We can all get jobs doing this. We can all have careers."

Peach ignored that and smiled at Raven. "Thanks."

Wolf grabbed his mike and flipped two switches.

Peach said, "Hey, let the loop run for a while. The idea is supposed to be . . ."

"This is Radio Free Seattle, broadcasting tonight on eighty-nine point seven. Wake up, sleepyheads! It's time to change the world. Radio Free Seattle is here to tell you how. Tonight, we'll be giving the city some of the medicine it desperately needs."

"That's right, we're here to . . ." Raven started to say. His mike was dead.

"We're here to tell you about direct action," Peach said into her microphone, "the kind of action we're taking ourselves, tonight, to take back the Earth from the corporations."

"And what exactly are we going to do?" Wolf prompted.

"We're going to kill machines," Peach answered. "We're

going to monkey wrench one small corner of the Evil Empire."

"You're so right, honey," Wolf said. "Come Monday morning, when the corporations start up their machines, at least one company is going to be in for a nasty surprise."

Raven had found the end of his mike cord. "This was plugged in when I left the van," he whispered to Wolf.

"Shit happens," Wolf said over the air. "But it doesn't happen nearly enough yet. It's going to take more than the efforts of Radio Free Seattle to shut down the machineries of enslavement. That's where you come in, citizens. We're on the air to urge you to join us."

Raven plugged himself in. "That's right . . ." His mike was still dead.

"Now maybe you're saying to yourself, 'Who are these criminals, and why in the world do they think I'd want to join them?' Well, we're just human beings who don't want to be slaves. We are the Resistance."

"In case you haven't noticed," interjected Peach, "our way of life sucks."

"Citizens, wake up! The air is foul. The water is poisoned. Concrete creeps foot by foot over the whole world."

"Cities suck," said Peach.

Raven flipped a switch. "Yeah," he said, but his mike still wasn't working.

"We're on our way to logging the last virgin forest. We're raping the planet with our mines."

"Mining sucks," said Peach.

"Some say it's time to go back to the land. But before long, there isn't going to be any land to go back to. We can't *see* our Mother Earth any more. We're blinded by money."

"Money sucks," said Peach. "So does farming."

"Citizens, the average hunter-gatherer spends three hours a day getting food and shelter. The rest of his time is his own. How does that sound to you, Mr. Suit-and-Tie? How'd you like to have everything you really need with three hours of work a day, Ms. Cell-Phone?"

Raven reached for a switch, but Wolf swatted his hand away.

"Asshole," Raven growled.

"The thing the corporations don't want you to know," Wolf continued, "is how vulnerable they are. If technological society falls apart, if it all breaks down, then it can't possibly be started up again. All the easy metals have been mined already. All the easy oil has been pumped. If we stepped back to an earlier time for just a little while, the poisonous technologies and the enslaving corporations would suffer a blow that they could not ever recover from. Are you a happy slave, citizen? You have the power to be free!"

"Every machine that breaks down is a step in the right direction," said Peach.

"A different life is possible," Wolf said. "Break the machines, stop the corporations, and we can start from scratch. How will we do it? We'll do it as free humans have always done it. We'll make it up as we go along."

"Don't give in!" Peach declared.

"Some people say to me, 'Man, don't you realize that what you're doing is criminal?' Hey, I'll tell you what a crime is. A crime is forcing people to be slaves while corporate advertising convinces them they are free. Most of you don't even see how far it's gone, how powerless you are until you try to resist."

Peach said, "So resist!"

Wolf opened a book to a page he had marked. He squinted in the dim light to read. "In the words of Chief Seattle, the Suquamish Indian whose lands were stolen to make this city, 'The dogs of appetite will devour the rich earth and leave only desert.' Chief Seattle saw what we were headed for. Money and technology aren't the answer. Their time is passing. No more machines. Earth and stone, muscle and bone. That's the world we're talking about. That's anarchy. That's freedom. And that's the future. We go out tonight to do battle. We go out in Chief Seattle's name. Long live freedom!"

Raven leaned close enough to Peach's microphone that

his voice chimed in with hers when they both said, "Long live freedom!"

"This is Radio Free Seattle. Good night." Wolf shut the transmitter off. "Okay. Take the antenna down and let's get moving."

"You take it down, jerk wad," Raven said.

Wolf looked at him. "What's your problem?"

"You *are* being a jerk," Peach said. "We're all in this together."

"What in the world are you talking about? The microphone? We were in the middle of a broadcast! I can't have Raven fiddling with stuff when we're on the air!"

"You really are unbelievable sometimes, Wolf," Raven said.

"You're cranky because you didn't get to talk on the radio?" Wolf said. "And I'm the jerk?"

"Yes! You act like . . ." Raven glanced at Peach, then he studied the floor of the van. "Just forget it," he said.

"No. Say it. I act like what?"

Raven picked his tools up off the floor. "Light."

Wolf just stared at him."

"Peach," Raven said softly, "kill the light."

Wolf switched off the red light. Raven opened the door and jumped out.

"Remember. You don't own me, Wolf," Peach said. Then she followed Raven into the rain.

Wolf slapped the side of the preamp with his palm.

*   *   *

When they set up again farther north, close to Carkeek Park, Wolf made a show of double-checking Raven's microphone before they went on the air. They broadcast pretty much the same message. But Raven didn't say much. He was sulking.

This time Wolf read at length from Chief Seattle's famous speech to the white invaders. Wolf invoked Seattle's name at the end of the broadcast. He did this again during their third broadcast from a location down south, toward Renton.

By the time they packed up for the last time and headed for the construction site, Raven seemed to have finished sulking.

"That Indian stuff is good," he told Wolf.

"The dude was righteous," Wolf agreed.

Wolf parked the van two blocks away. Then the three of them made a walking reconnaissance without any gear, just to check things out. The site looked the same as it had on other nights—a pit two stories deep, no security lights. There was a trailer down there with a light on, but they hadn't seen any sign of a night watchman. Two trucks. Four big earth movers. A couple of compressors. Plenty of targets.

Traffic was rare at three in the morning. Maybe half a dozen cars went by during their whole reconnaissance.

Back at the van, they put on the radio headsets, then covered them with hats so that only the little microphones showed, and those were subtle. Wolf put on black gloves and slung one of the packs onto his shoulder. Raven took the other. At the site, Raven helped Wolf over the fence and dropped the packs down to him.

"Sound check," Wolf said as he walked down the grade into the pit.

"Check," came Raven's voice in his ear.

Then Peach: "Check."

At the bottom of the pit, Wolf kept to the shadows and waited until Peach and Raven told him they were in position, that there were no cars or pedestrians that might spot him.

"Okay," Wolf said. "Keep an eye on that trailer, too. Just in case."

He went for the big machines first. Climbing onto the bulldozer, he found and unscrewed the crankcase lid. From one of the packs, he took a caulk gun that was loaded with the mixture they had made at Raven's apartment: oil-based grinding compound and salt.

Wolf said, "In Chief Seattle's name." Then he injected

the whole tube into the dozer's crankcase. On Monday, when the workers started the dozer up, the engine would do the work of grinding itself into junk.

The hair stood up on Wolf's neck even before Peach warned, "Car." Wolf crouched in the shadows of the bulldozer and watched the lights sweep by on Madison.

"Okay," Peach said.

Wolf still had the creeps. Someone was watching.

"You sure?" he said.

A pause. "Yeah. You're clear."

"Is *everybody* sure?" They didn't use names on the radio, not for their broadcasts, and not for their direct actions.

"You're clear," said Raven.

Wolf still didn't move. "I got a bad feeling."

"Nothing on the street, nothing in the trailer," said Peach.

"Quit being paranoid," Raven cut in. "You're clear."

Wolf slowly looked over the construction site. Nothing moved.

"Okay," he said. He went to the next bit of heavy machinery. "In Seattle's name," he said softly as he monkey wrenched the crankcase. And he had the same feeling again that he was being watched, that he was being betrayed.

Paranoid, Raven had called him. Well, what if it turned out that he had good reason to be paranoid? Maybe it wasn't some stranger who was creeping him out. Maybe it was Raven. Or Raven and Peach together. If they were messing around behind his back . . .

Would they turn on him? No, not Peach. Not his Peachy girl. Even if she were going to turn him out, she wouldn't do it this way. Raven, then.

Wolf opened the hood of the first truck. An engine this size only needed half a dose of corundum and salt. Chief Seattle had said that the white man lived like a snake eating its own tail, and the tail was getting shorter and shorter. This was like feeding shards of glass into the maw of the corporate snake. Wolf smiled.

"Die, snake!" he said.

"What?" This from Raven.

"Car," said Peach.

Wolf hopped down.

"It's a cop car," Peach added. "I don't think he can see you from that lane, though. Be cool."

Wolf felt his heart beating.

"On my side, now," said Raven. "He's slowing."

"Shit." Peach whispered. For a moment, that was all. Then, "Two more on my side."

"Tuck your mikes under your hats," Wolf said as he grabbed both packs and ran back to the bulldozer. "Walk away. They can stop you. And they can talk to you." He tripped, got up. "But they can't make you show ID. They can't arrest you for taking a walk on a public sidewalk."

He threw the packs between the dozer treads and crawled in after them. A car door slammed. A moment later, a powerful flashlight beam swept over the ground.

Wolf tried willing them to go away. *There's nothing here,* he thought. *The lock's still on the gate. Nothing's amiss. False alarm.*

Another flashlight beam joined the first. He heard voices coming over police radios.

"They're talking to her," said Raven's voice.

"Shut up," Wolf said softly. "What if they're listening?"

"If someone's listening in, then we're screwed anyway, aren't we?" said Raven. "She's cool. I can tell just looking that she's cool."

"Where are you?"

"I'm in an alley. They can't see me."

"They've got lights, asshole."

"Oh, so I'm an asshole for wanting to keep an eye on her?"

"Just keep walking. Get out of here."

"She's waving good-bye and walking away from them. Told you she's cool. I'll go parallel, make sure she gets back without a hassle. Sit tight, man. Maybe they'll pack up and go away."

"How did they know?"

"Tall buildings. Lots of windows. Maybe some janitor called it in."

"On the weekend? No way, you bastard."

Wolf couldn't see the flashlight beams any longer, but he could still hear the police radios up above.

"What are you saying?" Raven said, but his signal was weak.

"What I'm saying, asshole, is that I'm not so sure you want me around. If my ass is in jail, you've got Peach all to yourself."

"No names," said Peach. "You are totally losing your cool."

"You okay, baby?"

"I'm fine. Don't do anything stupid." Her signal, like Raven's, was thready.

"You neither," Wolf said. He heard another car arrive, something with a rough idle. He ventured a peek. Headlights shone on a section of the fence above. Somebody was unlocking and unchaining the gate. "Shit."

*   *   *

After the police dog had found him, after it was already too late because the cops had their flashlights on him, that's when he thought about his radio. What he should have done, while he still had time, was strip the thing off and feed it into the tread wheels. Or bury it. Anything to get rid of the evidence that he hadn't acted alone.

They hauled him out and read him his rights, which he already knew. He didn't have to talk to them. He didn't have to answer any questions. He could even make them stop asking, "Who was on the other end? Who were you talking to?" All he had to do was say he wanted his lawyer present, and they had to shut up.

He'd been over the procedures a hundred times with Peach and Raven. Get caught alone, take the punishment alone. The important thing was the movement. Even if one of them got sentenced to some prison time, the important thing was to keep someone on the outside doing the work that needed to be done, shutting it all down.

Now, however, he couldn't stop thinking about Peach and Raven. Even if Raven were innocent, which Wolf heartily doubted—there they'd be, the two of them. Peach would need comforting. Raven would know just what to do, just how to console her and take her mind off of poor old Wolf, sitting in some cell. There, there, Peachy baby. There, there.

So he gave them up.

Legal names. Addresses. The garage where they kept a drum of valve grinding compound. It all went so fast that it was still dark outside when the cops finally moved him to a holding cell.

It must have been a slow night. There was one other guy in the cell, and he was asleep, face to the wall, softly snoring. Wolf sat on the opposite side of the cell, on the edge of the shelf that served as a bed.

Wolf put his face in his hands. He was a jerk. He was an asshole. He was every name he could think of. Where was his commitment? After all that planning, he had caved right in and given it all up. Now they were all screwed. One stupid night of jealousy, and he had pissed it all away.

"It's better this way," said a voice from right beside him.

Wolf started. There was someone sitting next to him! Someone who hadn't been there a moment before. A man wearing a conical hat.

Wolf's heart pounded in his throat. "Who . . ." He stood and backed away.

The man's hat was dripping. Water puddled at his bare feet. Around his shoulders he wore a blanket and a sort of cape made of woven reeds. His face looked weathered, dark.

"When you keep speaking the name of a dead person, you hold him or her to this world. The Bostons didn't understand that. The Bostons didn't understand a lot of things." The dark man frowned.

"Bostons?"

"Your people. The white people."

"I don't . . ." Wolf's head felt light.

"Better sit down."

Wolf sat. "S–Seattle?"

"Close enough." The Indian frowned. "Even if they

don't ever say my name right, it's close enough to hold me here." He pulled the cape and blanket tighter. "I should be far away by now. But your people had the bad manners to give my name to this place."

"I don't know what to . . . I'm sorry." Wolf rubbed his forehead. "This can't be happening."

"Life is like that. Death, too. Things that can't be happening happen all the time." The Indian pursed his lips. "It's going to take a long time for me to leave this place now. It's going to take a long time for people to stop speaking my name."

"Seattle. Chief Seattle. I . . ." Wolf stood. Then he sat back down, the full realization finally sinking in. "Seattle! It's an honor!"

"Mmm." The ghost frowned.

"Oh, your name. I'm sorry. It's just . . . I admire your words."

"No, you don't. Not my words. But all night you were saying my name and sticking it into words that someone else said. That was the first thing that made me mad."

Wolf cocked his head. " 'Continuing to contaminate his own bed, the white man will one night suffocate in his own filth,' " Wolf quoted from memory. "Didn't you say that?"

"No! Some poet said that and mixed my name up in it. Ever since I died, this has been going on. Every time white people change their ideas about what they want Indians to be, someone makes a new speech for me."

Wolf swallowed. "But . . ." He rubbed his head again. Could he really be having this conversation? "But we're trying to take back the land. Maybe the words aren't exactly what you said, but what my friends and I want is a return to the old ways. Your ways."

"My ways? You don't know anything about my ways."

"I mean your people. Living off the land."

"Mmm." Another frown.

"See, the world is going to turn back to simpler ways of doing things. It *has* to. We don't need bulldozers and skyscrapers to be happy!"

"Those digging machines are pretty good for digging."

"We have our hands. We can make stone tools."

Seattle grunted dismissively. "I remember my first iron ax. Now that could cut!"

"Okay, but iron comes out of mines and mines gouge out the earth. Mother Earth, Chief! We need to live in a way that respects Mother Earth!"

"Mmm." The Indian deliberately looked away from Wolf and said very carefully, "Respect."

Wolf felt uncomfortable. Had he said something he shouldn't have? He thought about it. "Ah. Okay. So maybe you're thinking that what I was doing to those machines wasn't respectful. But, see, I respect the people who run the machines. They don't know they have any choice. It's the corporations. It's the system. It's the system that I'm at war with."

"Young men always like to make war. It's the first thing they think of."

"I've got to do *something*."

"When word came to me that the young men were planning a raid, I would go to the Bostons and warn them."

"Warn them? Against your own people?"

"Mmm. Young men make trouble." He looked at his feet. "This floor is cold."

Wolf had a thought. He didn't like it. "Did you . . . Chief, you aren't the one who . . ."

"Called the Boston soldiers. Mmm."

"The Boston soldiers? You mean the police? You called them? Told them about me and Peach and Raven? *You*?"

"I got inside the wire. There are things you can do when you're dead. Like this."

And he was gone. Vanished. The edge of the bed was still wet, though. Puddles still glistened on the floor.

Wolf sat thinking for a while. His living cell mate still snored. The man had slept through the whole conversation. When the puddles dried, there would be no evidence that Wolf had really spoken to the Indian Chief's ghost. *But he had.* What should he do now?

Raven would never believe this. But Peach might. Maybe, just maybe, there was something in what the Chief had said that would help Wolf figure out what to say to her when the time came.

Maybe. Wolf had some hard thinking ahead of him.

But the one clear lesson was this: Ghosts were real. They were bound to the world by their famous names.

Wolf went to the door of the cell. He gripped the rigid bars. "Houdini," he whispered. "In the name of Harry Houdini."

HATSHEPSUT'S REVENGE
by Peter Schweighofer

Peter Schweighofer lives in Williamsburg, Virginia, where he works at the Omohundro Institute of Early American History and Culture and continues his freelance writing and editing endeavors. He has published several science fiction and historical fantasy stories, edited two *Star Wars* anthologies, contributed to several role-playing game lines, and reported for a newspaper in Connecticut. "Hatshepsut's Revenge" capitalizes on his interest and amateur research in ancient and Victorian Egypt.

Robert Jones knew it wasn't smart for an Englishman to wander Alexandria's streets today. He was running an errand for his brother, George, who owned a shop in Cairo that peddled ancient Egyptian antiquities to European tourists. Despite all the trouble in Alexandria, he didn't want to let his brother down. But even more than that, Robert couldn't disappoint his Egyptian princess.

She began visiting his dreams after he did a few jobs for George: traveling to various cities up and down the Nile, buying ancient relics on the sly, and shipping them to Cairo. She came to him often, a thin figure shrouded in gauzy light. Her formfitting linen gown revealed just enough to tempt his fancy. Robert knew she was a princess from the diadem she wore, a golden band decorated with the sacred Egyptian cobra head. She wore jewelry similar to some of the pieces he saw in his brother's shop. Long, tightly curled strands of hair framed her face.

At night her delicate hands gently touched his chest, her lips whispered ancient words into his ears, and her eyes pleaded with him. Lined with dark makeup George had called "kohl," her eyes begged him to follow her. Sometimes she cried. He was certain she needed his help.

Robert didn't know her name. George taught him a little about ancient Egypt, just enough so he could effectively carry out his brother's errands. After a while, Robert just started referring to the princess as Nefer, the ancient Egyptian word for "beautiful."

Last week a telegram had arrived from an Egyptian living in Alexandria, a new supplier who wanted to negotiate a deal to sell George some choice treasures. As his brother's representative, Robert volunteered to go.

But the political situation was tense for foreigners. Egypt was a vital key in England's worldwide empire. The Suez Canal shortened the passage to her eastern colonies by weeks, and was built at considerable expense. It would be folly to lose it now to a mob of unruly Egyptian army officers.

Tensions between the Khedive Tewfik—who trusted England—and his rebellious minister of war, Arabi Pasha, had erupted, and sentiment against European interference in Egyptian affairs was nearing the boiling point. Egyptian soldiers had already attacked several Europeans a few weeks before. A combined British and French fleet now sat off the coast, ready to intervene in case any more trouble developed. In only a few weeks, the city that once hosted the world's greatest library of ancient knowledge had turned into a place of fear, anger, and violence.

Princess Nefer slipped into his dreams again. He saw her near the Pharos, the ancient lighthouse that once guarded Alexandria's harbor and housed her famous library. She held out her delicate hand to beckon him. Her rosy lips formed words he could not hear, though he knew they were in the ancient Egyptian tongue.

Robert didn't know why, but he woke determined to go to Alexandria. He told his brother he didn't mind all the tension brewing. He quite enjoyed wandering about in the face of potential danger . . . gave his life a sense of adventure he rarely felt. Yesterday, he'd taken the late train up from Cairo, checked into a decent hotel in the European quarter, and had a light supper before retiring.

Now Robert found himself walking alone through the city on a Sunday afternoon. He was far from the European quarter, and quite possibly lost. He reached into his coat pocket, removed a slip of paper, and read the address again. The antiquities supplier lived on one of these streets, but the paper couldn't tell him how to get there from the maze of narrow lanes, courtyards, and covered alleys into which he'd wandered.

Confusion flooded his senses. Salt air from the harbor mixed with the smells of garlic and paprika, someone cooking beans. The sound of a muezzin's chant wafted through the clear blue sky visible between the tall houses looming above. They seemed like sandstone cliffs imprisoning Robert in a dark chasm. A growling chorus from some angry crowd seethed through the streets nearby. Beggars stared at him from dark corners. Children rummaged through a pile of garbage. A veiled woman tottered up to him, yammering in Arabic, waved her hands at him, then continued on her way.

Robert stumbled down an alley, then burst into a small courtyard. He quickly glanced around, craning his neck to find some escape: a few covered passageways, an open lane leading toward a wider thoroughfare, several doorways. Robert noticed a familiar figure standing near one of the alleys, and he froze.

The princes stood beneath a darkened arch, light from the alley's far end pouring through her shimmering form. Robert shook his head, trying to dispel the chill creeping up his spine. Nefer had only come to him in his dreams, and now she was here, in the daylight shadows, beckoning to him, a terrified expression on her face. Her ancient Egyptian costume seemed out of place in the dingy streets of Alexandria. Robert wanted to step toward her, rush into her arms. But his legs felt paralyzed, his boots seemed fixed to the dusty ground.

"Ferengi!" The shout echoed from the entrance to the courtyard. A mob of angry Egyptians burst down the street, each brandishing some weapon, hate creasing their faces into furious masks. They charged down the lane, each one glaring angrily at Robert.

He was fit for an Englishman nearing forty. But at that age he was painfully aware of his own mortality . . . and it suddenly reared up and frightened him in the face of that mob. Their shouts flooded over him. Their heads bobbed like cackling goblins, arms waving above their heads, some with scimitars and clubs, others with muskets. The crowd seethed forward, driven by the violent euphoria of unbridled anger. They charged Robert. One man near the front lowered his musket and crammed the barrel into Robert's chest. The muzzle flashed.

Emotions burst within him. Robert clutched his chest, felt the blood gushing through his fingers. He saw his wasted life bleeding out his body. He wept inside at the years squandered at second-rate jobs, chasing futile dreams, living with no goal for family or career. No faces of wife or children passed through his mind. The only presence he felt steadying him was his gentle princess standing behind him, waiting to catch him in her arms.

*   *   *

Robert Jones dreamed while he was dead.

He lay prone on his back, staring up at a dark ceiling. At first he thought someone had dragged him to a hospital bed, that he had awoken past nightfall. But the surface was much too hard and cold to be a bed. Someone had trussed him up in sheets, for he could feel them clinging to his body.

Nefer appeared out of the darkness, bent over him, and stroked his face with her gentle hand. Robert felt the fine linen of her dress brush against his arm. The princess moved her lips softly, as if saying everything was all right now that he was with her. Nefer's eyes no longer held fear and pain, only dreamy affection, romantic longing for one kept so far from her in the waking world.

She rose abruptly as Robert saw another figure enter his

vision: a regal pharaoh wearing the double crown of Upper and Lower Egypt, bare-chested, gleaming with gold and blue faience baubles. He advanced menacingly on Nefer, his face twisted in an expression of rage, lips snarling words Robert could not hear.

The princess backed away, her eyes pleading for mercy, hands raised in supplication. Pharaoh halted his advance and loomed over her, shouting. Nefer continued pleading, tears running dark with kohl down her cheeks. For a moment it seemed Pharaoh's face softened in response to her appeal for compassion. Robert couldn't understand her words, though he heard them punctuated with sobbing. Nefer rose from her knees to approach Pharaoh, touching him affectionately on the cheek. Whatever she finally said only further enraged Pharaoh—he pushed her away, then lashed out at her with his fist.

Robert saw blood fly from her mouth as her delicate form arched back through the air. He heard her body thud against the stone floor. Pharaoh turned and marched off into the darkness, never once glancing back at the woman he'd struck down. Robert strained to look over the edge of his bed, to see what happened to Nefer. His princess. Was she curled up on the floor weeping, or was she sprawled on the ground, dead?

Robert strained as hard as he could, but discovered he couldn't move. He felt surrounded by silent rock, like someone was lowering his body into a cold, stone sarcophagus. Hieroglyphics carved into the coffin's walls danced in flickering light from lamps stationed at each corner.

A bald priest with a leopard skin draped over one shoulder approached the foot of the sepulcher. He gently set a box decorated in the ancient Egyptian style onto the stone edge. Robert examined the hieroglyph painted on the chest's side. Although he knew he couldn't read the ancient Egyptian symbols, Robert suspected they spelled out his name.

The priest chanted a long-forgotten verse while waving a censer of smoking incense over the box. Then he began lowering four stone jars into the chest, the stopper of each molded in the head of some ancient Egyptian god: a man, falcon, baboon, and finally a jackal. He carefully secured the lid on the box, then took it with him into the growing darkness.

As Robert succumbed to exhaustion, he tried dismissing his dreams as simply visions inspired by his time in Egypt, the various relics he so often dealt with, and his brother's lurid stories about ancient burial rituals. He sighed, comforted by this rational thought, and slipped into a cold sleep.

*　　*　　*

Robert woke surrounded by a glowing white aura. His mouth felt like it was stuffed with gauze. When the haze cleared from his eyes, he realized it was just morning light gleaming through his bed's mosquito netting. He turned to see his princess waiting at the bedside, the sunlight streaming through the window and outlining her body in a shimmering halo.

"Dr. Stephens," she called over her shoulder. "He's waking up."

Not his princess. The young woman who pulled the mosquito netting aside looked nothing like Nefer. She showed concern on her face, Robert was certain, but it masked deeper, more determined emotions. She possessed Eastern features—olive-toned skin, dark, almond-shaped eyes—yet exuded the regal posture of a British subject. She wore a simple linen shirtwaist with a high collar and smartly tied cravat. Her long, black hair was piled on her head with an abundance of pins. She was a vision of delicate yet assertive Victorian beauty.

An older gentleman in a frock coat appeared behind her. The man was bald and wore a stern expression on his face, like some priest come to administer last rites. His pale skin and haggard features impressed Robert as someone who'd stayed up night and day for several months.

"You are a very lucky young man, Mr. Jones," the older

gentleman said. "I am Dr. Stephens, and this is my ward, Miss Harriet Matthews."

Robert tried saying, "How do you do?" but his dry throat only allowed him to gasp, then cough.

Miss Matthews offered him a glass of water, which he greedily consumed. His mouth still felt dry, and the woman poured him another glass from a pitcher nearby. She handed it to him with a look of motherly concern Robert wouldn't have expected in someone so young.

"You're very weak," she said. "You'll still need a few weeks' rest before you'll be fit enough to move about." Robert felt dry all over. He looked down at his hands clutching the glass. They were pasty white and gaunt. Robert drank again, then handed the glass back to Miss Matthews. He coughed again, cleared his throat, and struggled to sit up on his own. She helped him, propping him up with an abundance of feather pillows. "What happened to me?" he asked.

"You were fortunate that Miss Matthews and I witnessed the mob assaulting you, that we took you in when the commotion dispersed," Dr. Stephens said, standing over the bed. "The musket must have slipped before it discharged. The ball passed right through the meat of your shoulder. Chipped your shoulder blade, I'm afraid, but I managed to clean the bone fragments from the wound."

Robert probed beneath the sheets covering his chest. His hand found the wound, now little more than a crumbly bump where he assumed Dr. Stephens had stitched it up. The skin felt stretched there, almost out of place.

"You've spent close to three months in a coma and delirious fever," Miss Matthews said, brushing the hair from Robert's eyes. He smiled back at her.

"There's been some trouble in Alexandria," Stephens said.

"All of Egypt, actually," Miss Matthews added.

"Yes, I somewhat determined that on my own."

"Arabi Pasha's treachery incited riots in Alexandria," she continued. "The British bombarded the harbor, then swept through the city to restore order. Arabi Pasha is on the run somewhere between Cairo and the Suez Canal."

"We hid in the catacombs beneath this house until the fighting was over," Dr. Stephens cut in. "Our home was spared the misfortune which befell other Europeans living here."

"It's only a matter of time before General Wolseley's army subdues these rebellious forces," Miss Matthews said.

Robert noticed something in her eyes that didn't fit with her youthful appearance—a weariness carried from more years and strife than someone in her mid-twenties should have experienced.

"We'll contact your brother in Cairo as soon as they've repaired the telegraph lines," she offered.

"You know George?"

She smiled. "My father visited his shop during his infrequent stops in Cairo. He fancies himself a collector of ancient knickknacks. Wanders through every bazaar and shop offering antiquities." Robert peered through the mosquito netting at the room around him while Miss Matthews talked. The Western furnishings were supplemented by an assortment of Oriental and ancient pieces: a papyrus scroll stretched out on the desk, a worn Persian carpet, some statuettes of Egyptian gods, a few painted glass mosque lamps, an alabaster vase in the shape of a lotus blossom.

"Where is your father now?" Robert asked.

"He serves Her Majesty as an administrator in India," she replied. "Dr. Stephens looks after me when he's gone."

"I must get back to my brother in Cairo." Robert tried pulling himself out of bed, but only fell back and floundered on the pillows.

"Easy, now," Miss Matthews said, soothing him back under the covers.

Dr. Stephens sat at the edge of the bed and held Robert's wrist. "Your injuries and the subsequent fever have left you extremely weak."

"You'll improve with time," Miss Matthews said, setting a reassuring hand on Robert's shoulder. "Just rest now. Are you hungry?"

Robert admitted he had no desire for food. He felt like he had a bellyful of sawdust and dried leaves. Miss Matthews asked Dr. Stephens to prepare some sandwiches and other light fare to leave at Robert's bedside, in case his appetite returned. She refilled the water glass and left it on the night table.

"You just get some sleep," she said, brushing his eyes closed with her hand. "Dr. Stephens and I will take good care of you."

He heard their feet brush the soft carpet as they left him. As Robert drifted off to sleep, he heard voices in the next room. "You told him too much," he heard Dr. Stephens say. Miss Matthews turned on him with a stern reply, though in a language Robert could not understand.

* * *

Robert was amazed how quickly his health returned, although his appetite had not. He'd only picked at the food Miss Matthews left for him, yet each day he seemed stronger and more alive. His brush with death and illness put everything in perspective. He began feeling more fit than he'd been in ten years.

She tended to him every day, and he soon felt well enough for her to help him out of bed and set him in an armchair. With a forceful determination that slightly frightened him, Miss Matthews sternly insisted that he not dwell on his injuries or his loss of appetite. "No matter what happens to us, we must carry on with our chins high," she'd say. "Don't pay any attention to the hardships other people throw in our path."

She had a patient ease about her, like someone who was used to waiting for the inevitable. She brought books from her father's library. He immersed himself in volumes about the Nile monuments, ancient rituals, tales of the pharaohs. One particular story that captivated his imagination told of an ancient queen who became pharaoh, a powerful woman who denied her stepson the right to rule even after he'd come of age. She took her trusted vizier as her lover, and together they maintained peace and prosperity in Egypt through a combination of her immense bureaucracy and a good dose of carefully applied force. And when the queen died, her vengeful stepson erased all traces of her rule from the kingdom, desecrated her grave, hacked her lover's body to pieces and fed them to the Nile crocodiles.

Robert had never spent much time reading books, but they hastened his convalescence and provided the fuel for several intellectual conversations with Harriet. And he quickly found himself speaking of his past misadventures—numerous petty opportunities vainly pursued and squandered. He told her how his teachers in school bored him with their rote and rhetoric, how he'd left more out of disinterest than ignorance. She listened intently as he described how he'd served as an agent for budding artists in Paris, until he sank all his savings into opening his own salon. The enterprise quickly turned into a disaster when the public panned his featured painters. He told of dozens of dubious ventures. He shared his feelings about the only woman he had really loved, who chose to follow her family to America rather than drift around Europe with a vagabond.

He spoke of his work for George, traveling up and down the Nile, meeting with dealers and other shady characters, personally shipping acquisitions back to the store in Cairo. In return George gave him a room in his house, fed him, and provided the meager stipend they could barely afford. The business was only marginally successful, the profits eaten by supporting the two of them and paying off his suppliers along the Nile. It was the latest of a life of dead-end opportunities, jobs that made him just enough to get by.

Encouraged by her kind interest and several books from her father's library, Robert discussed his future dreams. He thought he might try his hand at hunting big game out of Mombasa, or going down to the Cape to look for diamonds when he tired of working in Egypt.

When he could finally shuffle about on his own, Robert examined the treasures scattered around the house: the papyrus scroll, an illuminated manuscript of the Koran, a bronze cat statue, a plaster fragment from a tomb painting. Harriet explained each one, how she'd acquired it, and what purpose it served in the ancient or Mohammedan world. She even found a few relevant books in the study that Robert devoured in an afternoon's reading.

They spent one evening discussing the statuettes of Egyptian gods, the architecture of temples, and how the ancients prepared their dead for the journey to the eternal Western paradise.

"You mentioned the ancient Egyptians were buried with their innards packed into jars," Robert said.

"Yes," Harriet replied. "Canopic jars, each with the head of one of the Sons of Horus on top: a man, baboon, falcon, and jackal. Why do you ask?"

"I've seen such jars, placed in a box decorated with hieroglyphics." Robert tried shaking the cobwebs from his head. He knew he'd seen exactly such a thing, but he couldn't quite remember where. Perhaps he'd seen it in one of the books from the study. His eyes brightened with recognition. "I think my brother had something like that in his shop not too long ago."

"My father's been looking for something like that for his collection," Harriet said. "Did your brother sell it? If he still has it, I'd love to buy it as a surprise for Father."

"I can't remember whether he sold it," Robert said. "I suppose we'll find out when I get back to Cairo once all this political nonsense gets sorted out."

Harriet dutifully reported on the progress against the Egyptian rebels. He figured it was part of her assertive method to help draw his attention from his own injuries and focus it instead on the reestablishment of order throughout the land. He rationalized that she saw restoration of European rule in Egypt as a return of order in his own life.

She read newspaper accounts of the final action northeast of Cairo, at places like Tel el-Kebir and Kassassin, where the gallant Highlanders charged in the face of overwhelming enemy opposition. Harriet smiled sternly when news arrived that Arabi Pasha had surrendered the Citadel at Cairo.

"People like Arabi would seek to rule this world through riot and confusion," she said with an edge to her voice. "They manipulate people's fears, stir them into belligerent mobs, and direct them against established forces of order and peace."

"They certainly have no respect for other people's property or person," Robert said. "What kind of ruffians bend the Khedive to their will, then forcibly take over the country from the very powers who helped raise it from poverty and ruin?"

"Petty villains determined to infect the world with their selfish ideals and greedy motives," Harriet replied. "The British Empire has brought unity to the disparate peoples throughout the world. Her Majesty rules justly, with application of force only where needed to restore the right order of society."

Robert felt a tinge of personal anger in Harriet's voice, and saw her eyes staring icily into the distance as she spoke. He wondered if she, too, had been a victim of such lawless injustice.

Every night Robert dreamed that his princess returned to him, sitting at his bedside, holding his hand or gently stroking the hair from his face. She leaned over him, her breast just brushing his arm through her gauzy linen gown. She gazed at him with her deep brown eyes. At times they seemed like Harriet's eyes, but they were void of whatever edge lurked behind the woman's character. Nefer's eyes held hope, affection, peace.

The dream frequently transformed into the one visited upon him the day he was shot. Pharaoh inevitably emerged from the darkness, a sinister figure adorned with all the glorious treasures of ancient Egypt. His regal bearing quickly dissolved into rage as he tore the princess from the bedside. No matter how hard Robert struggled to protect her, Nefer always succumbed to Pharaoh's brute strength. His fist crushed her delicate face, sent her lifeless body flying through the air until it thudded against the cold stone.

On the last night in Alexandria, Robert woke violently, thrashing about the covers and screaming his princess' name. He gasped for air, a belly full of fear.

Dr. Stephens was at his side by the time he regained control of his senses. He settled Robert back into the bed, held his wrist for a moment, and made a grim face. "I was afraid you had slipped back into delirium."

Harriet burst into the room in her dressing gown. She rushed to Robert's side and embraced him.

"I'm fine, I think," he admitted. "Just haunted by nightmares, I suppose."

Harriet sat back on the bed. "What nightmares?"

Robert pulled himself from the bed and paced the room while he described the ancient Egyptian princess. "I don't know who she is," he said, shrugging his shoulders. "I see her in my dreams, and sometimes when I'm awake. I think she's called Nefer."

He explained how the princess came to him every night, how she kept a vigil at his bedside, and how her attentions were ultimately interrupted by Pharaoh's brutal assault.

Harriet burst into tears and ran from the room.

"It seems your time in Egypt has fueled your imagination like a bonfire," Dr. Stephens said. "Such dreadful nonsense upsets Miss Matthews."

Robert resolved not to mention it again.

As he tried drifting back to sleep, he overheard Harriet sobbing to Dr. Stephens elsewhere in the house. From his frequent dreams of the princess, Robert could understand their hushed tones despite the ancient language in which they spoke.

"Why didn't you tell me? All this time you kept it from me," Harriet cried. "Why didn't you tell me he killed his own wife, my beloved daughter?"

"It would have made no difference in the end," Stephens said, his voice void of any emotion. "Had you known the truth—that she died at his hands and not by the whim of the gods—you would have acted hastily. He was already plotting your own downfall and that of Senenmut."

"You rescued me, brought me back from the edge," Harriet sobbed. "But why would you not return my loved ones to help ease my burden?"

"I was commanded to act as I did. I am ruled by the same principles by which you yourself ruled: life, power, stability," Stephens said.

As Robert faded into sleep, the doctor's passionless voice took the tone of grim resignation. "And if you do not follow those same principles, the one who governs through lawlessness, chaos, and conquest will ultimately win the day."

*   *   *

When the telegraph lines were restrung and Egypt firmly under British control, Harriet and Dr. Stephens took Robert by train to Cairo. They'd sent his brother a telegram that he was safe and that they were accompanying him back to the city. Robert could move about on his own, and he felt a renewed vigor with each passing day; but still they insisted on taking the train to Cairo with him and delivering him into his brother's care.

George received them in his apartments in the European quarter. They were modestly furnished, reflecting the meager living he made doing what he enjoyed. The rooms were void of any antiquities, but contained various drawings George had rendered that reflected his amateur obsession with all things Egyptian.

He welcomed Harriet and Dr. Stephens into the house like old friends. "Things have been rather tense these past few weeks," George explained while serving the tea. "I'm glad to finally have visitors. Most of us Europeans huddled behind locked doors, fearing riots would break out here, that we'd all be rounded up and shot."

Harriet told how they'd hidden in the catacombs beneath their home in Alexandria.

"Not a bad strategy at all," George said, munching on one of the cakes he'd arranged on a tray. "I shut myself up in here and made like nobody was home. Kept the revolver loaded, but didn't have to use it. I'm glad I didn't leave the apartments. Turns out the fiends burgled my shop while I was hiding. Made a mess of it all, but didn't take much more than some cash."

Robert described his misadventures with the Alexandria riots, and how Miss Matthews and Dr. Stephens had rescued him and nursed him back to health. He noticed neither of them ate the cakes George had set out for them. Only Harriet accepted tea, and even then she took just one sip before setting the cup down. Robert didn't feel much like eating, especially while retelling his harrowing escapades.

"Well, I suppose Robert and I owe you both some debt of gratitude," George announced. "Whatever I can do for you, I am at your service."

"Actually," Robert spoke up, "Harriet was telling me the other day how she'd like to find a chest of canopic jars for her father's collection. Didn't we get one with that stash of relics I bought down in Luxor two years ago?"

"Yes, I remember the piece. A very rare find—intact and in perfect condition. I often wondered if it was purloined from that hidden tomb the authorities uncovered last year." He smiled at Harriet and Dr. Stephens. "But in my line of work, we don't worry too much about such things."

"Do you still have it?" Harriet asked.

George scratched his chin. "I'd love to give it to you, but I sold it to a fellow Englishman before all this rebellion business started. One of those dilettantes who was touring the Nile. He came back to Cairo just in time to hole up in Shepheard's Hotel until the unpleasantness subsided."

"I remember him," Robert said. "Young fellow, what was his name?"

"Nigel Carlisle, from an affluent family in Kent, I think," George said. "I believe he's still at Shepheard's. Now that General Wolseley has everything under control, I suspect Carlisle will be heading up to Alexandria or Port Said to catch a ship bound for the continent."

"Perhaps the gentleman might be interested in selling

this artifact to me?" Harriet said. "My father would be so pleasantly surprised to add it to his collection."

"I suppose there's no harm in going up to Shepheard's and having a talk with the fellow," George said. "Let me give you a letter of introduction, Miss Matthews, so he knows you've spoken to me about the matter."

Robert felt something stir nearby, like a delicate hand settling on his shoulder. "Why don't I accompany them to the hotel?" he suggested. "I can get about on my own, and can see them off at the station when it's time to leave."

Harriet placed her hand on Robert's. "That's very kind of you," she said, the affection in her voice masking a sharper edge.

"It's the least I can do to repay your kindness to me," he replied.

Dr. Stephens stood. "We must depart now for the hotel if we are to conclude our business and return to Alexandria on the late train," he announced. "Good day, Mr. Jones."

"Yes, thank you for your hospitality," Harriet said, offering her hand. George accepted and kissed it.

"The pleasure was all mine," he replied. "And thank you once again for saving my brother and nursing him back to health. Don't be too long, Robert. Take good care of Miss Matthews and Dr. Stephens."

*　　*　　*

They hired a carriage to take them the few blocks to Shepheard's Hotel. They inquired about Mr. Carlisle at the front desk, and a servant boy was summoned to escort them to his room.

Robert's knock on the door was promptly answered by a young man whose collar and waistcoat were undone.

"Mr. Carlisle? My name is Robert Jones. I'm sorry to disturb you, but you might remember me from my brother's shop. A few months ago he sold you a decorated Egyptian chest with four jars inside. I've brought some friends with me who'd like to have a look at it."

"Yes, of course, please come in."

Robert introduced Harriet and Dr. Stephens, and Carlisle ushered them into his room. Two steamer trunks sat on the bed. Clothes covered the chairs and couch, and an assortment of traveling articles littered the desk. White curtains fluttering gently near the open balcony doors enhanced the atmosphere of disorder in the room. "Pardon the mess, but I'm leaving in the morning to catch a ship out of Port Said."

"We were hoping to examine the chest for ourselves, and perhaps offer to purchase it from you," Harriet explained. "At a greater price than you paid for it, of course."

"As a matter of fact, I was just wondering how the damn thing would fit in all my baggage. It's awfully unwieldy, I'm afraid." Carlisle tossed some clothes off a chair, found the box, and brought it over to a clear spot on the desk. "New Empire, I think, covered with the cartouche for Tuthmosis III, if I'm not mistaken. You'd be amazed what you can learn from those travel books."

Robert followed Harriet to the chest. Colorful hieroglyphics decorated the surface, guarded by figures of animal-headed gods and ancient talismans. Harriet ran her fingers over the surface, lingering on the oval-shaped cartouche that contained the symbols for the pharaoh's royal name. "Born of the God Thoth," she whispered. "Lasting in the Manifestation of Re."

"So you read ancient hieroglyphs, too?" Carlisle asked. "I wasn't quite sure what it said when I bought it, but I had a bit of time on my hands waiting for the British army to sort out all this rebellion nonsense. Spent a whole week deciphering the cartouche."

Robert removed the chest's lid and looked inside. Four miniature heads started back at him—a man, baboon, falcon, and jackal—stoppers atop the four stone jars contained within.

Carlisle continued prattling on. "I don't care much for the jars, but the craftsmanship on the box is . . ."

Robert and Harriet turned to see Carlisle collapse, his hands clutching the throwing knife protruding from his throat. Bright blood stained his undone collar. He thrashed on the ground a moment before falling silent.

The curtains at the balcony doors fluttered. A stately man in a formal tailcoat glided past them and into the room, a walking stick firmly grasped in one white-gloved hand. Robert recognized his regal bearing, the cold face twisting into a mask of anger. He was the brutal pharaoh from his dreams, the one who had torn the princess from his side and mercilessly struck her dead. The fiend had somehow pulled himself from Robert's nightmares and stood before him as alive and real as any Englishman dressed for dinner.

Harriet withdrew her hands from the box. Dr. Stephens stood impassively by the door. Robert discovered he couldn't move.

"Oh, greatest of noble ladies," the gentleman pharaoh sneered, addressing Harriet. "Soul of Re's truth. Master of the Upper and Lower Kingdoms. The proverbial evil stepmother."

Harriet glared back at him, her eyes cold with ancient hatred.

"Who are you?" Robert managed.

"I think you know. I am *Men-kheper-re!*" he declared, his voice snarling with an inner cruelty. "Living incarnation of Re's divine power." The gentleman smiled coyly when Robert's face displayed recognition. "But for now you may call me Mr. Thompson, if it helps assuage your fear."

"I should have known you were behind all this," Harriet said. Her dark stare pierced Thompson, but he glared back with malice in his own eyes.

"It seems your schemes foiled my latest little enterprise," Mr. Thompson admitted. "My little rebellion here might have failed, but I'll have other opportunities to wreak havoc upon these European invaders. This is not their land, but ours." He turned on Robert. "The Nile and its people exist to serve me and whatever empire I choose to forge out of the ruins of your pathetic civilization."

"Your ambitions will always fail," Harriet staid. "Such are the rewards of ruling through conquest, terror, and death."

"And you, dear stepmother, rule through subterfuge, deception, and lies. Are you any more noble for it? You've even stooped to manipulating this sorry man to do your bidding." Thompson stepped forward, twisted his walking stick, pulled the handle out, and deftly swung the concealed rapier blade to point at Robert's chest. "Now, if you would kindly step away from my box. . . ."

Robert stood his ground, staring at this villain from his dreams, now framed in the gauze curtains rustling in the evening breeze. Beyond, out on the balcony, Robert noticed another person taking shape out of the evening mist. His princess. The ghostly woman buttressed his courage, gazing at Robert with her pleading eyes, providing calm reassurance.

"No. I'll not step away."

Thompson shook his head. "Bloody fool." He extended his arm, thrusting the blade deep into Robert's chest.

Robert instinctively clutched at his wound. He gasped—not at the pain, which did not flood his body, but at its absence. His legs held steady. His mind remained clear of the fog from the inevitable unconsciousness he expected.

Robert kept his footing even when Thompson yanked the blade from his chest. The tip drew no blood, just a small puff of sandy dust from his flesh. Robert smelled dried flowers.

"You cannot hurt him," Harriet declared, her lips curling into a sarcastic smile. She nodded to Dr. Stephens. "Hapuseneb has made him one of us."

"Traitor!" Thompson sneered at the doctor. "You've committed a beastly sacrilege."

"I obeyed the commands I was given," Dr. Stephens replied without emotion. "I do not question orders issued in the name of life, stability, and authority."

Thompson turned to Robert. "Don't you see what they've done to you?

"I see. They've saved me from an untimely death . . . at your very hands. I know that it was your schemes that ultimately caused my death." Robert's voice became softer, but charged with authority. "I have no need for food or water, other than what I please to eat and drink. Weapons cannot harm me."

"Can't you see?" Thompson snarled. "They've twisted you into an undead monster."

"Just like you," Robert said with a wry smile.

"You're nothing more than a heartless, mindless minion enslaved to their insidious plans!"

"We've made you immortal like us, Robert," Harriet said calmly.

"Shut up!" Thompson growled. He turned back on Robert. "Give me the box!" he ordered. "The jars inside. Hand them to me."

"Why such concern for these ancient trinkets?" Robert asked. He lifted the jackal-headed jar from the chest and hefted it in his hand. "Unless they hold the key to your own power and immortality."

"Stop him," Thompson ordered Harriet. "He's your plaything. Make him show mercy."

"You may be my stepson, but I know the truth," Harriet said, glaring at Thompson. "You murdered my daughter, your devoted wife, my own flesh, and for nothing more than a whim of rage."

"That was centuries ago," Thompson said.

"And yet the dead do not forget," Robert said, pointing to the balcony. Neferure, daughter of Queen Hatshepsut, wife of Tuthmosis, stood among the gauzy, billowing curtains, staring accusingly at Thompson. Yet at the same time, Robert felt the pain in her eyes, the hand striking her cheek in anger, the life ebbing from her limp body.

"You killed her!" Robert cried. In his rage he threw the jackal-headed jar against the wall, then sent the chest crashing to the floor. The jars shattered and spilled their ancient, dusty contents on the carpet.

Thompson dropped to his knees in agony. His face twisted into a mask of furious torment. His body crumbled inside the elegant European clothes, aging centuries in only a few seconds. Robert watched silently as the breeze from the balcony quickly scattered the wisps of gray dust until there was nothing left.

Harriet, Dr. Stephens, and Robert stood in silence, the pile of evening clothes little more than another crumpled heap of laundry waiting for someone to pack it into a steamer trunk. Robert looked to the balcony doors, but he just looked out into the dark night sky: the princess was gone.

"You lied to me!" Robert shouted, turning on Harriet. His hands tightened into claws. Robert imagined them closing around Harriet's neck, or the carefully hidden canopic jars containing *her* life essence.

"It was necessary." She pointed to the heaped dinner jacket where Thompson last stood. "He intended to rule through riot and strife. I prefer to exercise my power more discreetly, but no less effectively.

"It had to be done," Dr. Stephens added. "It was the only way to maintain stability."

"You manipulated me and my emotions to do exactly what you wanted." Robert said. You knew all along who I was, my connection to the chest, that I could lead you to it."

Harriet's expression hardened. "Yes, I used you, just as people have used each other for thousands of years. Through kindness or deceit, they forged a hold over others to obey their will. I have seen it time and again."

"I suppose you're going to tell me it all comes down to human nature."

"Humans betray one another," she replied. "To protect oneself, you must manipulate others. Find what they care about most and twist it to your own purposes. A very simple lesson to learn."

"Yet a painful one."

Harriet remained silent.

"And where are the canopic jars holding *my* innards?" Robert asked. "Have you hidden them for safekeeping, or are you just waiting to destroy me the same way, when I'm of no more use to you?"

"They're hidden and safe. And I'll destroy them if you force me to do so," Harriet admitted. "Indeed, it is against my nature to let you live. I should never have asked Dr.

Stephens to return your life." Harriet looked at the floor, to the crumpled pile of dusty clothes. "But I ordered him to, and you live now. It would not be right for me to take that away from you."

"Just leave me alone," Robert replied. He turned his back on Pharaoh Hatshepsut, ruler of nothing but lies, and left the hotel.

He wandered the dusty streets of Cairo all night, still shocked at what he'd experienced, what he'd become. When dawn streamed over the eastern horizon, Robert found himself across the river in Gizeh, staring up at the pyramids shining with the dawn's golden light. He saw his princess waiting for him at the base of the pyramids, waving to him, beckoning him to follow her into the great western desert. Her slender form shimmered in the sudden morning light, her linen dress radiant, her eyes warm and inviting. Robert approached Neferure, took her delicate hand in his, and continued walking out into the desert.

THOSE TAUNTED LIPS
by Leslie What

Leslie What has published more than fifty short stories in magazines including *Asimov's, The MacGuffin, Fiction Quarterly, Realms of Fantasy,* and in anthologies including The *Chick's in the Mail, Twice Upon a Time,* and *Bending the Landscape*: Volumes 1 and 3. She won the Nebula Award for best short fiction in 1999. Her first collection of fiction is entitled *The Sweet and Sour Tongue.* A complete bio can be viewed at: http://www.sff.net/people/leslie.what.

When Helen Keller first awakened to her death some thirty years ago, she was terrified. She found herself floating facedown in what felt like dry sand, with her consciousness pushed and pulled by forces neither seen, nor heard. The stench of crushed ants overpowered her. She knew she was dead, which only made things worse because it forced her to remember being alive.

The silence reminded her of those terrible years, before Teacher, when she was alone. The memories still taunted her; she screamed, unable to hear her own terror, though she felt the force of her anguish ripple the air.

She felt something else too, the tickling vibration of a fly walking over her skin. She detected a pattern in the sensation, but could make no sense of the repetitions. It felt almost like someone was trying to manually spell her name, just getting the letters wrong.

"Who's there?" she asked. She imagined the sound of her voice, thick as a heavy cloud. Suddenly, she was falling. Wind pierced her like splintered ice; there was no ground to break her flight through cold and dark. She screamed because screaming was the only way she knew to respond to the unknown.

A montage of images, thoughts, unrecognizable shapes and colors collided in her mind. "How does Helen Keller scream?" She had heard all the jokes, and now this one flashed through her memory. Others had always made fun of her. She had once joked with Annie about how death would be a welcome change, because in death, at least things couldn't get worse. Annie was the only one who had ever understood the irony of her situation.

Things had gotten worse. Not only that, but there seemed to be no one to help her face the trouble. *Annie!* she thought. *Where are you now?* She prayed. *Please, God, take me to the others. I don't want to be alone.* At some point, her awareness and her consciousness dissipated. Helen stopped falling to return to the restful sleep of death.

The dead exist for most of time in a "no world" of silence and dark, a peaceful stillness stretching beyond sleep and into the realm known as Heaven. They awaken, not at random, but because the living have chosen—at specific moments—to remember them.

Time passed without Helen's notice until the scenario repeated itself and someone thought of her or spoke her name. She awakened to feel something pulling her. It happened time and again.

Helen did not know enough to try and answer those early calls, but being gifted with an intelligent and playful, if ornery spirit, she soon took control of her afterlife. Remembering how to dance, she mastered her movement, learned to spin and turn. Instead of falling, it was as if she were diving from an island cliff and into a tropical pool. She somersaulted and twisted, not in the least startled to find herself dancing without a partner.

One day, a realization rushed her like a waterfall: that the tugging on her consciousness meant that someone from the living world had uttered her name. Instead of frightening her, she felt heartened, knowing she was not forgotten.

A spirit has no real body; she is more like the physical presence of wind. Because a spirit remembers the body, she envisions herself to be an entity contained within flesh. She imagines herself as a bodily apparition capable of following her mental commands.

Helen pictured herself as a graceful, beautiful being capable of flight.

She felt a thudding vibration and likened it to a pulse; she felt substance where her arms and legs had been. She imagined herself as a whole person, with hands capable of fluttering like wings, toes capable of wiggling in dirt, a mouth capable of tasting the world.

The tugging sensation continued. Someone was summoning her.

She could hear her name as if it were being written on the wind. She floated downward, slipping at times, but not tumbling uncontrollably. She stopped when she detected a scent—like sweet fried onions and fresh tomatoes—and knew her summoner was near.

Though Helen whispered, "I have come. What do you want?" he either did not hear or did not understand her. Her speech had always been slurred, and was probably worse now from however long it had been since she had last used it.

The caller was a man; she knew this from the way his voice moved the air when he spoke, a gentle rumbling that reminded her of an empty stomach. She sensed that the two of them were alone. Not knowing why, this sent pleasant shivers to her fingertips.

"Hello?" Helen called, to no response.

She reached out to talk to him, to spell her words manually against his skin. She found his hands, but they were callused from work. She doubted that he even felt the tickle of letters against his palm. She tried again, but he obviously did not understand her.

She kneaded her way up his arm. A fine powder blanketed his clothes—plaster. The chalky odor was like dirt. Her ghostly fingers moved upward and danced upon his cheek. "H," they wrote. "E-L-L-O." She imagined herself as a young woman, not the old one she had become. "Talk to me," she begged him. She imagined herself with soft

skin, her hair long and scented with roses, her lips moist
and full.

The man turned around suddenly, slapped at his neck,
shook out his hands. He was trying to push her away.

She held on tight. He pulled a cold blade from its sheath
and slashed at the air, but it could not hurt her.

Still, this infuriated Helen. Why had he brought her here
to be with him, only to scorn her? It had always been a
struggle not to seek revenge for all the slights, all the teasing. She forced herself to change her anger into curiosity.
This had always been her way of coping. If she stayed
angry, she could lose his company to her pride.

"Why did you call me?" she asked.

To hear his answer, she pressed her palm against his lips
and waited for them move beneath her touch. His hot
breath tickled as the air vibrated when he spoke. Tadoma,
it was called, this ability to feel words as they were spoken.
It was difficult to do, impossible, really, unless you wanted
to hear more than you wanted not to listen.

"What the hell?" he cried. He rubbed his mouth with
his arm and spat.

She had managed to get inside of him. This small victory
pleased her immensely.

He coughed and cleared his throat.

Her fingers danced across his lips and warned him to
stay calm.

He had called her here, so had better be prepared to
talk to her, to listen. "Why did you bring me?" she wrote.

She pushed her fingers into his mouth, and felt the moist
back sides of his lips. She remembered the confusion and
pleasure of similar moments of intimacy. There had never
been enough of them in life.

Now he was the one who screamed in terror. He lifted
his knife to his neck and she felt his choking gasp as its tip
broke through the skin. She forced herself to knock it from
his hand.

He was terrified of her.

She pulled back, suddenly ashamed at her wretched behavior. She had taken advantage of him. She took his hand and spelled her name into the palm.

"H-E-L-E-N. It's me," she said aloud. "Helen." She found the knife with her foot and kicked it away.

She could not hear her own voice, and did not know how close her words came to real language. She spoke again, trying to change her inflection so he would understand. "You asked me to come. Sorry if I frightened you."

She remembered having heard many sounds from her first two years, before the mysterious illness that robbed her of everything. She had lost her hearing too young to be able to attach names to sounds, and her earliest memories made little sense. It was possible that the thing she believed represented a dog's bark might really be the sound of a sheep's braying—no way to tell. A train whistle could have been the sound of wind.

But she could imagine the sound of her name. Teacher had showed her how to make an "H" with her breath.

"Helen," she repeated. "I'm Helen Keller."

He was trembling and sweaty.

She spelled her name again and again, touching him lightly on his arm, on his shoulder, on the back of his hand. He did not sense the pattern.

She suspected he was younger than she at first imagined and before long, his fear and immaturity became so strong it pushed away any other thoughts. She felt herself falling away from him, going backward toward the void. Though she fought to stay conscious, the death sleep overcame her.

                    *   *   *

Being awakened felt like a spider bite, slightly irritating at first, the discomfort steadily growing until the itching turned to pain and she could no longer ignore it. She was being summoned; by whom she did not know. She did not fight, and let herself be led into the world of the living.

It was he, the man who had called her before.

Her automatic response was to reach for him, to touch his lips and make her presence known.

He recoiled and she sensed his apprehension and smelled a slight change in the sourness of his odor. Like so many men she had yearned to be close to, he was afraid of her.

She could feel whirlpools rippling through the air as his breathing quickened.

He groaned. "Leave me alone," he said. He fondled his knife.

She willed the edge to a dullness of a grass blade. She tried to calm him by stroking his hair; that only made him more nervous.

"Why did you call me?" she asked. She could not read his thoughts, and when he did not answer, she spelled her name into his palm. "Why?" she wrote. "Why did you bring me here?"

His fragrance today was of cigarette smoke and paint; his shirt felt dusty. His body was lithe and there were blisters on both thumbs. He was wearing boots and when he walked, he made a clomping sound like a horse. He seemed slowed, as if he were drunk or drugged.

Construction, she thought. *He builds things. So do I,* she thought. *With Teacher's help, I build imaginary bridges.*

She found this young man strangely attractive. She brought her hand to his face and pictured his appearance with her touch. His nose was straight and his eyes deep. His chin was scratchy and his mustache soft.

His lips moved beneath her fingers. "Who's there?" he asked. "What's going on?"

"It's Helen," she said. "Helen Keller." Frantic, she spelled her name into his hand. "You called me," she said. "Why? How can I help you?"

He pulled back and when she tried to write her signs on his hand, she found his fists so tightly clenched she could not break through to reach his palms. She felt the puffy scars on his skin from where he had slashed his wrists.

She felt his will to live slipping away. Helen remembered the frustration of being unable to communicate. She remembered playing tricks on her friends—stealing their food, then pretending to have nothing to do with the thievery. She remembered being so angry with her mother that she had locked her in the pantry.

She fought to keep from growing as angry now, the way she had been whenever she felt helpless. This man was taunting her, forcing her to waken and then ignoring her when she came to him. After all she had done to try and help, how it hurt that the others laughed at her.

Had he brought her back here as some sort of practical joke?

She spelled, "I hate you," on his forehead and was gratified to feel the swish of air as he tried to wave her away. "I hate you," she screamed. "Hate!"

He tried to run from her, yet she followed closely, clinging to his touch. She spelled her name on the tip of his nose until he sneezed.

"It's Helen," she screamed, not caring if her words sounded sluggish or crisp. "Talk to me! Talk to me!" She touched his lips with her fingers and waited for his response.

"Get away!" was his only answer. "I don't believe in you anymore." He made it sound as if he believed that an angel instead of a ghost had visited him.

"I will not get away," she said, furiously spelling each letter onto his cheek.

"Why?" he asked. "Why, God? Isn't it enough that you are taking away my sight? Must you make me crazy as well?"

His anger made his muscles taut; deep lines creased his forehead. His mouth tightened. He was trying not to cry.

In her time, she had seen only a few men cry. Her father had been one of them.

She understood now why he had called her.

Something had happened, some accident or illness that was taking away his life. He was losing his vision. He had thought of her, or of the stories told about her, and he wanted her as his guide.

Her anger softened. She enjoyed being needed. Helen, robbed of any chance for a normal life, had been cast in the role of helper in life. How foolish she had been to hope it would be different in death.

"What can I do?" she asked, and wrapped her arms around

his waist to hold him close. Her embrace grew desperate; she clutched him, not wanting to let go. "It's not so bad, not being able to see the world." she said. She had lost her senses before the age of two; unlike her, at least he was old enough to remember all he had seen. She could only imagine the look of sunset, the color of roses, the look of happiness.

For so much of her existence, she had felt so alone. Her grip grew even snugger.

He was young, but she did not feel motherly toward him. She pressed her lips to his and whispered her name. "I will guide you," she said. "I will show you all there is to see in darkness." She tasted the vibrations in the air.

It had been a long time since she had felt this close to another soul. She brought her lips to his and took in his breath as if it were her own. She felt alive. She would willingly be his guide through the darkness, if only he would follow.

"Tell me your name," she whispered. She touched his face and found his eyes closed tight.

He clamped his mouth shut to breathe through his nose. He covered his ears with his hands and tried to shake loose of her.

She fell away, ashamed at her temerity. He had not called her as Helen, the woman, but as Helen, the role model. He did not seek her company, only her counsel. He did not feel about her as she did about him; it had always been this way.

Yet all she had ever wanted was to be like everyone else. Ironic, that in her attempts to become equal, she had sacrificed her humanity to become an icon.

"Come back," she called. "Please."

His fear compelled him to run away. She felt suddenly less substantial, a balloon, deflated and flying out of control. Her spirit rose, then sank, and spiraled into a crevice.

Her shame crushed her like a grave. She tried to make herself fall into the deep sleep, but couldn't shake the haunting feeling that no living soul had ever understood all she wished to say. No people had ever tried to listen to her the way she had fought to hear them. In spite of everything she had done to be a part of the living world, she had always stood just at the edge of it.

No one knew her for the woman that she was.

Except Annie, who, it seemed, had moved on, and abandoned her.

"Annie!" she cried. She felt as determined now as she had ever felt in life. She would rouse Annie's ghost from sleep, for it was time for Teacher to provide another lesson. "Annie!"

"How does Helen Keller scream?" Helen thought bitterly, and her agitation increased. For years they had made fun of her, not only her disability, but also her determination and spirit. She had struggled with the world most of her life, tried to help others less fortunate, yet still, they hated her.

"Annie!" she spelled, using the air as a chalkboard.

Since her fingers were not strong enough to call the dead, she used her hands and arms, frantically waving. It felt as if she were fighting to keep from drowning. The turbulence in the air pushed her, and she swam against the current. "Annie!" she cried. "Annie."

Not every ghost who is so called chooses to revisit the world. Some are frightened; some ignore their summons. Unsurprisingly, some ghosts choose to haunt instead of help, for death does not change the spirit, only the body.

A spirit who was whisperlike in life, remains a quiet ghost, seen only from a distance, like the hint of glitter on faraway waves. A spirit tormented throughout life is not easily silenced by death; she haunts like a hurricane, drenching anything in her path, destroying all she manages to touch. A spirit who was a helper in life, will be a helper in death.

Helen felt a warm trickle on her palm: a greeting, a question, and an expression of delight.

"Helen?" Annie wrote. "Helen!"

The dead embrace with all the passion and urgency of those who know that at any moment, they might lose each other for eternity. It was difficult to clutch what could only be imagined.

"You're here," Helen answered. A sense of calmness washed over her. She clung to Annie's spirit.

But something was awry.

"Why have you brought me here?" Annie asked.

Helen felt Teacher's irritation at being summoned. A stabbing pain, a sense of loss confronted Helen: that Annie could feel complete without her. As much as she wanted for Annie to stay, Teacher did not plan to remain with her forever. Being near, even if just for a while, would have to do.

Teacher had always been her helper, but help had its limits. As Helen held Annie, she did her best to explain about the young man.

"We must not fall asleep," she said, "or we could lose each other."

Annie reminded her of the time Helen had fallen and knocked her head against a tree, and Annie had kept her awake all night by tickling her and telling her funny stories.

Annie tickled her now, and Helen tickled back. In while, they felt the call.

Holding onto Teacher was like a slow dance through time. The two descended to the place where the young man waited.

"What does he want?" Helen asked, and Teacher pulled away for a moment to whisper in his ear. Helen felt the air vibrate with a cool breeze as Teacher spoke. The breeze grew warm when the young man answered.

"What does he want?" Helen asked. Before acting, she needed to be sure she understood him.

"He wants to know how you forced yourself to go on," Annie said. "He wants to know if you ever thought about committing suicide."

Helen gasped. Her first reaction was to smother him with affection, to somehow transfer the satisfaction she felt from overcoming challenges. But a darker reaction soon followed. If the young man killed himself, perhaps he would spend eternity with her.

She sensed the chill from his knife.

"What should I do?" Helen asked. She felt too ashamed to confess her secret longing to Teacher.

"Tell him he will never be alone," Annie said.

But that was a lie, and she could not force herself to say it. "You can go now," she told Annie. "I know how to help him."

Annie took Helen's hand and pressed it over her lips. "We'll meet again," she mouthed.

"Again," Helen answered. One moment, she was touching the cold essence of her friend, and the next, she was grasping at the empty air. She saw a flash—a glint of steel?

The young man had calmed. "I can feel you out there," he said. "Help me! Please."

Why? she thought. Why should I help you?

He was cowering, shivering, terrified. "I'm afraid of the dark," he said. She sensed his grip tightening on his knife.

She held his hand and pulled him toward her world, where lights were like bursts of energy, sparks to warm the soul. He could not understand her words, so she forced her thoughts upon him. "You'll learn a different way," she told him.

His breath was fast and shallow. She felt the catch as he shuddered with understanding. He dropped the knife, shattering the calm. "I can't imagine—never seeing the ocean again, never watching a storm, never reading poetry."

If Helen wanted to join her, he was ready to die.

She could not do it—put her needs above his. "It's not like that," she said. "You see it within."

He straightened, shook his head. "How did Helen Keller manage?" he asked. Where did she find the strength to go on?"

From Annie, Helen thought. *Once I found Annie, I stopped being afraid of being alone.* "I'm here," she said, and felt his tension lessen and his back slump as exhaustion overtook him. He yawned.

"Be strong," Helen said. "I will stay with you. Rest." She kissed his cheek and blew a gale of strength into his lungs. She took in his scent and committed him to memory. She would haunt him for as long as he needed, longer, if she could manage that.

WARRIOR IN THE MIST

by Lisanne Norman

Born in Glasgow, Scotland, **Lisanne Norman** started writing at the age of eight in order to find more of the books she liked to read. In 1980, two years after joining The Vikings!, the largest reenactment society in Britain, she moved to Norfolk, England. There she ran her own specialist archery display team. Personal experience has always provided inspiration for her writing, no more so than with this short story in which her experiences as an archer on the battlefield lend an air of authenticity to her story about the Battle of Hastings—where she in fact did play the part of a Norman archer in 1990. Now a full-time author, in her Sholan Alliance series she has created worlds where warriors, magic, and science all coexist. Her latest novel in the DAW series is *Stronghold Rising.* As mentioned in her tale "Warrior in the Mist," Lisanne's family name really is Normand—but the D was taken off seventy years ago. She traces her roots back to 1066, and claims her coat of arms is so old it breaks all the heraldry rules. She is indeed part of the MacLeod Clan.

I am Lisanne Normand, of the Clan MacLeod, and I first came to these shores in 1066 with Duke William of Normandy, heir of King Edward the Confessor of England. But it's not of that time I wish to tell.

It's of the evening of Saturday, October 13th. Dusk is falling on the slops of Senlac Hill. The year is 1990, and the event is the largest ever recreation of the Battle of Hastings, otherwise known as the battle of Senlac Hill. The site as aptly named Senlac—Sangue Lac—the River of Blood, because for years after, when it rained, the blood

203

that had been spilled that fateful day would rise red to the surface and its stench once more would fill the air.

Today's battle is over now and darkness is falling. I am the last of those who played the parts of Norman archers, and I am doing a final sweep of Senlac Hill with my young son for any lost arrows.

*　　*　　*

"Was this really where the Battle of Hastings was fought, Mum?" Kai asked as we trudged back toward the campsite where all through Friday night, from cities and towns across the length and breadth of Britain, some seven hundred re-enactors, most Warriors like me, had gathered on the wooded slopes to the east of Senlac Ridge.

I glanced briefly up the hill to my right where the Abbey, its ruined walls a forbidding presence, squatted on the brow of the hill.

"Yes, this is the place. The Normans defeated Harold up there where the Abbey now stands on the top of the Senlac Hill. They say he died where the altar stood."

"Did your side win today, then?"

"Of course. We're real Normans, aren't we?"

"Our family," he said with quiet pride.

"We didn't do so bad a job. Britain's never been invaded since." I looked down at his earnest five-year-old face and smiled, ruffling his shoulder-length fair hair. Then I stopped to pick up an arrow that lay concealed by my foot in a tuft of grass.

"How d'you know the arrow was there?" he demanded.

I shrugged, tucking it into the quiver that hung on my right hip. "A knack," I said. "Arrows take a long time to make, and they're too expensive to lose. The horses broke six of mine today."

"Tell me what happened in the battle," he said, losing interest in the arrow now that it was out of sight.

"We formed up at the bottom of the hill in three divisions," I began. "The Breton mercenaries, William's own Norman troops, and the French mercenaries. As archers, we were out in front with Roy. He was in charge of us all, but my unit was at the far end of the line, on the right, in front of the left-hand flank of Saxons. It happened in the second half of the show, after Harold's right flank had been destroyed."

"Did you follow the real battle plans?"

"More or less."

"How d'you know what happened that long ago?"

"The Normans left a history of it embroidered on the Bayeux Tapestry, and a Norman poet called Wace, who lived then wrote everything down in a poem called *Roman de Rue*. Oh, and there's the Chronicles of Battle Abbey, documents written about the battle and the founding of the Abbey," I added. "Now, shall I tell you what happened?"

* * *

I skidded to a halt by Roy on the damp grass in the gap between the Norman and Breton cavalry. "We're running out of arrows down our end," I yelled over the noise of the battle raging at the top of Senlac Ridge. "There's dozens of them lying ahead of us near the Saxon left flank but the scurriers can't reach them safely. If we don't get them now, they'll be trampled when the French do their second feigned retreat!"

Roy glanced across to the Saxon left, then behind him to where William's cavalry waited, the horses snorting and pawing the ground, impatient to be off again.

He leaned closer so I could hear him. "Do it," he said. "You've seven minutes before the next cavalry charge. If we don't get them, they'll be turned to matchwood by the horses. When the French retreat, the Saxon fyrdsmen will break ranks to follow. Let them through, then have your unit loose three volleys at the remaining Saxons to pin them down, giving our men a chance to turn on the fyrdsmen. Pull back to the trees until after the cavalry charge, then join us when we form up behind the Norman infantry."

                         *   *   *

"Fyrdsmen?" interrupted Kai. "What are they?"

"Ordinary men called from their farms to increase the size of the small permanent army Harold had. A militia. It's thought Harold only had about two thousand fully trained and armored men, the remaining five thousand were his fyrdsmen, most of whom didn't have armor or even a shield."

"And William?"

"Probably about the same number, but they were a well armored and disciplined army, and twenty-five hundred of them were his knights on horses. Now, hush, I thought you wanted me to tell you what happened to me?"

                         *   *   *

Giving Roy a thumbs up, I quickly checked the watch in my pouch as I ran back to the far end of the line of archers. "Follow me!" I yelled, heading toward the woodland bordering the battlefield. "You, too," I said, touching two scurriers as I passed. Twenty yards from the tree line, I stopped.

"Everyone got at least four arrows?" I demanded, looking 'round my group of ten men and women. Getting nods from everyone, I briefed them and gave the order to move out.

In a loose file, keeping to the rough ground, we ran up the hill until we were just beyond the scattered arrows. I pulled out my watch again.

"Katie, Kevin, you got two minutes. Get as many arrows as you can, then get back to the French lines. We'll cover you. Colin, form an open order line in front and just to the left of the arrows. Space yourselves to let the French and the Saxons through," I ordered, leading the way out onto the field, my eyes focused on the combat sixty yards ahead of us.

I placed myself beside Colin, but slightly in front of him, checking my watch every now and then. The French line was wavering, getting ready to retreat.

"Thirty seconds!" I yelled, looking back at the scurriers to find Katie beside me, holding half a dozen arrows.

"We're finished," she said breathlessly. "You've all got six more."

"Well done. Now go!" I grabbed the arrows, pushing them easily into my almost empty quiver. The large rubber blunts on the ends usually made this a task that needed both hands. "Rest of you, hold fast and let the French and Saxons through!"

The gap between the two lines was getting larger. I pulled out two arrows, and holding one against the bow with my left hand, I nocked the other, latching my left forefinger over it to anchor it to the bow. Having an extra arrow ready had saved me from enemy reenactors many a time. I fell back in line with Colin and glanced to my right at the other six archers, making sure they were ready and far enough apart. All we had to do now was wait.

As the French line broke and began to run downhill, I knew I'd placed us well. They, and the Saxons, should pass at least five feet clear of us. I hadn't been happy at the thought of standing like trees in the middle of a hurricane of fleeing armed warriors. Accidents happen, and apart from helmets concealed beneath soft hats, we were unarmored.

Suddenly, something heavy slammed into me, sending me reeling. I was dragged violently to one side. The ground shook as the huge dark shape of a horse thundered past.

"Looks like Delon got bored," said Colin's voice calmly in my ear.

Stunned, I could only watch in horror as five more mounted knights followed the first, each of them sending clods of grass and earth flying into our faces as they passed.

Colin let me slide down to the ground. "You all right?" he asked. "You look a little pale."

"I'm fine," I said shakily, one hand tightening on my bow, the other going automatically to check that my quiver was still hanging at my side. Numbly, I looked across at the others. Their faces were as pale as mine probably was, but everyone was still there and unhurt, thanks to Colin's quick actions.

*   *   *

"You nearly got run down by a horse?" interrupted Kai, his face scrunched up with worry. "Didn't the rider know you were there?"

"He didn't care. He expected me to get out of his way."

"But you couldn't see him!"

"I know, but I'm here, aren't I? Let me finish the story."

*   *   *

"Thanks, Colin," I said as he went back for his bow. "Dammit! The man's a maniac! What the hell does he think he's doing? He could have killed me! He's not supposed to go yet! His cue is to wait for the French to turn and kill the fleeing Saxons, then all the cavalry charge to destroy what remains of the Saxon left!"

Colin shrugged as he came back, nocking his arrow again. "That's what happens when you use display riders like Delon as cavalry. We've had trouble from him before, at the Isle of Man Millennium show."

The shock of what had nearly happened to me was just beginning to penetrate. On autopilot, I looked over to the far side of the field where Roy stood with the rest of the archers. With Delon messing up the script, I knew I needed to check for fresh orders.

Roy raised his arm, making the signal for me to carry on. I gestured my acknowledgment and turned my attention back to Delon and his riders. Discovering the Saxons hadn't yet broken ranks to run after the French, they'd obviously charged to the other side of the field where the Norman and Breton infantry were attacking the Saxon center. From behind their lines, Delon and his riders shouted insults and taunts at the Saxons while making their horses rear up and prance on their hind legs.

The French had almost reached us now, and the Saxon

left had begun to split with more than half of its force following our fleeing soldiers. "I hope Delon's not completely forgotten his cue," I muttered, checking again on the maniac. An adrenaline rush had kicked in, and I was getting increasingly bad feelings about our position. "Pull back, Colin," I said abruptly. "Head back to the trees!" I began to run in front of my archers. "We'll wait there till they're all past us!"

"Incoming!" yelled someone.

Stopping in my tracks, I instinctively ducked, turning my head away to look behind me, praying the others would do the same. I glanced sideways along our line—in time to see Stewart look up, and an arrow smack him hard in the center of his forehead.

"Jesus!" I swore, then "Go!" I yelled to the others, rushing over to him.

With a look of incredulity on his face, Stewart staggered back a few paces, then fell like a stone. Dropping my bow and arrows, I flung myself on the ground beside him, holding him down when he began to struggle to sit up.

"How many times have I told you to keep your head down when you hear 'Incoming'?" I raged at him, checking his face, relieved to find the skin on his forehead unbroken, though a large lump was beginning to form. Around us, the French foot soldiers were streaming past, thankfully giving us a wide berth. Reaching out, I snagged my bow closer to my side. "Stay put. You could have a concussion. At least you kept hold of your bow."

Jumping to my feet, I grabbed the nearest man. He swung 'round, eyes staring, mouth set in a snarl of fury as he raised his sword to hit me, then hesitated.

"Take him to a medic! He took an arrow on the forehead!"

His breathing labored, he glanced briefly over his shoulder. The Saxons were only thirty yards away and closing fast. "Take him yourself," he said, trying to pull free of me. "I got Saxons to kill!" Sweat was running in rivulets down his face, and as he shook his head, droplets sprayed onto me. The light of battle was fading from his eyes.

"Unit commander, I can't," I snapped, pointing to the band of red I wore round my upper arm. I let him go and pushed him toward Stewart. "Got a volley to do right now!"

He nodded and reached down to drag Stewart to his feet.

"Watch out for the cavalry!" I yelled after them, as I grabbed for my weapons and the arrow that had hit Stewart, then I sprinted back to the others.

"Is he okay?" asked Judith, face creased in concern.

"Trust him to do a Harold," grinned Pete. "Told you that Stewart the halfling was on the wrong side. He should have been a Saxon."

"Yeah. Well, maybe it'll knock some sense into him, but I doubt it," I said, gesturing them to follow me up the hill as I stuffed the extra arrow into my quiver. "Let's move out. Keep level with me. We've got to shoot before the cavalry charge."

The hill was steeper now, and by the time we'd out-flanked the Saxon fyrdsmen following our soldiers and taken up our positions opposite the remainder of the Saxon left, we were all short of breath and sweating in the heat of the October sun.

Behind us, the French had turned on the Saxons and were slaughtering them. There'd be no danger to us from that direction. I checked the Saxon center, but Delon's horses had returned to the bottom of the hill with William's infantry. I suddenly realized that the battlefield was empty and we'd be virtually alone in the center. The eyes of the audience of ten thousand people would be on us.

This better look good, I thought. "Show time," I said, glancing over my shoulder at my unit. "In single file, we jog out and line up with an arrow ready. Make it look nice and military. If you miss my call, don't loose, wait for the next volley just as we've practiced. Nothing looks worse than a trailing arrow."

Heart pounding, I led us out to face the Saxons.

They greeted us with yells and screams of anger and derision. They only had four archers, there just to provide return fire so we didn't run out of arrows like the real Duke William's archers had until this final stage of the battle. And yet, despite all our plans to avoid it, so had we. It was strange how our show was actually paralleling the real battle.

"Open order. On my command, three volleys, then fall back in good order to the trees. Low shots, aimed at their shield wall. Try to get some kills. It's about time some of those Saxons died." I searched for a Saxon to target in the front rank. I found one, and as we locked eyes, he began to strike the back of his shield with his sword pommel, yelling, "Out! Out!"

"Nock," I commanded, "Draw. Loose!"

Like a wave, our arrows flew, bouncing harmlessly off their shields. Twice more I gave the command, and with the last volley, as the warriors lifted their shields slightly in anticipation, some of our arrows hit home. Two front line soldiers, mine one of them, were reeling backward, their comrades immediately closing to fill the gaps in the shield wall.

"Yes!" I yelled exultantly as we ran back to the trees. "Good shooting!"

This time I could feel the ground vibrating beneath my feet with the beat of the horses' hooves as all the cavalry charged up Senlac Hill, encircling the Saxons and cutting them off from their central unit.

"The whole Saxon left will collapse now," I said, crouching down to catch my breath, watching our French infantry surging up the hill in the wake of the cavalry. "They'll run for their lives, a few of them breaking to come this way. Let them pass unchallenged. A small group actually escaped the Normans, and they're scripted to be it. As soon as they're gone, we watch for Roy and the rest of the archers. Get an arrow ready, we've got to look like we mean business."

The cavalry wheeled about, pulling back to let the Saxons break and run—straight into the waiting French infantry. Six fyrdsmen broke from the rest, heading toward us. They hit the rough some fifteen feet below and crashed into the cover of the trees.

* * *

We formed up at the end of Roy's line of archers, behind the combined ranks of William's infantry, facing the remains of the Saxon army which had now regrouped closely 'round Harold's banners of the Fighting Man and the Red Dragon of Wessex. The huscarls were packed so close together they really would be unable to lift their shields to protect themselves from our arrows.

Stewart rejoined us as the arrow scurriers rushed up and down our line handing out fresh arrows. Katie and Ken, remembering my earlier instructions, made sure that as many of my distinctive turquoise, blue, and white fletched arrows as possible were returned to our unit.

"I'm fine," he said, touching a hand gingerly to the huge swelling in the center of his forehead. "Couldn't miss the final part."

"You'll have a shiner tomorrow," I said, hiding my anger at the Saxon archer who'd injured him. High lobbed shots were only to be used at scripted sections of the battle, and none were warranted by the Saxons. It had been deliberate. There was one archer up there who'd been targeting our little group throughout the battle, and I knew who he was. He was in the center now, and he was mine.

"Six volleys, then hold your ground," yelled Roy. "High angle lobs to fall down on them from above, then shoot at will. On my order!"

There'd be no incoming fire this time. All four Saxon archers would have downed their bows for the final assault on their position.

We were about halfway up the hill, and with our underpowered bows, which were all the safety rules would allow, we'd be hard-pressed to reach the Saxons on the brow of the hill—if it hadn't been for my speed-fletched blunts. Having only three feathers like a regular arrow rather than the four we normally used, we had an edge over the other archers. I knew that Roy, being a member of the Ancient Guild of Bowmen and Fletchers, planned to use one of his more powerful bows to enable him to reach the top of the hill.

I called my seven archers into a huddle. "We've six called

volleys. Get a rhythm going and try to punch your bow forward as you draw back on the bowstring. Don't aim too high or the arrows will go into the Abbey grounds or the woodland and be lost. We did ranging shots from here this morning, so you know the angle of shot you need to make to reach the top. Track your own arrows and adjust your aim accordingly. Use the speed blunts first, those are the shots the audience will be watching, so we want them to count."

They nodded and fell back to their positions.

"You punch the bows forward?" asked Colin as we readied our arrows. "That's a new one on me."

During the break in the middle of the battle, while we'd waited for the water carriers to come 'round, Colin and I'd shared a surreptitious cigarette, puffing the smoke down into a small pothole beside us, and chatted about archery. I'd been surprised to find out just how much he knew. I remembered then had it not been for the fact his armor hadn't passed the authenticity check that morning, he'd not have been doing archery with us—and wouldn't have been there to pull me out from under the hooves of Delon's horse. I shuddered, glad that I'd followed my instincts and spoken to Roy about him joining my unit.

"Roy lent me a book about the history of archery in warfare," I said, reaching down to pluck a tuft of grass and throw it up into the air to check the wind direction. I knew it had veered slightly. "He taught me how to set up and run my specialist archery display team. Punching the bow away from you was a trick they used with the longbows to get more power behind the shots. I know ours are only lightweight self bows like the Normans actually used, but it does work. I've only been able to do it a couple of times, but then we don't usually have such a large arena to shoot in."

"I'll have to give it a try," he said.

"Wind's changed," I said over my shoulder to anyone who was listening. "Coming across the field from right to left now."

Then all talk ceased as Roy gave the command to nock arrows.

*   *   *

The arrows flew high, like a dark cloud over the heads of our army, out into the field, many falling spent at the feet of the Saxon shield wall, but not our arrows. Straight and true, they dropped down into the Saxon center.

It was our fifth volley before a cry from the Saxons signaled that the man playing the part of King Harold had been hit. A small gap opened up in the middle of their ranks, and as we loosed our last volley, we could plainly see him staggering, holding his hand to an arrow protruding from his head.

The cavalry, led by Jim Alexander who was playing Duke William, passed safely between us, in an ordered charge this time, and headed up the hill, followed by the rest of William's infantry.

I began shooting at will, thinking of the Saxons up on the brow of the hill—Chris from my own group, so proud to be chosen to be one of Harold's huscarls, John himself, and his wife Gina, Ralph, and the others. They had no way of protecting themselves from the arrows falling down from above, they were too tightly pressed together to lift their shields. But they'd been trained as well as my own people— better, probably—to keep their heads down when under a barrage of arrows. I thought then of the archer who'd shot Stewart. It hardened my heart. We all had our jobs to do today, and mine was to rain arrows down on the Saxons, hopefully hitting the man who'd targeted Stewart.

I started to build a rhythm with my shots: as soon as I loosed one, I plucked another arrow from my quiver, nocking it, raising the bow, and punching it forward as I drew back the bowstring. Each arrow flew true, soaring high above the shield wall before the weight of the blunt pulled it down in a sharp arc to fall in the center of the remaining Saxons.

It was a different kind of battle fever I experienced, and

it was exhilarating. For the first time I understood what the others meant when they said it was hard to control the fighting spirit of the ancient Saxons that filled them whenever they fought at Battle Abbey. Only what I felt was the battle fever of the Normans.

Before long, like the others around me, I'd run out of arrows.

We watched the cavalry retreat to let the infantry close in. The Normans ran forward, shouting enthusiastically, then the whole line seemed to hesitate, to waver briefly before engaging.

The fighting was fiercest in the center. But then, John had chosen his men from among the best warriors across the length and breadth of England.

There was nothing left for us to do now, save to pick up what arrows we could and wait for the end, then go up the hill to help in the final slaughter as we gave the *coup de grace* to the dying Saxons and pulled our arrows from their bodies.

* * *

"Why did the Normans not go rushing in?" asked Kai.

"I found out when I got to the top of the hill."

* * *

"Let go of the arrow, Ralph," I grinned, putting my foot on his chest to give me extra leverage as I tried to tug free the arrow that he was holding firmly against his chest.

His bearded, blood-spattered face leered challengingly up at me. "Shan't! You want it, you got to pull it free!"

"C'mon, give it to me."

He let go suddenly, sending me staggering back. I recovered my balance and went back to him, pulling out my battle knife and kneeling down to pretend to be looting his corpse.

"What's with all the fake blood?" I asked.

He laughed, a great, deep belly laugh that went all the

way to his eyes. "Did you see the Norman line falter?" he asked.

"Yeah. What did you do?" I asked suspiciously.

"Just before the final charge, the whole front line, which was us of course, stepped back and we squirted stage blood into our helmets. Then when the Normans charged, the front line opened up and we stepped through. The first thing they saw was us, covered in blood! They thought it was real. Gave them a hell of a fright!"

"You're a bunch of mean bastards! We could see the line waver even from our position half way down the hill."

"Well, if we had to die, we were going to do it in style."

*   *   *

"Did they really do that?" laughed Kai, delighted at the gory tale.

"Yes, they covered themselves in lots of fake blood," I said as we headed back to the fence that divided our campsite from the battlefield.

"And you're going to do it all again tomorrow?"

"Not quite all of it," I said. "Tomorrow is the actual date that the real Battle of Senlac Hill took place. October 14th, though it happened on a Saturday, not a Sunday."

Full darkness had fallen as we'd been talking. A low mist was beginning to rise from the ground, and moonlight filtered down through the scudding clouds, giving the land an unearthly quality. As we reached the fence, the small hand within mine clenched, pulling me 'round.

"Mum! Over there! One of our knights!"

I looked. Emerging from the mist was a horse, its rider dressed in full battle kit.

"The horses have all been stabled for the night and aren't due out until tomorrow morning," I said, frowning as I looked in the knight's direction. Around him the mist eddied and swirled, hiding him from clear sight.

A tug on my arm and, "I want to go back to our tent now, Mum."

"I need to see who it is first. He might be lost, wondering

where they're camped." My voice was as quiet as Kai's had been.

A breath of wind and the mist parted, allowing me to see the knight clearly. He wasn't alone. I shivered, and not because of the rising wind. Two outrunners were with him, one on each side of his mount. Holding fast to the stirrup straps, they were using the momentum of the horse to help them keep pace with the knight. They were barely fifteen meters away, keeping close in by the trees.

The knight reined in, bringing his horse to a stop, then gestured silently toward Senlac Hill. The runners dipped their heads in obedience, then sped off through the mist toward the woodland on either side of the ridge, one to the right, one to the left.

I remembered to breathe. These couldn't possibly be our people. During all the years I'd been coming to battle recreations in this area, several times before I'd caught sight of shapes in the darkness, ghosts if you will, especially on the coast at Norman's Bay. When we'd arrived last night, I'd seen the flicker of campfires in the surrounding woodlands, fires that I knew didn't exist—in our time.

The knight looked so real, so unlike the other shapes I'd seen. Transfixed, I stared disbelievingly. I could see every detail clearly; the dark gleam of his long mail hauberk, reaching down to cover his knees, his conical helmet, darkened, probably with soot from a campfire—even the nasal showed dark against his skin. I could even hear the muffled jingle of his horse's tack despite the bindings wrapped round it as the horse snorted gently, tossing its head.

Leaning forward, the knight patted his mount's neck, murmuring reassuringly to it.

At my side, Kai shifted, dropping his small bow. As he bent down to pick it up, the knight sat up and looked sharply, his gaze suddenly meeting mine.

I gasped. He could see me! Whirling 'round and grabbing Kai, I thrust him through the gap in the fence. "Run to John's and Gina's tent and wait for me," I said urgently, pushing him into the field. "Hurry, Kai!" Heart pounding, I blocked the stile entrance with my body, bow gripped tightly in my hand, wishing I had the comforting weight of my sword at my side. Tomorrow—if there was a tomorrow for me—I would wear my sword during the battle.

As if he heard my thoughts, the knight's hand clenched around the pommel of the sword hanging from his right hip as he urged his horse toward me. I could feel his fear, twin to my own, reaching out to touch me as if it was a living thing.

He barked words in a language I didn't understand. I shook my head, too terrified to look up at him.

He moved the horse closer and spoke again, this time more harshly. "What are you doing here?" he demanded. "Scouts and foragers were told to be back in the camp before nightfall."

I understood him this time, and understood more: this was no chance meeting. Somehow, this real Norman knight from nine hundred and twenty-four years in the past and I had been brought together for a reason.

"I'm not with your people," I began, raising my face to his, then stopped as, with an exclamation of shock, he recoiled from me in fear. Trusting my instincts, I leaped forward. "I need to tell you about tomorrow," I said.

* * *

Duke William's camp, Wilting Friday October 13, 1066

"God's wounds! Why will you not believe me?" I yelled in exasperation, gripping the pommel of my sword tightly in anger as I looked round the circle of barons seated at the table. "I tell you, he was dressed as one of our archers! It was a true vision of tomorrow I saw!"

"Watch your language, Ranulf!" my father snarled. "We'll have no blasphemy here!"

"Peace, Corbet," said Bishop Odo, the Duke's half-brother, sitting back in his seat, his eyes not leaving my face. "This archer you saw, Ranulf—how did you know he was a Norman?"

"I knew," I muttered, looking away so they'd not see the anger blazing in my eyes.

"You said the archer was clean-shaven, and darker-skinned than the Saxons," my father said forcefully.

"Have the pickets been checked? Could one of them have strayed so far?" murmured Fitz Osber. "Or a forager, returning late?"

"Archers don't do picket duty, and none were sent out foraging alone," said Mortemer. "And certainly none with a child."

"It was a fetch, a sending! Saxon witchcraft—or marsh gas! How, in truth, could one of our archers be there? This Godforsaken land with its mists and marshes reeks of the devil—even the heavens are full of it with that hairy burning star earlier this year! No good'll come of this plan, mark my words!" someone muttered darkly.

Anger surged through me as I peered through the flickering candlelight in the direction of the voice, but I couldn't make the speaker out. How dare these barons—and my father!—doubt my word! I wasn't some virgin boy with an unblooded blade and a wild imagination on the eve of his first battle! I knew what I'd seen, and it hadn't been marsh gas, or a fetch, or a ghost.

"An archer with a child? Hardly an image to strike fear into our hearts, Tesson. And the fiery star we saw in the spring was a sign of God's favor," murmured bishop Odo. "When the Holy Church is with us, how could it be otherwise? I'm inclined to agree with young Normand here that he was sent a vision of the future."

I looked up to find the bishop eyeing me thoughtfully. "And he said that the side striking the first blow would win?"

I nodded. "And that our archers will run out of arrows. He said there will come a point in the battle, late in the day, when we can safely send them forward to collect their spent arrows. After, they should shoot high in the air, from behind the safety of our infantry, so the arrows fall down on the heads of Harold's men. My Lord Duke would know the time to do it, he said, because Harold's men will be pressed so hard together they cannot lift their shields to protect themselves."

"We'll carry the field tomorrow, Odo," said a deep voice

from the far end of the tent. "By all that's holy, I'll be crowned king in London by Christmas as I said I would!"

I blanched, having quite forgot in the heat of argument that I was in the Duke's own tent.

"The Lord is indeed showing us the way," the Duke continued, emerging from the shadows. "He's telling us that my archers hold the key to this battle, as I've said all along they would. You've done well, Ranulf," he said. "I'll not forget this. What news have you from your scouts?"

Recovering from my embarrassment, I boldly met his gaze. "They reported that the Saxons have lit many campfires in an attempt to make us think their numbers are larger than they are. Each fire is tended only by some five or so men."

The Duke reached out, pushing the parchment on which he'd drawn the lay of the land toward the center for all to see. "The archers will be in the front line," he said, touching the map with an imperious finger, "acting as an offensive unit as well as supporting us from behind our shields." He stood there, his dark eyes regarding each one of us from under a creased brow, daring us to disagree.

"They'll like as not shoot our men in the backs," objected the voice I'd heard before. "Just because Le Normand's son saw marsh gas and thought it a fetch isn't a good reason to change our plans at this late stage!"

"I believe him," said a voice I knew well. Taillefer. I turned to look at the bard. He held his cup up to me in salute. "A toast to you, Sir Knight! You are blessed to be singled out for such a vision! If God and the heavens are with us, how can we possibly fail? I, for one, will fight with a lighter heart tomorrow. Sire, a favor if you please," he said to the Duke. "For many a year I've sung of great heroes in your court. Let me be the one to strike the first blow that others may sing of my deeds in years to come."

"Granted, Taillefer," said the Duke.

I quickly lowered my head, lest anyone see the look of shock on my face.

My father signaled me to leave. As I saluted and turned to go, Bishop Odo rose and walked with me to the entrance.

"A vision is rare, indeed, Ranulf," he said quietly as he pulled the tent flap aside and we stepped outside into the damp night air. Seeing the guards, he waved them aside that we might talk privately. "Did this archer tell you anything else?"

I hesitated, not knowing what to say.

"It will go no further, I give you my word."

"He said two more things," I admitted reluctantly. "That we would know he spoke the truth because tomorrow, when the Duke's hauberk is brought to him, it will be offered the wrong way 'round and seen as an ill-omen. But the Duke will say that it means only he'll change his title of Duke for that of King, just as he'll turn his hauberk 'round."

"And the second thing?" Odo asked after a moment's silence.

"That Taillefer will ask to strike the first blow and will be the first to die, your Eminence," I said quietly. I liked Taillefer, who could not? He was a man of good humor and even better songs.

The Bishop said nothing for a moment. Then, "I thought you overly concerned when Taillefer asked his boon of the Duke." He held his hand out to me. Taking it, I knelt to kiss his ring.

"Rest easy, Ranulf. God's will be done tomorrow. It's not your place to worry about what you learned in your vision. You were merely the messenger, and you've discharged that duty with honor." His hand touched my bowed head and he murmured a benediction.

From within the tent, I heard Duke William addressing the barons.

"Good night, Ranulf," said the Bishop.

*   *   *

As I made my way back through the campsite to my tent, I shivered—not from the cold, but from fear for my very soul. I'd still not told the bishop everything. How could I? How could I possibly tell anyone that it hadn't been a *vision?* That the face of the Norman archer I'd seen before me—a face the very mirror image of my own—had been that of a real flesh-and-blood woman, one who shared my family name and claimed to live in the future? I could doubt her words no longer because already the things she'd told me would happen were beginning to come to pass. One thing alone kept my spirits up. If she was from the future, then I knew that I'd survive tomorrow. But it was going to be a long night.

*   *   *

Coda

Harold's plan was simple. He fought war the way his people had learned from the Vikings, by forming a static shield wall and holding fast and relying on the huge two-handed Dane axes that could fell a man or a horse in one blow. But William was a tactician, adapting his plans to meet the changing situations in the battle. It was he who had introduced archery to the battlefield. He had a well-trained and fully armored army of about eight thousand men, more than two thousand of whom were his cavalry, plus heavy infantry and archers. The Saxons had only some two thousand fully trained and armored huscarls, or hearthtroop, who were supported by some five thousand local levies, or fyrdsmen, untrained and in the main unarmored peasants, some using only farm implements as weapons. Their lack of cavalry and archers allowed William to use the advantages of his troops to the full. But there were disadvantages.

The Norman style of fighting was to use William's innovative archers to soften the enemy up first. After the archers' barrage, they would follow this up with the heavy infantry with their spears to open up gaps that the cavalry could use to their advantage. The presence of the Papal Banner and the knowledge that those who fought against William would be excommunicated must also not be ignored for these were very superstitious times. This would cause a huge loss of morale to the Saxon troops.

After Taillefer's fatal single charge at the Saxons, the archers opened fire—but to little effect, as the Saxons took the arrows on their shield wall. William sent in his Breton heavy infantry next. However they were met with an onslaught of missiles from the Saxon slings—rocks and lumps of flint, throwing axes, anything they could lay hands on, following it up with the fearful Dane ax. This panicked the Bretons, and they fled, followed by many in the Saxon right flank who thought the battle nearly won.

William, seeing this, sent his cavalry in support. The Bretons turned, cutting the Saxons off from their lines and slaughtering them. It is unlikely that Harold authorized this, as he had used the tactic of a feigned retreat successfully against his brother Tostig some two weeks previously at the Battle of Stamford Bridge. It's probable that the charge was led by Harold's brothers, Leofwine and Gyrth, who were killed. This was a personal blow to Harold.

Later in the day, William intentionally used the feigned retreat successfully on Harold's left flank, as they hadn't witnessed the slaughter of their comrades on the right. This forced Harold to pull back what remained of his men to the center where they formed a tight wall around him.

Now was William's chance to let his archers, who had run out of arrows earlier in the day, reprovision themselves from the spent arrows on the ground. This done, from behind the safety of the infantry, they shot high into the air, raining arrows down on the heads of the helpless Saxons who were so tightly packed together that even the dead were held upright on their feet. It is at this point that Harold is said to have taken an arrow in the eye.

It was growing dark by now, and many men had been lost on both sides, the Saxon Dane ax doing great damage to both William's cavalry and infantry. Hearing news of Harold's injury or possible death, William risked all in a full frontal attack, knowing that if the battle was not won before night fell, then he had lost everything. There was no retreat possible. He succeeded, and all but the huscarls protecting the now dead Harold were driven into the woods and back up the road to London.

The remainder of Harold's huscarls fought ferociously to the last man, but were finally overcome. And so, the last conqueror of England, William, Duke of Normandy, was crowned King of England on Christmas Day of 1066 in London.

This year will be the Millennium Celebration of the Battle of Senlac Hill, and it falls on the exact day and date of the original battle, Saturday, October 14th. I will be there to meet Ranulf again.

With many thanks to Pete James of "The Vikings!" for his technical help.

WHERE THE BODIES ARE BURIED
by Pierce Askegren

Born in Pittsburgh, **Pierce Askegren** now finds himself held captive in a postage-stamp-sized Balkan nation, where he toils in the service of that land's iron-masked ruler—a madman hell-bent on ruling the world! In between obediently conducting forbidden scientific experiments and scheming to escape, Pierce pecks out stories for various fiction markets. He's written six media novels (mostly based on Marvel Comics properties) and a similar number of media-based short stories (ditto). He also wrote "Foxy Boxer Gal Fights Giant Monster King!" for *The Chick Is in the Mail,* the fourth in Esther Friesner's popular series of anthologies.

"What this outfit needs is a new Jimmy Hoffa."

Marty winced at the other man's words. "That isn't a name we throw around lightly these days," he said mildly.

Chuck Kurilla, seated on the other side of Marty Greimm's cluttered desk, snorted in reply. Kurilla was a big man with broad features and callused hands—the kind of hands that built things and broke them. He looked uncomfortable in the suit and tie. "Don't know why," he said. "Jimmy's long dead and long gone. If he was still around, he'd be running the joint now."

"He's gone, at least," Marty said. He took a breath, held it, then let it go. He wasn't enjoying this conversation, but he hadn't expected to. He had made Kurilla's acquaintance more than once, at various union functions, never finding much common ground with the other man. He had never expected to see him here, in the basement office in local headquarters that he had occupied.

"Dead and gone," Kurilla repeated. "And I want to put his methods to work for me."

Marty stared at him blankly. "Excuse me?" he said.

Kurilla passed the coffee cup he was holding from one hand to the other, then back again. He shifted in his chair. "I'm gonna run for union president, Marty," he said. "This outfit needs someone like Jimmy back at the top. A working man, a guy who's willing to get his hands dirty."

" 'Jimmy'?" Marty asked. "When were you on first names with Mr. Hoffa? 'Sides, he was before your time."

"Never met the guy," Kurilla acknowledged easily. "Back then, I was an apprentice puke in a machine shop outside of Lansing. But I knew he was what I wanted to be."

Marty didn't like the way the conversation was going. His stomach suddenly hurt. There were crackers in his desk drawer and milk in his small refrigerator. He wanted both, but putting out the fire in his belly would mean breaking bread with Chuck Kurilla, and he did not want to do that.

"You knew him, though, didn't you, Marty?" Kurilla continued.

"Not well," Greimm said. That wasn't entirely true. He just didn't like talking about Hoffa or his times. They were things better left buried and unmentioned. "But I did a little work for him."

"Yeah, I heard about that," Kurilla said smoothly. "More than a little. Nothing rough and tumble, though, right?"

Marty's stomach hurt worse, but he didn't say anything.

Kurilla continued. "I'm gonna run for president," he repeated. "I may not be management's golden boy, but I can win."

Marty thought that he just might, too—not in the next election, but maybe the one after that, after Kurilla had made even more of a name for himself. Certainly, the man had risen swiftly through the ranks, from near-anonymity to in-house prominence, even if the public at large had never heard his name. In the past ten years, Chuck Kurilla had built a reputation as an effective organizer and a skilled negotiator.

Greimm had heard something about just how Kurilla had won that reputation—muttered rumors about broken legs and missing teeth and gasoline-filled bottles with burning rags stuffed in their necks. But there were always rumors like that.

And Marty always heard them.

"It's a free country," he said. "There are folks ahead of you in line, though."

"I can jump the line," Kurilla said. "If I have your support."

So it was coming to this. Marty felt as if a fist had been rammed into his gut. "I don't know what you're talking about," he said. "I'm just a glorified accountant."

"You? You ain't just no accountant, Marty. I know about you."

Marty remembered another man who had spoken words like those, what seemed like a lifetime ago. The words, the cadence, the casual tone that promised equally casual brutality—he had heard all these before.

Kurilla sounded like Jimmy sounded.

"You don't know anything about me," he said.

"I know enough," Kurilla said calmly. "You're a hold-over, a fossil. Maybe you keep books now, but that's not what you did in the old days—not all that you did, anyway." He gazed at Marty and grinned. "How many administrations have you seen? Ten?"

"Twelve."

Kurilla nodded. "Twelve. That's a lot of water under a lot of bridges. Presidents come, presidents go—you stay. The Feds come in with a big broom and they sweep the joint clean, but they miss a spot—*your* spot. Nobody talks about you, but everyone knows who you are." He snickered, grinned. "I figured you must know where a lot of bodies are buried, Marty. Maybe all of them."

Marty tried to laugh. "Or maybe I'm just good with numbers," he said.

Kurilla snickered again. "Nobody's *that* good, Marty."

A long moment passed. There had been a time when

Marty Greimm could outwait anyone, but now he realized suddenly, sadly, that the time was gone.

"I want your backing," Kurilla continued. He gestured at the mountain range of locked cabinets that ran along one wall of Marty's office. "Your files."

Greimm shook his head. He had held onto his hard-won role for so long only by maintaining scrupulous neutrality. No one bothered the old man in the corner if the old man didn't bother them. "I can't do that," he said.

"You can."

Marty's head was throbbing too, now, and he found himself staring at Kurilla's thick neck, at the fleshy part just above his collar. "I can, but I won't. Why should I?"

"You're an old man, Marty. You're a holdover. The guys who brought you in are gone, and the guys who keep you here don't do it 'cause they like you. You get to stay because you don't make trouble. But your muscle's gone." Kurilla's eyes went suddenly hard. "I'm not part of the old guard. Maybe you can make trouble for me, but I can make more for you."

"Is that a threat?" Marty forced himself to speak calmly.

Kurilla smirked faintly and shrugged.

Marty stared. There was a brushed-finish aluminum letter opener on his desk, not much edge but plenty of point. Marty, even without looking, knew precisely where it lay and how many inches his fingers would have to move to seize it and how much force it would take to drive the blade into Kurilla's neck. He had never been much for muscle work, but he knew the old way of doing things.

Then what? There would be blood and a body to deal with, and investigations. Would management back him, or would he end up in a little gray room with a barred door, like so many other old-timers?

"What exactly is it you want?" he asked again.

"Headlines," Kurilla said easily. "Not now, but later. I'm running as a reformer. I wanna know where the bodies are buried and I wanna be the one to find them."

"A run like that could bring the house crashing down," Marty said. "Again."

Kurilla continued as if he hadn't heard. "There's folks who have overstayed their welcome, and I want to help them go." He grinned again, a predator's smile that stretched his broad features. "Most of all, Marty, I wanna be the guy who hands you your gold watch and pension certificate so you can't help anyone else the way you're gonna help me."

"I'll think about it," Marty said. He couldn't think of anything else to say.

"You'll do it." Kurilla stood, straightened his jacket. "Don't worry, Marty. It's gonna be just like the old days."

Marty shuddered.

* * *

After Kurilla left, Marty lurched out of his chair and to the small refrigerator. He gulped milk and swallowed crackers, but the fire in his stomach lingered. There was a bottle of the pink stuff in his coat pocket, so he gulped some of that, too.

Four years. Four years were all he needed. Another four years and he could go on full retirement with a bonus and a decent pension, not the crumbs he would get if he quit now.

Kurilla wasn't going to give him those years. Whether he cooperated or not, Kurilla wasn't going to let him hang around much longer.

He forced himself to breathe slowly, thinking of mountain lakes and midnight skies. The unwelcome fury that had swept through him so suddenly a few moments before faded until it was just a memory. Finally, he reached for the phone.

"Nick?" he said a moment later. "Marty, in Accounting. Something's come up, and I need to see you." He listened for a moment. "Ten minutes, then."

In one corner, near the refrigerator, was a small wash basin with a mirror above it. Marty glanced in the polished glass and made a look of disgust at the old man's face staring back at him. Nervous sweat had pasted what was left of his hair flat against his scalp, and his lips were crusted with milk and antacid. He ran a comb through the hair and dabbed at his lips with a moistened paper towel, then ran hot water to wash his hands. He was looking down, watching the lather grow, when he heard the voice.

"Bastard."

The word came from somewhere behind him.

"Son of a bitch thinks he can come in and tear down what I built."

Marty knew the voice, and he knew that he couldn't be hearing it.

"Don't turn around," the speaker continued. "You won't like what you'd see. It ain't easy on the other side, Marty. Things get ugly pretty fast. You look in the mirror, instead."

Slowly, careful not to glance in any direction other than dead ahead, Marty raised his eyes to the mirror's slightly mist-clouded surface. His face and one another were reflected back, one with broad features and hard eyes. For a split second, Marty clung to the hope that Chuck Kurilla had come back to bother him some more—but he knew that the hope was futile.

"Hiya," Jimmy Hoffa said.

For a dead guy, he sounded pretty good.

"H–hello, Mr. Hoffa," Marty said slowly. It was not a name he said lightly.

The dead man's head swung from side to side. "C'mon, Marty. We're pals. It's Jimmy, remember?"

"Hello, Jimmy." Marty flinched as he saw the dead man's lips part in a grin as wolfish as Kurilla's.

"Good. That's better. It's been a long time. Too long."

"Yes, Jimmy—much too long," Marty lied. He didn't know what else to say. All he knew was that his skin suddenly felt three sizes too tight, and his fingers, even under the hot water, had turned to ice.

Hoffa's reflection nodded. "I just wanted to let you know I'm still on your side. This mook, this Kurilla, he's trouble. You're gonna need help with him, and the pansy upstairs isn't going to give it to you."

"Nick isn't a—"

Something that cast a reflection like a hand but didn't feel like one slapped Marty on the back. "Hah!" Jimmy Hoffa said, his voice suddenly jovial. "Same old Marty! Always with the rose glasses! I love ya, kid!" His image began to waver and fade. "When you come back from meeting with the pansy, we'll talk some more, okay? I'm gonna show you what you have to do."

Marty stared carefully at the mirror. When, at last, only his own image stared back at him, he rinsed his hands. Moving with great precision, he adjusted his collar and straightened his tie. Panic and disbelief and terror and worry surged though him, warring for dominance. Somehow, he found it in himself to smile faintly

It had been many years since anyone had called Marty Greimm "kid."

*   *   *

"You have a problem?" Nick Wulfekuhle asked. His office was on the top floor. Behind him, the Chicago skyline stretched into the distance; three of his four office walls were glass. To one side, Marty could see the construction site for the new wing.

In the best of times, Marty didn't like calling on his boss. The title of the lean blond man with soft clean hands changed almost every week, but Marty knew that his duties did not. No matter where they put him on the org chart, Wulfekuhle was one of the union's real powerbrokers, a man who could cause a lot of trouble for a lot of people with a few well-placed words. That was bad enough, but making things worse was the fact that Wulfekuhle came from an entirely different tradition that Greimm, or Kurilla, or even Hoffa. Wulfekuhle hadn't built his power the old-fashioned way, by building coalitions and breaking jaws; he had come to the Brotherhood fresh out of college, and climbed most of the way to the top with nothing more than a degree.

That frightened Marty.

"Does the problem have a name?" Wulfekuhle prompted. He had a soft voice, and he spoke cleanly and neatly.

Marty nodded. "Chuck Kurilla," he said. "Regional Director for the Machi—"

"I know who Kurilla is." That was another Wulfekuhle knack that Marty found unnerving. The younger man knew almost every name on the union rolls, or at least any name that Marty had heard. "What about him?"

"He wants to make a play for the presidency," Marty said.

"So?" Wulfekuhle obviously wanted to get back to the single sheet of paper that occupied his otherwise barren desktop. Not for the first time, Marty wondered where he kept the phone. "Let him be president if he wants," Wulfekuhle said. "It makes no difference to me."

"There's a problem. He wants to run as a reformer. There are some cages he wants to rattle."

"Ambitious." Wulfekuhle said the word with mild distaste.

"He thinks he's gonna be another Jimmy Hof—"

Wulfekuhle raise his hand and cut him off. "There are names better not to mention. We've worked very hard for years now to clean shop. The unfortunate gentleman you started to mention would have no place in the current organization. His memory haunts our operations enough as it is." He paused. "But there are still many rugs with dirt—old dirt—under them, and I don't want Kurilla sweeping it back out."

"So what do I do?"

"You say there's a problem. I say you solve it."

"But I can't just—"

Wulfekuhle cut him off again. "Marty, I don't mind telling you that *your* name comes up fairly often in budget and staffing meetings. Some of us see you as an unpleasant reminder of days better forgotten. I see you that way, for that matter."

Marty winced.

"But you've devoted most of your life to the unions,

doing whatever it is you do. It seems contrary to the spirit of the enterprise to let you go—as long as you can make yourself useful."

Marty didn't say anything.

"Solve the problem," Wulfekuhle repeated.

"Yes, sir," Marty said, choking back his fury at having to kowtow to a man half his age.

"Good." Wulfekuhle nodded. He picked up his paper and began to read.

Marty knew that it was time to go.

* * *

"See? I knew the pansy wouldn't be any help," Hoffa said from somewhere behind Marty's left shoulder.

"I really don't think he's—"

"Ah. You know what I mean." Hoffa was in full fettle. He shot Marty a reflected grin and a wink. "Never did an honest day's work in his life. Never worked with his hands."

While Marty had been upstairs, the ghost had done some rearranging. The mirror had been propped up on Marty's desk. Hoffa's profile moved back and forth on the silvered pane as the ghost spoke, and Marty realized with a start that his visitor was pacing.

"Never thought it would come to this," Hoffa continued. "You spend your life building something—hell, you give your life for it—and they turn it over to the pansies to run."

"It took a while," Marty said slowly. "And it isn't all bad. The world's changed a lot, and men like Wulfekuhle—"

"Hah. Men." Hoffa snorted. "Ain't no *men* like Wulfe-kuhle."

Marty decided it was time to change the subject. "What brought you back, Jimmy?" He was very much afraid that the answer would be "old business." Marty knew a lot about the old days, but didn't know what had happened to Jimmy Hoffa or who had made it happen.

And he very much didn't want to know.

"Brought me back?" Hoffa asked. "What? You think

I'm here for revenge or somethin'? Hah! I'll tell you what brought me back, Marty." The ghost paused. "*You* brought me back."

Marty blinked. Keeping his eyes fixed on the mirror and working by touch, he opened his desk drawer and pulled out a bottle that had languished there for more than a year, ever since a misunderstanding but considerate temp had given it to him.

"That's the ticket," Hoffa said as Marty poured most of the bourbon into a coffee mug. "Milk's for kids. Man, I wish I could still drink. And what I wouldn't give for a good cigar!"

"How did I bring you back, Jimmy?" Marty asked. He drank, and felt some microscopic percentage of tension seep out of him. He wasn't supposed to drink anymore, but his stomach was making no complaint.

"The thing with the letter opener. When you wanted to ice pick Kurilla."

Marty remembered the sudden fury he had felt at the thick-necked machinist. "That—*that's* what brought you back?" he asked.

"Yeah. Or brought me the rest of the way. I was never very far away," Hoffa said. "Not from this outfit."

Marty could understand that.

"So, what are you going to do about Kurilla?" Hoffa asked again.

"Do about him?" Marty asked.

"He's a clever son of a bitch, I'll give 'im that," Hoffa continued. "Fuckin' Machiavellian."

The reference came as a surprise. "I didn't know you read Machiavelli," Marty said.

"Read him, hell," Hoffa said. "We fight like cats and dogs on the other side. See, he's got this screwy theory about what a general should do when—"

"You talk with Machiavelli?" The very idea was staggering.

"Yeah. And Patton and all the rest. It's not like you think on the other side," Hoffa said. "It's not like anyone thinks. But some things stay the same. The stuff that interested you most in life, still interests you there."

Marty shuddered. He didn't want to think about it. "I don't know," he said.

"Don't know?"

"Don't know what to do about Kurilla."

"That ain't what I asked," Hoffa said. "I'm not worried about what *you're* going to do—just about what *we're* going to do."

Marty drank some more bourbon.

"I know guys like this Kurilla," Hoffa said. "I know how they think. Cock of the walk, big boy on the block, right?"

Marty nodded. He couldn't think of anything to say.

"Guys like that, they give me a pain. I can respect 'em, but they give me a pain."

Marty almost laughed. Once upon a time, he had said the same thing about Hoffa.

"Well, I know how to deal with that," Hoffa said. Still somewhere behind Marty, he leaned closer. The big face that was reflected next to Marty's wore an amiable expression. "Close your eyes," Hoffa murmured. "I gotta do some stuff, and I don't want you should see me."

Marty closed his eyes. He felt no fear. The booze had made him calm. He sat there without speaking, watching the faint trace of sparks that always came when he closed his eyes. He sipped whiskey from his coffee mug—half empty now—and listened to Hoffa's ghost open file cabinet drawers and close them, humming tunelessly all the while. Finally, after a period that could have been seconds or hours, the voice came again from behind Marty.

"Okay," Hoffa said. "You can look."

Half a dozen file folders sat perched on Marty's desk now. They were old, battered manila of a style that he hadn't used in years. Even without looking, he knew what they held. Atop the stack was a revolver.

"I didn't even know I still had that," he said softly, sadly.

"Yeah, it took some looking. You had it in the archives." The ghost paused. "It's a Colt, though. Why did you have it under 'S'?"

"Stood for 'security,' " Marty said.

The ghost laughed. At least, Marty hoped it was a laugh. Whatever it was, it wasn't a sound anything human should be able to make.

"The hell with that," Hoffa said. "Don't worry about security. Go looking for control—control and power. You'll get security in the bargain. And you don't have power if you don't use it."

"More Machiavelli," Marty said.

"Heh. Yeah, he's got his point, all right," Hoffa said. "Now fix yourself some coffee. There's some calls you got to make and some work you have to do, and I don't want you tripping all over yourself."

* * *

The night was colder than it should have been, and the wind cut through Marty like a chainsaw as he shuffled along the battered planking that ran along the main foundation forms. He trembled as he walked, and he peered carefully into the night. At least the night was clear and free of fog, a rarity for Chicago at this time of year. The moon was full and Marty could see every girder, every scaffold, every bit of idle equipment that ringed the deserted construction site. From nearby, he could hear the steady rumble of the diesel mixer that kept the concrete flowing and available to pour. Earlier that day, workers had completed the first of three pours for the annex foundation. Tomorrow, they would begin their day by pouring a fresh Niagara of cement.

Marty's left hand gripped his briefcase's worn handle; his right, hidden in his jacket pocket, was curled around the revolver's reassuring grip.

"That you, Marty?" Kurilla's familiar voice hung in the cold air. Near the lip of the main foundation, the big man stepped out from behind a skid of cinder blocks.

"It's me," Marty said sadly. He felt a sudden sympathy, maybe even affection for Kurilla. At the very least, he felt pity.

White teeth glinted in the gloom as the big man smiled. "Not like the movies, is it?" he asked.

The question confused Marty. "Huh?" he asked.

"Not like the movies," Kurilla repeated. "It's easy to think about doing something like this, but it takes real stones to pull it off."

Marty didn't like where this was going. "I don't know what you're talking about."

Kurilla hit him.

His big callused right hand came up in an open slapping motion. Kurilla moved fast for a man his size. A sound like breaking wood echoed in Marty's ears and fireworks erupted in his eyes. The world spun crazily, and when it righted itself, Marty had fallen to the dirty wooden walkway and was looking up at Kurilla, who had Marty's gun in his hand.

"You're an old man, Marty," Kurilla said softly. "This isn't the time to learn new tricks."

"I don't know what you mean," Marty said. From behind him, he heard a muttered curse.

It was in Hoffa's voice.

"You got somebody with you?" Kurilla asked.

Marty shook his head. "No. Nobody."

"Okay," Kurilla said. He held the gun loosely in one hand while he used the other to grab and open the briefcase. "See, one thing I've learned is to be careful when a guy starts doing something that doesn't seem right for him. And an accountant, four years from retirement, offering to meet a tough customer at a construction site . . . that accountant—even if he's not just an accountant—he's doing something that don't seem right." He grinned again. "And I *am* a tough customer, Marty."

Marty had to nod at that.

"Now, let's see what you got," Kurilla said. He held the papers at an angle, making maximum use of the strong, clear moonlight. He made approving sounds as he skimmed one document and then another. "Nice, Marty. Very nice," he said. "Who would have thought it? All this good stuff, sitting dusty and forgotten in the basement for all these years."

"Some things are better forgotten," Marty said hollowly.

"Yeah, well, I'd like to forget about this little bonehead play of yours, Marty," Kurilla said. "Seeing as how you've done me such a favor and all. But I can't."

"The night watchman will hear the shot," Marty said. That was a lie; he had pulled the man off duty himself, with a call that supposedly had come from Wulfekuhle's office.

"I'll take that risk," Kurilla said.

Marty felt something like hands rest gently on his shoulders. He felt the presence behind him lean closer, and he heard Hoffa's voice whisper urgently in his left ear.

"Don't look back, Marty," the dead man murmured. "You look straight ahead, and you'll come out of this all right."

"Who is that? Who else is here?" Kurilla, all humor fled from his voice, barked the words. His eyes darted from side to side. "Show yourself!"

"Not such a good idea, you stupid mook," Hoffa said from behind Marty. "But since you're calling the shots—"

Kurilla's gaze shifted. His eyes bulged in their sockets as he stared at something behind Marty. They bulged— then exploded.

Marty gasped in horror.

Kurilla screamed. He dropped Marty's gun and files and clawed at his ruined eyes. Kurilla sobbed and babbled words that might have been prayers, stumbled and fell, toppling over the edge of the construction dig and into the blackness that yawned below. There was a thudding impact. Then silence.

"Pansy," Jimmy Hoffa said. The word hung in the darkness long after he had spoken it.

Marty trembled.

"You gonna be okay, Marty?" the ghost asked.

Marty's heart raced and his breath came in rapid gasps, but it was nothing he couldn't handle. He realized with surprise that he felt more alive than he had in many years.

Slowly, his tremors became a nod, and his moaning became a muttered acquiescence.

"Yeah," he forced the words out. "Yeah, I'll be okay."

"Good," Hoffa said. He laughed. "This business, it takes me back," he continued. "Just like old times. What's it that the ballplayer said? Déjà vu, all over again?"

Marty managed to laugh at the words.

Hoffa continued. "We ain't done yet," he said. "Gather up your gun and files and help me with the cement mixer. Then you and me got more work to do."

*　　*　　*

"No trace," Marty said a few days later. "Kurilla left town, but he didn't leave a trail."

His voice sounded a little strained to him, but Wulfe-kuhle didn't seem to notice. The slender man had risen at Marty's entrance—a first—and now he stood silhouetted against the Chicago skyline. It was a dramatic pose, and one that he had probably practiced for many hours, but Marty was not impressed.

"How is that possible?" Wulfekuhle asked.

Marty shrugged. "He got in a car and he left."

"Why? Kurilla didn't strike me as a man to cut and run."

Marty shrugged again. "I don't know," he said. "I thought he'd stay and fight it. That's what he said, when I confronted him."

"You're talking about a lot of money," Wulfekuhle said.

"He must have been at it for a long time. Maybe to finance his run for office. It was a complicated scam."

"Surprising that Kurilla would find such an elaborate way to siphon funds from his division's accounts. Even more surprising that he could make them so difficult to trace," Wulfekuhle said. He gazed levelly at Marty. "That's more of an accountant's crime."

Marty thought about the long hours he had spent during the past few nights. He thought about labyrinthine paper trails and hastily improvised money-laundering processes, and he thought about forged signatures and doctored papers of incorporation. He thought about every dirty accounting trick he had learned in his long years on the sidelines, and he thought about seven hundred thousand dollars and change, waiting for him in a Venezuelan numbered bank account. He thought about the kind of life that money could buy.

He smiled. "We're all capable of surprises, sir," he said.

Wulfekuhle turned to gaze out the window. "So we have a scandal and a mystery, but on a scale we can handle. We have another Hoffa after all, though."

"Only if we treat it that way. Kurilla was—isn't well known."

Something outside had caught Wulfekuhle's attention. The big crane at the center of the new annex had pivoted and was lowering a cage of steel girders into place.

"There was a disturbance on the construction site earlier this week," the blond man said slowly, still gazing into the distance. "Trespassers."

Marty kept his voice carefully neutral. "What did the watchman say?"

"Nothing. He was on an errand. Someone had told him—well, never mind what he was told." He turned to face Marty again, and this time there was something odd about the expression he wore, some nuance that Marty had never seen on his features before.

Fear?

"You say there's no way to find Kurilla?" he asked.

"No way that I know, Nick," Marty said. "But I'm no expert at that kind of stuff."

Wulfekuhle nodded. "Too bad, really," he said. "You and I may not like them, but men like Kurilla are the very heart and soul of any labor movement."

"The very foundation, sir."

*   *   *

Marty stepped into the elevator and thumbed the *B*. He faced resolutely ahead as thick metal doors slid together and the elevator cage began to drop.

"Hah. I like to bust a gut when you made that crack,

Marty," Jimmy Hoffa said. His face grinned out from the doors' polished metal surface. "If I had a gut to bust."

Despite himself, Marty grinned.

"How many years you got to go, Marty?"

"Four until full retirement." Not that he needed to worry about the pension anymore. Not that he was sure he wanted to retire. "Six until mandatory."

"Guys like that Wulfekuhle pansy don't have to retire, do they?"

Marty shook his head. "No. They're exempt."

"Something to think about, Marty."

Marty nodded again and watched the lighted numbers on the elevator control panel change.

It was, in fact, something to think about.

AN ANSWERED PRAYER

by Gene DeWeese

While a tech writer, **Gene DeWeese** produced everything from cleaning instructions for U.S. Air Force computer ball bearings to NASA space navigation texts. Since Robert Coulson recruited him to help out on a *Man From U.N.C.L.E.* novel thirty-odd years ago, he's also produced thirty-odd books, including two—*The Wanting Factor* and *Something Answered*—that explore themes similar to those in his tale in this volume, "*An Answered Prayer*." Another book, on doll-making, explains how to make dried-apple shrunken heads. He lives in Milwaukee with his wife Beverly and two one-eyed cats, Toughie and Suzilla, and two "normal" ones, Octavia and Roscoe.

When Olivia Wilson awoke and saw the figure, standing silent and translucent in the near darkness of her bedroom, she assumed it was a result of the tumor. Visual hallucinations were among the symptoms she could expect, Dr. Waverly and others had warned her.

Reminded, she grimaced, imagining once again that she could feel the tumor itself, expanding like a slowly inflating balloon deep inside her brain. Impossible, of course. The brain couldn't "feel" anything that happened to itself, only interpret what happened to the rest of her. That was another thing the doctors had told her, one among many, and she had no reason to disbelieve any of them, no matter how much she wished she could.

"Inoperable" was another of their unwelcome but believable pronouncements, along with "resistant to chemotherapy" and "largely inaccessible to radiation."

And, finally, when she had demanded a specific prognosis, "six months, give or take."

Another wave of guilt swept over her, as if the malignancy were her fault, as if she had done something to bring it into existence. It was virtually the same reaction she had had when Doctor Waverly had broken the news to her two months ago in early February. After a shocked, stomach-wrenching silence, her first question—her first concern—had been "Will I be able to finish out the school year?"

Waverly had looked at her oddly for a moment before catching himself and restoring his professionally bland facade. "Perhaps," he had said, "but that's not something you should be worrying about. I'm sure Father Haggerty won't have any trouble finding someone to take over your classes."

Intellectually, she knew he was right, of course, but that knowledge hadn't helped then and it didn't help now. It had *never* helped. Even as a child, when a cold or flu or some other ailment kept her from school, she felt guilty about each and every day she missed. It was even worse once she became a teacher. A commitment was a commitment, and when you broke one, no matter what the reason, the ones you made the commitment to had the right to be disappointed in you. Particularly children.

She looked at the robed hallucination again, consciously willing it to go away.

To her surprise, it obliged, undulating like gentle waves on a pond, imposing ripples on the door frame visible behind it for a few moments before it vanished altogether.

*   *   *

Two nights later the figure was standing closer, bare inches from the side of her bed, when she awoke, chilled despite the extra blanket she had pulled over herself while she slept.

"Go away," she said softly as she pulled the blankets more tightly around her. "You're not real."

The face, shaggily bearded and sharp-featured, perhaps slightly more solid-seeming than the first time, tilted forward to look down at her.

And was gone.

But not before the close-set, piercing eyes met hers for just an instant and she saw—imagined she saw—the pain that lay buried in their depths. A reflection of her own? she wondered.

Hallucination or not, this time it took her more than an hour to drift back into a fitful sleep.

*   *   *

Twice more it came to her in the night. Each time it was a little more solid-seeming but still vanished at her command. Each time, however, its pleading eyes kept her from sleep a little longer.

A sign that the end was nearer than Waverly and the others had estimated?

But before she could work up the nerve to call Waverly and ask, the question answered itself, though not in a way she had expected.

It happened near the end of her ten o'clock English class. As usual, she was in front of her desk as she talked with the twenty-odd fifth graders. Her only concession to the tumor was that, instead of standing halfway between her desk and the front row, she half leaned against it, bracing herself in case one of the increasingly frequents bouts of dizziness struck without the usual warning. She had just glanced up at the clock on the back wall and was about to tell them to expect a quiz the following Monday when the entire class literally gasped, their eyes swiveling in startled unison toward a point a few feet to her right.

Frowning, keeping one steadying hand on the desktop, she turned.

And froze, her heart suddenly pounding thunderously.

The robed hallucination stood in front of the dusty green chalkboard, the next day's assignment just barely discernable through it.

And it had changed. Or perhaps she was now able to see certain details that had been obscured by the darkness of her room.

Details such as the drops of translucent blood, black against the green of the chalkboard, that dotted its forehead and dripped from its dangling fingers.

Olivia swallowed audibly and looked back at the class. "You see it, too?" she asked softly.

A few of them nodded. A few began, inexplicably to her, to cry.

And then, as she caught a shimmering movement out of the corner of her eye, one of the children screamed, and then another.

A moment later, half of the children were bolting for the door, leaving books and backpacks and pencils scattered in their wake, while the other half sat motionless, eyes wide.

Olivia felt a tingle, like an electric charge, on her shoulder. Looking down, she saw a ghostly hand streaked with blood sinking slowly into her flesh. Involuntarily, she jerked away, the way she would have done if it had been a spider.

"Go away!" she said in a trembling voice, falling back on what had worked before.

But this time it didn't. As she backed away, the figure—mass hallucination?—seemed to grow more solid, not less, the blood on forehead and hands taking on, finally, a reddish tinge.

Behind her, she heard footsteps coming rapidly down the hall and into the back of the room. Then a gasp.

Turning, she saw Sister Angelique, the gray-haired nun who had a social studies class in the next room every day at this time. The tiny woman had dropped to her knees and was crossing herself vigorously as she bowed her head.

Father Haggerty arrived five minutes later. He went paper-pale as he came through the door and saw the apparition, still just insubstantial enough for the chalkboard to be visible through it. An instant later he joined Sister Angelique and five other nuns on their knees. Olivia, having collapsed into one of the chairs that lined the back of the room, was still willing it to disappear but no longer speaking the words out loud, not even in a whisper.

When it became obvious the figure was not going to do anything but stand silently, its pain-filled eyes fastened on

Olivia, Father Haggerty, his head still bowed, got to his feet. He was still pale but his normally ruddy color was beginning to return to his face as he took Olivia's arm and led her into the hallway, leaving the nuns to continue kneeling.

"What—" he began, but before he could finish the question, the story of the previous nights' hallucinations came flooding quietly from Olivia's lips.

By the time she had straggled to the end, his face had turned ashen once again. Haltingly, apologetically, he told her of the group prayers he had been leading at late-evening services since her illness had been diagnosed, services that were held at approximately the time she had been awakened by the apparitions.

*   *   *

A news crew—one reporter, one cameraman—from Channel 7 showed up twenty minutes later, smirking and rolling their eyes in what they probably thought was a discreet display of how they felt about having been sent out to give some wacko his or her fifteen minutes of Warhol time.

But then they entered the classroom.

For a long moment there was dead silence as the smirks gave way to gapes. Then the reporter jabbed the cameraman in the arm hard enough to make him wince.

"Get this on tape!" she snapped. "Now!"

Snatching her cell phone from the pocket-laden jacket she wore over her fashion-statement, stand-up outfit, she hit the top number on her speed dial list.

"Pete, this is Gail," she said when the news director picked up on the first ring. "Get Walt the hell over to St. Benedict! I don't know what we've got here, but it'll bring in more ratings than that piddly warehouse fire you sent him to."

She paused, grimacing, then plunged back in. "Just take my word for it, Pete! Whatever this is, you don't want Channel 9 getting it on the air first!"

Regretting the fact that you couldn't hang up a cell

phone by slamming it down the way you could with normal phones, she disconnected and stuffed it back into one of her many pockets.

Resisting the temptation to approach the figure—vision? apparition?—and try to touch it, she hurried back into the hallway. Father Haggerty was still there, still talking to a pale, middle-aged woman. Must be the nun who goes with the room, she thought. Olivia, someone had said her name was. Better get to her first, before everyone and his brother shows up.

And before that thing, whatever it is, vanishes.

* * *

Whatever it was, it didn't vanish. Virtually everyone and his brother did show up, however.

By noon, news crews from all the local TV stations were there, *with* their remote feed equipment, as well as reporters and photographers from the local newspapers, not to mention someone from each of a dozen radio stations, be it a talkative drive–time dj or the owner of the anonymous voice that reads the headlines and traffic reports every half hour.

By midafternoon, the networks, no longer satisfied with parasiting the local coverage, began to arrive with their own news crews, starting with CNN. Long before network evening news time, the St. Benedict parking lot was jammed with what looked like semi-trailers with satellite dishes on their roofs and heavy cable snaking every which way.

And every single producer, reporter, and anchor wanted to talk to—and photograph—Olivia. To her great relief, however, Father Haggerty had, in effect, thrown himself into the breach right at the start, successfully sidetracking Gail Sandler of Channel 7 and blocking everyone who followed. With the help of the other teachers, he even arranged for her to slip out of the building, unnoticed, and reach her upstairs flat a few blocks away.

But her relief was short-lived. Her phone started ringing within minutes, and after giving identical answers to the first ten callers—"I have no idea who or what it is or why it appears!"—she unplugged the phone.

Within minutes, the first of the cameras and curiosity seekers showed up on her front lawn, still soggy from last weekend's quick-melting early-spring snow. The forcefully cheerful lies of her landlady Marge Whelan, who lived in the downstairs flat, sent many of them on wild goose chases around town long enough for Father Haggerty to talk Chief Gordon and Sheriff Andrews into posting enough patrolmen and deputies to force the growing crowd to keep their distance and their composure. Even so, it took nearly a dozen arrests for "disturbing the peace" to convince them that trampling the lawn and shouting questions at closed, second-floor windows wasn't a good idea.

Inside, behind blinds drawn before sunset for the first time in months, Olivia watched television with a growing sense of dread that the entire world was going mad. Every station or network that had anything even remotely resembling a news department was covering the "miracle" nonstop. The figure itself, once it had become clear that its image could be captured on tape and film and that that image could be successfully broadcast to billions of TV sets around the world, was on the screen continuously, even if occasionally reduced to occupying a small window in one corner. Father Haggerty's early afternoon press conference, staged in the St. Benedict auditorium, was almost as popular, being replayed and analyzed again and again on every channel.

He had kept it as simple as possible, ignoring all questions and refusing to make any claims about the identity of the "figure." His main message, stated a dozen different ways, boiled down to "Stay calm." He had told Olivia he would try to keep her name out of it, but it had been too late for that when the first reporter arrived on the scene. Since Father Haggerty was the only one she had told about the earlier manifestations, however, he was able to at least keep *them* a secret, along with the disturbing fact that each one had coincided approximately with one of the group prayers he had been leading during evening services since he had learned of her terminal diagnosis. He couldn't, however, keep the members of the congregation silent about the special morning service he had been conducting at the very moment the classroom manifestation had appeared.

Nor was the congregation nearly as reticent as Father Haggerty when it came to answering questions. Most were more than willing to share the few facts they had and to speculate endlessly about what, if anything, those facts meant. And if that weren't enough, they were soon joined on screens everywhere by the professional talking heads that came out of the electronic woodwork whenever they were needed to fill air time, which was whenever the network news organizations latched onto a story and decided it deserved continuous coverage despite the fact that nothing was really happening.

As a result, every channel treated Olivia to endless and sometimes rancorous discussions as to why this particular prayer from among the millions uttered daily had apparently been answered in a form more concrete than any had been answered in hundreds, if not thousands, of years. When it was revealed that she was not only not Catholic but not even a Believer—an agnostic, at best—the faces of some of the St. Benedict parents hardened, and the questions of many shifted to why she was even teaching at St. Benedict in the first place.

"An excellent, dedicated lay teacher, " Father Haggerty and several nuns insisted, but that was never enough to soften all the faces nor to stop the questions. Carolyn Musgrave, who had just recovered from surgery for ovarian cancer, looked particularly grim as she demanded to know why *she* had not been the subject of such prayers rather than having a few candles perfunctorily lit for her. She wasn't mollified when it was pointed out that no one knew—or could even make an educated guess—whether or not Olivia had been "cured," either by the prayers or by the apparition's appearance.

Olivia herself, now completely exhausted, certainly didn't *feel* cured. In fact, she not only agreed with Mrs. Musgrave but resented the fact that Father Haggerty had gone behind her back to conduct these prayer services, something in which she obviously hadn't believed. It was one thing to try to convert her openly, face-to-face, or to banter with her now and then about her "lack of faith," as both he and half the nuns had done routinely, but this was altogether different, no matter what the results, no matter how good his intentions.

And to do it for her and not for others, particularly for those who believed in such things and would have *wanted* it done for them, struck her as especially unfair. And there were almost certainly others in Father Haggerty's flock who had similarly serious illnesses and who resented the special treatment Olivia appeared to have gotten.

But there was nothing she could think to do about it now.

Except to wait out what remained of the six months and, as she still assumed she would, die approximately on schedule.

* * *

The first of what one of the anchors quickly dubbed "supplicants" appeared at the school in late afternoon: Harry Brockman, fifty years old with advanced ALS, in a wheelchair for months. His daughter Audrey brought him and, when the wheelchair was blocked by the permanently mounted classroom seats, struggled to help him to his feet and supported him as he shuffled painfully down the aisle while an apprehensive Father Haggerty and hundreds of millions of TV viewers watched.

As Brockman's barely controlled hand passed through the apparition, the entire figure seemed to shimmer as if, Olivia thought, it was about to vanish.

But nothing happened, and as the hand was withdrawn and the figure steadied on hundreds of millions of screens and Brockman was helped back into his wheelchair, a collective sigh of sympathetic disappointment flowed out across the world.

But despite the seeming failure, Brockman was followed by at first a trickle and then a flood of supplicants of all kinds who, while waiting their turn, joined together in prayer. For the majority, however, things went about as they had with Brockman: No apparent results.

But for a growing number—those with psychosomatic ailments, Olivia, still forcing herself to watch, was certain—there were modest successes. Crutches thrown away. Backs straightened. Migraines banished.

And with each supplicant, cured or not, the number and fervor of prayers grew. Crowds began gathering everywhere around the world, in churches, town squares, auditoriums, anywhere that could hold a large-screen TV set and a few dozen people. And more and more people, the cameras and anchors reported, were lining up to touch the image on the screens, just as the supplicants in St. Benedict's were lining up to "touch" the figure itself.

Just after ten, less than twelve hours since the apparition had first appeared in Olivia's classroom, Reverend Terrence Walker, a lean, silver-haired televangelist whose organization owned more that a dozen TV stations throughout the Midwest, arrived with cameramen, technicians, and his own satellite truck. Olivia's stomach knotted as she watched the other networks, both cable and broadcast, cover his arrival as if he were a visiting head of state. She could finally take it no more when Walker, in effect, called a press conference and began it with a prayer, his actor's voice, resonant and booming, invading every corner of the world as he called for everyone to join him, not only the faithful watching his own mini-network but everyone watching him on other channels. Once again the figure seemed to waver, as if about to disappear, but it didn't.

Turning off the TV in disgust, she slumped down, exhausted, on the couch she had been sitting on most of the evening.

But in her darkened room she could still see the figure in her mind's eye, even more clearly, it seemed, than when its image had been on the screen. Particularly clear were its eyes, almost glowing as they seemed to burn into hers. They were still filled with pain, but now she saw—imagined she saw—that the pain was turning to despair.

As the sleep of exhaustion claimed her, her last thought was a puzzled and heartfelt, "Why *are* you here? If you're real, *what is it you want?*"

*   *   *

Olivia came awake with a shiver sometime during the night. She was, she realized blearily, still lying on the couch, one arm twisted painfully beneath her.

For a moment she wondered if the last few hours had been an elaborate nightmare, just as she had in the weeks before awakened and wondered briefly if her illness might have been only a dream. But then she heard the murmur of the crowd beyond the windows of her apartment, and she knew it was all true.

Her hand stricken with a pins-and-needles prickling as she freed her arm, she lurched into a sitting position—and saw out of the corner of her eye that she was not alone.

The apparition, almost completely transparent, stood just beyond the end of the couch, leaning forward, one hand stretched out to where her head had lain only moments before.

Heart pounding, not yet trusting her legs to hold her, she inched toward the end of the couch. The apparition straightened, letting its arm float down to its side as it began to move slowly toward her, floating as much as walking as its lower body passed through the couch as if it didn't exist.

As it came closer, it stretched out both of its arms toward her. The motion caused the sleeve of its coarse robe to slip back, revealing jagged wounds in both wrists, the sources of the translucent blood that had become increasingly obvious hour by hour as it dripped from its fingers on hundreds of millions of TV screens around the world.

You're real, she thought, finally coming to grips with the concept. *You really did exist, and now . . .*

Looking up, into the nearly transparent eyes, she spoke aloud, in a trembling whisper, the question that had filled her thoughts as she had fallen asleep. *"Why are you here? What is it that you want?"*

Her entire body tingled as its hands touched her brow, then passed through it like mist through gauze. A moment later, its tortured face only inches from her own, the entire apparition shimmered and faded slowly from sight.

But it was not gone.

She could still feel its presence in every part of her own body, in every corner of her mind.

She could feel its remembered pain, but the agony in its wrists and feet and chest were as nothing compared to the anguish, the feeling of utter helplessness that had gripped it ever since.

And she heard its wordless plea, not once but endlessly as the night wore on and she shared its torture.

Until, finally, as the light of dawn began to filter into the room, she felt it fading and slowly realized that she was once again alone.

But it had left a legacy behind.

She knew what it wanted.

She knew what it had sought so desperately for so long.

Countless others down through the centuries *could* have known, indeed *should* have known, but none had ever truly *wanted* to know.

Until now.

But there was nothing she could do. She was just one person, and what it needed was far beyond her power to give, no matter how hard she tried, no matter how deeply she wished she could.

Unless . . .

The images that had finally prompted her to turn the television off flashed through her mind: Reverend Terrence Walker.

Forcing herself to ignore the dizziness that set the room to spinning, the weakness that nearly turned her legs to rubber, she got to her feet and turned on the small TV set. The apparition was still there, in her classroom. The network had added a digital elapsed time in the lower right corner of the screen. It was approaching twenty hours.

Wondering how she could go about getting in touch with Walker or any of the dozens of others like him, Olivia located the phone and plugged it in.

It rang almost instantly.

Slumping limply back on the couch, she pressed the TALK button on the handset.

She couldn't help but smile faintly as she discovered that it was one of Walker's assistants on the line. She wouldn't have to find Walker after all. He had found her. One of his assistants had been dialing and redialing her number for hours, starting even before they had arrived in town, and now he begged her to stay on the line while he fetched Reverend Walker himself.

While she waited, she tried to think how best she could convince Walker that the apparition was not what it seemed but was, in fact, the work of Satan himself, the ultimate trickster.

As she quickly discovered, however, a simple statement to that effect was more than enough. To Walker—and to most of his followers and countless others—it was instantly obvious. God would never have selected a non-believer for such an honor.

It could only be the work of Satan.

A trick.

A test.

A test that Reverend Terrence Walker was ready and willing—eager—to take on.

Within minutes, he began his own personal version of an exorcism, an exorcism that would cast out this demon that had tried to trick the entire world. Walker's audience had never been larger or more attentive as, by the millions, watchers switched from praying for help from the apparition to praying for it to depart and never return.

Slowly, sharing hundreds of millions of TV screens with Walker, the apparition began to fade from view.

But only Olivia, at peace with herself for the first time in her truncated life, saw the gratitude and serenity that gradually replaced the pain and desperation in its eyes.

*   *   *

Spirits, out of their element, are fragile things, and his was no exception.

The strength he had had as a man had drained out of him as he hung on the cross, dying slowly and excruciatingly.

The strength he had felt as death released him, the strength that allowed his spirit to soar effortlessly into the sky, looking back upon the bloody thing that had been his body, the strength to ascend to the heavenly realm he knew awaited him, had been overwhelmed by the weight of the relentless entreaties of those who professed to be his followers but had become in reality his jailers, a leaden anchor to this stifling plane of existence.

But now, as those same millions prayed for him to go rather than to stay, a growing sensation of lightness enveloped him and he could feel the 2,000-year-old chains weakening.

Soon, very soon, they would fall away and he would at last be free . . .

STARS, WON'T YOU HIDE ME?

by Tom Dupree

Tom Dupree is a native Virginian who grew up in Mississippi. He's a former rock critic, wire-service reporter, advertising creative director, and public relations man. As a book editor, he has worked on projects with the likes of Lucasfilm Ltd., the writers of *Mystery Science Theater 3000,* and NASCAR; and alongside an eclectic slew of authors including Tom Robbins, Norman Spinrad, Richie Havens, Dan Simmons, Christopher Moore, Bill Fitzhugh, and tons-of-manuscripts'-worth more. He currently lives in New York City with his wife, Linda.

The pale golden liquid pricked needles against his throat as he swallowed, and it stung all the way down. God-*damn*. Ice-cold Pabst Blue Ribbon. At least you could still count on a few things in this fucked-up world.

Lee Jefferson Williamson III crushed the red-white-and-blue can in a meaty paw, cocked his wrist against the prodigious belly that PBR had damn near made all by itself, and took aim at the waiting garbage can. Swoosh! Nothin' but net. Only thing that had gone right today.

The flicker from the TV screen emphasized the hard lines on his face. Sadness and desperation gripped him like the biggest deputies in the worst drunk tank in the state. He was only thirty-five, but today he felt like fifty.

Lop off several decades, say all the way back to Lee Jeff's granddaddy's day, and it would have been a different story, yessir. A different story entirely. You couldn't have found five people willing to stand in front of the Copaloma County Courthouse and yell for the county to take it down. But this—a fucking disgrace. Lee Jeff hadn't been able to put together even five people willing to take a stand and yell to keep it up.

Where was everybody? Sitting in front of their own TV sets, drinking their own PBRs. Afraid to come out in public and speak up for their heritage. Afraid they might offend somebody who might have a job to offer them one day. Afraid of their shadows. And they should be, buddy. Because there was a great nation lying uneasily under their feet, moaning in eternal disgust at the shameful betrayal at the hands of their sons and daughters.

"It's the flag of slavemasters!" The pretty octoroon had screamed in his face this afternoon. "Well, yeah, sure," Lee Jeff found himself sputtering, "but that's not why you honor it. You're keeping the memory alive of the people who died to defend it. You don't see anybody forcing Japs to take their flag down, and we killed the shit out of them."

Lee Jeff felt for the Japs. He could relate. After all, the Southerner and the American Indian shared something important with them. They were each conquered peoples. But now we were doing everything we possibly could to kiss the Indians' asses, they were getting rich off casinos everywhere—even in Mississippi, for Christ's sake. And with no more army to pay for—thanks to Douglas MacArthur, and there ought to be a statue of him in every lousy Jap village—Japs had been able to concentrate on business. Now they were walking around in suits, with cell phones and briefcases, fighting back and hitting us where it hurts the worst: in the wallet.

But what of the children of Dixie?

The last conquered people that had *stayed* conquered.

Even queers had their own flag. Lee Jeff had seen it. A big rainbow-colored piece of shit that he wouldn't hang in a whorehouse. Yet the banner that had waved over the gallant boys who had dared to create their own sovereign nation was soon going to fade from this earth, like everything else that Lee Jeff's granddaddy had held dear. Communist, that's what it was. Denying the truth, forgetting history. And not a handful of people, not a tiny handful, willing to stand up in public and say something about it.

Lee Jeff stood with a great sigh. He decided to look inside Granddaddy's box again.

He walked to the closet, slid open the door, and stood on his toes to grab the ancient Dutch Masters box that never failed to rescue him from a funk. The lid faintly groaned as he flipped it back and reached inside. There were a few old shells, some filthy gray fabric, and the postcards.

The postcards.

Lee Jeff took one in his hand and held it up close. It showed what looked like a great summer picnic or a church social—men in white suits and boaters, women in gowns that spread prettily as they reached for the ground. Black and white, stark, revealing, like a modern snapshot taken at night. About fifty adults, and a few youngsters, were standing stiffly and staring at the photographer: some smiling, some wearing that stern pained expression of people who aren't used to having their pictures taken. In contrast to the otherwise unanimous attention paid to the recorder of this occasion, a bony man looked backward and pointed to the only three people in the crowd who failed to regard the camera. The three men dangling from ropes slung over a broad oak tree branch.

There had been dozens of socials like this, all over the South—hell, all over the country—in the early years of the century. Lee Jeff knew that well. There was no telling what the three jigs had done to deserve this kill party. Grab at a white woman on the street? Maybe. Steal some groceries from the general store? Could be. Get likkered up and turn a nice quiet town square into a jungle-music dance hall?

They had trespassed in a foreign world somehow, just as if Lee Jeff had gotten drunk and gone into Darktown yelling that Cassius Clay was a fairy. They got what was coming to them. No fancy lawyers, no bleeding hearts begging to open the jail doors and let the scum out on the streets. Just a little Southern justice, quick and true. The big constable grinning into the camera had made examples of them in front of the whole citizenry. And far from hiding, as the good ol' boys started to do a few years later, these folks were proud of themselves. The picture taker, like many others before him, had turned the event into a souvenir, printing up his prize shot as postcards that went out far and wide. This one, and several others like it, had showed up in granddaddy's mailbox.

CLAYTON, GEORGIA, JUNE 23, 1907, it said under the photo. And on the reverse, the handwritten note to Lee Jefferson Williamson the elder: THEY HAVE REAPED THE WHIRLWIND. BE A GOOD BOY ALWAYS. LOVE, UNCLE HARMON AND AUNT SUE.

Hell, the post office probably wouldn't even touch the damn things today.

Lee Jeff reverently shut the Dutch Masters box, cracked another Blue Ribbon and stood wearily, dizzy from the brew. He lazed into the bathroom, unzipped, and aimed for the doughnut hole. But not a drop came out when he heard a sharp crack, for all the world sounding like it came from outside.

If that was a twig, somebody was damn close. Somebody who might have had an objection to today's little one-man demonstration downtown. But Lee Jeff's trailer was the only one in the campground today.

He stepped back into the living room and checked the TV. Just a couple of talk-show hosts that you had to sit through before it was time for Jerry Springer, yapping about some other damn smoking regulation in the office. Hell, in granddaddy's day, you could *chew* at work, and just about everybody did. You don't like it, stay clear of the spittoon.

The crack sounded again, faint, echoing.

Not close.

Not a twig.

Lee Jeff grabbed his .38 special and eased outside slowly, pistol in the air, just like he'd seen on the TV cop shows. The late afternoon sun cast deep shadows that fooled folks into thinking that the stifling humidity might take a break sometime soon. He inched his way through the thick pine and made it about fifty yards when . . .

YEEEEEEEEEEE!

He backed into a tree so hard he saw lights.

The screech sounded like an angry animal at first. But then there was shrieking laughter, more than one person, and wild shouts: OW! OOOOW! YEEEEEEE!

Lee Jeff moved closer, with his finger on the trigger. Just past the last pine stand, in a little clearing, was a campfire. Parked by the fire, a dusty old pickup. Now he could hear steel guitars and fiddles coming from the truck's radio. Howling around the pickup were five men in the unmistakable grays of the Great Conflict. Confederate soldiers. Another crack, louder this time. A rifle blazed into the air. One of the soldiers threw an empty beer can into the fire.

"Hey!" Lee Jeff stepped out from behind the tree, and hit the ground as a branch exploded six inches above his head.

"Goddamn! Come out here, son!" One of the Rebs leveled a rifle at his chest.

"Hold it, boys." Lee Jeff walked forward slowly, hands in the air. "Calm down. Just comin' over to see what all the ruckus was about." As he moved closer, he heard a muffled groan from behind a big tree. Rounding it, he saw the great canvas banner of red, white, and blue. The Stars and Bars, the proud states of the Confederacy locked in stern embrace like two crossed swords, ready for battle against any foe.

Wrapped around a bound and gagged nigger, fighting to free himself.

"Drop that shooter, friend." The riflemen gestured to the .38 that was still in Lee Jeff's hand, and down it went.

"W–what's going' on here? What's them costumes for?"

A weasel-thin guy stepped up. "You might say we're . . . reenactors."

"Been a long time since the war, boys."

"Hundred years."

"More than that."

"Have it your way, pup. But we just decided to have ourselves a little commemoration."

Lee Jeff walked closer to the tree. It reminded him of

omething granddaddy's kinfolk might have seen. Maybe
hey even posed nearby, one fine summer's night. The
hought filled him with a strange shot of anticipation and
nxiety, but then his head seemed to clear. The big black
nan snorted like a bull.

"He's a fancy one, all right." The rifleman set down his
veapon and pulled out a hunting knife. "Tell him, Rastus."
Ie slit the gag with one economical motion. The captive
aised his head slowly, and piercing white eyes looked at
he gathering with disgust and resignation. "Tell him what
ou said."

"I was teaching my kids about this piteous piece of garage." He made a violent back-and-forth motion, but the
ond of the Confederacy remained secure around his torso,
lown just past his knees. "How it's a symbol of everything
hat's wrong with this society. That the war's been over for
century, but the struggle has just begun." His clear, con-
ident baritone sliced through the woods.

"Well, you know, Sambo, when we see that flag, we think
omething different. We think," the rifleman winked at his
nates, "HOTTY TOTTY, GOSH ALMOTTY, WHO IN
THE HELL ARE WE? HEY! FLIM, FLAM, BIM, BAM,
JLE MISS, BY DAMN!" By the end of the cheer, all five
oldiers were jumping up and down like monkeys. Lee Jeff
ad to smile. The strange tension he'd felt was long gone.
They were just good ol' boys, with a little too much beer
n their bellies.

"Have a cold one!" One of the Johnny Rebs threw Lee
Jeff a can and a metal church key.

"Haven't seen one of these in years." Lee Jeff cracked
he can open. "Didn't know they even made 'em like this
ny more."

"Son, where you been? Africa?" The soldiers howled,
nd the man wrapped in the flag continued to stare.

"Just what are you boys reenactin'?"

"They're trying to hold onto something, but it's moving
way from them." A smirk darted across the black man's
ace. "They can feel it in their ignorant redneck bones.
Things are about to change, son, and nothing's gonna hold

it back. But there's rivers of blood that have to spill first, and you're fixin' to see some of it."

"Aw, nobody's gonna hurt you, boy." Lee Jeff pulled on the beer. "Besides, what do you mean, *about* to change? Hell, the godforsaken South's changed already. They're afraid to fly that thing down at the courthouse."

"They're not afraid. They're ashamed."

"Ashamed? Of what? Of a generation of people who fought for their way of life?"

"Some of them did." The prisoner looked away with a strange wistful glance. "Some of them were well-meaning folks. And it takes a real man to look death in the eye, no matter what you're doing it for. They were brave, I'll hand you that. But they were wrong."

"Shut up!" A fat, bearded Rebel sauntered toward the tree.

"What's that way of life you're so proud of, anyway? Living off the sweat of another human being? Making him break his back in a cotton field, serve you iced tea on the verandah, raise the children you claim—even bear the ones you won't? Those were your rules, for your own little world. Your people offered a double handful of nickels and dimes from a fishbowl at Christmas and expected us to be grateful."

Lee Jeff perked up. "My folks treated their help like family. They told me that."

"That's right. The Yankee loves the race and hates the individual, but the Southerner hates the race and loves the individual. I've heard all that shit. Listen to me. Your family was free to come and go. Anybody who wasn't, wasn't your family."

"I never owned no slave. What's that got to do with the price of tea in China? What's that got to do with that robe they got you wearin'?"

"Looks right smart on him, too!" The Reb leaned up against the tree and trickled beer on the captive's head.

"Ever stopped to think, who's waving this flag? Lonely old fools barricaded on mountaintops, wishing time ran backwards. Shitkicker college students spending their dad-

dy's money at football games, wouldn't know a cause if it
bit them in the ass. Frustrated clock punchers who tick off
their days at the lumber mill and can't figure out how life
got away from them. Just look at these drunken pencil-
licked clowns."

The soldier gave him a quick shot in the gut.

Lee Jeff hollered and pulled him away. "Hey, pal, lighten
it up." A look passed between the black man and the soldier that Lee Jeff couldn't figure.

"That's what they do." The prisoner wheezed to catch
his breath. "That's what they're here for."

"Bullshit," Lee Jeff spat. "Nobody's waving the goddamn
flag! That's the goddamn point! Everybody else in this
country has people screamin' so they won't be discrimi-
nated against. But what about the white man? Who's
speakin' up for *our* rights?"

"Your rights were bought and paid for by the blood of
my people. Generations' worth. And I understand flags better than you think, sonny. I served in Germany during the
last great war. Ate more dirt and watched more buddies
turn into goo than anybody who ever wore that gray. There
was a flag waving over there, too, another one that I never
want to have to see again as long as I live."

"I don't think that'll be much longer, spearchucker." The
soldier with the rifle stopped to pick up Lee Jeff's .38.
"Fine little shooter—never saw one like 'is before." He
tossed it to Lee Jeff. "Well, son, do it. Take this pretty-
talking nigger."

"What're you talkin' about?" Lee Jeff looked up in
horror.

"You think we brought him out here for a square dance?
Shoot him, boy, or we'll put you right up there beside
him!" The .38 glinted in the firelight.

Sweat poured off Lee Jeff's face. "Hey. Hey. He ain't
doin' nothin'. Nothin' but talk."

"Talk is how it starts, son." The black man struggled to
stand up to his full height. "You talk back. And then your
talk gets loud, and then it gets mad. And then, one day,

you look up and there's more of you talking than there is
of them. And that's when the time for talk is over."

"He ain't gonna do it." A soft, sober voice came from
one of the soldiers Lee Jeff hadn't heard before. He peered
across the flames in the deepening gloom, but could barely
make out the soldier's shape through the rising smoke. "He
ain't got the fire."

"Listen here, boy." The rifleman grabbed Lee Jeff's chin
and shook it. "The War of Northern Aggression's lost. The
goddamn Yankee carpetbaggers have raped our country
like it was a schoolgirl. They've fouled everything we ever
believed in and laughed at us while they were at it. But
there's still people here. People who understand the only
way to win is to fight back. And you're one of 'em. We
know you are. 'Cause we were there with you today."

"I didn't see shit for friends down at the courthouse.
Nobody was there with me."

"We was there all right." The bearded fat Reb leaned
down and picked up a twig. "We was there because you sent
out the call."

"Just for people to stand with me and honor a flag. Not for
killing."

"Like those poor massacred boys at Sumter? Like the men
Sherman stepped on all the way to the sea? Like the young'uns who could barely tote a rifle and wound up fertilizin'
their own farmland? They weren't wastin' time standin',
son. They were killin'. You called for us, and now you got
us! And what we stand for's a lot more serious than any
pissant flag. We stand for shootin' this boy right goddamn
now!"

"THE NIGGER AIN'T DONE NOTHIN'!"

"Oh, yes, he has." The fat Reb bit down on the twig and
grinned. "Just like them other niggers on your ol' postcards."

Lee Jeff took a quick breath and felt dizzy.

"What postcards?"

"Come on, son." The rifleman brought Lee Jeff's .38 up
to his face. "The ones you moon over to give you some
guts, make you feel like you're part of something. Go back

to your granddaddy's day and try it on for size. Well, here's your chance. Here's what you've been waitin' for. You're with us now, so do it!" He shoved the pistol into Lee Jeff's hand. "DO IT!" He pointed to the tree, and the gesture looked familiar, but not in a way that made Lee Jeff feel warm inside.

"Who are you?"

"Aw, boy, don't you recognize us?" The fat Reb grinned obscenely, and Lee Jeff imagined him wearing a constable's badge on a summer night long, long ago.

"It ain't possible."

"Anything's possible to folks who believe. And you do believe, don't you? Like that ol' license plate says: 'FORGET? HELL!' Come on, son. You're with friends. Nobody will ever know. You know you want to. You know you do. Be one of us. You can do it. Just do it. DO IT!"

Lee Jeff whirled to face the man wrapped up in the Stars and Bars. "Boy, say something! Why don't you just tell 'em you're sorry, or you're crazy, or whatever shit they want to hear? Why don't you save yourself?"

"I am sorry, young'un. I am very, very sorry. But I'm not crazy. And I am saving myself. God help me, I'm gonna save myself from the likes of you. You stupid cracker. You poor ignorant dumbass."

And then the nigger hawked and spit, all over the Confederate flag.

"Black bastard!" Lee Jeff cried.

"Untie me and I'll wipe my ass with it!"

"FUCK YOU!" Tears fogged Lee Jeff's eyes and a sound roared louder than anything he'd ever heard before. He stared as the white and blue slowly gave way to red, red, red.

"You gutted him, boy!"

Lee Jeff crawled, heaving, toward the dying man. There was no pain on his face, only a grimace that was trying its best to turn into a smile. He whispered something and Lee Jeff moved closer.

"God help you, son . . . freedom." He coughed once, gurgled, and slumped over.

"By God, we got ourselves a winner!" The soldiers moved toward Lee Jeff, and one made to put his arm around him. Lee Jeff stepped away, raising the .38 to his face. The burned-iron smell of the barrel rose to attack him, and he vomited his last two beers to the ground.

"Oh, my God, my God. I killed him."

"Deader than hell. I really didn't think you could do it." A trick of the firelight made the fat Reb's eyes glow red, like a cheap snapshot.

"Oh, my God. Why'd you have to bring that nigger down here?"

"We brought him for you, boy." The soldiers moved in slowly. "He was for you. That's what we do."

"What the hell are you talking about?"

The rifleman rested his weapon against the tree. "See, the bigger a thing is, the slower it changes. So slow, most people can't even see it. Because it has to happen one person at a time."

"One at a time." The fat Reb stuffed his shirttail under the fold in his belly. "I got to say, Lee Jeff, I did not believe you'd really do it. We fix most folks here and now. Worst nightmare they ever had, is all it takes. But you seem to be a regular hardcase, son. You went over the edge, by God if you didn't. So now it's your turn."

Lee Jeff backed numbly into the tree. It barely registered, deep in the back of his mind, that the dead man, the flag, the blood, his .38, were gone.

"What are you gonna do?" He looked from soldier to soldier. Their faces had gone hard, and he realized the crimson glow from their eyes was no trick at all.

Two of the Rebs unfolded something great and billowy, something red, white, and blue. Another brought a length of rope. Lee Jeff raised his hands to push them away. Long, angular, black hands.

"No. God, no." His voice had become deep and muscular, even as he whimpered.

"You're the temptation now, boy. Every night. From now on. As long as it takes. And you're gonna hug this tree until you can convince somebody else to put you down.

So get thinking about what you're gonna say." The fat Reb snickered and spit.

"It's gettin' harder and harder every time we change." The rifleman shook out the banner like an apron. " 'Course, that's what we're here for, after all. The last one, the very last one, will be there forever. Glory."

The crossed stars rose up in front of Lee Jeff like scimitars and blotted out the sky as they wrapped around his body. The world seemed to shimmer as the gag fell into position.

"Don't worry, pup. There are still lots more where you came from. It's just tougher to find them these days. But don't worry. We'll do it. We will."

The pickup truck's wheel spun and dirt poured out toward Lee Jeff's face. He leaned against the tree, and the last thing he saw was the license plate:

MISSISSIPPI
MAGNOLIA STATE
JUN 1961
FORGET? HELL!
Then he saw nothing.

*   *   *

He woke to the sound of a rifle, fired into the air. Lee Jeff tried to reach for a beer, but he was bound tight. He tried to yell, but there was something over his mouth. He looked down to see the flag wrapped around him, and bare feet. Black as night. He moaned through the gag.

"Hey!"

One of the Rebs fired into the pine thicket.

PRETENDER OF THE FAITH

by James Lowder

James Lowder is the author of a half-dozen novels, including *Prince of Lies* and *The Ring of Winter*. His short fiction has appeared in various anthologies and magazines, often alongside his essays and reviews about genre films. A longtime devotee of the Matter of Britain, as you might guess from his story in this collection, he also serves as executive editor for Green Knight Publishing's Pendragon book line.

The Holy Grail was the last straw. When the *People* article turned its decidedly short attention to that most elusive of artifacts, Grant Chambers twisted his copy of the magazine and pitched it forward over two rows of airline seats. He should have seen it coming, of course, but he hadn't, no more than the young woman had who took the abused and discarded weekly to the back of her head.

"A fair shot," noted the red-bearded bruiser wedged into the seat across the aisle from Chambers. He nodded in a way that was both sympathetic and judgmental. The gesture was as grating to Chambers as the man's exaggerated Scottish burr. The brute folded the sports section of *The Orcadian* and gently slid it into the seat pouch ahead of him. "Not very courteous, though."

Chambers ignored him. He'd recaptured his lost composure and was sizing up the situation. The recipient of his rejected magazine was out of her seat, scanning the passengers for her assailant. When her eyes lit on the Scot, he tilted his head in Chambers' direction. For an instant it seemed as if she might hurl the slick back. Chambers smirked, hoping to provoke just that response. Tit for tat, and the problem would be solved. But a steward was suddenly at her side. As the woman explained what had occurred, her moue of annoyance jumped to the attendant's previously placid features.

"Is this yours?" The steward asked, presenting the rumpled issue of *People* to Chambers.

"Yes," he sighed. "Though I suppose I forfeited ownership when I threw it."

The blunt answer took the steward by surprise, which made Chambers feel just a bit better. Still, the attendant maintained his facade of official disdain as he leaned over the empty seat between the aisle and the offender. "The young woman would like an apology."

"No doubt." Chambers leaned back against the window. "I can't apologize, even if I were so inclined. It wasn't an accident—tossing the magazine, I mean. I purposefully hurled it. She got in the way."

Chambers had honed his demeaning, pedantic tone to razor sharpness on many a hapless undergrad and even a grant committee or two. It was a common enough weapon in academia, but the steward had no armor against it. His mask of reserve fell away in tatters, and the magazine slipped from his fingers onto the empty seat. "We aren't so far from Boston that we can't turn back," he said in a voice loud enough to be heard five rows in either direction.

Perhaps he thought to draw the passengers to his side, set them against the offender. Instead, the threat prompted a chorus of groans. Even the victim of Chambers' outburst rolled her eyes. "Forget it," she said. "Just don't leave him with any hardcovers."

Chambers laughed, a burst of genuine good humor. As the woman turned to sit down, he flashed a well-practiced, thoroughly charming smile and said, "I only packed paperbacks."

Silent accord deemed the matter dropped, and the tension that had settled over that small section of the cabin dissipated. The steward stood there for a moment, bemused and fuming, then retreated.

"You're a clever lad," the Scotsman said. "Serpents and foxes are clever, too. Only men can be courteous."

A cutting reply flew to Chambers' tongue, but he swallowed it. Browbeating a flight attendant was fine enough sport; insulting a man who looked quite capable of snapping him in two was foolhardy. Grant Chambers had long ago recognized his own penchant for creative self-destruction—it was a trait that was hard for anyone to miss—but that bent did not usually include physical recklessness. He mumbled something noncommittal and turned to stare at the cloud tops.

"What did you read in there that set you off?" the big Scot pressed. He reached for the abused magazine, still resting on the empty seat where the steward had dropped it, and flipped through a few pages. "I can't think of anything that would make me—" He paused as something caught his attention. "Could I borrow this?" he asked sheepishly, like a child who had stumbled across something wonderful and unexpected.

"It's all yours," Chambers replied, thankful for a reprieve. As he turned back toward the window, he noted with more than a little annoyance that the article now captivating the Scotsman was the very same one that had prompted his own outburst. With loving care and callused hands, the man smoothed the wrinkled full-page photo of the Reverend Ambrose Aurelius Hunter.

Chambers spat a few choice Anglo-Saxon obscenities with a vehemence worthy of Beowulf himself. Reverend Hunter had used the fawning *People* profile to announce a new goal for his TV ministry: the quest for the Holy Grail. With the cup from which Christ drank at the Last Supper, in which Joseph of Arimathea later captured the blood of the crucified Savior, Hunter planned to establish a holy community. This small settlement would serve as the foundation for a genuine City of God. Chambers could picture it now—a holy habitat with water slides and time-shares.

Normally, Chambers paid little attention to such nonsense. His area of academic expertise was the historical Arthur, not the literary character garbed in the cloth of

French romance and Christian pseudo-history. To be sure, he found the whole topic of the Grail annoying; it tended to sidetrack even the most grounded researchers in his field. But it wasn't just the subject of Reverend Hunter's crusade that upset him. The televangelist had credited Chambers himself with prompting it.

In the article, Hunter had called Chambers "a misguided soul, but a champion of our new City of God nonetheless." Chambers had hoped to elicit a rather different response when he sent his book, *The Illusion of Camelot*, to the teleministry offices.

At the time, the reverend was using Arthur's mythical capital in all of his advertisements. He had dubbed his donation-built glass cathedral "the American Camelot," a redoubt capable of standing firm even in the face of Marilyn Manson and Must-See-TV. His Fellowship of the Cross—full membership available for a love offering, operators standing by—was cast as a force capable of rivaling the Round Table for valorous deeds. Never mind that a large percentage of Hunter's "knights" were elderly shut-ins.

Hunter was tapping into every Arthurian archetype Chambers dismissed as fantasy in his monograph. The televangelist should have taken one look at the book and declared its author not just misguided, but heretical. That's what Chambers had hoped for anyway; an attack by the Religious Right would have done wonders for his floundering academic career. But Hunter had taken the book as a sign that he had lost his way. Like the scholars Chambers chided for looking in the wrong places for the historical Arthur, the preacher had turned his eyes from the sacred and become mired in the profane. His attention should be taken up with goals more worthwhile than fund-raising quotas and a greater cable market share. What more worthy aim than the Grail itself?

That topic haunted Chambers for the rest of the flight, which was otherwise spent dodging conversations with the devout Scot, ignoring the material he should have been reviewing for the London Arthurian conference, and shrugging off the smirks directed his way by the spuriously titled hospitality crew. Only when he made his way off the plane did he come to understand the reason for their smugness. A grim-faced band of middle managers and security staffers met him in the terminal. After a brief recitation by the aggrieved steward of the airline's policy on disruptive behavior, they revoked his return ticket. He didn't protest, but as the triumphant group disbanded, he leaned close to the steward.

"You know how to hold a grudge," he said quietly. "But you need a lesson or two on vengeance. Losing my luggage would have been a better blow. I'm flying on someone else's tab."

Savoring the annoyed, defeated look on the man's face buoyed Chambers' spirit as he made his way by cab from Gatwick to the bed and breakfast near the conference center. That happiness proved rather fleeting, though. When he opened the information packet the organizers had left for him, he discovered that he'd been removed from every important panel. They had also managed to misspell his name every time it appeared. He might have chalked it all up to simple snobbery—he'd always believed his British counterparts considered any American researcher something of an intruder—but his name had been mangled differently each time, and the panels on which he was now to appear placed him squarely in the academic limbo populated by amateurs and New Age nutcases. To his mind, that slight took real effort. It also conveyed a clear message: *Even among the pretenders to this heritage, you are, at best, a bastard son.*

"Just wait till they see that *People* article." He glanced down at the most outrageous misspelling, then dumped the conference packet into the trash. "Or maybe they already have . . ."

Before half an hour had passed, Chambers was speeding in a rental car toward Glastonbury. Between the canceled plane ticket, the conference committee's calculated slights, and the whole Hunter situation, it seemed unlikely that the university would fly him to England again any time soon.

There were some things he wanted to do—or, rather, statements he wanted to make—while he still had the chance.

He had only a vague notion of the form those statements would take when, at mid-afternoon, he reached Somerset. The sun that had struggled with the threatening clouds all morning ceded the field just before Chambers entered the hill cluster known as the Isle of Avalon. By the time he reached Glastonbury village, drizzle had begun to fall from the bruise-purple sky. Chambers was happy for that. Rain would cut down on the number of tourists milling about. The fewer witnesses the better.

A large group unhappily awaited their bus driver's return outside the gardens surrounding the Chalice Well, the spring where Joseph of Arimathea had supposedly stashed the Grail itself. Chambers decided to come back later and continued to drive down Chirkwell and Silver streets to Glastonbury Abbey's all-but-deserted parking lot. He stalked through the ruins, and an unexpected surge of envy flashed through him; whatever mischief he might do here would be nothing compared to the havoc wrought by Henry VIII when he seized the place from the Church, or the later owners who used the structure as a quarry. He walked quickly, pausing only to scowl at the knot of tourists standing with bowed heads before the former High Altar. Upon that site had once stood a black marble tomb, the final resting place of King Arthur and Queen Guenevere. The rains came harder as Chambers passed by the tourists.

He finally stopped to the south of Lady Chapel, near the intersection of two footpaths. Here, in 1191, monks had discovered Arthur's grave. The spot had no marker, unlike the site by the altar that had held the tomb until King Henry's men shattered the coffin and scattered the remains. Chambers, however, needed no placard. He knew the site well.

The scholar lowered his eyes, but the words that spilled from his lips as he looked upon Arthur's grave were no prayer: "You had it easy," Chambers said bitterly. "You had enemies you could hack up."

He dug a heel into a well-tended turf, then again and

again, until he dislodged a sizable divot. At first he only grunted in anger with each stroke. Then a torrent of accusation spewed forth, as cold and biting as the rain that was transforming the fresh-turned earth to mud. "This is how you reward the faithful," Chambers growled. "With dirt. We quest after you, and you can't even leave us your bones!"

A strong, gentle hand on his shoulders made Chambers start. He spun around, all wild-eyed and sputtering, to find himself face-to-face with a small crowd. In its van stood the Scotsman from the plane flight. "Easy, brother," the big man said. That familiar sympathetic yet judgmental expression spread across the Scot's features even before he recognized the vandal from the plane.

"It's him," gasped one of the Scotsman's companions from beneath an umbrella. "Gawaine, it's the one Reverend Hunter talked about. The guy who wrote that book about Camelot."

"You're right," added a woman with a southern drawl. "His picture's on the jacket."

Boldly the Scotsman extended a hand to Chambers. "Gawaine of Orkney."

The scholar rolled his eyes. "Oh, sure. Is Merlin here, too?"

The big man drew him close. "I'm sure this all seems a bit silly to someone as important as you," he admitted in a conspiratorial whisper that was suddenly free of any burr. "I mean, we're all just trying to be worthy of the quest. My name's actually Gary Porter, from Cleveland. I didn't think that was so good for a member of the Round Table."

Chambers turned his face to the sky and let the rain wash away the shriek he felt welling up. When he faced Hunter's faithful again, he found Gawaine of Orkney—or, rather, Gary of Cleveland—on his knees, carefully repairing the savaged holy ground.

"I'm the only one who sees it," Chambers said at last. "He wouldn't want *your* worship. Arthur was a warlord. He didn't drive back the Saxons by modeling himself after Rome's priests, but their soldiers. He idolized the same military that carried out Pilate's sentence and crucified Christ."

The sky opened up. To Hunter's followers, the susurrus sounded for all the world like the shocked and disapproving gasp of heaven. To Chambers, the downpour's sudden, steady hiss was nothing less than a satisfied sigh of relief. With one muddy foot the scholar knocked Gary back. When he saw that the big man would take the abuse, that his fellows were too frightened or awed to act, Chambers kicked him again. "Warriors don't turn the other cheek. You're weak, all of you." He scanned the shocked faces of Hunter's meek and unworldly faithful. "Arthur would have no use for—"

The tirade died in his throat, killed by the sight of a phantasmal figure at the rear of the knot. Chambers blinked and rubbed the rain from his eyes. The man, armored like a Roman cavalryman, remained. Slowly, the figure raised an elaborately hilted sword and pointed its blade-tip toward the scholar, though whether the gesture was intended as a warning or a salute was unclear.

"Is he all right?" Chambers heard someone ask. The crowd moved together to peer at the scholar's stricken face, and their clustered umbrellas obscured the armored specter. When the black domes divided again, thrust apart by Chambers' mad rush forward, the figure was gone.

"The armored guy—is he one of your lot?" Chambers cried. "Some accountant from Spokane playing dress-up, I suppose." With a parting burst of obscenities, he stumbled off into the downpour.

None of Hunter's followers tried to stop Chambers as he staggered away, though they did bow their heads in prayer for him. He surely would have told them to save their breath had he not been consumed by the realization that he must be experiencing a breakdown. *But I can't be crazy if I'm still worried about my sanity*, he decided. *Isn't that how the saying goes?*

"Face me, if you would fight at my side."

Translucent and wavering like heat haze, the specter stood once more before Grant Chambers. It was clad in a

shirt of black metallic scales, heavy cloth leggings, and a
pale gray cloak that fluttered at the edges as if the day's
weather were dry and breezy. Its features were largely hidden by a helmet of Roman design—a plain iron cap with
flaps to protect the cheeks and a movable member to guard
the upper part of the face. Only the hard line of the specter's mouth, encircled and emphasized by a dark, close-
cropped beard, remained visible.

Chambers looked around and was not surprised to find
himself alone with the ghost. He laughed a laugh edged
with hysteria, and struggled to remember the line from *A
Christmas Carol*, the one about undigested potatoes or
badly done beef or some such.

"You are ready for the truth about my kingdom," the
ghost said solemnly. "About Camelot." The phantom's horrible, hollow voice drove all the facetious replies from
Chambers' mind. He heard the echo of the grave in each
word.

"My world was as you said—brutish and violent—and I
a warrior well suited to my times. I would have you, who
is no man's servant, as my voice in this age." The phantom
again unsheathed his sword, a strikingly beautiful admix-
ture of Roman *gladius* and Celtic leaf-blade, and gestured
for Chambers to kneel. The last of the scholar's resistance—or perhaps it was his sanity—fell away.

"Tell me the truth," Chambers whispered, "and I will
relay it to the world."

"As ally, not as servant. And you must have credentials.
A badge of office to open those portals barred to you."

The phantom sword touched Chambers' shoulder. *Excali-
bur*, he realized dully. *It can be nothing less.* No sooner had
the thought faded that a vision blossomed in his mind. He
saw quite clearly what his badge would be and how he
would obtain it. He left the Abbey dazedly in its pursuit.

Some sixteen hours later he entered the convention hall.
A night of frantic digging had left his clothes torn, his fingers filthy and bleeding. He limped from his long walk back
to the city from the spot where he'd abandoned his petrol-
bereft rental. Despite his lack of sleep, or perhaps because

of it, his eyes blazed with a mad glee. The fire was so notable that one of the convention staff called the police for fear the American was planning something dire with whatever it was he carried wrapped in grimy oilcloth.

The gathering was the first of the conference, so most of the members were in attendance. Chambers barely noticed the commotion stirring around him as he strode to the front of the hall.

"I won't take up much of your time," Chambers began. "Just wanted to let you know that I will be discussing my latest finding at three o'clock today. You'll have to re-arrange the schedule, as I'll need the main hall." He opened the oilcloth and produced a small metal cross, little more than a foot long. "Arthur's burial marker," he declared simply and started away from the lectern.

After a few steps Chambers paused, then returned to the microphone. "No fee for entry, but you will be quizzed at the door on the correct spelling of my name."

*   *   *

"Our guests this half hour are Professor Grant Chambers," the BBC host announced smoothly, "and Sir Denis Kaufman, noted scholars and specialists on the subject of the historical King Arthur."

Chambers didn't try to hide his satisfaction at being introduced before the venerable Sir Denis, the leading light of Arthurian academia. *Until now,* he corrected silently. The past two weeks had seen many such victories, but few as satisfying as this. Chambers considered it a partial payback for the form letter the old man had use to deny him a promotional blurb for *The Illusion of Camelot.* It was the first of many payments he planned to exact.

"Professor Chambers can be credited with the renewal of popular interest in this subject," the host continued, "thanks to his recent discovery of an artifact known as Arthur's Cross."

The broadcast slid seamlessly into a prerecorded segment outlining the cross's history. A computer-generated sequence detailed its first recorded appearance in 1191, with animated monks uncovering Arthur's grave in the Abbey's oldest burial ground. The leaden cross was found on the underside of a great stone slab, which faced down toward hollowed-out oaks serving as coffins for at least two figures. In a strange, archaic letterform, an inscription on the cross identified the grave's most eminent occupant: *Hic Iacet Sepultus Inclitus Rex Arturius In Insula Avalonia.* "Here lies the famous King Arthur, buried in the isle of Avalon."

The cross remained part of the region's historical record, even after the Abbey's Dissolution during the English Reformation. The usually reliable chronicler John Leland reported handling it around 1540. William Camden even sketched the artifact for the 1607 edition of his work, *Britannia.* By the early eighteenth century, it had passed to William Hughes, an official of Wells Cathedral. From there, though, the cross vanished from all reputable recorded history.

"Until now, that is," the host noted as the prerecorded segment ended. "Professor Chambers has already turned the cross over to the British Museum for examination. However, as the artifact has been the subject of several notorious hoaxes—including one as recent as 1981—those experts have greeted the discovery with skepticism."

"The cross was very likely born of a hoax—or, rather, a public relations gimmick," noted Sir Denis. He was a mild, gray-haired man with the sort of tweedy air of authority old Hollywood movies attributed to all college professors. "The original Glastonbury Abbey, which included on its grounds the oldest Christian church in England, burned down in 1184. When the replacement was built, it needed a new attraction to draw pilgrims and donations. This need quite likely brought about the miraculous discovery of Arthur's grave."

"Nonsense," Chambers countered. "Had the monks wished to manufacture an attraction certain to draw tourists, they would have created a Grail, which legends also placed in their care. They uncovered the grave based upon information that had been kept by generations of Welsh bards. A colleague of yours examined the grave site in 1962 and confirmed that an excavation had been conducted there in the twelfth century, just as the chronicles report."

Sir Denis nodded. "Quite correct. But the dig proved only that the monks had made a hole in the ground, not what was in it."

"So you don't believe that King Arthur was buried at the Abbey?" the host prompted. He quirked an eyebrow to indicate his piqued curiosity.

"I don't think we'll ever know," Sir Denis replied. "We certainly can't dismiss the stories as false, but like every discovery linked to Arthur and Camelot, the Glastonbury grave can be interpreted in other ways. The monks surely had motive to create the discovery. How the bardic legends Professor Chambers mentioned a moment ago reached the Abbot also remains a mystery. When studied in that light, it's all just a bit too convenient."

Through his earpiece, the host had already received orders from his producer to liven up the exchange. That last comment afforded him the perfect opportunity to do so. "The objections raised by Sir Denis to the original Glastonbury grave sound very much like the criticisms leveled at your discovery, Professor Chambers."

Sir Denis recognized the moderator's intent. "That's not at all—" he began.

Chambers cut him off in mid-correction. "Pending a hearing to determine legal ownership of the cross, I have been directed by counsel to refrain from revealing where I located it. However, I have made the cross available for study. It will, I am certain, prove to be authentic."

The station cut away for a commercial, and the segment producer chimed in on the studio intercom. "A bit dull at the start, but nice energy toward the break. Keep it up."

Sir Denis had other ideas. "You're taking everything I say personally, Grant, when that is not at all what I intend." He spared a withering look for the moderator, who acted as if he were suddenly invisible. The elder scholar turned back to his colleague. "Forgive me if—"

"I don't believe in forgiveness," Chambers noted, "either giving it or asking for it."

That comment set the tone for the rest of the segment. Even the host, who had sat through the scholars' exchange with the same vapid affability he affected when on the air, took a more adversarial stance right from the start.

"Is King Arthur's Cross an historical hoax, another Hitler diary? Or has Professor Grant Chambers discovered tangible evidence that the legendary ruler of Camelot existed? Sir Denis Kaufman, England's most celebrated authority on the subject, seems to think the former. Sir Denis?"

"Not at all," replied Kaufman forcefully. "It will take years of study to unlock the artifact's secrets. Professor Chambers has made a potentially important discovery. The cross by itself cannot prove or disprove Arthur's existence, for it was likely placed on his grave decades, even centuries, after his death. It could bring us a bit closer to the historical figure of Arthur, but it cannot reveal his identity or the nature of his kingdom."

Chambers smirked. The ghost had whispered the truth about Camelot to him in their hushed twilight meetings. "In the coming months I'll reveal enough to end all debate," he said. "First, I will be seeking dig permits to prove that there was no single castle called Camelot. As I suggested in my book, *The Illusion of Camelot,* Arthur used a number of forts and thought of them equally as his base of operations. Cadbury, Caerleon, even Dinas Emrys in Wales served in this capacity."

"If it could be proved, the theory carves out a nice middle ground for quieting a rather fractious debate," Sir Denis offered. "*All* the scholars who identified these places as Camelot could claim to be correct."

"Not all correct," said Chambers. "All wrong. Only I put forward the theory of multiple capitals. If you'd read my book, you would know that."

Sir Denis accepted the barb without comment, for he had indeed left the monograph unread upon his crowded library shelf. Chambers, though, could not let this silent admission of guilt pass unexploited. The ghost had made it clear such weakness was abhorrent, that it had no place in the heart of anyone connected to Camelot. "You closed your mind to the truth years ago, Sir Denis," he began. "You see Arthur's kingdom as some sort of idyllic faerie realm, but you must base your conclusions upon the reality of sixth-century Britain. To drive back the barbarians, Arthur had to be cunning, evasive, brutal—a tyrant by modern standards."

The host cut in. "Yet he has come down to us as a noble monarch."

"As has Henry V," Chambers replied. "Thanks to Shakespeare and Olivier and Branagh, we see Henry's brutal campaign in France as a heroic struggle. Those chroniclers fail to mention how he starved the populations of cities, refusing to let even women and children exit a siege. So, too, with Arthur. But he was unapologetic for his actions. He knew the fate of civilization rested in his hands. He did what was necessary to preserve it."

"Good God," exclaimed Sir Denis. "That's fascist nonsense. Even if you could prove what the man thought about his battles—which I daresay you cannot—you miss the heart and lifeblood of the subject entirely. We still talk about King Arthur today, regardless of the truth of his reign, because he has come to stand for steadfastness and nobility in the face of adversity. He is a symbol of the quest for sacredness in a profane world."

"Which is exactly the topic for discussion in the next segment," the host interjected, apparently oblivious to the anger saturating the air around him. "We will be talking about the pursuit of the sacred, in the form of the Holy Grail, with the Reverend Ambrose Aurelius Hunter, who is in London for a rally of his followers, and John Eschenbach, associate director of education for the Glastonbury Abbey Trust. Now, you were saying, Sir Denis?"

The interruption had not cooled the elder scholar's fury. "I was saying that this young man has no business discussing this topic. He can't seem to address even the simplest scholarly problem connected with the cross or the Glastonbury grave."

The greater his opponent's exasperation the calmer, more controlled, Chambers became. "What academic puzzles could I clear up for you?" he asked, almost sweetly.

Sir Denis fumbled for an example. "The variant accounts of the grave's discovery," he said at last. "How many coffins did the monks find? If there were three, as some chronicles suggest, why no mention of Guenevere or Mordred on the cross itself?"

"Guenevere's coffin was on the top, with the wife-stealing Sir Mordred in between her and her king," Chambers said in his most condescending voice. "I'm surprised you haven't brought up Lancelot yet." He turned to the host. "Those elements are pure romantic invention, added to the original accounts to maintain the illusion of Arthur's civility. A favorite topic of pathetic daydreamers everywhere."

The camera crew shifted nervously, and there was movement in the control room and on the studio floor. A powerfully built man in an expensive suit—doubtless some gym-obsessed executive, Chambers mused—crossed his arms over his chest. The stooped man next to him cringed at the gesture, as if he expected a blow. Chambers couldn't make out either man's features, haloed as they were by the glaring studio lights, but he knew somehow that both wore frowns. It was almost as if he could feel their disapproval.

Sir Denis remained stonily silent as the segment closed, and the host left without shaking Chambers' hand, but that was of little consequence. The network would come crawling to him to set up another appearance after his next few discoveries were revealed. It would cost them, too. As he made his way from the set, Chambers calculated how much he should hike his speaking fee.

"You were rather hard on Sir Denis," said the man in the expertly tailored suit.

Out of the glare of the lights, Chambers could see now that he'd been mistaken. He had incorrectly labeled the man a mere network executive; the imposing figure was none other than Reverend Ambrose Hunter.

It's said that the television camera adds twenty pounds to the person upon which it turns its unblinking eye. The opposite was true of Reverend Hunter. To be sure, the camera loved him, yet it diminished him, as if the equipment were incapable of reproducing his form or, more precisely, his power. In person, he radiated the sort of potency and charm that politicians would—and sometimes did—kill to obtain. No one who met Hunter failed to recognize what it was about him that made millions accept him as God's agent on earth.

Grant Chambers spat on the minister's shoes.

The cringing little man next to Hunter gasped, as did the knot of studio staffers watching the exchange. The frown on the reverend's face deepened to a full-blown scowl. The expression did not sit well on his handsome features. Then, an instant later, Hunter dismissed the insult with an absolving wave of his hand.

"They needed a shine," Hunter said cheerfully. "Thanks for pointing that out." He turned to the man next to him, a scrawny fellow who looked only the worse for his proximity to the minister. "Mr. Eschenbach, have you met Professor Chambers?"

Eschenbach craned his head forward a bit. "Do you know when we get paid for doing this?" he asked. "Are they prompt in sending out checks?"

The scholar ignored the little man, instead poking Hunter in the chest with one accusing finger; it was going to take a lot, it seemed, to unsettle the minister. "I don't want you using my work to bilk old ladies out of their Social Security checks," Chambers said hotly. "Mention my name again, and I'll sue you back to the revival tent circuit."

"I respect your passion," Hunter replied. "Even if it is misdirected sometimes, that fire allowed you to forge your clever solution to the Camelot question. And since we are, I believe, working toward the same goal now, why not work together? Our Grail is not so far away, I think. Perhaps even within arm's reach."

That last comment had rather different effects upon Eschenbach and Chambers. The little man broke out in a noticeable sweat and suddenly excused himself to return to the makeup table. Chambers, on the other hand, was dumbstruck with fury.

"I've had a vision. God directed me to you," Hunter continued, with sincerity even Chambers found impossible to dismiss. "Accept my guidance, Grant. You may be lost if you turn away."

Chambers did just that—turn away. And when Reverend Hunter laid a restraining hand upon his shoulder, the scholar spun about, right hand already crushed into a fist, and broke the minister's perfect Roman nose.

*　　*　　*

That night, high upon the lonely sweep of Glastonbury Tor, Chambers spoke into the fog-choked darkness. "I have proved myself worthy of your trust and capable to fight for your cause. Give me something else to wield against them, something that will silence anyone who questions my identity as your true ally."

The rolling fog parted for a moment, and Chambers glimpsed a figure clad in armor blacker than the surrounding midnight. "Yes," said the specter. "You are my herald, heir to my kingdom. I will give you the Grail."

*　　*　　*

"Who did you say you were, love?" the cleaning woman asked. She squinted at Chambers through the partially opened door, one rubber-gloved hand firmly on the jamb to bar his way.

The elaborate and glorious scenarios Chambers had constructed during his night-long vigil on the Tor dissolved like so much mist. This dreary little Glastonbury cottage was no Grail castle, the dowdy woman with the bad teeth no Grail maiden. He might have found the disparity laughable, but he had exhausted his capacity to recognize irony hours ago in a futile attempt to reconcile his long-held beliefs about the Grail with his quest.

The cleaning woman drummed her fingers impatiently.

"If you're trying to sell something, don't bother. He ain't paid me in three months." She sighed through the alarming gaps in her front teeth. "I only come 'round 'cause I feel sorry for him."

"Money, yes," Chambers said at last. "I'm here with his check from the BBC, for his appearance."

She ushered him inside without another word, directing him to a study that might more properly be labeled a storeroom. In places, teetering piles of books reached from the floor to the water-stained ceiling. A partial suit of plate armor slumped in one corner. Near the soot-choked fireplace, an elephant foot umbrella stand bristled with swords and walking sticks. A painting of the tower atop the Tor hung at a kilter above a mantel heaped with everything from chunks of stone to crystal figurines. Three glassfronted display shelves hulking in various spots were similarly overpopulated.

The cleaning woman disappeared up the stairs, then returned a moment later. "I'm on my way to my next job, but he'll be right with you," she said, shrugging on her coat. As the woman headed for the door she called back, "Be sure to remind him that he's got bills to pay when you hand over the check."

Chambers set about searching the room, lifting box lids and peering into the shadowy corners. Images of the remarkable stardom that would soon be his filled his thoughts, even as he sorted through the junk and relics jumbled together on the mantel. He was so caught up in the hunt and his daydreams that he didn't hear the soft footfalls on the stairs, didn't abandon his investigation until a moan shuddered through the room.

When Chambers looked up, John Eschenbach staggered back a step. "I kept it safe," the little man said, though his tone betrayed his actual opinion of his own competency.

"That's my duty now," Chambers said. "Where is it?"

Eschenbach entered the room on unsteady legs, muttering furiously. "The old man was dying when I took the thing, or nearly dying. It wasn't so bad, that, not like burning down God's own house." He stopped suddenly and stared at Chambers. His watery eyes were wide with terror. "Have you earned it yet?" he whispered, dropping to his knees.

Chambers snatched an iron-tipped cane from the umbrella stand. "Where is it?" he shouted. With his free hand he pulled Eschenbach back to his feet. "Where?"

"Sorry for the interruption," said a voice that was familiar, but rather more nasal than usual. "The front entry was ajar so I let myself in." Reverend Ambrose Aurelius Hunter, eyes circled with bruises pooling out from his broken nose, positioned himself in the study's sole doorway.

"You've been following me," Chambers snapped.

"Not me," Hunter supplied. "Until last night, anyway. My people had been doing the detective work up until then, even before you left the States. God really did give me a vision of you, Grant. You, as well, John."

Eschenbach wheezed, "I'm calling the police."

As the little man pulled away from Chambers, the cane came crashing down upon his head. Eschenbach and the broken bits of oak hit the floor simultaneously. The blood seeping onto the carpet testified to the blow's fury.

Reverend Hunter moved toward the stricken man, but Chambers quickly pulled a sword from the stand and warded him off.

"You cannot keep the Grail from God's true servant," the minister said. "Eschenbach was almost ready to admit that." As he spoke, Hunter scanned the clutter with his piercing blue eyes.

"You don't serve God. You serve yourself," Chambers said. "Just like everyone else."

"If you believe that, you are truly—" Wonder filled the minister's eyes and he stepped forward, heedless of the scholar and his rusty weapon. Hunter reached out one hand, trembling with expectation. Something on the mantel flared with a brilliant crimson radiance that lit the room and drove the darkness from the corners.

Chambers glanced over his shoulder, to a spot he had himself searched just a few moments earlier. The unearthly beauty of what the scholar saw brought tears to even his eyes. A chalice, jewel-spangled and golden, had lifted itself on a blood-red radiance from the mantel's jumble of junk, as if it yearned for Reverend Hunter's outstretched hand.

"The Grail," Chambers breathed.

With a viciousness that surprised even him, the scholar lashed out with the rusted sword. The blow snapped the bones in Hunter's forearm. Had the blade been sharper, it would have severed the man's hand completely.

The crimson light faded, and shadows reclaimed their momentarily lost ground. "But the City of God," Hunter hissed, his savaged arm cradled to his chest.

"Why build your kingdom? I have another in mind."

Reverend Hunter looked up at Chambers. "Your city already exists. It's all around us. But if you ask, another kingdom might be yours. Even this—" Hunter raised his shattered, bloody arm "—even this would be forgiven."

Grant Chambers noted the pair of spectral eyes glinting from the corner behind the minister. The color of their fiery glow was totally unlike that of the Grail, which was hardly a surprise. After all, their unearthly light was born of a source that could be no more distant from the holy relic's place of origin. Yet Chambers knew that those infernal eyes saw him as he was, had been drawn to him by his suitability for the task at hand. It was up to him to prevent the creation of the City of God.

Chambers should have seen it coming, and perhaps he had. Perhaps he had understood his role right from the start. In any case, he accepted it now.

With a single, brutal thrust, Chambers split Reverend Hunter's heart.

The phantom abandoned the darkened corner, hovering first over Eschenbach, then the minister. "Take the Grail and leave," it said.

"A fire first. The less evidence the better." Chambers tossed the rusty sword onto Hunter's corpse. He stared for a moment at the preacher, searching the while for some trace of regret in his heart. He found none. "Then I'll track down the housekeeper. She can identify me."

The ghost remained silent as Chambers went about his

work, scattering books and rags, spilling bottles of wine and cans of chemical cleaner, anything that would burn. It had watched similar preparations centuries ago, though not so very far away, when another ally readied Glastonbury Abbey itself for the torch. That wretch had been like Eschenbach, drawn into service with promises of glory, of earthly and spiritual riches. Only after he had damned himself did he realize how vital it was to exhume Arthur's grave and remove the Grail hidden there before the Welsh bards could recruit someone equally righteous to wield the vessel as God had intended.

"Was it buried with you, Mordred, or with Arthur?" Chambers asked casually as he used a Malay war club to finish his work on Eschenbach. The specter seemed surprised that it need not reveal its true name, that the scholar had somehow come to understand its plan on his own. They were, after all, much more alike than even it had suspected.

"With the woman," said Arthur's bastard son. "And like her, always out of my reach."

Chambers flipped a burning book of matches onto Eschenbach's corpse and reached for the Holy Grail, once more an ordinary leaden cup upon the mantel.

The fires that had driven Grant Chambers were left that day to devastate the decrepit country cottage. In their place he took with him the Grail, which granted him no insight into what might be, only a cold and comfortless understanding of what was not.

KNOWING SHE WOULD
by Donald J. Bingle

Donald J. Bingle, a corporate attorney, has written a wide variety of material for science fiction and fantasy role-playing games, as well as authoring movie reviews, short stories, and an action-comedy screenplay. He is also the world's top-ranked player of sanctioned role-playing game tournaments. His gorgeous wife, Linda, is ranked #2 in the same category. Try as he might, he has been unable to get their Shar Pei, Smoosh, to take up gaming. You can contact him or check out his writing resume at www.orphyte.com.

"**N**ijammeh!"

Caroline sat up with a start, anxious and confused and tangled in the sheets. She wanted to holler for Mom, but at eleven she figured she was really too old for that—unless what she heard was more than a dream. Or rather, more than a nightmare. The odd-sounding voice had spoken so urgently and sounded so near. And that couldn't be good, could it?

She took a deep breath. After a few panicky movements, her wide eyes flitting about to search the darkened room, she had to admit there was no one there. No bogeyman, no looming specter, not even a friendly ghost, like in the cartoons she used to watch.

Nothing.

She got up and looked under the bed to see if her obnoxious brother, Skip (his real name was Ralph, but no one called him that), was playing some horrible trick. Instead, she found only her slippers and a collection of dusty jigsaw puzzles.

She listened intently again—just to make sure. But she heard no voice, no breath, no step. However, there was an infinitesimally faint background hum, like a chord from the church organ that lingered on—or, quite frankly, that droned softly like the whir of the furnace fan.

Still, Caroline sensed *something*.

"I wasn't dreaming," she whispered. She was certain she had not yet fallen asleep—the excitement of a young girl's day had her awake well past her bedtime. It was no dream, she told herself again. It was definitely a voice, a word spoken in some strange tongue or accent. She lay back down and worried over it until she finally did fall asleep.

Later, she would realize that it was the first time her abilities had manifested, that a spirit indeed had been present in her bedroom. But for now it was just another night in the life of a young girl in a small suburban town in 1963.

Nothing happened the next night. Or the next. Or the one after that. And for a while the strange voice and the even stranger word were forgotten.

There were teen magazines to peruse, homework assignments to do, boys to ignore or discuss with her girlfriends, favorite songs to listen to, and all manner of things to gossip about.

She read *The Hobbit*, giggled over schoolyard pranks, and talked intently with her best friends over important topics—like whether Dennis was the dreamiest of the Beach Boys, whether Ringo was cute or ugly, and how late she could stay up and how loud her parents would let her play that "noise" she called great music.

Actually, Caroline's parents were more tolerant than most. Her bedtime was nine, but she could read or play her radio softly until a half hour after that. She could watch television with her folks if she had her homework done. Dad had even set up his clunky reel-to-reel tape recorder so that she could capture the Beatles' appearance of *The Ed Sullivan Show*. She suspected he had figured he could save the cost of several 45 rpm records if he simply taped the program for her.

The effort was pretty much a waste, though. The screaming fans drowned out the songs, Mom clucked disapprovingly during the quiet parts about the length of the Fab Four's hair, and Skip just kept saying "They're stupid!" every time the cameras moved in for a close-up. So she listened to the tape once and put it away in a shoebox with her other treasures. Besides, it was not long until the Dave Clark Five and the Monkees were competing for her attention. Young girls are fickle, after all, and none too serious.

Eventually, however, Caroline became quite serious.

The "incidents," voices mostly, became more frequent. Some were still odd and unrecognizable, spouting words she couldn't hope to decipher. But others were coherent whispers in English. All were accompanied by a sensation of a presence of some kind. There was nothing evil about them. Most of the speakers seemed to simply want a little recognition. The tone almost always became less fevered once they knew she had heard them. A few she was able to converse with appeared to be lost, asking her about people or places she didn't know. And when she said she couldn't help them, they just went away.

Eventually, she mentioned the voices to a few of her friends. From that day on there was still plenty of schoolgirl giggling, but now most of it occurred with fingers pointed at her.

She had opened up a new Beatles album, when a spirit rushed upon her so suddenly and so deliberately that she had dropped the double album and gasped. Caroline broke into a fit of shivering as if someone she knew had died, even though no one had. Her friends, her family, even the Fab Four were all okay. But in that moment of panic, she told everyone around her about the strange sensing. Her best friend freaked out and walked away. Others distanced themselves more politely and gradually, but with the same ultimate effect.

As Caroline grew older, she became increasingly isolated. She dreaded Halloween, a time when her erstwhile friends would mock her and play stupid tricks. Even Skip, just enough younger than her to never grow out of being obnoxious, ruined her old tape of the Ed Sullivan Show by winding the tape backwards onto another spool and leaving it on the recorder with a crudely printed note reading "Turn Me On." At least she had recognized that doing that would probably wreck the tape, so she returned it to her memento box. She was certain Skip hoped the backwards noises of the tape would spook her.

For the most part, neither the pranks nor the voices of the spirits ruffled her. But there were exceptions. Several times in 1968 she woke up screaming. Caroline didn't remember in any vivid detail what had scared her, but she did know that it was one of the voices urgently assaulting her mind. The only phrase she could remember was "Namded," or something like that. Of course, the screaming had brought the incidents to the attention of her parents.

Dad suspected drugs and had spent an hour searching her room for marijuana.

Mom probably suspected the same thing—after all, her bright little girl had turned into a loner who listened to Ravi Shankar records.

Mom tried to be supportive, however, pointing out that Caroline's "bad dreams" occurred early in the evening, when her clock radio was still playing. Perhaps it was the news reports about all the poor dead boys in Vietnam that were traumatizing Caroline. And who wouldn't be concerned about all the "Vietnam dead." Then Mom said something about it being such a terrible war and Dad got mad, and nothing was resolved—except that Caroline resolved to do what she could to become even more sensitive to the voices. Maybe that way she would know why the spirits talked to her.

It was harder than she thought, though.

Mom and Dad got pretty concerned when she admitted she heard voices on a regular basis. She was institutionalized for a while in '69, but eventually learned to say what she needed to get out, graduate from high school, and head for college where she could focus on what she really wanted to learn.

Time passed in the regular world. The Beatles broke up. The Rolling Stones kept on rocking and rolling and rolling, though Mick Jagger never got any "Satisfaction"—not that she paid much attention to popular music anymore.

The country reelected the President.

The Vietnam war ended in a loss.

Nixon resigned amid the revelations of the Watergate scandal.

The Arab oil embargo created lines at the gas stations.

The Bicentennial minutes appeared on television every night for two years.

And a peanut farmer was put in the White House.

Through it all, Caroline studied—but not just the regular subjects that were required to get through college and keep her parents off her case. She read book after book about parapsychology, ghosts, obscure religions, and extrasensory perceptions. She learned that some people are born with the ability to sense spirits and that the spirits seek out those "gifted" individuals. She learned that some spirits apparently just want to be remembered, but that some are trapped on the wrong plane and seek guidance or a simple task to be performed that will send them on their way.

And, over the years, Caroline learned to listen to the spirits and sometimes even help them.

She discovered that once a connection is made with a medium, the spirit often returns to visit and that subsequent connections are easier and more extensive, and the spirit more able to be helped.

Most spirits Caroline helped just wanted to locate those they had known in life and be with them—commune with them, if you will—and continue in life through them. But the ability of spirits to affect the real world was limited and required great practice. Even poltergeists rarely moved anything more than a few ounces—a task seemingly as simple as picking up a phone book to look up an address was beyond the abilities of most of them without the help of a medium. Such as Caroline.

Caroline enjoyed helping the spirits. She understood their loneliness. She even studied languages so she could communicate with those who did not speak English.

But there was still one voice she couldn't understand.

The urgent one that came to her when she was eleven and had made her realize her special sensitivity. It had visited her from time to time later in life, but never as insistently as that first night. Eventually, at some point in the early eighties, she realized that it had stopped visiting altogether. She hoped it had found peace at last.

Caroline lived in a world apart from her family and school friends, traveling to places of historic and psychic confluence and lecturing on arcane subjects to the curious and others like herself. Her parents were troubled by, but tolerant of, her life choices. Skip had grown up to be a minor executive at a sportswear company back home. He never called.

Home became more foreign to Caroline than the spirit world.

Perhaps it was because she had gotten so used to reaching out to others that she decided to attend her twentieth high school reunion. The folks were getting on, Skip was still living nearby, and she hadn't kept in touch with anyone from home—it was time to connect again. If she didn't, she feared that when she died she would not have anyone to live through when she walked the earth as a spirit.

Mom and Dad were pleased with the unexpected visit. They put her up in her old room. It had long since been turned into a sewing nook, but still had a few things in the closet which she had never carried away after college. Dinner was great, though Dad didn't understand why she insisted on being a vegetarian. Dad even hauled out old slides and movies for a show after dessert.

Skip had mellowed a bit and did not seem nearly as obnoxious as when she was young. The next day, before the reunion, he even took her to lunch, followed by a bit of shopping on his company discount.

The reunion was not fancy—a local hotel ballroom with a deejay and some modest decorations and photos from high school days. The deejay played old records while the attendees talked about kids and careers and who kept up with whom.

Sure, the old cliques still congregated together, but for a

while Caroline felt almost normal and accepted. She was mingling her way over to the punch bowl when she heard an interesting piece of conversation. She couldn't make it all out, but the phrase "Paul is dead" was clear. She headed over to where Nancy Gantz was taking to local deejay Larry Lobob.

"Paul who? Was he in our class?"

"Paul McCartney, Caroline," said Nancy. "But he's not dead. Larry was just pointing out the clues on the album covers to the Paul is Dead hoax of the Beatles. See, there is the hand of death on Sgt. Pepper, and the black carnation Paul is wearing in this picture. . . ."

"I have no idea what you're talking about."

Larry's eyes gleamed at the thought of someone new to impress with his historical musical expertise, especially since he did not see a wedding ring on Caroline's hand. "It was a complicated hoax, really. Most people think John masterminded it, but he denied everything. Strange things on the album covers, like this O.P.D. badge on Paul's Sgt. Pepper outfit—that's the English equivalent of D.O.A. here. It means 'officially pronounced dead.' The band later said it was a badge they stuck on that they got from the Ontario Police Department when they were doing a photo shoot up there. Funny thing is, there is no Ontario Police Department. They call it the Ontario Provincial Police." He interjected a clipped laugh. "Then there's all that stuff on the records themselves, mumbled phrases at odd speeds and the whole backmasking thing."

Caroline was confused. "Backmasking?"

Larry puffed himself up. "Weird stuff recorded backwards on the record. Gee, where were you in '69?"

Caroline stiffened. "Away."

"Hey, no offense, sister. Even most people who heard of the hoax actually haven't heard the backmasking. You have to turn the record backward manually at just the right speed. And it can ruin your record if you're not careful. I was smart and used an old reel-to-reel, then made a cassette off that."

"Reel-to-reel," she whispered.

He handed Caroline a cassette recorder and a pair of headphones. "Take a listen. It's from 'Revolution No. 9.' Pretty weird song. Some guy repeating 'number nine' a lot of some strange sounds and music. Extensive backmasking would have been too obvious on simple songs and melodies. Backwards, it sounds different. Try it. I brought it for Joe, for his Beatles' collection."

Nancy looked disappointed that Larry had not given her the headphones first, but Caroline was too curious to defer. With a flourish, Larry hit the PLAY button.

It was weird listening to music in reverse, though Caroline vaguely remembered someone had once mentioned an old 45 that had a silly song called 'They're Coming to Take Me Away, Ha, Ha' backwards on the flip-side, but she couldn't recall ever listening to it. Then her attention was pulled fully back to the deejay's tape as she heard a repeated voice saying "Turn me on, dead man. Turn me on, dead man." Or perhaps it was "Turn me on. Dead Man." There was no context to figure out the punctuation.

She tried to imagine how that would sound backwards and fit into the song playing normally, but it was hard to concentrate on reversing the sounds with the tape still playing. She took the headphones off just as her mind conjured up the phrase "nam ded nah eem nret." She gasped.

"Pretty neat, huh?" said Larry. "Nobody does this kind of stuff anymore."

"Nam ded," mumbled Caroline as she fled the reunion.

"There she goes again," announced Nancy, pointing at her own head and circling her finger.

Caroline's mind raced over the theoretical basis as she drove unsteadily back to her parent's house. She knew that many spirits trapped on this plane sought to live by watching the lives of those they had left behind—in effect continuing through them. The endless tedium of their spirit world is made bearable by watching the future unfold and by viewing the farthest permutations of the impact of their life on the world.

Some seek to find heaven or hell, but some are content to merely remain on Earth and watch over their loved ones.

But what if someone died and their spirit moved backward in time? The spirit wouldn't be able to communicate effectively, even with a medium—all the words would come out reversed.

And the spirit wouldn't be able to build on any connection it made with a medium, because the two were moving in opposite directions in time. The next encounter for the spirit would be before the connecting encounter for the medium.

She parked crookedly in her parents' driveway and rushed into the house. Her mother looked at her in surprise. "What, home so . . ."

Caroline ran upstairs to her old room. There, in the shoebox, was a tape . . . her tape . . . of *The Ed Sullivan Show*. It was still wound backward. The note that had been attached to it fluttered to the ground as she grabbed it up.

"Turn me on," the note read in awkward block letters that she now realized were not written by Skip.

She headed to her Dad's study, where the reel-to-reel still sat, mostly unused these days. She loaded the tape and paused over the controls.

"Is it possible?" she breathed.

There was no reason to fast-forward, she realized. The voice would not be in the songs. It would be in the audience noise, the chaotic sound of screaming girls. That would hide a backmask. She hit PLAY and watched the reel begin to run. The sound of applause and screaming backwards was strangely soothing and rhythmic.

On the ninth revolution of the reel, she heard the voice—a voice she had heard a thousand times before in her generation's most popular song—a voice she knew she had heard in the dark of night. The first time when she was eleven.

"This is John speaking to . . . anyone, I guess . . . anyone listening at all. It took me a bit o' time, but I finally think I have it reckoned. Not just that I'm dead and a spirit and all, but that I am bloody hell moving backward in time. They always say that your life passes before you as you die, and I s'pose that's true for some. But mine . . . mine's passing backward before me, has been ever since I was shot. It's made contact hard, it has. I can't get through to my mates. Only a few people can hear me at all, but even then the words are all twisty and jumbled to them. Their's are to me, anyhow. I picked some young birds who were in tune with the spirits, and I've done my level best to insinuate myself enough into their history, in my own obnoxious way, so that one of them is bound to figure it out eventually. But this show is probably my last chance. It's hard enough getting someone to acknowledge me as a ghost in a time before I'm dead, but it's going to be even harder in a time before I'm known. I won't be John Lennon to those folks. I'll just be some dead man. I guess that's it. . . . Peace."

Caroline sat in the darkened study as the empty reel kept turning. How and why had this happened?

Divine vengeance for John's proclamation that the Beatles were more famous than Jesus?

A sinister supernatural twist for all the backmasking pranks that John had pulled?

A confirmation of John's assertion that there was no heaven and no hell?

He was right about one thing, though. Soon, no medium would know him or be able to help him. Already this tape, this message, was close to thirty years old. He had haunted her as a child, believing she would become a medium . . . knowing she would. But unsure if she would ever identify who was haunting her.

After all these years, twenty-seven years more in reverse, he was haunting a world in a time before he was born. Eventually, he would haunt a world before man, before time. Dark, formless, without interaction, without music, without sound, without words, without any other spirits—or at least any other spirits he believed in.

Soft tears glimmered down Caroline's cheeks. Imagine the loneliness then . . . imagine.

"Nijammeh."

DIVING THE *COOLIDGE*

by Brian A. Hopkins

Brian A. Hopkins is the author of *Something Haunts Us All, Cold at Heart, Flesh Wounds, The Licking Valley Coon Hunters Club,* and about seventy stories published in a variety of professional and semi-professional magazines and anthologies. He won a Bram Stoker Award and was a Nebula Finalist for his 1999 story, "Five Days in April." He appreciates feedback and can be reached via email at brian_a_hopkins@sff.net. You can learn more about him on the Web at http://www.sff.net/people/brian_a_hopkins/.

The water of Espiritu Santo harbor was a thick, chalky cobalt against which our diving lights struggled in vain. At a depth of sixty feet, motes of tiny marine life hung like stars in the ethereal glare, vanishing toward the bottom where the U.S.S. *President Coolidge* reposed in the gloom. Except for the bubbles from our regulators, it was deathly quiet. The silence of a grave. The silence of a museum. The silence of half a century and more.

The ship lay on her port side, empty lifeboat davits reaching toward the surface. She was coated with a thick shag of marine growth: sponges and coral and great purple sea fans. Her bow lay just below us, near the top of the reef, while her stern lay downslope, held against the sandy harbor floor by two hundred feet of sea water. The holes where U.S. mines had gutted her starboard hull were still visible.

Edward ran the headlights of his sled along the *Coolidge*'s promenade, while I shot photos. We'd been diving together for six years, Edward locating the wrecks with that eerie combination of sixth sense and sonar sensitivity that I'd come to expect (and even take for granted), me shooting my photos. I remember when he spotted that B-17 lying off Rabaul. We hadn't even been looking for anything that day, but the depth finder had been running, plotting a rough outline of the sea floor in blocky LCD pixels. Without a word, Edward had slowed the engine and brought the boat around. He pointed at what, to me, appeared to be nothing more than another stretch of coral reef.

"That's an airplane," he said. "A *big* airplane."

"I think you're full of shit."

"A hundred dollars says I'm right."

So we dove, and we found the B-17 embedded in the reef 150 feet beneath the surface. The photos I took made the cover of *Newsweek*. The B-17 had gone down in 1943, caught in severe weather after skip-bombing a Japanese cruiser. I paid Edward his hundred and bet him double or nothing he couldn't locate anything else on the crude depth finder. In rapid succession, he found several more wrecks. First, a Japanese Zero, teeming with tiny silversides and encrusted with sponges and coralline algae, completely unrecognizable from more than twenty feet away—but as soon as it appeared on the depth finder, Edward had pointed to what he said was the prop and identified not just that it was a plane, but the exact type of plane. Ten minutes later, I was sitting in the cockpit of the Zero, accompanied by an iridescent blue parrotfish, and staring at the butts of the twin 7.7 millimeter machine guns, wondering what it had been like to fly her, to hear the roar of those guns whipping past. How had she come to rest here, I wondered, cupped in the maritime museum of the sea? Had she been outmaneuvered by an F-4U Corsair or a P-38 Lightning? Had she been forced to ditch when she ran out of fuel? With better equipment, we'd find many more Zeros in the days to come—nearly three hundred of the Japanese fighter planes were shot down over Rabaul—but that first one was special.

National Geographic saw the photos and commissioned a story. I was suddenly an expert on World War II wreckage at the bottom of the South Pacific. The assignment for a coffee table book came next. Edward and I were suddenly inseparable. We shot long forgotten Japanese warships like the *Hakki Maru* in Simpson Harbor, placed there by B-25s on January 17, 1944. And one of those same B-25s, not a hundred feet away, had bullets still racked and ready to fire from her twin .50 caliber guns. I photographed tractors and jeeps and tanks lost from the holds and decks of battleships and cargo vessels. Scuttled submarines. Torpedoed patrol boats. The flotsam and jetsam of the last great war. Throughout the Solomon Islands, across New Guinea and Vanuatu, we searched and we found them, one by one, each with its own story to tell.

Edward would find them. And I would photograph them.

I don't know how he did it. Sometimes, he didn't even look at the equipment. Sometimes we weren't even *near* the equipment. I remember the Kawanishi flying boat he found just off shore. We were sitting on the beach at Rabaul, watching Papua New Guinean children playing in the surf. Edward's wheelchair was firmly entrenched in the loose sand. I was dreading the struggle involved in getting him back to the Bougainville Resort, when Edward suddenly sat up and stared out at the turquoise water.

"What is it?" I asked.

"There's something out there," he said. His face had that haunted look I had come to know. "A plane."

I got to my feet and looked. The waves curled white and foamy, broke around the brown legs of the children, and scattered tiny bivalves on the beach. "I don't see anything."

He called over some of the children and tried to talk to them, but of course they didn't speak English. Somehow he got through to them that he thought there was something on the ocean bottom, there just outside the breakers. They rolled their eyes. Of course there's something out there, their expressions said. One of the older boys held out his arms and soared around the beach making airplane noises, his rags flapping in the breeze, while the other children laughed and jabbered in Malaysian. Edward bribed them to ferry us out beyond the surf in their outriggers—

dangerous, as we didn't have our dive gear with us. The children were careful with him, though. Besides, they lived their lives in those canoes, tooling about the islands the way an American child would ride around town on a bicycle. We stood more chance of being swallowed by a whale than one of the children tipping a canoe and letting Edward drown.

Not more than eight feet beneath the surface, we found the Kawanishi. The children had played in it all their lives.

As I said, I don't know how he found them. He would laugh about it when I insisted there was something paranormal about the whole experience. He would point to the sonar and the depth finders and all the fancy equipment that the National Geographic Society had bought us. He would deny that there was anything strange going on.

And then we dove the *Coolidge*.

* * *

In January of 1942, Japan captured Rabaul on New Britain Island and established a garrison of 100,000 troops, five airstrips, and a naval base. From this vantage point, Japan attempted to invade Port Morseby, an allied base in New Guinea. They were turned back in the Battle of the Coral Sea. In July, Japanese troops took Guadalcanal in the Solomons. U.S. Marines attacked a month later and for twenty-six weeks a channel called the Ironbottom Sound accumulated the detritus of war. American reinforcements were sent in from Espiritu Santo in the New Hebrides (now Vanuatu). It wasn't until March 1943, in the Battle of the Bismarck Sea, that Allied forces skip-bombed the Japanese Navy at Rabaul to ribbons. In November, U.S. aircraft from the carriers *Saratoga* and *Princeton* entered Rabaul's Simpson Harbor and bombed the Japanese fortress to impotency. But from 1942 on, Espiritu Santo, protected by a series of underwater mines, was the staging area for our operations against Rabaul.

It was one of those mines—*one of our own mines*—that sank the *President Coolidge*.

Sometimes life works that way. The mine you step on is the mine you laid years ago, the trap you set for someone else, not realizing the ultimate target was yourself. Long forgotten, but still waiting.

Sometimes you are your own worst enemy. And the most grievous of injuries are those which are self-inflicted: the guilt you carry with you, the lies you tell yourself.

*   *   *

Edward sipped his rum and tried to look comfortable, but I knew him too well. He fidgeted with the wheel brakes on his chair and made a great show of adjusting his bicycle gloves. Public places make him nervous, especially places like this remote bar which had never heard of accommodations for the handicapped. It had been a struggle just to get the wheelchair maneuvered through all the tables and, once there, our table was too low, meaning that Edward's chair had to sit out in the aisle, a good arm's length and a stretch from his drink. He'd told me before that it seemed everyone stared at him in places like this. That he could feel a million eyes on him, wondering how he'd ended up in the chair, wondering just how wasted were the remnants of his legs, hidden beneath the tweed throw. Edward was most comfortable in the sea, where the Farallon DPV gave him greater range and speed than any diver I knew. Even before he'd been able to afford the Diver Propulsion Vehicle, though, his powerful arms had made him an accomplished diver. Here . . . in the resort's surfside bar . . . he was truly a fish out of water.

"You want to go on up to your room?" I asked. "I can take care of this."

He shook his head. "No, I'll stay. I want to make sure Gunter knows he has to have room for the Farallon."

"After six years you don't trust me?"

"Oh, I trust you, Mickey. It's your memory I don't put much faith in. Sometimes," he snickered playfully, "I think you might have skipped a decompression or two."

I pointed at him with my shot glass. "Don't make me have to come over there and let the air out of your tires."

"You'd have to catch me first. We both know I can outrun you on land, too."

It wasn't true, but I laughed as if it was. I thought it ironic that Edward would joke about speed, when it was speed that had made him a paraplegic to begin with. According to him, he'd been outrunning a speeding ticket, his Camaro Z28 clocking over a hundred when an old woman had pulled out in front of him. He'd chosen a roadside ditch over her Chrysler LeBaron, and the rest was history. He joked that the Highway Patrol had still written him the speeding ticket.

"How'd you find this Gunter guy anyway?"

I shrugged. "Phone book. We need him. No one dives the *Coolidge* without a guide." Vanuatu laws were very specific about this.

"Well, you could have found one who knew how to tell time."

I let it go. He was just irritable because the bar made him uncomfortable. "You want another drink?"

"Tell me that's not our man," he said, pointing.

Gunter was fortyish. Long hair. Khaki shorts. Flip flops. Hawaiian shirt, mostly hidden by the fact that his right arm hung in a white sling. He spotted us, waved, and made his way through the tables. "Mick Beai?"

"It's pronounced *bay-eye*," I told him, taking the offered hand. "You're our guide?"

He nodded vigorously. "Yes. Guide. That's me. Gunter." His accent was the thick guttural of Northern Germany. Hamburg maybe. His w's were v's. The end of each word was clipped off. His vowels came from somewhere deep within his gut. How he'd come to be in the South Pacific was probably quite an involved story.

I introduced him to Edward.

"Forgive me for asking," Edward said, "but how the hell do you plan to dive with your arm in that sling?"

Gunter cocked an eyebrow. "*You* would ask Gunter such a thing?" Then he laughed, a great hearty bear laugh, and slapped Edward's wasted thigh (an offense for which I surely thought Edward would actually rise from his chair and kill the German). "I'm kidding, friend. Gunter will not dive." He pulled out a chair. "Sit? Yes?" He dropped into the chair, which groaned under his weight.

"The law," Gunter said "says you need guide. Need Gunter. Law does not say that Gunter must dive with you." He grinned, knowing we knew he was full of shit, but that we wouldn't say anything. "Gunter take you out to mooring at bow of *Coolidge*. You dive. Gunter wait up top. You bring nothing up with you. Law say that everything must stay in wreck. First dive, you maybe go as far as the Lady, but no further into ship, no further down toward stern. Depth maybe 45 meters. You use safety lines inside, cause Gunter does not like to dive for corpses, and the *Coolidge* . . . she is very possessive. Very often there are silt-outs. Next day you swim to stern. Over 70 meters."

"Decompression?"

"Forty minutes."

It was a bit much by my quick mental estimate, but I understood his caution. The nearest chamber was in Australia. "Gunter show you deco stops. Lovely coral garden. Lots of fish. Maybe moray eel." He tried to sound sinister, but his voice was already a nightmare. "Maybe shark or two!" He laughed. "You take pictures. You swim around and look at fish. Decompression time go very slow for you."

"Fast."

"Oh. Yeah. Time go fast." He laughed again. "You have great dive, Mick. Tell all friends Gunter is the best guide 'cause he not breathe over your shoulder the whole time." He patted his injured arm. "Dislocated shoulder."

"Do you have maps of the interior?" Edward asked. We had our own, but local guides usually have maps that they've annotated. The interior of a ship that's been on the bottom as long as the *Coolidge* would hardly match her original blueprints.

"Gunter show you maps. First day, though, no further than the Lady. Everyone wants to see the Lady. Toilets, too," he guffawed. "Everybody wants to see the toilets!"

"The two divers who died in '96," I asked, "what happened?"

Gunter shrugged. "No guide. No safety lines. Caught in silt-out . . . and drowned."

*   *   *

The *President Coolidge* began her career as a luxury liner in 1931. Built by Newport News Shipbuilding, her interiors were paneled in rare woods, draped in silk, lit by skylights of cathedral glass. She displaced nearly twenty-two thousand tons and was more than six hundred and fifty feet long. Her two steam turbine engines were capable of sustaining twenty knots. In 1942, just after the Japanese entered the war, she was converted to an Army troop transport and put into service in the South Pacific. Her finery was ripped out. Her promenade deck was crowded with three rows of extra toilets to accommodate the large number of troops onboard. Guns were mounted on her decks.

On her seventh voyage for the military, while entering Segond Channel on approach to Espiritu Santo, staging base for hard-pressed Allied troops on Guadalcanal, the *Coolidge* missed a warning signal from shore and hit two U.S. mines. She was carrying more than five thousand men, most of them from the 43rd Infantry Division. The ship's Master, Captain Henry Nelson, ran her aground on a coral reef to give the men time to abandon ship. Just over an hour later, the *Coolidge,* which had listed almost completely over on her port side, slipped off the reef and sank. By this time, nearly all the men on board had been evacuated. Dead were a fireman, Robert Reid, killed by the second explosion, and an Army Officer, Captain Elwood Euart, whose death remains something of a mystery. He and another Army Officer, Warren Covill, were instrumental in saving hundreds of lives by rigging a line to guide men across the treacherously tilted deck. When everyone was clear, they went to make their own escape, but Euart turned back and went below. The ship slipped from the reef. Covill was sucked under and barely escaped alive. Euart was never recovered. It's believed that, in the confusion, Euart thought there were still men below decks. He was posthumously awarded the Distinguished Service Cross.

Today, the *Coolidge* is the largest, intact, accessible shipwreck. And she's certainly one of the best known. People have come from around the world to see the last bit of refinery left to her: the Lady. The Lady waits in the main smoking lounge, over the marble fireplace, an Elizabethan figure with a unicorn. The rare woods of the fireplace have been eaten by teredo worms, and the unicorn has lost his horn, but the marble and the Lady remain. In her fine white gown with its gold ruffles and brocade, she watches, a somber sentinel to the waste at the bottom of the sea.

* * *

Shipwreck divers can't help but believe in ghosts. You don't spend your life diving ocean graveyards such as the South Pacific without acquiring an affinity for the drowned. It's always there, the possibility of death, just an equipment failure or stupid mistake away. Nor can you photograph such wreckage without imagining the last minutes of those who've gone before you: the frantic haste to abandon ship, the crushing weight of all that water sweeping over the deck, the agony of waiting for that last breath and then seeing that final air bubble squeezed from your lungs, meandering, fading with your darkening vision, toward an impossibility distant surface.

World-renowned underwater photographer David Doubilet has said, "the minute a ship crosses that final barrier between air and surface, as it settles into the sea, it loses the heat and the pain and the blood and the smell, and it becomes a sculpture."

The *Coolidge* lay beneath us like a surreal work of art in the murky depths. Descending the mooring line, with Gunter waiting above in his boat, I was aware of the demarcation of light and dark. The scintillating surface above. The gray-green hue of the sea between. And the black mass of the wreck below us, her stern vanishing in the gloom. Edward hit the lights on the Farallon and they played over the *Coolidge's* bow. I snapped a photo, capturing the chain locker, a three-inch gun battery, and the dark opening of her forward cargo hold. Her masts were still in place on the foredeck, their tips buried in the sand. The crow's nest was still in place. A massive anchor leaned against the nearly vertical deck, replete with fairy shrimp and feather duster worms, its chains tangled with the masts and metal cables and several long silent hoists. Everything was coated with heavy marine growth, a veil of wet, brown-green dust that swirled murkily in the eddies behind Edward's sled.

We proceeded to the cargo hold where Edward let his lights penetrate the gloom. The hold was crammed with the mechanisms of war: six-wheeled Studebaker trucks, Jeeps, huge artillery guns, aircraft drop tanks, rifles, Thompson submachine guns, helmets, barrels, mysterious and mostly-decomposed crates, and even a typewriter. Everything was jumbled together against the port bulkhead, seething with marine life.

I snapped my pictures, trying to capture the ghosts and the voices. Such a picture should do more than tell a story. Such a picture should haunt, should echo with those final moments.

We entered through the gaping windows of the bridge and worked our way aft along the promenade. The deck here was littered with discarded equipment: rifles, gas masks, metal ladders, helmets, .303 cartridges, plates, cups, cooking utensils . . . a single inexplicable tuba, now the home for an octopus. The famous toilets—tightly spaced with absolutely no concern for privacy—gleamed white, their porcelain surface immune to the assault of the reef.

From the promenade, we entered the main dining hall. Here, the quarters became too tight for Edward's sled. Also, there was the very real danger that the Farallon's fan might stir up too much of the silt in the wreck. Though the walls of the promenade had collapsed, leaving an easy escape through the remaining steel girders, technically this was still a penetration dive with all due caution. Divers had become confused and died in similar conditions. Silt can be blinding. With no easy orientation, a man can become confused, can forget all the basics, and wind up joining the vast number of dead in the sea.

Edward removed one of the spotlights and proceeded by arm strength alone, propelling himself from different surfaces like an astronaut in zero gravity, his dead legs trailing behind him. When he couldn't reach a surface, he pulled himself through the water with his arms, his upper body strength more than a match for the dead weight below his waist. While he swam, the spotlight hung from a strap around his neck, its light playing madly across the canted interior of the *Coolidge*, sweeping across the skeletal ribs that separated us from the open sea. I would tap my tank to get his attention and indicate a shot I wanted. He'd hover then, the light casting its own ghosts. With hand signals we'd worked out years ago, I'd move him around until I had just the effect I was looking for. The underwater Nikon would whir and click in my hand, the noise of its tiny motor magnified tenfold by the pressure of all that water. Another ghostly image recorded. Another piece of history laid bare.

Beyond the promenade, moving steadily deeper as we ventured astern, we entered the main dining hall, the tables and chairs long gone to rot, now just a deep bed of silt to port. Beyond that massive room, we entered the smoking lounge and found the Lady. She stood guard over a dangerous looking rampart of bed frames. The beds had been brought in to house the troops. Looking at the twisted mass of rusted metal, like some mad fence around a concentration camp, I couldn't even begin to guess how many thousands of men must have been crammed into this one room. Like the toilets, there couldn't have been any privacy.

With Edward holding his light, I photographed the Lady. Her colors were remarkably bright for her age: red dress with gold brocade and ruffled collar; yellow hair pulled back from a high Elizabethan forehead; green vines and pink flowers behind her. The unicorn was still as white as porcelain of the toilets on the promenade. He was reared

up on his hind legs, his tail raised and his mane, though
hidden behind the long, trailing sleeve of the Lady's gown,
appeared swept by a strong breeze. The Lady's expression
was one of beatific benevolence, her arms raised as if she
were welcoming all those who came to visit, as if she was
grandly gesturing to the splendor all around her. Only the
splendor of the *Coolidge* was long gone. Nothing but
ghosts remained.

I didn't realize Edward was gone until the light rolled
free of where he'd wedged it. I was turning to frown at
him for not holding it still, when I caught movement from
the corner of my eye. In the threshold of an aft exit, I saw
something white slip around the corner and vanish. Edward's neoprene suit was black, like my own, so it couldn't
have been him. I'd chalked it up to some sort of fish turning
the corner, my peripheral vision making it larger and
brighter than it probably was. The light continued its roll,
playing across the exit, revealing a dense cloud of silt rising
from the floor, tossed up by whatever I'd seen.

Edward was gone.

With the camera housing, I tapped my tank three times
in rapid succession, then did it again—our distress code.
The silt cloud by the doorway expanded, all but obliterating
the opening. Setting aside my mounting fear, I turned and
swam for the abandoned spotlight, moving carefully so as
not to create any additional turbulence in the room. When
I'd retrieved the light, I immediately focused it on the doorway. The light reflected back from the cloud of silt, blinding me.

I tapped my tank again.

Nothing.

Damn you, Edward, if—

But there he was, pulling himself back through the open
doorway, pushing off the frame and gliding through the
expanding silt. I let the light blind him, wanting to see his
face. Just before he squinted his eyes and turned his face
away from the light, I saw fear, an expression I'd never
known Edward to wear, not in all our diving experiences.

When he was close enough, I caught him by the vest and

dragged him toward the bow, ignoring the great clouds of silt that billowed up from my flippers. We outran the silt into the dining hall and then onto the bridge where I shoved Edward rather too harshly toward his sled. He didn't look back at me as he powered the thing up and shot for open water. I can well imagine his rage at being handled that way.

We made the decompression stops. Edward fiddled with his sled, showing me his back. It took forever to reach the surface.

Gunter checked his watch when we broke the surfaced.

I stripped off my mask and spit out my regulator, grabbing for Edward. "What the hell were you doing down there?" I screamed at him.

"You didn't see it?" He was hanging onto the Farallon and it was still running. He was using it to keep himself afloat. I'd never seen him do that before. He looked exhausted. He was shaking.

"See what?" I asked, some of my anger subsiding.

"The ghost."

*   *   *

"I lied to you."

"About what?" I asked, signaling our waitress for another round. It had taken two to get Edward talking.

"Everything," he said without meeting my eyes. "The accident that put me in this chair. About my father."

I tried to recall what he'd told me over the years about his father. Very little. I knew the man was dead, but couldn't recall how he'd died. In the rare conversations in which either of our parents had been a topic, I'd gotten the sense that Edward's father had been one of the absentee types, that Edward had seen very little of the man. He'd never given me any indication that this had been a problem for him, though.

"I never owned a Camaro. Never owned *any* automobile, for that matter."

The waitress brought out drinks. As she turned away, I

pushed Edward's closer to him, using it as an opportunity to lean out and squeeze his forearm. "Hey, man, forget it. We all tell little white lies from time to time. Remember that time I told you about feeling up my older brother's girlfriend? Hell, that was really my brother and his best friend's girl. He used to tell that story all the time. I just kind of adopted it as my own when I was younger and it's stuck with me all these years. Hell, I've been telling that lie for so long that it really seems as if it did happen that way."

"In time we all come to believe our own lies," Edward said with a slight nod. He still hadn't looked at me.

"No lie," I said, still trying to lighten the mood. It didn't work. "Look, Edward, why don't you just tell me what you saw on the *Coolidge* and—"

"When I was young," he said, looking up at last, "my father and I were inseparable. I told you I grew up on the Outer Banks? That was the truth. But I lied when I said my father was a carpenter. He was a fisherman."

A chill ran up my spine. "Look, Edward, I think I know where you're going with this. If you're just trying to pull off some elaborate hoax . . ."

"Shut up and listen, Mickey. For once, just shut the fuck up."

I pushed back a bit from the table. "Sure. But if you're going to tell me your father's boat went down at sea one day, all hands lost, and now you've seen his ghost swimming around in the *Coolidge,* I'm going to be forced to remind you how far we are from the Outer Banks. If the old man was such a great swimmer, then he never should have drowned in the first place." I regretted it as soon as it was out, regretted it even more when I saw the hurt and anger in Edward's eyes, but I'd always been quick to put my foot in my mouth.

Edward reached for the wheels of his chair.

"Wait," I stammered, catching the arm of his chair. "Damn, but I'm sorry, Edward. You know what a stupid fuck I can be sometimes. Please forgive me. Let's start over, okay? You said you never owned a Camaro. Why don't you start by telling me how you wound up in the chair?

Let's get that out of the way first. Then we can talk about your father. Okay?"

He said nothing. The thick cords of muscle in his forearms were set to propel the chair backward. I knew I wouldn't be able to hold onto it if he did.

"You have to agree to go back to the *Coolidge* with me tomorrow."

"Sure, Edward. I'll go back with you." It was, after all, what we'd come for.

"And this time, we do a deep penetration. Past Gunter's maps. Down into the stern, all the way into the bilge hold if necessary."

I nodded. "If you promise me that we'll follow proper safety procedures. Rig guidelines. Run a safety line between us. Carry some extra lights."

"Agreed."

I leaned back in my chair. "Tell me then. Start from the beginning."

* * *

The *Coolidge*'s third cargo hold had been used for medical storage. More serious than the loss of the vessel itself or the equipment of the 43rd had been the loss of the medical supplies stored there. The *Coolidge* had been carrying Atabrine to fight malaria on Guadalcanal. Most of the supplies have been salvaged, but they say if you dig around in the silt against the port bulkhead, you can still find a few intact phials of Atabrine and morphine among the eye droppers and syringes, tubing and surgical clamps and so on. Edward and I passed through the hold without probing her mysteries, tethered by thirty feet of nylon line. I only shot a few halfhearted photos without fussing over the lighting or the angls.

We were both carrying flashlights this time. I had a spare clipped to my vest, along with two spools of iridescent monofilament line, one of which was already reeling out through a hatch that led to the promenade.

Edward took a corridor astern, heading deeper. I followed, checking to make sure the guideline didn't become entangled behind me, kicking easy so as not to disturb the silt. In the tight passageway, it would be all too easy for a diver to create a blinding cloud with his flippers.

The passageway brought us to the ship's swimming pool, mosaic tiles still in place. Beyond it waited the soda fountain and beauty shop. Stranger even than the swimming pool turned vertical was the barber's chair standing out from what seemed to be the wall. The soda fountain was littered with old Coca-Cola bottles. Edward continued past all of this, barely allowing me time for a single photo. When I delayed too long, the line between us snapped taut, and I was forced to continue or be dragged.

"Though I loved him dearly, my father was an alcoholic," Edward had told me last night. "The only time he didn't drink was when he was working on the boat, which made those times with him at sea the best times in my life. Oh, it was a lot of hard work, especially for a kid, but I didn't mind.

"I was ten when he stopped off that night in the bar after a day on the boat, leaving me to wait outside. The night he wrecked the car because he was drunk. The night he put me in this wheelchair for the rest of my life." There was no bitterness in his voice, just a deep regret and a comfortable resignation. Edward had come to terms with all this years ago, had hidden whatever anger and resentment he still felt behind the lies that had come to be more real to him. But the lies spoke of guilt, and I wondered if somehow Edward didn't blame himself.

We were beyond the annotations on Gunter's maps now. Edward moved deeper into the bowels of the ship, ever astern and toward the keel on our left. The line on the first reel of monofilament was almost gone: nearly 250 feet of line strung out behind us through the twisting warrens of the vessel.

"Guilt ate the man alive," Edward continued, as if he'd read my thoughts. "He never took me out on the boat with him again. 'It's no place for a cripple,' he'd say, not meaning to be cruel, just stating fact in the unvarnished manner that he'd always used. Yes, it would have been difficult, but not impossible. The real reason he didn't want me on the boat is because it would have reminded him of all those times before the accident. It would have driven home the fact that his son would never be whole again and the fact that it was his fault.

"He drank more than ever. He even started drinking while working the boat."

He was getting careless, stirring up more and more of the fine silt that littered the *Coolidge*. I tugged on the tether to signal for him to slow down. He ignored me. I checked my air supply, checked the time, checked our depth. We were a hundred and seventy some odd feet beneath the surface. At this depth, I had maybe twenty minutes of air left. It was time to turn back, head up to our first decompression stop where our remaining air would last longer.

"You guessed the rest. There was a storm. He'd been drinking. He never came home." The pain I'd expected to see in Edward's eyes wasn't there. Instead he shrugged and said, "He's been haunting me ever since. It's Dad who whispers in my ear, tells me where things are at the bottom of the sea. Oh, don't look at me like I'm crazy, Mickey! I don't mean that literally, but even you've said there's something unnatural in my ability to find these things. I get these intuitions that manifest themselves as a voice in my head. It's the voice of my father."

I'd tried to laugh it off, told him I wished his father would tell him where the *Santa Maria* was laid to rest. Having broken apart on a reef off the coast of Hispaniola and never found, Columbus' flagship is something of a Holy Grail to underwater archeologists.

"He's not really interested in shipwrecks," Edward replied. "My father wants me to find *him*."

I tugged the line again. The silt and the gloom and the narrow corridor prevented me from seeing Edward, but his weight was still there at the end of the line. I needed to stop, tie off the guideline, and start the second spool. More importantly, we needed to turn back. I braced a flipper against the bulkhead and hauled back on the tether, attempting to stall Edward. As I did, I saw the end of the monofilament slip from the empty spool and slither back toward the bow, vanishing in the dark and the swirling silt.

"So," I asked, my blood gone cold, "you saw your father in the *Coolidge?*"

"No. I saw a cat."

"A cat? What do you mean, a cat? What would a cat be doing underwater? And I thought you said you saw a ghost?"

"I did. I saw the ghost of a cat. A white Siamese."

"Edward, this is getting ridiculous . . ."

I pulled on the tether, but it wouldn't give. I tapped the distress code on my tank with my flashlight. I kicked furiously, attempting to draw Edward back down the corridor toward me. My actions stirred up great billowing clouds of silt.

"Used to be, all I ever heard in my head was my father's voice, but over the years I've started hearing others. Now I've begun to see them."

"But really, Edward—*a cat?*"

"I know it sounds crazy, but it's just the first step. My eyes have been opened now. Somewhere on the *Coolidge* there are other ghosts—I've heard them. I have to find them. If you see one ghost, it indoctrinates you. Before long, you'll be seeing more."

The tether went slack. The pounding in my heart eased somewhat. Since I wouldn't let him advance, Edward must have turned back. I reeled in the line, waiting for it to pull taut again against his weight. It never did. Thirty feet of line coiled in the muck swirling about my feet . . . and then came the end of the line . . . with nothing attached.

Edward?

I plunged aft, heedless of the silt thickening about me. My light was useless. I couldn't see the bulkheads, the ceiling, the deck. My panic contributed to my disorientation and in seconds I was unsure which way was up. I no longer knew if I was heading fore or aft, if I'd turned to port or starboard at the last intersection of passageways. I tapped my tank. I banged the walls. I removed my regulator and screamed Edward's name.

We were going to die down here.

I couldn't see my hand held out before my face.

I searched for the monofilament guideline, praying for its bright strand to flash back from the beam of my light. Nothing. I hung suspended in a directionless void, my oxygen bubbling away with every—

My air bubbles! The *Coolidge* lay on a steep incline. The bow was at the top of the reef. The bow was up. My air bubbles were rising . . . up!

I followed the bubbles to the nearest surface, which logic said had to run parallel to the starboard hull. Teasing the bubbles to run along the surface rather than adhere to the marine growth, I followed them to the next intersection, where I faltered. Left had to be the direction of the upper deck, but there were also salvage holes that had been cut to allow access to the engine room and the lower decks. Was one of those holes closer to open water than working my way back up to the promenade? I didn't have time to debate it. I didn't have the air to hesitate. I turned left and pressed on, propelling myself at top speed, ignoring the additional silt that I disturbed behind me.

Forgive me, Edward.

Another intersection. I proceed straight through. The beauty shop should be ahead with its barber chair. Beyond that—

The corridor came to an end against a series of unrecognizable doors. All closed. All rusted shut. I turned and made my way back to the corridor, took the left turn. The beauty shop should be—

Another intersection. I turned left again.

I checked my depth. Somehow I was moving deeper, which meant I was heading aft. No . . . wait. It could also mean I was heading to port. The port side of the ship was down. I retraced my path, came to the intersection and couldn't remember which way I had come from.

I was lost.

Bubbles flow up. Up is toward the bow. But up is also to starboard, isn't it?

I was running out of air. My panic just made it worse. At this rate, I wouldn't have enough air to decompress.

Something brushed my face mask. A long, thick strand of brown. I caught it, ran my light over it. It was the end of a rope. What the hell—" It tugged in my hand, nearly escaping. I wrapped it in my fist and hung on.

Hand over hand, I climbed the length of the rope, even as it drew me through the ship. The clouds of silt swirled and eddied about me. I couldn't see anything but the rope where it vanished into the thick soup ahead of me. Then the dark faded to gray, and the gray to the green of the deep ocean. I could see it ahead, just the other side of the thinning silt and the splines of the girders surrounding the promenade. The rope played out, slipping through my hands. I floundered for a second in the silt-out, but then my hands found something . . . no, that's not right.

My hands found *someone*.

Edward! I'd found Edward! He'd pulled me to safety with the rope.

But where had the rope come from?

And why, when I should feel the neoprene of Edward's diveskin, was I feeling cloth that tore in my hands, cloth long rotted by the sea?

I clutched at my savior, but he was slipping away. Clothing parted in my fingers. My hand came up against something solid in the midst of the shredding cloth, and I wrapped it in my fingers, squeezing it tight.

Then the silt cloud dropped behind me. The *Coolidge* stretched up toward daylight, toward the mooring line at the bow. I checked my gauges. To rise now would mean death. But I didn't have enough air to make all the decompression stops. I wouldn't even make the first one, unless—

Edward's sled was where we'd left it on the promenade. I switched it on, gave it full throttle, and allowed it to carry me the length of the bow toward the coral garden and the first deco stop. There I paused, checked my air gauge, checked my watch. There wasn't enough time. There wasn't enough air.

I was a dead man.

A moment later, he came out of the sunlight, trailing a pony bottle, his arm still in that silly sling. Gunter.

*   *   *

While I decompressed, Gunter went down and brought out Edward. Hanging there, waiting for my friend's body, hoping for a miracle but knowing the sea rarely permits miracles, I examined the object in my hand. It was a name tag.

Euart.

He and Covill had used a rope to pull members of the 43rd Infantry to safety. The ship had listed so badly to port that it was impossible to cross the steep deck and reach the lifeboats. Without their heroic actions, many men would have gone down with the ship. Covill escaped, but Euart had gone back after something.

It would take me six months of research and phone calls, but I eventually located Warren Covill. He was old, but still alive. He remembered those days on the *Coolidge* like they were yesterday. He confirmed what I had already guessed. I know why Euart went back.

Army mess officer Captain Elwood Euart had kept a cat in his kitchen to keep the ship free of mice. A Siamese cat.

Edward, when Gunter brought him up, looked at peace. I wondered if he'd found his father. I wonder if they're both out there somewhere, haunting the South Pacific—or perhaps the Outer Banks.

In the folklore of many seafaring countries, those who drown depart their bodies and commend their souls to the sea, where they live forever, drifting with the tides, carried by the currents, the upsurges, and the swells. Is Edward there somewhere, relieved of the crippling weight of land and a physical body? Do he and his father enjoy the sea together as they did when he was young, before the accident and the guilt and the lies that Edward made of his life?

I can't be sure.

But I do know this.

What Edward said was true. There are ghosts in the

depths of the seas. And once you've learned to see one, you eventually see them all.

I don't do freelance underwater photography anymore. I've taken a permanent job for a yachting magazine where I spend my time on the surface, shooting sailboat races and charter boat ads with lovely ladies in bikinis. Even there, though, I see the occasional ghost, perched on the rail of a passing merchant vessel, waiting on a pier, awash and alone in the surf. They're easily avoided. But the ghosts below the surface are all too real for me.

And far too insistent that I join them.

for Dietmar Trommeshauser, 1955–1998